Golden Emerald

Treasures in Life and Relationships

Rex Rian

Camile R. Rigby

Mention of specific companies, organizations, or authorities in this book does not imply endorsement by the author or publisher, nor does the mention of specific companies, organizations, or authorities imply that they endorse this book, its author, or the publisher.

The author of this book does not dispense medical advice or prescribe the use of any technique as a form of treatment for physical, emotional, or medical problems without the advice of a physician, either directly or indirectly. The intent of the author is only to offer information of a general nature to help you in your quest for emotional, physical, and spiritual well-being. In the event you use any of the information in this book for yourself or others, which is your constitutional right, the author and publisher assume no responsibility for your actions.

Any information contained in this book is purely for informational purposes. It should not be considered financial advice. The authors/publisher thereof are not financial advisers, nor is any claim, guarantee, or promise made pertaining to the results that may be obtained from any of the aforementioned materials/discussions. You should consult with a financial adviser to determine what may be best for your individual needs. The author disclaims, to the maximum extent permitted by law, any and all liability in the event that this information proves to be inaccurate/ineffective. Your use of the specified information/materials is at your own risk.

This book is a work of fiction. Names, characters, organizations, events, and incidents either are the product of the author's imagination or are used fictitiously. Any resemblance to actual persons, living or dead, events, or locales is entirely coincidental.

ISBN – 978-1-6896-2137-3

Cover design by Andrew Balls

Golden Emerald and the books of the Golden Copper series are dedicated, with the utmost gratitude and love, to the Highest Power in the Universe. Without that inspiration, these books, and the principles taught in them, would not be possible.

Acknowledgments

Thank you to Camile Rigby for her patient help in the creation of this story. I could not have done it without her.

To Jackson Bylund for his insights and amazing talents in the editing of this book. It is greatly appreciated.

A big thank you to the Cache Valley Community Writing Center and Nate Hardy for teaching and sharing your gifts with us.

My appreciation also to Andrew Balls for his assistance in producing the cover design.

Finally, thank you to my wife and family for their love and support for the past two years while I've been creating this work.

Preface

Things to consider before you begin: This is not a typical book. It is a fictional story and I hope you find it entertaining. However, it is primarily a self-help novel.

People throughout the world have certain types of emotional issues and limiting beliefs. Almost all of these issues come back to three primary root beliefs. These three beliefs are based on the "Three Great Lies" that have been perpetuated for over 1,600 years. The first three books in the Golden Copper series each address one of these lies.

The Golden Copper series was written to bring greater awareness to the three great lies and then empower the reader to move forward into a thriving life in a new and transformed world. The more you are aware of yourself, the better you will understand the world.

In *Golden Emerald* – Treasures in Life and Relationships, I discuss the second great lie, which is, that femininity is weak and sexuality is evil, wrong and bad, and the cause of many problems in relationships. Issues pertaining to gender and sexuality have plagued cultures and countries as well as individuals and families for generations.

My intention is to present a fictional story that discusses some of the issues associated with this lie. I have intentionally written this book in such a way as to induce emotions in the reader pertaining to this topic.

In writing this story I have tried to be sensitive of the subject matter and still convey the importance of the material.

As you read this, please consider the principles it teaches. If you have your own tools for releasing negative emotions, limiting beliefs and false paradigms, you may want to use them. You may also want to consider letting go of negative emotions and limiting beliefs: energetically, emotionally and physically, then replacing them with knowledge and positive emotions such as gratitude and love or anything else that serves your highest good.

May you come away from this story more free of baggage and limiting beliefs and be filled with peace as you experience joy in all the relationships of your life.

"The cave you fear to enter holds the treasure that you seek." – Joseph Campbell

"People become great exactly in the degree in which they work for the welfare of others."
"You must be the change you want to see in the world." – Mahatma Gandhi

Prologue

Mount Ararat, Eastern Turkey, 2313 B.C.E.

The mountain peak loomed large above them as Noah came to stand beside his wife, Emzara. It had been months since the prophesied rains had abated. Now, as the strong winds moved the massive vessel sideways towards its final resting place, the matriarch of this new world wondered what life would be like for her and what was left of her family.

She held one of the last remnants from their old world in her left hand: an ophanim. It was the only piece of technology they'd brought with them through the deluge that had destroyed the rest of their civilization. It had the appearance of a polished emerald and fit comfortably in her palm. Her thumb stroked the raised images of their sacred and ancient language.

The huge craft heaved to one side. Emzara knew her sons were releasing the anchor stones, large rocks that hung from the ship to keep it stable during the worst of the many waves that crashed over this vessel, an Ark that had taken them years to construct.

She took her husband's hand, to keep them both stable and to reassure him of what they had embarked upon.

It was then that she noticed something in the sky. A magnificent, arching bow rose above the horizon. She could see it ascending into the heavens and falling to the farthest points to either side. It was not a single color, but all colors, a ribbon of vivid light.

"It is beautiful," her husband said, his voice barely a whisper. "This is the sign God promised us. Our new life. Our new home."

Chapter 1 – Grand Canyon

Arizona, USA, Modern Day

The rain pelted the helicopter as it flew through the fierce black clouds. *We shouldn't be attempting this mission in such terrible weather*, Taylor thought, a feeling of alarm growing within her.

Yes, Arizona is a desert, but really? No one even bothered to pull up a weather app? Taylor shook her head as water poured down the window in thick streams that made it nearly impossible for her to see the ground below. Even under the best conditions, this was a dangerous mission; she hated to think of the perils below.

Taylor was ashamed to imagine her mentor Nicholas Ryan's reaction to this kind of serious oversight. She'd been trained to plan meticulously and account for her surroundings at all times.

A voice came over the helicopter's intercom system, interrupting her mental fuming. "We're one minute from the drop point. Get ready."

Taylor felt the throbbing beat of the helicopter blades clear to her core. She had ridden in one at a fair with her father before he died. All she recalled was the eardrum-shattering noise.

The side door flew open and the blowback from the wind and rain assaulted her. Grit stuck to her face and became ingrained in her fatigues. She pulled on her goggles to clear her vision.

"Alright, it's go time! Taylor, you're up next!" came a shout from behind her. In the blur and chaos, Taylor couldn't tell who snapped her carabiner into place. The next thing she knew, she was out of the helicopter and clinging to a rope ladder for dear life.

Taylor forced her eyes open and quickly caught her bearings.

"Come on! You're slowing us all down! We have a deadline, Taylor!" a voice said in the howl of wind. The erratic winds made it difficult as she descended the ladder. She found herself shaking from the cold and rain that sliced through her like a knife. Without the sun, the Arizona climate had drastically changed to something unforgiving.

She descended as fast as she dared. It took longer than expected, but she finally dropped on semi-solid ground. The rains had churned the red soil into a paste that clung to her boots.

Taylor hurried under the shelter of a nearby pine tree. She pulled up her collar against the relentless downpour that seemed to be coming at her sideways. She could just make out the canyon in the distance. Even obscured by the misty rain, the sight was breathtaking.

She snapped her attention from the majesty of the canyon and scanned the area for her teammates. *Which team am I on? Talia's? Joseph's?* Frustrated by the poor planning of the mission, she kicked a pine cone. *Where is everyone?*

Taylor shook her head to clear her thoughts. Her mind felt clouded. She couldn't seem to find her team, or anyone else for that matter. She checked her bag, but it didn't have anything useful. She left it hanging on her shoulder and checked the pockets of her fatigues. She then became aware of the binoculars slung around her neck.

"How on earth did I miss these?" she said out loud, her voice muffled by the white noise of torrential rain.

The sky lit up and thunder clapped almost instantly. Taylor inched away from the tree as she put the binoculars to her eyes, and she was amazed by what she saw. The lenses cut straight across the canyon through the storm and gave her a clear view of a small group. *Is that my team or the other team? Did I get separated?* She increased the zoom. She could barely make out a figure standing apart from several others. *Is that Joseph? It is! Does he see me over here?*

She scanned the area and saw that the group was standing near a cliff that overlooked the water. She could see the imposing river beginning to swell in mighty torrents. The zoom on the binoculars was incredible. As Taylor peered at the people across the chasm, she identified Logan, Miranda, and Ching huddled under a copse of trees. She saw a few others standing in the elements, gesturing and talking.

Joseph seemed to be trying to project the confidence that he hoped would assure his team, but Taylor could tell he was fighting his own fears.

No one moved. Putting the radio in his pack, Joseph stepped closer to his friends huddled under the trees and tried to urge them to action. They just stared at him mutely. Joseph watched the faces peering back at him, gauging their hesitation.

Taylor couldn't tell what he said to them, but she could see the effect of Joseph's words. Their eyes drew up from the muddy ground to Joseph's face and they seemed to rally together. The team gathered their gear and followed him to the edge, preparing to descend.

Taylor gasped. From her vantage point, she could see that traversing down the cliff to the rising river was a terrible idea, maybe even a deadly one. She tried to call to them while she scanned furiously for another option. Lightning cracked across the sky and startled her. Dropping her binoculars in fright, she braced herself for the thunder to follow. She waited, but it didn't come. Confused, she fumbled for her binoculars in the mud, wiped off the lenses and searched for Joseph. In her frantic zooming and scanning, she spotted the other team. This group, led by Talia, was across the canyon from Joseph. *Do they see each other?* Taylor could see that the heavy mist and punishing rain prevented the teams from making visual contact.

Looking up at the sky, she knew the downpour was not going to end anytime soon. Watching Talia's team, she saw they were in disarray, arguing and yelling at one another as they suited up to rappel into the canyon.

They can't do this! Don't they see what's happening to the river?

Taylor watched in growing horror as Joseph's team started their descent into certain peril. She split her attention between both teams as they secured their ropes around pine trees on their respective sides.

It was so strange. Their movements mirrored each other so much and yet the team members couldn't work together. They simultaneously cast their ropes into the canyon and began snapping onto them like clockwork. Joseph and Talia took anchor for their respective teams.

Shouting at them to stop, Taylor tried fruitlessly to warn them that it was too dangerous. She waved her arms and yelled at the top of her voice, but was drowned out by the wind and raging storm. Hot tears stung her eyes as the rain soaked her to the marrow.

They can regroup and try another day with the right gear, Taylor thought as the teams continued on. She gave up shouting and returned to watching through her binoculars.

The deep rumble of thunder reverberated in the air around her, but it didn't come from above. It came from down below, near the river. Taylor couldn't help but turn her attention there. A cloud of smoke was fading and she could see the river was flooding, surging uncontrollably.

Taylor felt all of the blood leaving her body. In shock, she turned her gaze back to her friends. She could see that the first rappellers on both teams had fallen into the canyon, having lost hold. Joseph and Talia were scrambling and shouting at their remaining members.

She saw Pajori snap his carabiner onto the rope and leap off the cliff. Talia screamed at him to stop, but slipped on the wet rocks and went cascading after him into the thick mist, down to the flooding waters below.

The remaining members of Joseph's team were securing additional ropes to the tree to go after their fallen comrades. Taylor could see Ching screaming into the radio for help.

As both teams scrambled in panic, another bolt of lightning struck the canyon wall right below where they stood. The entire side of the cliff gave way, taking the remaining members of Talia's team with it.

Taylor watched in horror as she turned her attention to Joseph's team. The tree they were using as an anchor tore loose. It ripped free from the ground, roots and all, sending the remaining team members into the vapor below.

She scanned the floor of the canyon, praying she'd find her friends alive, but to no avail. There was no sign of either team anywhere.

Subconsciously, she turned her eyes up to the sky for inspiration. Somehow, she knew Mr. Ryan was watching them from afar. She couldn't see him, but knew he was aware of what was happening. She could feel his immense disappointment in the failure of this mission. Taylor felt a wail rise in her throat. She had just watched her friends vanish and probably die, and Nicholas was watching and hadn't helped. *Where is he? Why isn't he helping?* Taylor screamed...

The alarm on her phone blared as her eyes flew open. She flailed in panic, knocking her phone to the floor. *Both teams are dead! I have to tell someone,* she thought as she leapt from the couch.

After a moment, logic began to dissolve her fear. She sat back down. *A dream. It was only a dream. A very horrible and vivid dream.* Taylor took a couple of calming breaths as she said out loud, "Your friends did not just die in the Grand Canyon. That didn't really happen." She tried to reassure herself. "It felt so real, but it wasn't."

Still breathing deliberately, she took in her surroundings. She was at her grandparents' home, where she had spent so much of her time growing up. Walking out of the room, she ran her hand along the walls, savoring the texture of the wood paneling.

Climbing the stairs, she let her bare feet glide over the grain in the wood, until she came to the door of her bedroom.

Opening the door, she was assailed with photos of her father, her brother, her grandparents—her fondest memories, all happy, all positive. Slowly, the pain of the nightmare faded. Taylor dropped into an overstuffed chair and wrapped herself a blanket. The army of stuffed animals that had guarded her childhood dreams now absorbed the final shards of her nightmare. Comforted,

Taylor drifted back to sleep, swaddled in her childhood memories.

Chapter 2 – Back to the Estate

Taylor's peaceful rest was broken by a persistent rapping sound. She opened her eyes and slowly became aware of where she was. She looked down at the blanket and remembered everything: the dream, why she'd sought comfort in her childhood bedroom, and even who was likely at the front door.

She wrapped herself tighter in the small blanket and hurried to the door before the noise woke up her grandmother and sixteen-year-old brother.

The door swung open and she gestured for Austin to both come in and be quiet. Austin froze on the doorstep, taking in Taylor's bed head and pajamas with a sideways, perplexed expression. Even confused and slightly bewildered, Austin was handsome. His dark wavy hair was brushed off his forehead and his blue eyes gleamed bright in the morning light.

"You forgot, didn't you?" Austin said.

"No, no," Taylor answered, escorting Austin into the front room. "I overslept. I'm nearly packed. I just want to jump in the shower really fast. We'll be at the Institute in time for our check-in, I promise."

Austin folded his long, athletic frame onto Grandma's floral couch as Taylor ran to get ready.

As she stepped into the shower, she allowed herself a little bit of excitement. She realized how happy she felt at seeing Austin.

Taylor recalled the eventful past half-year while she shampooed her long brown hair. She could count on one hand the number of times she'd seen Austin since Christmas. Truthfully, she hadn't seen much of anyone in the five months since the Christmas holiday—a truly awful time for her family.

Since her father's passing six years earlier, her paternal grandparents had been her surrogate mom and dad. They had warmly taken in Taylor and her little brother, Connor, and raised them in a loving, happy home. Then her grandfather passed suddenly in December, right in the middle of Taylor's final exams.

The grief was suffocating; Taylor had already lost so much of her family. Her mother left them when she was eight-years-old, right after the birth of Connor. With the death of her grandfather, Taylor felt like she was being orphaned all over again.

Taylor turned up the hot water and closed her eyes against the heat and the building tears. It was an agonizing loss, a physical pain, and Austin had stepped up beautifully. He'd spoken to all of Taylor's professors for her, packed up her things, and driven her home. He stayed by Taylor's side at the funeral home, at the burial, and in the sad aftermath instead of spending Christmas with his own family. He'd even bought a Christmas tree, decorated it, and brought poorly wrapped presents for each of them in hopes of bringing some of the Christmas spirit to their home.

Austin's service to Taylor and her family had been a surprising life raft in an ocean of grief. When Taylor first met him a year earlier, he was a hothead who was flunking out of college and blaming others for his troubles. Austin hired Taylor as a tutor to help him turn things around academically, and then the two attended a seminar headlining the ultra-successful Nicholas Ryan. In a series of events Taylor still didn't understand, both Austin and Taylor had been invited to attend Nicholas's Estate that summer, and Austin had been personally mentored by Nicholas himself.

As Taylor rinsed the soap from her thick hair, she couldn't help but smile, remembering Austin's ridiculous antics from the summer before. *Who but Austin would challenge a billionaire to a footrace?*

The change in Austin from the beginning to the end of the summer was nothing short of remarkable. Taylor found herself beginning to really like him. They began dating, hanging out almost every day of fall semester.

That had been Taylor's senior year. Austin should've graduated the year before, but his major-jumping and failed classes meant he only had enough credits to be a junior. After a summer with Nicholas Ryan, Austin was motivated to graduate quickly and do his best in his classes. At her graduation ceremony, she wanted to feel excited about the day she'd worked toward for so many years, but instead she felt apathetic. At least, until Austin text her a screenshot of his straight A's, and then she'd felt a surge of pride for how hard he had worked to change his life.

Taylor turned off the water and stood for a moment in the shower, watching the steam rise. Sighing, she knew Austin must be confused about her feelings for him. After her grandfather's death and the bleak Christmas break, Taylor had cocooned herself through spring semester. She felt numb and uninterested in just about everything. She still found Austin attractive and wanted to spend time with him, but she often couldn't bring herself to answer his texts or calls and had no interest in doing anything outside of what had been absolutely necessary: classes, study, eat, sleep. Austin had backed off, but continued to send Taylor texts, letting her know he was there for her without being pushy or selfish.

They both felt lucky to be invited back to attend another training summer at the Institute by Nicholas Ryan. Taylor hoped she would regain some of her enthusiasm for her future. And for Austin, as well.

Taylor dried herself with one of Grandma's plush pink towels. *We'll talk through things on the ride there*, she thought, and felt a tiny glimmer of excitement to be on an adventure with Austin.

Dressing quickly, Taylor grabbed her suitcases and made her way to the family room to find Austin sitting with her Grandmother, talking quietly.

"Oh, Grandma. I didn't want to wake you," she said, bending and giving her a gentle kiss on the cheek.

"I couldn't miss a chance to say hello to Austin," Grandma said with a smile that had more than a tinge of concern when she looked at Taylor, "and to wish my Taylor well."

"Grandma? Did you make bacon?" Taylor asked, turning her head in the direction of the kitchen and the savory aroma. "How? When?"

"It's a few hours' drive. You kids need to keep your strength up," Grandma said, rising and grabbing a large paper sack stained with bacon grease.

Austin stood and took the suitcases from Taylor's hands as well as the offered sack. Taylor smiled and even felt a little bit of a blush rising in her cheeks. She pulled her damp hair in front of her face to hide her pink cheeks. Taylor held her by her shoulders and gazed into her face.

"Are you going to be okay?"

Her Grandmother took Taylor's hands in her own and smiled bravely through shining eyes, "Don't you worry about me, sweetie. I've got Connor. I'll be okay. You focus on your job and learning and..." her voice broke a bit, "can you try to have some fun, dear?" She hugged Taylor tight, then ducked her head to conceal her tears. She quickly hugged Austin and walked them to the door.

Austin was respectful of Taylor's space, driving in silence for about a half-hour. He didn't know what else to do for her. He looked over at her profile, reached out, and wiped the tears that slipped down her cheek. He felt his grip tighten on the steering wheel, the now-familiar feeling of powerlessness, the fear of losing her bubbling up within him. It hurt him to be unable to help her, and he felt the distance that had opened up between them in her grieving might never be breached. He had been mourning the loss of his best friend and girlfriend since December, but he hoped this summer at the Institute might change all that. He'd been pleasantly surprised to learn that she wanted to return to the Institute when he'd been sure she'd feel duty-bound to be with her grandmother and Connor over the summer. And he'd felt even more delighted when she'd asked if they could drive together.

"Were you okay this morning? Usually you are the prompt one. Anything you want to talk about?" he asked.

"I had a horrible dream, and I'm not sure what it means. Can I tell you about it later?"

"Of course," Austin said.

"Do you know your assignment at the Institute?" Taylor asked. "I got an email from Sheena inviting me back, but have no idea what I'll be doing."

He took his eyes off the road to look at Taylor for a moment, and the intensity of her eye contact took his breath away. Turning his attention back to the road he said, "I don't know, either, but if I know Nicholas, it'll be about moving heavy objects." He chuckled ruefully, remembering clearing a field of rocks by hand, for Nicholas the previous summer.

Taylor allowed herself a small smile, too. "It wasn't so bad. Remember your awesome rock-throwing muscles?" Austin felt his face get warm at the compliment. "I wouldn't mind being back at the greenhouse," Taylor said, "but I would also love a new challenge."

"Maybe we'll be working together this time?" Austin said.

"Hm...maybe?" Taylor replied, returning to another long bout of silence.

Austin sighed and let the conversation drop. He hoped Taylor would play a role in his job at the Institute that summer. If he was being honest, he hoped Taylor would play a big role in the rest of his life. He'd worked hard this school year to show her he could be diligent and deliberate in setting and achieving goals, traits he knew were important to her. His growing love for her had intensified through her distance, but he had no idea what to do with that love or the heavy sadness that clung to her.

He rolled down his window and let the wind catch his hair. The warm summer breeze danced through the wooded area and filled the car with the white noise of rushing wind. Taylor rolled down her window, too, and smiled as the fragrance of spring wafted into the car. They drove in silence for the remainder of the two-hour drive, Taylor dozing off for most of it.

Austin knew he was getting close when he came to thick, fragrant woodlands. Nicholas Ryan's Estate was massive, but also some of the most serene land he'd ever had the pleasure to see. He could still feel a knot of doubt and fear about his and Taylor's relationship, but he tried to stamp it down and take in the peacefulness of his surroundings. As he rounded a bend, the Estate came into view.

Taylor let out a gasp. She'd also forgotten the majesty of the Ryan's Estate. The large windows caught the sun in a way that made the mansion glow like a sanctuary from a higher plane, nestled in the woods where only a select few would ever see and know of its existence, like a Shangri-La for the chosen.

They drove through the front gates and parked in one of the subterranean parking annexes. Sheena, Nicholas's officious executive secretary, was already waiting for them. She gestured impatiently for them, and Austin and Taylor jumped out of the car and followed her brisk walk to the elevator that would take them to the main house. Her long black hair was braided intricately, and her tailored business dress suit and trademark stilettos were polished and immaculate.

"I trust you had a productive school year?" Sheena asked the two, not bothering to turn and face them. Taylor answered for them both, becoming rather chatty with Sheena about Austin's grades, her graduation, and the feat she'd pulled off: graduating without any debt. Sheena didn't respond in any way. Austin realized this was the most talking he'd heard from Taylor in five months.

Haltingly, Taylor even mentioned the death of her grandfather. At this, Sheena stopped their progress to the lobby, turned, and took Taylor's hand with a loving squeeze.

"Loss is never an easy thing to deal with," Sheena said. "If you'd like to talk about it, there are plenty of people here who can help."

Taylor smiled at her. It was a warm and vibrant smile, and the way it filled Taylor's face reminded Austin of the girl he'd fallen for the summer before. "That would be wonderful," she said.

They walked the few remaining yards to the lobby, where they found Nicholas Ryan himself, walking briskly from the other direction with his assistant, Benjamin, in tow. At almost six feet tall, Nicholas was a work of chiseled perfection. His clothes accentuated every fluid movement of his powerful frame. The man emanated power in a way that demanded respect, but carried himself in a serene and even approachable manner.

Benjamin was reading off a list of some kind. Upon seeing Taylor and Austin, Nicholas stopped midstride. "Ah. You made it."

Austin and Taylor both beamed as the owner of the Estate made his way to them. He shook both of their hands firmly.

"I trust Sheena is taking care of both of you?"

They both nodded and started speaking at once about their gratitude to be there. Nicholas chuckled at their enthusiasm. "Yes, it's a good place to spend a summer with the very best people to help you learn some big ideas. Have you received your assignments yet?"

Before Austin or Taylor could reply, the lobby filled with students and trainees, apparently just released from a class. Some of these pupils were friends they'd met the previous summer. While Taylor and Austin were excited to see old friends, they were confused that the group didn't acknowledge them or even Nicholas, as they walked morosely through the lobby, plodding past them with their eyes on the ground directly in front of them.

Taylor and Austin exchanged a perplexed glance. Nicholas cleared his throat.

"They're working through some things. They had a training mission this week that *did not* go as we hoped," Nicholas explained.

"I think I get how they feel," Austin said. He remembered how rough it had been moving rocks the previous summer, and how frustrating that had been. Taylor nodded, also remembering the difficulties she had adjusting to her training last summer. But something else about that group and their overall disposition that reeked of failure tugged at her. She felt like she knew why they were dejected, but it was just outside of her memory. Her mind went to the dream she'd had that morning.

"Are they all alright?" Taylor asked.

"Physically, yes," replied Nicholas. "But emotionally they still have a long way to go."

Nicholas waved a hand, dismissing the gloom. "No matter. They may try again. In the meantime, why don't you two settle in? I have some matters to attend to."

"Of course," Sheena said, accepting for them. With that, the trio watched Nicholas depart. While Sheena pulled two folders from the front desk, Taylor's thoughtfulness sharpened into intense curiosity and her head snapped back to see where Nicholas had just exited.

"Sheena?" Taylor asked.

"Yes?"

"Do you think I can set up a meeting with Mr. Ryan?"

"I should be able to arrange that. What matters would you like to discuss? And is it a private appointment, or is it for both of you?"

Austin turned to Taylor and fixed his gaze on her. *What did she need to talk to him about?*

"Oh!" Taylor said. "I hadn't thought about..." Taylor trailed off, and Austin tried to puzzle out what she was thinking.

Sheena snapped her fingers. "Well?" she asked. Both Austin and Taylor wordlessly looked at her. "Shall we get you two to your rooms so you can get settled?"

"Uh, sure," Austin said.

"Both of us," Taylor said, her moment of hesitation gone. "Can we both get an appointment to talk to Mr. Ryan?"

Sheena nodded and put a note in her calendar, the three of them then headed to the stairs that lead to the dorm rooms.

Chapter 3 – Austin's Bold Request

It didn't take them long to unpack and settle in. Before they knew it, Sheena had an appointment with Nicholas for them. She had informed them that Mr. Ryan's schedule was tight, so they would have to spend a few moments with him between meetings.

Neither Austin nor Taylor objected as they made their way through the elegant, yet comfortable halls of the Estate. Austin took the lead and knocked on the door to Nicholas's office. They could hear the hushed sound of voices through the heavy wooden door. It cracked open a sliver, and Austin and Taylor ushered themselves in.

"Ah," said Nicholas. "Come in, you two. Have a seat and I'll be with you in a moment."

Nicholas returned to discussing some important matters with the gentleman on a video screen in front of him. Austin and Taylor sat as they were bid. Both of them attempted to take in their surroundings to give Nicholas and his other guest some privacy. It was much the same as last year. Austin began to study some of the Feng Shui of the room, and Taylor's eyes went right to the ring Nicholas is wearing on his hand. It was jet black with a brilliant red stone set in it. There seemed to be engravings around the edge that she couldn't quite decipher.

Taylor vividly remembered that particular ring, except the last time she had seen it had been on the hand of Nicholas' lovely wife, Vivian. Taylor remembered it so well because it had seemed to accentuate Vivian's fluid grace much as the highlights in the woman's blonde hair had made her face that much more inviting. However, she did not remember the center stone being red. Vivian's had been a light blue stone. But, then maybe these were their wedding bands.

Despite her interest in the ring, Taylor couldn't help but see who it was Nicholas was speaking with. The image of a confident and professional man with bright green eyes and dark brown hair touched with gray at the temples, filled the screen. He was immaculate in a tailored suit that rivaled Nicholas's in quality.

"Thank you, Kaleb," Nicholas said. "The proposal you sent me that would liquidate the oceanic exploration rights to that particular portion of our holdings should prove beneficial. I look forward to further updates of your negotiations with the potential buyer."

"Thank you, sir," Kaleb said. "If you'll excuse me, I would like to get the ball rolling on this as soon as possible."

Taylor found the man's eyes staring directly at her. She gave him a small smile and a nod before he looked away.

Nicholas sighed. "Alright, Kaleb. We'll talk soon."

"Very good, Mr. Ryan. Adieu."

The screen went dark. Nicholas chuckled to himself and turned to face Taylor and Austin. Somehow, during that exchange Nicholas seemed simultaneously relaxed and gripped with interest. Taylor was puzzled at how someone could be so ambiguous and mysterious about such a deal.

Nicholas steepled his fingers and smiled. "I guess you two caught the tail end of my wheelings and dealings there," he said.

"We heard a little bit, not enough to really understand—" Austin said, and was cut off as Nicholas waved away his excuse.

"It is asinine to think either of you two brilliant young people did not gather some information from that conversation," Nicholas said. "Well, let me set the record straight. That was Kaleb Mitchell, the CEO of one of my parent companies. He was just discussing a deal with me that would sell off one of my salvage companies to a competitor at an incredibly lucrative price."

"I gathered as much," Taylor said by way of admission.

Nicholas smiled. "Yes, I can tell. What else did you pick up, Taylor?" Nicholas said.

"I don't know," she said. "But you did seem both interested and uninterested at the same time."

Austin looked back and forth between them. Had he heard the same conversation? *How could someone be simultaneously two different things?*

"Ah," Nicholas said. "You caught that, did you? Mr. Mitchell is a brilliant and capable business man, and generally I trust his instincts. I just can't place why this particular property will be going for such a handsome sum. However, I am at peace with it. Does that make sense, Austin?"

Austin shook his head. It was like Nicholas had reached into his mind and scried out exactly what he had been trying to process. "I think so."

Nicholas smiled at the two of them. "Enough with work. How are you two? Has the school year treated you well?" Taylor shared her experiences over the previous nine months. Nicholas leaned forward, his arms rested on his desk as he listened.

She told of how they had gone back to school, and focused on their studies. She also spoke of how her Grandfather's death had impacted her. She misted up as she recounted the confused and lonely Christmas.

"Austin was there for me, and my family," Taylor said. "I am grateful for that, but it was still so empty."

Nicholas nodded his head. "Grief is not an easy obstacle for anyone. I am sorry you had to go through the loss of a loved one, especially at such a festive time of the year. The world doesn't stop, not even to grieve."

"Thank you," she said. "And thank you again for the lovely gift you sent me and my family after Grandpa's passing."

"It was the least we could do," Nicholas said. "You and Austin mean a great deal to everyone here. We were glad to help."

Taylor nodded, then continued her discussion about the remainder of the school year. When she had finished up with her graduation, she told him about how Austin had been a huge support for her.

"That is quite an eventful year, Taylor," he said. "And I am very happy you two are supporting one another. I am also happy to see you have graduated, but I do have to ask: what about you, Austin? What did you learn over the past nine months?"

Austin had gotten so used to having Taylor tell the whole story that he hadn't really thought about his own perspective on the past school year. He cleared his throat.

"To start off, let me say it went well," he said. Austin proceeded to recount his version of the events of the past nine months. His schooling had not been easy, but it had gone better. He had implemented the principles he had learned the previous summer. Nicholas smiled warmly as Austin recounted his meeting with the admissions board and his guidance counselor on why he believed he should graduate and how the exercise he had done in proclaiming his intentions had actually benefited his drive to do so.

"That is fantastic," Nicholas said, his voice had a charged layer of enthusiasm. "Have you considered what you want out of this summer?"

Austin didn't hesitate. "I know I have some serious catching up to do with school to graduate. I was thinking, and I've decided I want to do more training like last summer," he said. "I am willing to work for you for the summer like last year to pay my way. I just know I need to train more and learn what I can here. I feel it's the key to my success."

Nicholas smiled. "Indeed. So what can I do for you?" he asked.

Austin smiled at Taylor, who looked at him with bewilderment. They had not discussed what he was now asking Nicholas. "I want to do the Genius Program," he said. "The one you teach here at the Institute during the summers."

"Really?" asked Nicholas. He was trying to act surprised, but knew Austin was going to ask about that very thing. To his credit, his mock-surprise had fooled Austin.

"Yeah. Taylor and I saw the program online," Austin said, hooking a thumb to indicate Taylor. "And not only that, I want to do the Ascension Program, too, like the other guys were doing last summer. I hope it's possible to do them both at the same time."

Nicholas started to laugh. "Let me describe the Genius Program we have here at the Institute first. The average age for those in the program is *fourteen-years-old*," Nicholas said. "These young people are already very gifted in their various fields. They are beyond their peers at an international level. Each program is tailored to the individual for where they are and what they want to become. They are very self-motivated, and their parents pay handsomely for the relatively few spots we have in this program. The average price their parents pay is about a million dollars a year."

Austin's eyes went big at the mention of the average tuition for the program. If it cost a cool million for one program, how in the world would he ever afford two separate programs?

Nicholas paused to allow the silence to permeate more completely. He hoped it was more than mere dollar signs that Austin was thinking about. Meanwhile, Taylor watched Austin with a growing concern. He was stubborn and driven, but a roadblock like this might crush him.

"In fact," Nicholas said. "Some students will be in the program for up to four years, and when they are done, these kids will be the best in the world. True geniuses in their respective fields on the level of people like Einstein, Newton, Da Vinci, and Ramanujan. Is that really what you would like to do?"

Austin pondered what Nicholas was saying. "I don't know who Ramanujan is," he said, denoting his lack of knowledge as a sign of humility. "But yes, that is what I am asking. I would like to do the program, even though I had no idea how expensive it is."

Nicholas smiled and chuckled slightly to himself. "The Ascension Training is a separate program. It is for the greatest masters on the planet and, ultimately, the avatars that change the whole world."

Austin hung his head and pondered that. Was he being turned away now that he was committed to becoming his best self?

After a tense pause, Nicholas cleared his throat. "And how do you expect to pay the tuition for the Genius

Program?" he asked. He looked from Austin to Taylor and back again. "Are you going to get a million-dollar student loan?"

Austin exhaled slowly, with an expression of defeat. "I can't come up with that kind of money," he said. "Honestly, I was sort of hoping you would make an exception in our case."

Taylor was flabbergasted. Austin wanted this to be a handout? She started to protest, but Austin spoke up first.

"I know it sounds greedy to ask for such a huge favor, but I feel I needed to at least ask," he said. "I mean, if I never asked, then I know the answer would be no. At least I followed my promptings and asked. Thank you for at least hearing me out." He promptly stood up, preparing to leave.

Taylor looked over at Austin, who seemed so dejected. *What did he expect?* He had just asked for a million dollar freebie. She shook her head and turned back to Nicholas, who was gazing at her intently.

Finally, Nicholas asked, "What would you like, Taylor?"

"Honestly," she said, "I would love to do the Genius Program, but I'm no master or genius. Really, I'm just grateful to be here."

Nicholas sighed and sat back in his chair. "You know genius is relative, right? Think about it. You could specialize in one area or another like math, music, athletics, or in general intelligence, like multi-dimensional thinking that can be used with everything.

The options are available and tailored for your best fit. So, it really is a question of what you would like."

Taylor was taken aback. "Well, I still figure it's so far out of my reach, why even try?" she said, trying to be equal parts blunt and humble. "I'm fine with working here this summer like I did before, for real. We both know I don't have that kind of money, and besides, I know I can learn a lot from simply being here."

Nicholas shook his head. "Taylor. That sounds like you're giving up before you've even started," he said. "You know you have more in you than that. You are amazing. You need to give yourself permission to be that amazing woman you already are."

Taylor searched his eyes, then looked away, almost wishing she could be as daring as Austin. Austin turned to see what she would say.

"Maybe," said Taylor, "but, really, if I could have what I want from you, it would simply be a good paying job here at the Estate."

"That's it?" asked Nicholas.

"Yes."

"I will see what I can do, then," said Nicholas.

"Thank you," Taylor said. "We really appreciate the opportunity to be here."

Nicholas nodded and they both turned to leave.

"Wait," said Nicholas, "Austin, you haven't given me the chance to give you my answer."

Austin turned back to him, expecting chastisement for his bold request. He could see it now, his brazen request might have cost him his summer here and left him flipping burgers or digging sprinkler systems somewhere else, without Taylor.

He braced himself. "I know I don't have the money," said Austin. "So I guess I'm out of luck. I didn't mean to seem greedy, thinking I could just ask and receive such a huge gift." Austin sighed, his shoulders slumped. "But if you're offering me a paying job here this summer," he said, forcing a smile, "I would love to take you up on it, but that's about the best I can do until I graduate next year."

"After making such an admittedly bold request," said Nicholas, "you are just going to give up that easily?"

A glimmer of hope sparked back to life in Austin's eyes. Nicholas smiled. "I will consider your request for the Genius Program."

"Thank you!" Austin said. "I really appreciate this."

Austin was frankly surprised at how levelheaded he had been. The emotional clearing he had done over the past few weeks had really paid off.

"Wait, you two," Nicholas said, as he directed his eyes toward the ceiling for a moment. He looked back down and met Austin's gaze. "You said you wanted to do the Ascension Training, as well."

"I do. In fact, would like to do them simultaneously, if possible."

Nicholas had a somewhat puzzled expression on his face. "The Ascension Training Program is not even on the website," he said. "It's not even technically part of the Institute. How did you know about it?"

This time it was Austin's turn to smile knowingly. "I talked with some of the other guys last year, and they said it was what they were doing."

Nicholas nodded. "In the last twelve years, around three hundred people have done the Genius Program, including the thirty-six we have in the program now. In that same time, only thirty-three have done the Ascension Training. Twenty-two of them are still in the process."

Nicholas paused, letting his words sink in. "If you thought the Genius Program was intense, the Ascension Program is ten to a hundred times more so."

Austin's face blanched, realizing how hard it would be to do one of the programs, let alone both at the same time.

"Well," he said after getting up the courage, "I would like to at least give it a try."

"Do or do not, there is no try," Nicholas said.

Austin smiled at the pop culture reference, and responded, "Yes. I want to do it."

Nicholas looked up at the ceiling again, deliberating. "I will give you my answer tomorrow. In the meantime, I recommend you do some soul-searching and make sure you really want this. It's not something one goes into half-heartedly. If you choose to do the Ascension Training and are accepted, you would be doing the most intensive training possible. More than you can imagine right now."

"Mr. Ryan, if you will let me do the Ascension program, I promise you, I will not fail. I can do it. I'm not afraid." Austin responded, using what he had learned about declaring his intentions.

Nicholas smiled, nodding towards the door. Austin and Taylor took their cues and left Nicholas's office. As they did, Austin could have sworn he heard a faint voice in the back of his mind. "You will be. You will be."

Austin shook the words from his mind. He instead replaced it with the hopeful idea that he could do both the programs and show Nicholas and Taylor just how smart and capable he really was.

Nicholas sat musing over the conversation with Austin and Taylor. Although they had since left his office, something about their conversation still lingered in his mind.

Alchesay sat on the couch in the far corner of the office. He was in plain view, so Nicholas found it interesting that neither Austin nor Taylor had noticed his personal assistant and bodyguard. Al stood about six foot five inches tall, had dark skin and was a muscular, bald, Samoan tank. The man could be silent when he wanted to, a fact Nicholas had come to know very well.

Al had been pulled from the verge of death by Nicholas eighteen years earlier, and felt a fierce sense of loyalty ever since. In turn, Nicholas put great trust in this man and what he had to say. "So what do you think, Al?" he asked. "Can they do it?"

"I don't know," said the loyal bodyguard. "Taylor sells herself short. If she would commit to it she would do it at one-hundred percent. She seems like an all-or-nothing type of girl. I'm not so sure about Austin. Even with all he learned last summer, he still has a long way to go."

"You're right," Nicholas said. "Austin has the dark gifts of doubt and fear." The mention of these gifts caused both men to fall into a state of silence as they pondered the conversation independently, both looking at the ceiling.

"So, what are you going to tell them?" Al asked.

"Well, Taylor definitely has a job here doing something. She has far too much talent to waste," Nicholas said.

Al nodded and both men stared off into the silence a moment more.

Nicholas sighed. "And you're right about her being one-hundred percent. If she asked to do either program I would say yes. But she has to ask for it, so she would do it at one-hundred percent. She has to believe in herself."

"And Austin?" Al asked, scratching his chin.

"I'm still not sure. He made a lot of progress last summer, but he's still really headstrong, unaware, and naïve to what he's really asking."

Al smiled slightly, which was unusual for him. "It kind of reminds me of you when you first started doing the training."

Nicholas returned a knowing smile. "Was I as rough and undisciplined as Austin?"

"No, you were worse," Al said. They both laughed.

"You're right," said Nicholas, his smile fading. "I was such a broken man then. So desperate I would have bit the head off a live chicken if I knew it would have helped."

"But you didn't have the three months of pre-training that Austin has," Al added.

At that, Nicholas nodded.

"Think of what the other masters have said about Austin," Al said. "His potential. They believe in him. That it's his time. You even recommended Austin to the Council last month. He's not perfect, but who is? That's the beauty of it." Al paused. "You once told me a long time ago, that it's about the journey, not the destination."

Nicholas remained quiet.

"They can do it," Al said. "They both can."

Nicholas nodded in agreement.

Chapter 4 – The Construction Site

Austin tried to stay positive on the heels of his meeting with Nicholas the previous morning. He could still stay and work at the Institute, even if he didn't get to participate in either the Genius Training or the Ascension Training. That and it guaranteed him a chance to be around Taylor all summer and to try and figure out why she had been so hot and cold about their relationship lately. She still confused him.

He finished the apple he had snagged for breakfast as he headed out for a jog. He had seen vast improvements in his school schedule by adding a run to his morning routine. He tossed the apple core in the trash and stretched a bit to loosen up.

As he straightened up he saw Benjamin come around the corner. He smiled and signaled for Austin to hold up. Austin shrugged and continued stretching as Benjamin approached.

"And how are you this morning, Austin?" he asked.

Austin smiled. "Can't complain."

"Good. Good," Benjamin said. "Hey, Mr. Ryan wanted me to invite you and Taylor on a tour of the rest of the Institute later this morning."

"Oh," Austin said. He was taken aback by the bluntness of the request. What did he mean by the Institute? *Wasn't the Estate all there was?* Come to think of it, Austin didn't remember seeing any Genius Training-age kids around.

"Sure," he replied.

"Sure, what?" Taylor said, as she jogged up to join them.

"Oh," Austin said. "Mr. Ryan has set up a tour for us to see the Institute."

"Actually," Benjamin said with a wry smile. "He plans to give you the tour himself."

"That sounds fantastic," Taylor said. "Tell Mr. Ryan we're in. Right, Austin?"

"Sure," he said, a little surprised that Nicholas would take the time to show them around. "Hey, last one to finish today's jog buys the other a protein shake. Deal?"

Taylor opened her mouth to answer Austin's challenge, but he was already gone. She clicked her tongue and jogged hard to close the gap. *He was going to be the one buying the protein drink.*

Nicholas Ryan waited on the curb by his Mercedes S400 Rolls Royce Edition limousine. He had a fleet of cars and various vehicles at his disposal, but he had chosen this one today, not because he had to impress his young guest, but for a practical reason. This vehicle would allow them to focus on chatting with one another without having to focus on the drive. Nicholas wanted to study both Austin and Taylor today. It would inform the decisions he was planning to make.

Both Austin and Taylor strode out of the front of the Estate at ten o'clock sharp. Austin let out a low whistle as they came near Mr. Ryan.

"A limo? You are taking us on a tour of the Institute in a limo?" Austin said.

Taylor rolled her eyes. *Boys and their toys, they never grow out of them*, she thought.

Austin walked around admiring the vehicle until Nicholas cleared his throat to get his attention and opened the door for them. Austin jumped in, giddy as a child on Christmas morning, and Taylor climbed in, unable to fight the small thrill only a quality vehicle could afford.

Nicholas smiled and nodded to Al, who was sitting in the driver's seat. He climbed into the back and sat facing the two young people who he had grown to care for last summer and had kept tabs on during their school year. He had such high hopes for them. Nicholas studied both of them while they pulled out of the drive. He had instructed Al to take it slow so he and his friends would have adequate time to talk. The Institute was not far, but it would take them at least ten minutes to get there.

The limo pulled off the road and onto a recently graded gravel drive. The surrounding area was forested with stately maples, their green leaves fluttered in the morning breeze. The lodge pole pines stood tall and straight, a grand backdrop for the pink wood rose, red dogwoods, and the wild raspberries.

"It's so beautiful out here," Taylor said, enthralled with the scene before her. "It's peaceful and serene on so many levels."

"That is why Vivian and I selected it to be the site of the Institute," Nicholas said. "The connection one can feel with nature here is essential to unlocking latent potential. The sacred geometry of nature is unparalleled in our modern world."

A perplexed expression spread over Austin's face. *Sacred geometry? Connections? What were they talking about?* He decided not to ask and resumed peering back out his window as he said, "The pictures online don't do this place justice."

Nicholas smiled and made a mental note that Austin was trying to appear more knowledgeable than he was, probably to impress him. *The boy definitely has drive, that was obvious, but will it be enough?*

As the trees parted, Austin could see a huge construction site. Giant mounds of dirt and tall cranes were strewn about the side of the mountain.

"What's being built here?" he asked.

Nicholas smiled. "Would you like to see it?" He had planned this all along. It was one of the reasons he had insisted on showing Taylor and Austin around personally.

Austin didn't hesitate, "Sure. What is it, though?"

Nicholas smiled as they made an unexpected turn. Taylor and Austin exchanged a glance before turning back to Nicholas when they began to head down a road they had not previously seen.

Austin wanted to ask if this was the way to the Institute. *Was it off in these woods? Was it still being built?* He had a million questions formulating, but noticed Taylor was staring out the window, so he thought better of it. Nicholas always seemed to have his reasons for doing things, so Austin relaxed and decided to enjoy the experience.

Meanwhile, Taylor had noticed the road quality improved, as if it were freshly paved within the last week or had experienced hardly any traffic. Her suspicions were confirmed that it was rarely used when she noted the dust on the center line where traffic lines would generally be painted. The woods here were so thick that Taylor couldn't see very far on either side of the road. She could barely make the mountains out as they headed west towards them.

The limo came around a bend and they found themselves at a large, imposing gate with a guardhouse beside it. The high fence behind that was going off in both directions into the woods—not that they could see very far in either direction because of the dense foliage spilling out through the gate.

The entrance gate was wide. However, the gate itself was made of reinforced steel that looked like it had enough stopping power to halt anything shy of a tank. Taylor noted that this was only the first such gate. Another gate lay roughly twenty yards ahead, equipped with its own security station just beyond the fence. *What is this place?*

The door to the security station slid open with a slight hiss that they more anticipated than heard or felt. A somewhat handsome guard came walking up to Nicholas' window and peered in with a smile on his face, recognizing Nicholas instantly.

"Hello, Mr. Ryan!" the guard said with a note of familiarity. Austin noticed the Glock 41 Gen4 strapped on the guard's belt. He knew the type because it had been the starter weapon in a game he had recently played with Taylor's brother, Connor. The guard seemed very relaxed though, so the piece must have been a precaution more than anything.

"Hello, Jake," Nicholas said returning the guard's genuine smile. "How are things going today?"

"They're going great. Things are moving along quickly, sir." The guard handed Nicholas three work helmets as he did. "I think we're ahead of schedule." Jake glanced at Taylor, who was sitting in the seat kiddy-corner to Nicholas and then shot a brief glance through the window at Austin.

"Great," Nicholas said. "How are Carrie and the kids doing?"

"They're all doing well. Our youngest is starting school in a few weeks."

"Kylie is already starting school? They sure do grow up, fast don't they?" Nicholas said. "Hey, do me a favor and give them all a hug for me."

"Will do, sir."

The vehicle began to roll forward. "Tell Lyle hi for me, too" Nicholas said as he gestured to the other guard in the gatehouse. The guard stepped back and saluted.

"You got it, sir."

Both Austin and Taylor noticed there was an older guard, likely Lyle, in the gatehouse as they rolled by. He was on the phone, and he had some sort of automatic rifle slung over his shoulder, barrel down. Austin couldn't quite make out the model through the limo's tinted windows. He could tell that it definitely had stopping power, though. Lyle nodded his head towards Nicholas as both large heavy gates rose, and they were on their way again.

The limo drove a little further west through the beautiful wooded tree-lined road before it bent to the north. Taylor cleared her throat.

"I'm curious," she said. "Were you planning on bringing us here?"

"Not really," said Nicholas matter-of-factly. "Why do you ask?"

"Because," Taylor responded. "That guy back there—Jake seemed to be expecting us."

"Interesting. What makes you say that?" Nicholas said, handing out the construction helmets

Austin took the helmet and added, "Yeah, like he knew three of us were coming. I felt the same way."

Nicholas smiled keeping his eyes trained out the window on the road as he set the third helmet on the seat next to him. The cab grew silent for a moment, until the road began to turn back to the west.

"So, were they expecting..." Taylor let the sentence end abruptly as her attention was absorbed by the scene in front of her. The trees gave way as they came around the last corner to the massive construction site. Gigantic hills of excavated soil were piled on either side of the site, and three enormous cranes loomed over a gargantuan hole in the ground. It seemed more like a quarry than a construction site at this point.

The vehicle came up to a lighter-duty construction truck and stopped. Nicholas was the first to get out of the back, not even waiting for Al to open the door for him. He nodded to Al, then looked back at the two still seated in the back with their mouths agape.

"Well, come on," Nicholas said as he put on his hard hat. Austin and Taylor quickly got out of the limo and put on their hats. Nicholas had already begun making his way towards the construction activity.

A line of cement blocks acted as a barricade between them and the enormous pit. A mountain rose on the far side as the two followed Nicholas past the barricade. They came up to another fence with three-foot gaps spaced every fifteen yards. Many construction workers milled about the site, doing their jobs like ants working around their hill.

Several of them noticed Nicholas and his guests, but they just nodded and continued their work. Whatever they were up to must have been of the utmost importance. For the most part though, Austin and Taylor were still transfixed by massive hole in front of them as they passed through the fence line. Nicholas guided them along the ridge around the site, allowing them to see down the hole, only ten feet from the edge.

Their astonishment at the size and magnitude of the space only grew. Nicholas smiled and put his hand out. "This is one of my latest projects," he said.

Austin and Taylor looked into the abyss of the pit until Taylor finally found her words.

"What is it?" Taylor asked.

"Why, it's a hole," Nicholas said with a playful smile.

"Yeah," she said. "But what's it for?"

Nicholas smiled. "Ah, now that's a better question. It's going to be a healing center unlike any the planet has known for thousands of years."

Austin looked at Nicholas incredulously. "That's going to be a healing center? It's enormous!"

"Do you mean like a fully staffed hospital?" Taylor asked.

"No. Not really," Nicholas said with a sly smile.

Just then, Taylor noticed a fidgety older man hurrying up to them. Nicholas seemed to not notice him at first.

"Mr. Ryan," said the man. He appeared to be in his mid-fifties, with an average build.

"We weren't expecting you today, sir. I mean it's okay that you're here, but..."

"Relax, Karl," Nicholas said, turning to him. "This is not an official inspection. It's just a tour for some of my friends."

"Oh. Okay then," Karl said, a little relieved.

Austin and Taylor had gone back to surveying the site before them. That was, until Taylor noticed Nicholas glance at the band on his left wrist. It seemed so mundane, yet she could not recall when she'd ever seen him concerned about time before.

"Karl," Nicholas said, looking up from his timepiece, "would you do me a favor and give my friends a tour of the site?"

"Sure, Mr. Ryan," Karl said as Nicholas walked quickly back to the limo. He passed through the gates and Al opened the door to the car.

Karl turned to Austin and Taylor. "Well, do you youngsters want to see one of the most amazing things ever built?" he said with a smile. The impression Taylor had was that he was rough on the outside with most of people, especially the workers, but that he was actually very kind and showed that to Mr. Ryan's guests.

"Well, come along then," he said as he started to walk in the opposite direction of the gates, "and mind your step or it will be your last." His dark humor was disarming. They followed after him as he walked along the edge heading towards one of the large cranes.

"What we have undertaken to build is unlike anything you have ever seen," he said, his voice taking on a lecturer's tone. "On this side, the drop is 250 feet to the bottom, where we are putting in the footings for this..." he paused, not knowing exactly how to describe it, "thing."

Karl took them further and stopped where the cliffs climbed to the mountain only to drop off over 350 feet to the floor. Austin and Taylor continued to look around. Three large cranes extended far over the gaping expanse. One of them was lowering a huge gray bucket into the hole. A second crane held another bucket that was being filled with concrete from a large mixing truck on their far left. Taylor noticed cement trucks coming and going on both sides of the expanse. She couldn't tell where they were coming from.

"The opening is more than 600 feet wide and across. It's over a third of a million square feet," Karl said with a note of pride. He stopped at an overlook and leaned on the guardrail, gesturing to Austin and Taylor to come see. They could easily see the bottom of the hole.

A third crane was lowering a bundle of long steel rods down to the square concrete footings that ran around the perimeter of the opening at the bottom. Cement forms ran directly east, west, north, and south, creating a checkerboard pattern. In between the square openings, Taylor thought she saw moving water, but she wasn't sure because of the distance.

The path along the northern perimeter was still verdant, even as workers continued covering it with long steel rods and fresh concrete. Taylor noticed the massive amount of steel that seemed to be all over the place. It was a hive of activity. Trucks buzzed around along the top, and some sat along with the sheets of steel stacked on their side and huge bundles of twenty feet long pieces of steel being readied to lower into the hole.

Austin had to consciously pull his attention away from the activity below in order to see how much soil had been excavated into towering hills. The mounds rose like mini-mountains beside the vastness of the hole.

"So, what is this going to look like when it's finally done?" Taylor said into the odd silence of the construction site.

Before Karl could answer, Nicholas was at their side. Karl jumped.

"Sorry," Nicholas said with a wink. "And sorry to cut this short, but we need to get going with the rest of the tour."

Taylor and Austin had more questions for Karl, but turned to follow Nicholas back to an SUV. There was no trace of Al or the limo from before, but neither of them questioned it. They hopped in, holding on to their myriad of questions as Nicholas simply said, "Don't worry. I'll explain more later. Right now, we need to get to the Institute as soon as we can."

Chapter 5 – Tour

On the drive to the Institute, Taylor took the front passenger seat and Austin sat behind her. Nicholas was uncharacteristically quiet. The drive was a short four miles, which the SUV seemed to be making considerably quicker than the luxuriant limo.

"You will probably notice," Nicholas said, breaking the silence, "That the Institute is laid out differently than nearly any other school you will ever have the pleasure of seeing."

Taylor and Austin nodded, soaking up what Nicholas was telling them.

"I trust Dr. Johnson's program, and so do many of the world's richest and most brilliant minds," Nicholas continued. "I had the pleasure of constructing this bastion of higher learning with the good doctor. You will find none more focused on teaching young minds the correct principles they need to have a successful life."

Austin recalled his last summer at Nicholas' Estate. If Nicholas Ryan gave his seal of approval to the Institute, then it was top notch. It made him all the more serious about getting into the Genius Program. He knew success was more than dollar signs now, and he wanted it. He had proclaimed to the universe, to his higher power, that he wanted it.

Taylor drew in a quick breath as the tree line cleared. Austin pulled his attention to the road. True to Nicholas's word, the Genius Institute was like no school he had ever seen before. They were greeted by two finely crafted dormitories modeled after antebellum southern plantations, but that was where traditional architecture ended. Austin's eyes were drawn to the grand outdoor amphitheater in the heart of five buildings, shaped like octagons and made out of exquisite glass and metal work. The trees and natural surroundings of the area did not seem disturbed by any of the learning structures. In fact, these may have been the most organic buildings either Taylor or Austin could remember seeing since the hobbit holes in *The Lord of the Rings.*

Nicholas smiled. "Austin," he said.

"Yes?" Austin replied, distracted by what he thought was a soccer field hidden among the trees and brush.

"I want to tell you a little more about the program before we park and take a tour of the grounds."

Austin swung his attention back to Nicholas, as did Taylor. "Yeah?"

"Yes," Nicholas said, hiding a smile. He loved to see the excitement in young people when they were awed by things he had worked so hard in creating. He also loved teaching them how to obtain their own dreams. "Typically, Dr. Johnson's program here at the Institute is for younger people. The general students don't begin the program later than age fourteen."

Austin stared numbly at Nicholas. He felt like his world was coming undone.

"Our oldest student is almost eighteen," Nicholas continued. "The adults have different programs in a different set of buildings."

Austin steeled himself. He knew this was coming, but Nicholas changed the subject. "Alright, shall we go take a look at the Institute?"

Austin was dazed as he got out of the SUV. He'd been ready for the knockout blow to his dreams, but maybe he still had a fighting chance? Hope redoubled in his chest, as he held the door open for Taylor. She smiled at him and seemed to be having the time of her life.

Nicholas motioned them onto the path and they continued the tour. "At the Institute," he began, "they teach the regular textbook school subjects, so the student body can graduate from high school if they desire. We are a state accredited and recognized institution. However, we also specialize in certain areas of expertise. That is where we are different from other conventional education programs."

"What types of things does the program teach here?" Taylor asked. She couldn't help admiring the grace with which the grounds were incorporated into the woods.

Nicholas smiled "Well, a lot of child prodigies come through our program. So, while we cater to their fields of interest, we teach them in areas outside of their comfort zone to broaden their knowledge and increase their education."

"Wow," Taylor said. "That is incredible! But how do you have such a specialized program for each student?"

"I will answer that, but first," Nicholas said indicating the antebellum style buildings as they passed. "These are our dormitories capable of housing fifty people comfortably. We have them split into a boys' dorm and a girls' dorm. The staff housing is separate, just a ways east of here."

Taylor had no issue seeing how these three-story structures could house so many people. In fact, it gave her an inkling as to what Nicholas was going to tell her next.

"Back to your question, Taylor. The program currently has over eighty instructors for forty-two students. We are able to tailor their individual experience based on the fact that they have about a two teacher to one student ratio. In fact, a number of our instructors are former students and are some of the very best in the world in their respective fields."

Taylor mulled that over, and Austin tried to take it all in. He could hear a symphony of music wafting toward them as they neared the first of the class buildings. The sounds of harmonious piano, harp, violin and flute music, among other instruments, gently enveloped them.

Nicholas stopped and closed his eyes, taking in the sounds. Taylor emulated him, and Austin quirked his head trying to decipher all the instruments before finally succumbing and closing his eyes.

"Peaceful tranquility," Nicholas said. "We host twelve students in the music program. Seven of these students are in piano, but are also taught astrophysics and mathematics."

This is incredible. The music was some of the finest Austin had ever heard, and most of these kids weren't even old enough to drive. "How much did this all cost?" Austin asked before he could help himself.

"Ever one to talk brass tacks aren't you, Austin?" Nicholas said with a hint of chastisement.

"Think about it, Austin," Taylor said. "Those in the math program are also taught the arts. We saw the athletic fields, so they are obviously taught at the Institute. There's so much here, of course it cost a lot to build."

"She's quite right," Nicholas said giving Taylor an approving smile. "Even our prodigy athletes are taught advanced courses in physics, geometry and other sciences, so it's not just our intellectual students being taught advanced fitness skills. And all students are taught emotional clearing and mental exercises."

Austin fell silent. *How in the world can I ever pay for this?*

Nicholas continued the tour. One of the buildings was dedicated to healing arts and non-traditional medicine. This, Nicholas explained, was an entirely separate program from the Genius Training. As they passed through several of the buildings, they witnessed some of the different subjects being taught.

Austin remembered the Reiki session he'd received the previous summer, and pushed aside his financial woes to watch as further demonstrations of the techniques were displayed. There was Foot Zone Therapy. An herbalist was lecturing about the beneficial properties of common herbs and a few other different types of alternative medicine that made Austin ponder about the healing center they were building not that far away.

They concluded the tour back at the SUV. It had certainly been enlightening, and despite the fact that Austin was close to a decade too old for the program, he still wanted to try.

"Alright," Nicholas said as they backed out of their parking stall. "Taylor, would you still like to work at the Estate?"

"Definitely," said Taylor. "I would love to."

Nicholas smiled at her in the rearview mirror. "You're sure you don't want to do any of the programs?"

"Oh, I could never ask for that," Taylor said. "I don't have that much money, and what with my Grandma being a widow and my brother..."

"Alright," Nicholas said nodding. "It's settled. Tomorrow morning you will report to Sheena and she can hammer out the paperwork and get you on the payroll."

Nicholas then turned a sidelong glance at Austin. "And I suppose you still want to do both the advanced trainings as old as you are?"

"Old!" Austin replied. His early twenties were not where Austin considered himself to be over the hill. "Age is just a number, right?"

Taylor snickered. "Austin, you act younger than your age, anyway."

Austin's face reddened as Taylor chuckled at her rejoinder.

Nicholas had a half-smile on his face. "Alright," he said. "Austin, you can do both the Genius and Ascension trainings as part of a scholarship program."

Austin nearly jumped out of the car in elation.

Chapter 6 – Austin and Incident

Nicholas had left, taking off with a team for an international obstacle course competition. Austin found himself accompanying Taylor to the Equine Center at the Institute. It was Austin's first morning off since Nicholas had told him he would be working at the Estate until he got back. She had told him about how awesome the center was and how much it helped with the kids who went there. Austin got a feeling that she secretly loved horses. He wanted their relationship to progress, so he had agreed to come.

The drive over had been short, and Taylor had regaled him with equine facts, and center tidbits. He was beginning to wonder if she hadn't memorized the pamphlet on this place when they pulled up.

Austin quickly hopped out of the car and got Taylor's door. She smiled up at him and climbed out.

"I can get my own door, you know," Taylor said as she swatted Austin's hand away playfully. "It is the twenty-first century, after all."

Austin held out his hands placatingly. "I just wanted to show off the fact that I do have manners."

Taylor clucked. "Right. Chivalry doubles as manners, then?"

Austin dropped his hands, he wasn't sure if he was heading into a trap or what. "Tell you what," he said. "You can get the door to the building."

"How magnanimous of you," Taylor said a mirthful laugh punctuating her statement. "It's a stable."

Austin made a show of looking over at the Equine Center. "So it is."

Taylor punched his arm as they strode over to the entrance. Austin was impressed by the grounds inside. Though, if the Estate was any indicator, this should have been on par with what he could expect from one of the healing facilities Nicholas Ryan had constructed.

Taylor was in awe as they watched the horses helping children with physical issues and even some less obvious mental and emotional issues in the healing process. She dragged Austin closer to watch the cavalry of equine pediatric healers working their miracles on their patients.

Luckily, a trainer came up to them and cut Taylor short. He was a stocky man who came up to Austin's shoulder. The man was made of thick ropes of muscle.

"Howdy, folks," he said. "The name's Laramie. You must be Austin and Taylor."

"How did you know that?" Austin said.

"Sheena phoned ahead and told me you were coming," Laramie said.

Taylor smiled and shook his hand. "Nice to meet you, Laramie, I'm Taylor."

"Shoot, ma'am," Laramie said. "I never would have guessed." He winked at her and she giggled.

Austin stuck out his hand, trying not to show his annoyance. Laramie took it. "That makes you Austin, I reckon."

"Reckon so," Austin said. The trainer's smile was contagious. If Austin had had any ill will toward the man, it was gone now.

"Y'all wanna meet some of the stars of the show?" Laramie asked.

Taylor didn't even give Austin a chance to respond and, before he knew it, Laramie was walking them around the stable showing them the horses. Austin noticed Raul, Joseph, Mani and Will, friends from the previous summer, there. He was glad to see he wasn't the only one roped into this.

Laramie came up short and patted a nut-brown filly on the neck. She nuzzled close to him. "This one is a new addition to the pack," Laramie said. "Incident here is a special horse. She has an even temperament to help children with severe forms of emotional trauma. Might say she is the gentlest critter in the bunch."

"That so?" Austin said before he realized he was talking. The flippant comment bought him a sidelong glance from Taylor.

Laramie let out a deep belly laugh. "Well, if'n you folks have any more question y'all can find me at the stalls or ask any of the other trainers."

Taylor thanked Laramie as he left. She turned back to Incident and ignored Austin as she stroked the filly's mane. Joseph, Mani and Will had made their way over to welcome their friends.

Austin turned back to the Taylor after taking another look around the stable. She seemed a little perturbed, *but why?* Did he do something to embarrass her?

"What's up, Taylor?" he asked, quickly deciding it was better to inquire than worry.

"I think I left my phone in the car," she said. Austin held back a chuckle. "I wanted to get a picture of us and one of the horses to send to Grandma and Connor."

Before Austin could offer his phone for the photo, Taylor turned to him with big doe eyes. "Can you go get it for me?"

Austin didn't have it in him to turn down her request. It wasn't that difficult, and it got him out of the constant smell of horse manure. He cracked a smile.

"I'll do it, but you owe me," he said.

"Seriously?" she asked.

"Hey," Austin said keeping up his playful ruse. "This isn't pro bono, I'll think of something fitting as a payback on my way back with your phone."

Before she could protest, Austin was off like a shot out of the stable. Even the lingering smell could not dull his mood.

Austin had been thinking about this for a while now, and if he spun this just right, things could work out. Honestly, with him and Taylor becoming more friendly again, why wouldn't this be a great time to take their relationship to the next level? He wouldn't go for the coup de gras with this favor. No, he'd start smaller.

Austin was going to ask for an innocent kiss. The plan was a sound one in his mind by the time he reached the car. He would start with a kiss in just the right location, and the romance would sweep her off her feet and then they really would be to that next level. *Girls always seem to love stuff like that. Seemingly spontaneous romantic gestures and random, but quaint locations,* he thought. It was a formula Austin had used to his advantage a time or two.

The trick was planning. *If I stack my cards just right, and make her feel special enough, she's going to feel obligated to return the kiss and maybe more.* Austin smiled smugly to himself as he retrieved Taylor's cell from the car.

The best part about this was Taylor had given him the opportunity. Austin hurried back to the stable to give Taylor her phone and deviously tell her he needed more time to think about what she could repay him with. However, as he walked in, he noticed that Joseph, Mani, and Will were circled around Taylor. They were all laughing.

The warning hackles on the back of Austin's neck stood at attention. This was the exact opposite of what he was planning. He watched unnoticed from outside the stable yard as Joseph demonstrated a fluid motion that saw him in the saddle of one of the horses. Then Mani said something and they all laughed.

Austin ground his teeth and put Taylor's phone in his pocket as Joseph, with as much grace as before, dismounted and gave a flourishing bow to Taylor's apparent delight.

She likes cowboys, eh? Austin looked around the stable yard and spotted Incident, the horse they had seen with Laramie earlier, and smiled an impish smile.

Joseph, Mani, and Will still hung around Taylor, chatting as Austin stormed into the yard like a thunderhead. He marched up to Incident, who stomped nervously, and attempted to climb onto her back. Austin could still salvage this. He just had to show Taylor he could ride, too.

After an inordinate amount of time, he finally was in the saddle. The horse snorted, but Austin paid the creature no mind.

"Hey Taylor," he said as loud as he could. "Check this out!"

Taylor's jaw dropped and the color drained from her face. Will, Mani, and Joseph looked over at Austin after seeing her expression change.

"Austin!" Taylor said, practically screaming. "You don't even know how to ride!"

Austin ignored her and grabbed the horse's reins. *It's now or never.*

"Ya!" His exclamation echoed he whipped the horse with reins. Incident didn't move.

Austin blushed and tried to spur the horse on, but Incident wouldn't even budge. He exhausted everything he could think of, everything he had ever seen a cowboy do in the movies—nothing. All the horse did was begin to fidget nervously.

Fury rose in the pit of Austin's stomach. The guys he had considered friends were laughing and coming over now to help him down. No one seemed to have the issues he was having right then.

Austin had passed his boiling point. He had been made a fool of in front of everyone, but most of all he had been shown up *by this dumb animal* in front of Taylor. He'd had enough.

Suddenly, and without warning, the horse bucked violently. Austin, momentarily airborne, crashed back down hard, sideways in the saddle. Off balance, he fell to the ground getting a face full of dirt. The other guys roared with laughter.

He waved them off as he got up. No one was going to make him a laughingstock, *e*specially not *some stupid horse.* Enraged, Austin charged and went to jump on the horse's back. Incident shied away then turned and whipped her head knocking him into a bale of hay.

The laughter had stopped, but Austin wasn't paying attention anymore. He only saw red. And the horse. Getting up, he strode back over to the animal. Everyone watched unmoving.

Taylor was sure she could hear a pin drop. She watched in abject horror as Austin reared back and socked the horse in the side of the head as hard as he could. Taylor was mortified. This was the guy she was dating?

The guy she even considered a future with had punched a poor, defenseless horse in the head. Taylor was about to tear into him herself when Incident reacted, and jerked her head again, knocking Austin to the unforgiving ground.

He lay in a heap, defeated. Will and Joseph grabbed the reins, calming the horse as Mani checked on Austin. Taylor just stared, then turned and stormed off.

Through his pain, he watched her go. He knew he'd screwed up big time. He'd only wanted to impress her. Instead, he was beat up as bad as his ego. He closed his eyes, partly due to his realization and partly to shut out the pain in his arm.

"Bro," Mani said. "I think your shoulder is dislocated. What *were* you thinking?"

Austin winced as he sat up. "That horse was making a fool out of me!" he said.

Mani shook his head. "Let's get you over to the medical building and have them take a look at you. Then maybe you should stay away from horses for a while."

Austin's eyes glinted, but the pain in his shoulder won out and he allowed Mani to help him.

On the way there, the two of them didn't exchange a single word. *If that damn horse hadn't been so stubborn,* Austin thought, *Taylor wouldn't have left.* Austin had never hated anything as much as he did that horse.

When they got to the building Mani helped him inside. "Give this to Taylor for me, will you?" Austin asked handing Mani Taylor's phone.

"Sure thing," he replied.

It wasn't long before one of the medical assistants had Austin's shirt off. "What happened to you, Austin?" Dr. Mac said upon entering the room.

Austin shot him a painful glance from where he sat on the examination table.

Mani explained what happened as the doctor examined the injured shoulder. Austin saw stars as the intense pain shot through him when Dr. Mac, with the help of the assistant, adjusted his shoulder back into place.

"Just relax and Kara will be in shortly."

After Austin's Reiki session, the pain had turned into a dull ache. Kara left, and he found himself alone in the room with his thoughts. *How will I ever make this up to Taylor and save face with the others?*

It did not take long for Austin to have his first visitor. Nicholas strode into the room.

"You're back," Austin said trying to make small talk.

"I am," Nicholas said. "How are you feeling?"

"I've been better," Austin replied. "But I'll live."

There was a tense moment of silence between the two. Nicholas idly scratched his chin, a gesture Austin had never seen him do before.

"Do you know what I heard when I arrived?"

Austin didn't answer. He was sure he didn't need too.

"What happened?" Nicholas said sternly.

Austin sighed. "I decked a horse because it wasn't cooperating," he said. "And if you ask me—"

"Stop," Nicholas said with a fiery glint in his eyes. "I've heard Mani, Joseph, Will, and Taylor's accounts of your attack on one of my animals. Now start at the beginning and tell me why."

Austin got a similar steely glint in his eyes. He grit his teeth. That stupid horse had him in a pack of trouble.

"Like I said, I'm okay. It was the horse who had the problem."

"Austin, Incident is a trained therapy horse. She instinctively tried to help a foolish young man, who then repaid her with injury." He looked Austin dead in the eye. "*You* are the one who has the problem."

"You're not seriously going to side with the horse?" Austin said.

"That horse has been thoroughly trained to help people, mostly children, let go of their emotional baggage, and she does it quite well. Many horses and some dogs are best at doing this," Nicholas replied.

Austin could not believe what he was hearing. That dumb creature had not only messed up his relationship, it had bought him this tongue lashing as well. Before he could dig himself a deeper hole, Nicholas spoke.

"You started out with negative emotions and you weren't letting go of them. From what I gather, Incident was trying to help you. That's why you got bucked off. And in repayment you hit her. Of course the horse released the emotions the same way you did—by force."

"I didn't have any negative emotions until the horse bucked me off," Austin said, ignoring the heart of what Nicholas was saying.

"You were trying to show off in front of Taylor and the others," Nicholas said. "The horse reflected back the emotions and tried to dissipate them. You hit her first. She was responding emotionally to you not letting go of your emotions the easy way."

"But—."

"I don't want to ever hear that you hit another horse, especially one of mine," Nicholas said. "If I do, I'll knock you on your ass myself, faster than the horse did. Understood?"

Nicholas had not shouted the words. He didn't change his cadence. His tone had been calm and metered. There was no mistaking the fact that he was dead serious. Austin simply nodded, too afraid to say anything else.

"There," Nicholas said. "Now that we are done with that unpleasantness, I want you to finish up here, and then go and clear on the emotions of that experience and this conversation as well."

Austin nodded. *It sounded like that would be for the best anyway.*

"And one last thing," Nicholas said as he turned to go. "You will then go back to the Equine center to the stall where Incident is and apologize to her."

Austin gapped at Nicholas's last request.

"I'll talk to her later, explain the situation, and see if she has accepted your apology," Nicholas said. "If so, then we'll let go of this whole experience with no negative residual emotions and move forward. Is that clear?"

Austin nodded, and Nicholas left without another word.

He found a blank notepad and spent the next ten minutes writing out his emotions. The paper ended, shredded in the trash. He then walked back to the Estate. He probably could have got a lift from one of the guys, but he needed the time to think.

He arrived as dinner was ending, and Taylor steered clear of him as he came in. *I probably deserve that.*

For the rest of the night, Austin allowed himself to feel miserable. Not because of punching the horse, or the confrontational conversation with Nicholas. He felt miserable because he couldn't apologize to Taylor.

Austin did the only thing he could. He turned in early and set his alarm for an hour before breakfast so he could apologize to the dumb horse.

Austin awoke from a restless sleep and dragged himself out of bed. He quickly tied on his running shoes. He had planned to jog to the center. It wasn't all that far away, and he needed the exercise.

With an apple in his mouth and a bottle of water in his hand, he stretched, never really considering that he might have offered it as an olive branch to the horse. He threw it into a compost bin and began his jog at a light pace.

Even while he was in school and at home, Austin had kept up his morning jog. The fresh air and exercise had invigorated him to a level no amount of caffeine or energy drink could. Plus, he didn't have to worry about a crash in the middle of the day. *It was awesome.*

It didn't take Austin long to reach the Equine Center. The door swung open and he noticed Laramie feeding the horses and waved hello.

"Incident's in the back, slugger," Laramie said.

Austin winced. "Thanks."

He followed Laramie's directions and came to Incident's stall. The horse was not alone. Nicholas was there brushing her down.

"Right on time, Austin."

Austin quirked an eyebrow. "What do you mean?"

"Judging by how angry Taylor was at you," Nicholas said. "Plus our discussion last night, I'd say you wanted to get this out of your way as soon as possible, am I correct?"

Austin was surprised. He had never stopped to realize how predictable he was, but all of what Nicholas had said was true. "Yeah. I came to get this over with."

"Alright," Nicholas said. "Say your peace."

Austin sighed, put a hand on the horse's mane, and looked into her eyes. He could not help the anger welling up within him. He turned to his mentor.

"I just don't see this as a problem," he said. "It's only a dumb animal."

Disappointed Nicholas said, "That is not what I asked you to do, Austin."

"But why? I feel so silly talking to an animal that I am pretty sure hates me," Austin said.

"Would you like a person who had hit you for no reason?" Nicholas said bluntly.

"How is that even the same thing?"

"I told you to clear your emotions before this."

"I did," Austin said. "I am not angry at the dumb thing anymore."

"Somehow, I don't believe you," Nicholas said. Incident shook her mane in agreement.

The frustration returned abundantly. As it started to turn to anger, he literally had to bite his tongue. *This is so stupid and embarrassing!* "Unbelievable," Austin said, turning to go.

"If you walk out that door, Austin, you will be on suspension," Nicholas said, emotionlessly. "And that means you will not be allowed to do any training until you have made amends with the horse."

Austin didn't even reply as he walked out.

It was all he could do not to blow up. "Guess I'll just go stay with Collin or something," he said under his breath.

Chapter 7 - Austin's Suspension

In the aftermath of his incident with Incident, Austin found himself bunking with Collin, his roommate from college. Collin was taking summer classes and staying in the off-campus housing near the school. There was no way Austin would go home and risk his parents siding with that stupid horse or anyone else. He knew he needed a sympathetic ear to hash this all out. However, now that he was watching as pixels flooded his vision, he was having second thoughts.

Austin knew Collin liked to game, so it was no surprise when he found himself in front of the TV at 6:30 that evening with a controller in his hand, playing a death-match in the latest first-person shooter game. At one time, this would have been all the catharsis he needed, all the validation he could have asked for. Life was so much more now.

Austin allowed himself to be taken out quickly, and since this particular game had no respawns, he knew he had a minute. "Collin, man, can you believe what happened?"

"I know right, bro?" Collin said. "You got sniped like a newb. My grandma has better skills! Your talent is wasting away, dude."

Austin pinched the bridge of his nose. "Not that. I mean what happened with the dumb horse."

"Huh," Collin said. "Could have sworn you got dropped by a P90."

Austin took a deep breath, trying not to sigh too obviously. "I meant about my fight with a horse."

"Oh, come on!" Collin said, as his avatar was taken out. "No way, you, cheaters got me! Not a chance in he—"

"Collin?" Austin said.

"Oh, right," Collin said. "Good game, you freakin' cheaters."

Austin looked up to the ceiling. "Have you heard a word I've said?"

"Yeah, dude," Collin said. "Your buddy Collin has your back. You want a soda?"

"No, thank you," Austin said. "Can you believe I got suspended over a dumb horse?"

Collin came back in from the kitchen, guzzling a can of neon green energy-enriched liquid. He belched. "Dude, it's totally harsh. Like, getting sniped by a bunch of ten-year-olds in a death-match. Brutal."

Austin felt slightly better, but not much. "Thanks, man. At least you have my back."

Austin then lit into his litany of issues he had with the whole situation, from Taylor being so hot and cold toward their relationship, to Nicholas siding with Incident, to the horse hating him, because it was a dumb animal. Collin nodded and gave him the affirmation he wanted between loud drinks of his high fructose game fuel.

An alarm went off on Collin's phone. "Crap!" Collin said. "I have a class in ten minutes!" He staggered to his feet, knocking over the empty energy drink cans. "Bro, I'd love to stay and help you game through this, but some of us have credits we need to make up from last semester."

Collin had missed one of his finals when his phone died because he had forgotten to plug it in before an all-night death-match session. He'd slept right through the exam. Now he had to repeat the class this summer or he wouldn't be able to take all the classes he needed to graduate next school year.

"Thanks for letting me crash here," Austin said.

Collin nodded as he bit into a jerky stick. "No problem. Hey, if you're still up when I get back, you want to game some more?"

Austin had forgotten how much gaming could take over your life. He had been so wrapped up in getting his GPA up and getting to know Taylor last school year he'd not paid a lot of attention to his roommate. Seeing Collin like this now was a real eye opener. Austin shook his head.

"Your choice, broski," Collin said, shrugging as he slipped out the front door. His head ducked back in for a moment.

"Hey, it's none of my business, dude, but you should totally call Taylor, at least. That ain't gonna to work itself out."

Collin was gone before Austin could reply.

Austin sighed. His friend was right. He needed to call Taylor. He glanced down at the phone in his hand. He wasn't sure when he had taken it out, or when he'd selected Taylor's contact information. He gulped though and hit the call button.

The phone rang for less than ten seconds before it picked up.

"Austin?"

"Hey, Taylor," Austin said, hoping he didn't sound lame.

"I heard about your suspension," she said.

"Yeah," Austin said. "It was a lame excuse too."

"Lame?" Taylor said cutting him off. "You punched a horse in the head! You are so lucky all you got was suspended!"

"What?" Austin asked, his voice going deadpan.

"Mr. Ryan could have sued you for that!"

"Sued me for hitting a stupid horse?" Austin said with a scoff. "That horse had it coming!"

"You have got to be joking, Austin!" Taylor said, her voice reaching a higher octave. "You should be getting jail time for animal abuse! That sweet, intelligent animal did not deserve that!"

"Sweet? Intelligent?" Austin said, his own voice raising. "That damn thing should have been turned into super glue long ago with how belligerent it is!"

"Oh, and you would know, Mr. King of Serene?"

That rejoinder wounded Austin right in his pride, and he abruptly hung up. *How dare she? She took the stupid horse's side over her boyfriend?*

Austin balled his fists together and shook. His emotions were surfacing as he tried not to put a hole in the wall or chuck his phone.

All because he hit a horse that was being a jerk and making him look bad. He needed to clear his head. He could tell these negative emotions were getting the best of him. He checked the time. *The campus gym should still be open.* Hitting something was probably his best hope of working out this bottled aggression.

The girl he wanted to marry had sided with *a dumb horse.* Austin pushed it down as best he could and changed into his gym clothes. *Of all the nerve!*

He snapped up the spare key and a water bottle. *Since the horse was Nicholas's property, didn't that make this his fault?*

Austin slammed the door and started jogging. He needed to get his blood pumping now, and not just from his seething anger. He would get that out at the gym.

The jog seemed to help take the edge off Austin's mood, even though it was as if he was running from his problems instead of resolving them. The college gym was still open when he arrived, and he was glad they let him in for free, considering the fact he wasn't taking any summer classes. His luck held out, and there were only two or three other people on the machines.

Austin warmed up with a few incline dumbbell curls and preacher curls before making a beeline to the punching bag. He wanted to make sure his body was pumped so he could get it all out. He unleashed the fury of his emotions into the bag, and it absorbed every one of his hits as he hammered away. He had no sense of time as he smacked the weighted bag until a voice came over the com system telling him that the gym would be closing in ten minutes.

Austin caught the bag and could feel how rubbery his arms were, how shallow his breathing was, and how drenched in sweat he was. He had been punching at the bag for over an hour, but he still had a lot of negative emotions. *How had things gotten to this point?* He toweled off the bag and headed for the doors.

The walk back to Collin's place might cool his head, since blowing off steam had only left Austin spaghetti-armed and tired. *What was he going to do about the rift that was growing between him and Taylor? Was their relationship worth it? Did he actually love her? They hadn't even spent the night together, yet. How serious was it?* He shook his head.

And what about the Institute? Austin had eaten a lot of humble pie by asking Nicholas for a ludicrously large scholarship. *Was he going to give it up?* He wrestled with indecision the remainder of his walk. At last, when he was climbing the stairs that had become so familiar to him over the previous two semesters, he put his back against a wall.

A lone tear rolled down his face. *This was all so frustrating.* He'd fallen for his dream girl and been given the chance of a lifetime, and it had all been thrown into jeopardy when he had socked *a glue factory reject. It wasn't fair! Things had been so perfect!*

Austin calmed himself and made his way back to the apartment. He opened the door and found a note from Collin saying his class had been canceled and he was headed out to an all-night death-match. Austin stopped reading and went to the bathroom. There was only one way to get out of this funk. He had to use the tools he had learned the previous summer. He showered off the sweat of the vigorous exercise before finding a piece of paper.

Austin scribbled down all of his negative emotions about the entire Incident experience, about his argument with Nicholas, and about his hurt feelings in regard to Taylor. Then, while tapping on his sternum, he lit them on fire. New tears slid down his face as he tried desperately to let it go, to refocus and to be free of his negativity.

In the end, Austin found himself exhausted. All the clearing had done was leave him drained. He was out before his head laid down on the couch and slipped into a deep and dreamless sleep.

Chapter 8 – Taylor's Duality experience

Taylor, unlike Austin, didn't shirk her responsibilities so lightly. The day after they had spoken last, she was right back to work. Taylor was driving to the nearby town to pick up some packages for the Institute. Taylor was nothing short of furious with Austin because of their previous conversation and then he had the gall to hang up on her.

No, Taylor was not ready to let this go yet. She had consciously decided not to do her emotional clearing after talking to him on the phone. Austin had been a punk after all. She had a right to be mad at him. *What kind of relationship did they have, anyway? It was not like they were married or even engaged.* Sure, they had gone through a lot of good experiences the previous summer here, but there were some bad ones as well.

Were they signs for Taylor to get out of the relationship while she could? It's not like she was looking at it pessimistically. She was being a realist. She and Austin were so fundamentally different. Was she lying to herself, thinking there was a chance this could ever work?

Taylor shook her head. She had been lost in thought as she drove. *Maybe I should do the emotional clearing*, she thought. *After all, Austin was a knucklehead, but aren't most guys his age?* Maybe she should be using the tools she'd learned the previous summer, but wasn't she entitled to her anger? She was right after all. Austin had been a bully when he hit that poor horse.

Taylor had not spoken with anyone, but Sheena all day, and that was how it remained after she returned. Freed up for the day, she tried to avoid as many people as possible.

Nothing abated her righteous fury. She wouldn't let it. Taylor was right, and she had the right to be mad about it. It was all becoming clear to her as she snuggled down in her bed that night. Taylor needed to break things off with Austin for good. Then, and only then, would she be free to completely let go of all this baggage. She could then move forward and stop wasting her life.

Through her fitful musings, Taylor gradually found sleep. However, it was not sound. At 3:33 a.m., Taylor rolled over and looked at her clock. She had been wrestling with a dream, but now she couldn't remember it. Sleep was not going to be coming back anytime soon and she knew it. Quietly, she headed downstairs for the kitchen. *Comfort food after dark was the best way to deal with sleepless nights*, her Grandpa had always teased.

It wasn't like Taylor was even hungry. She just needed something to fill one of the voids inside her. Missing Austin was worse than she had thought, even though she was still mad at him. She got a cool glass of water instead of a piece of leftover cold quiche. She was sad, but not that sad.

Taylor finished her water, but still didn't feel tired. She decided to go for a walk. This early in the morning, she found the halls of the main house completely empty. Even the lights were dimmed so low, that the Estate took on a different and almost enchanting demeanor.

For a moment, the quiet solitude of the Estate after dark allowed Taylor to shut out everything else and enjoy her walk. That was, until she saw Miranda and Mani quietly leave the library. *What on earth were they doing up at this hour?* Taylor edged closer, realizing that a lamp had been left on. She shook her head, and decided to turn it off. It didn't take long to get to where the lamp stood and that was when she realized she wasn't alone. Nicholas was there, in an overstuffed chair reading a book.

Taylor tried not to disturb him, but Nicholas immediately glanced up at her, placing his finger on the page he was reading. He wore a tight white t-shirt and a pair of black flannel pajama pants. It seemed almost out of character to her.

"Hello Taylor," Nicholas said in his best library attuned voice. "What gets you up this early? Surely you are not an early morning reader like myself?"

Taylor relaxed a little. "I was having a rough night sleep," she said. "So, I guess I was just wondering if Marti had left some chocolate milk in the fridge."

Nicholas smiled. "I am not sure you are going to find anything for your apparent sugar craving in here," he said.

"No," Taylor said.

Nicholas flashed her a disarming smile.

"Well," Taylor said, feeling a little sheepish. "Yeah, I guess I was having a carb craving, and didn't want to give in, so—"

"What's on your mind that you couldn't sleep?" Nicholas asked. "Craving empty carbs isn't like you."

Taylor was surprised at how comfortable she felt talking to Nicholas. She felt absolutely no judgment from him whatsoever. He genuinely seemed to care. *Austin could take some pointers from him*, she thought.

"Well," she said. "I talked to Austin last night."

Nicholas nodded as he listened patiently to the rest of Taylor's story. He demonstrated he was listening by repeating snippets and asking questions to encourage her. He didn't even get emotional about the experience of Austin hitting the horse or putting Austin on suspension from the Institute.

After Taylor finished, there was a moment of silence. Nicholas quirked an eyebrow at her and she began to vent again. This cycle continued until Taylor became aware that she had been feeling a whole bunch of negative emotions, more than she thought she had, emotions she was trying to dump on Nicholas. To his credit, Nicholas remained patient and actively listening until she'd finished her ranting.

When Taylor finally stopped, Nicholas said, "Would you like me to help you?"

"Please," Taylor said, slumping her shoulders.

Nicholas didn't disappoint her. "You need to use your emotional clearing tools. Hanging onto low frequency emotions, like anger and frustration, isn't helping anyone."

Taylor realized the wisdom in his words. She had been nursing the hurt senselessly, and now it was starting to show through. She may have the right to be angry, but she also had the right to be happy and let it go as well. She felt foolish. It was her choice how she felt and she knew it.

As if Nicholas had read her thoughts, he smiled and said, "You do need to do your emotional clearing, but do you want to try something different."

"Sure," she said curiously.

Nicholas retrieved a small clear rock from his pocket and placed it in Taylor's left hand. "Here," he said. "Go to your room and lock the door. Then lay down on your bed and place the stone over your heart."

"Get in bed and hold this over my heart?" Taylor asked.

Nicholas nodded. "Just lay there and breathe. That's all you need to do."

Taylor looked down at the stone, and Nicholas went back to his reading. She turned to go, her eyes refusing to leave what lay in her hand.

Taylor turned to thank Nicholas, but he was gone. Puzzled, she looked around the room. *Had he even been there in the first place?* Surely, he had. The stone attested to the fact.

Taylor shook it off and went back to her room, locking the door behind her, as instructed. Climbing back into bed, she rested the stone over her heart and waited for sleep to come. She had to admit she felt better after talking to Nicholas. Even if this rock technique didn't work for her, at least there was that.

When sleep did not immediately come for her, Taylor decided that she might as well do some emotional clearing. Perhaps doing that would help her get tired enough. She started to try to unravel her feelings, but the idea of going much further with it, let alone getting up and doing a write and burn left her mentally drained. She'd do it first thing in the morning.

Taylor continued to hold the rock as Nicholas had instructed her. She felt the weight on her chest. It was somehow comforting. It brought to mind thoughts of coming back to the Estate, Nicholas's warm greeting, and the tours of the other facilities. Gradually, her mind drifted to Austin. Him beating that beautiful animal still infuriated her, so she turned her mind to their experiences the previous summer. That took her right back to her family, and especially her dad.

Taylor found herself slowly opening her eyes. If she had to guess, she had briefly drifted off, after all. As the world came into focus, she realized she was not in her bed anymore. Tall trees rose majestically around her. These were woods behind the Estate. Had she been sleepwalking? She puzzled it in her mind. She seemed to be uninjured, and why was she here right now?

Taylor got to her feet as she took in her surroundings a little more. After a quick glance up and down, she confirmed that everything seemed safe enough, and started walking through the woods in the direction she assumed would take her to the Estate.

A multitude of beautiful birds chirped and whirled above Taylor in such a way that it came out like a symphony instead of a cacophony. She found herself enjoying the free concert immensely. She even caught sight of a flock of ducks flying in an iconic V pattern overhead. Instinctually she knew they were ducks, in part because of the V, but also from somewhere deep in the reservoirs of her mind.

From that same recess, Taylor realized that it was odd to see ducks flying overhead near the Estate. She could not recall if there was a pond or lake nearby. At least, according to her previous experience, there wasn't one. *Were there bodies of water around the Estate that no one knew about?*

Taylor pondered this as she continued her walk back to the Estate. A twig snapped, and she turned to her right to see a delicate, yet majestic deer. If she hadn't looked up when she did, she would've spooked it, if not run right into it.

The fact that the deer wasn't scared amazed Taylor. She made her way towards it. The deer seemed blissfully ignorant, or completely at ease with her. It was hard to tell which.

However, Taylor stood still when the beautiful creature came to her without hesitation. She found herself gazing into the limpid pools of radiant black that were its eyes. If eyes are the windows to the soul, then this deer had a limitless depth inside. Taylor could feel the magnetic pool of this creature's pure essence. It was the deer who broke the gaze. It turned without ceremony and started walking down a path. Taylor could only marvel at the grace with which it moved unencumbered through the trees.

Taylor moved swiftly to follow. There was no way there wasn't something more to this. Never had she had such a deep and immediate connection with any animal.

She pondered this, watching the path, trying not to lose her precious guide. A large brown and white bird flew above the trees where the deer had stood. Its circle may have begun above the deer, but it quickly included Taylor. She could just make it out high above her. She made a mental note, along with the strange feeling inside her. Taylor could not place the feeling, but she knew it wasn't fear or concern. It was like a bizarre type of curiosity. She stopped at the thought and took a look around with sharper awareness. The deer was gone. The path that she had been following had grown cold and was beyond her meager tracking skills to find.

As she pondered her next move, Taylor caught a faint sound in front of her. It was startling, but only a rustle in the undergrowth. At least, that was what she tried to tell herself, until a large brown bear broke through at a leisurely pace.

Taylor froze, fear coming over her. Was this how she was going to die? Mauled to death because she had been sleepwalking through the woods? She missed Austin right then. In fact, she probably wouldn't hold it against him if he struck this bear. It sniffed the air and continued in a direct path toward her.

If stones could freeze, it would not begin to describe how still Taylor stood. She had no idea what to do. Her fear was nearly paralyzing as the frightful creature got closer to her. The bear didn't even seem aggressive in its gait. It just meandered slowly up to her.

As it neared her, the bear reared back on its hind legs. Taylor was caught in a moment of awe. It was huge, standing almost twelve feet tall, at least twice her height. The majestic creature didn't make a sound as Taylor stood paralyzed with fear, trying to decide if she should run or not.

The bear put a paw out to her. Taylor stared in astonishment. Was this fearsome creature asking her to follow it? For a moment it stood there, but when she didn't move, it went back down to all fours.

Taylor steeled herself, then moved cautiously to one side of the massive bear. The creature didn't take its highly intelligent eyes off her as it moved to continue on down the path. Taylor held her breath. The bear seemed indifferent to her decision.

Taylor was relieved as she watched the bear begin lumbering down the path. She watched the beast recede as she began to calm down. No sooner than she did, she was startled to see Nicholas right in front of her.

"Don't worry. She won't harm you," he said, putting his hand out to her.

To say Taylor was surprised would be an understatement. She had thought she was lost in the woods, far from the Estate. Had she stumbled upon one of his clandestine meditation sites? She tried to say something, anything. Instead, she took Nicholas's hand as he beckoned her. She found herself continuing on the path beside him. Incoherent questions went through her mind. She didn't get the chance to voice them as her emotions changed from fear to peace.

Being in the presence of Nicholas right here, right now, was more serene than Taylor could have ever imagined. The incident with the deer, the bird, and the bear seemed like a lifetime ago. She felt a comforting safety in holding Nicholas' hand. It was almost like how holding her father's hand had been when she was little.

That thought shattered the spell of peace. The raw and partially processed emotion at the death of her father came bubbling up to the surface. The immense sadness at his loss threatened to overtake her. She was on the precipice of despair.

In Taylor's moment of dark reverie, she found Nicholas wordlessly staring at her. Somehow, his bearing witness to her sorrow eased the pain of it. He smiled, and she felt the sadness soften, a feeling of comfort beginning to replace it. They continued in silence.

Taylor found herself relaxing more as the beauty of the woods enveloped them. She wished that the experience would never end. She turned to Nicholas again, but his focus was on the path in front of them. She unabashedly continued her gaze, trusting his guidance.

Taylor hadn't really noticed how young Nicholas looked before. It was odd, because she had the distinct impression she knew him for a very long time, maybe even a past life. He seemed more akin to an older brother in this moment than a mentor.

As if aware of her thought, Nicholas looked into her eyes and smiled. It was one of the most real and pure things Taylor had ever seen. Her breath caught in her throat.

"Yes. I am your brother," he said. "But not older. I am your younger brother."

An image of Connor flashed through her mind's eye. She was pretty sure he was her only brother. At least, the only brother she knew about.

"What?" she said as confusion creased her brow.

Before Nicholas could speak, a beautiful white dove flew across their path. He looked at her and smiled again.

"Do you know what a white dove represents, Taylor?" he asked.

Taylor puzzled, considering the bird, which had landed on a tree branch above and ahead of them. "I thought a dove was just a bird."

"Here in this place, animals are totems. Symbols that represent something greater," Nicholas said. He was her teacher once again.

"Here?" she asked, motioning with her hand to the forest about them. She stopped, letting go of Nicholas' hand.

Nicholas walked a few steps ahead of her on the path, then turned to her. Taylor continued to scan her surroundings. This place was beautiful. Incredibly beautiful. She could see further down the path. The deer she had seen earlier stood waiting for them.

Somehow, she was not surprised. Then she saw the bear standing right next to the deer. And neither of them seemed bothered by the other.

Taylor turned to Nicholas, who stood a few feet in front of her on the path, his face emotionless.

"What's going on?" she asked, pointing at the two animals calmly standing next to each other.

"Like I said, animals are totems here. A symbolic representation of something greater." Taylor looked at the two animals peacefully beside each other as Nicholas continued. "The deer is a messenger for you. The bear is a guardian of this realm."

"This realm? What do you mean, 'this realm'?" Taylor asked. This was beginning to sound like one of Connor's video games instead of reality. She skeptically narrowed her eyes. "Where are we?"

Nicholas smiled and put his hand out to Taylor, indicating the creatures behind her. She turned to see the deer a few inches from her right shoulder. She was startled for a brief moment. Nicholas calmly began stroking the docile animal's head. She had not heard him move past her, but Taylor still found herself oddly at ease.

"Wow! That's..." Taylor said.

"That's not something you see every day," Nicholas said. He gently took Taylor's hand and put it on the neck of the still calm deer. She could feel its warm, thick fur. The animal was so peaceful.

"Yes," said Nicholas. Taylor realized that she hadn't said out loud what she was thinking, and yet Nicholas had again responded as if he had heard her thoughts. Intentionally keeping her lips tightly closed, she very deliberately wondered if he could hear what she was thinking.

Nicholas smiled and, with his mouth closed, said, "Yes, Taylor. I know exactly what you're thinking."

Startled, Taylor stepped back. This was something straight out of a movie. At the same moment, she realized the deer that had been standing next to her was now gone. Instead of seeing the deer, she froze. The large bear was now standing on its back two feet directly behind her. She hadn't heard its approach, but there it was, standing less than three feet from her.

Taylor could not stop her emotions from rapid-fire shifting. She wasn't sure if she should feel fear or not. She carefully stepped back beside Nicholas and, without thinking, got behind him.

Nicholas smiled, then walked forward to the large beast. He put his left hand out towards the bear. Without a sound, the bear put her massive paw forward, touching

Nicholas's hand. Taylor could see the four-inch-long claws.

"Do you think she needs a manicure?" Taylor heard in her mind. Nicholas was looking at her, still touching the paw of the bear. He started to smile. Taylor couldn't help but smile, too. The humor helped her calm a little bit.

The bear went back down to all four. "Do you want to pet her?" she heard in her mind.

"No, that's okay." she said, speaking out loud. She was still concerned. As if her words had broken whatever spell had held the beast captive, the bear turned and began to walk off back down the trail again.

"I don't understand," she said. "Are they always like that?"

"Not always," said Nicholas. "But things are different here."

Taylor looked around, still puzzled. "Where is here?" she asked.

"You're in another dimension right now, Taylor," he said matter-of-factly.

"Another dimension?" she asked. This was getting to be way to sci-fi for her.

Nicholas could see the confusion in her face. "Do you remember last summer when we talked about duality and the other dimensions that exist outside of regular time and space?" he asked.

Taylor searched her memory, "Yes. I remember you taught us about that," she said. As she took hold of that thought, a light came on in her mind. She remembered learning about length, width, and depth. The three dimensions that mortals exist in. The realm that the five senses detect. And the fourth dimension of time—the past, the present, and the future.

"Yes," Nicholas said. "We are in the seventh dimension right now. And I use the word 'now' very loosely."

"Now?" she asked.

"Yes. Now denotes a present moment in time which is actually in the fourth dimension," he said. Taylor was trying to make sense of all this. "You body is actually in your room asleep right now. Do you remember our conversation in the library?"

Taylor remembered having a hard time sleeping. She remembered Austin and her decision to end their relationship. She remembered going to the library and seeing Nicholas reading a book and their brief conversation.

"Look in your hand Taylor," Nicholas said.

Taylor realized her left hand was closed, grasping a small object. She opened it to reveal the stone that Nicholas had given her in the library. She had fallen asleep with the rock on her chest. All feelings of fear or concern began to leave her. The feeling of unconditional love that she felt in this place and from Nicholas, brought her peace even though she had so many questions.

She directed her thoughts toward Nicholas. "Please. Help me understand."

"No need to shout," Nicholas said with a chuckle. "After our conversation, you went back to your room and fell asleep. At least your body fell asleep. Your spirit stretched out and, with the help of some tools, you reached into the higher, less dense dimensions. It's okay. You're still safe but, what you're experiencing here is not physical. The bear and the deer you saw are symbols to teach you." Nicholas looked up, hearing the sound of the dove above them. "Do you know what the dove represents?"

"No," said Taylor. "Teach me."

Nicholas smiled again. "The dove represents cross-world communication. It is a spirit messenger. It also represents peace, gentleness, and unconditional love. She is one of your spirit guides."

"Spirit guides?" Taylor asked.

"Animal totems have different purposes. Sometimes the animal is a messenger such as the deer is for you. They come to deliver their message and once the message is delivered, they are done and they go. Like the deer," Nicholas replied.

"What's the message?" asked Taylor.

"You tell me," said Nicholas and turned to see the deer back standing next to Taylor. This time she was not startled by its presence.

Taylor leveled her gaze steadily at the beautiful creature. She focused on discerning why it had come to her.

"So what does it have to tell me?"

"Ask to her," said Nicholas.

"How do I even begin to talk to a deer?" Taylor said. "I don't know what language they speak, or if they even have speech."

Nicholas was amused. "In these other dimensions there is only one language," he said. "This language is known by everything and everyone here. It is the language of thought. Sometimes it comes across in symbols and imagery, like this path we are standing on, which represents a journey. Specifically, your journey, Taylor."

Taylor had to think about that for a moment. "The deer is telepathic?"

"Just talk to the deer with your mind, don't bother assigning labels here," Nicholas said.

Taylor focused on the deer. "Got it. But what do I say to her?"

"She's a messenger," said Nicholas. "Ask what message she has for you."

Taylor felt a little silly talking to the animal, but Nicholas had never led her astray before.

"Uhh, Mrs. Deer," she said, not knowing the proper way to address a creature in this dimension. "Is there something you came to tell me?"

Taylor felt her cheeks starting to flush as she finished speaking. She was startled as she distinctly heard the word "Yes" in her mind. It had burst into her mind almost as if *she* had thought it, but she could distinguish it from her own thoughts. She marveled at the deer.

Taylor looked at Nicholas and then back at the deer. "What do you want to tell me?" she tried thinking.

The deer didn't flinch as it peered at her, almost into her. However, she heard nothing in her mind. She gave the deer a moment, but nothing came. She turned again to Nicholas, who was still smiling.

"What do I do?" she asked.

"Listen with your heart," Nicholas said.

"My heart?"

"Yes. What do you feel in your heart?"

Taylor closed her eyes and focused on her heart. She quickly tapped into her emotions like she had learned to do, and immediately she felt a feeling of peace, compassion, gentle kindness, and caring.

Taylor's breath caught in her throat—if she was even breathing here. Then she became aware of a strange sense of innocence that began to mix into her feelings with a timid adventurous spirit. She surrendered to a smile, and kept her eyes still closed. The feelings had become more intense. They were new senses of femininity and graceful power in blossom in the heart of the feeling.

The power continued to grow, evolving from the feelings in Taylor's heart. It was confident power that began to spread through her whole being. She opened her eyes as the deer turned to walk forward on the path.

"It's you, Taylor. It's you." She heard in her mind, and then the deer was gone.

Taylor could feel tears on her cheeks. Without thinking she put her arms around Nicholas. She didn't know why she was crying, but a feeling of compassion and unconditional love was emanating from him. She felt no judgment from him as he accepted her hug.

After a moment, Taylor pulled away and tried to regain her composure.

"Is this a dream?" she asked.

"Your conscious mind thinks it is," Nicholas said and nodded. "So, yes."

"Then how can I feel you if my body is asleep in bed back at the Estate?"

"It's a perception," said Nicholas as he turned back to look up the trail. A tall tree had formed in the center of their path. Taylor hadn't seen it before. She was curious how she could have missed such an obvious obstacle in their way.

Nicholas walked up to the tree. "Under some circumstances, you can bring your body with you into the other dimensions, but most of the time it's just your soul or spirit that is reaching out to experience things in these other realms," he said, and stretched out his hand to touch the tree. As he made contact, his hand went into the tree and started coming out the other side.

Taylor stared. She could actually see his fingers moving on the opposite side of the tree. He waved his detached hand at her. She couldn't help but be slightly amused. It did look kind of funny. She allowed herself to laugh. It just felt right, and then Nicholas started laughing as well as he pulled his arm back through the tree.

"Wow!" she said

"That's not the half of it," said Nicholas. He put both hands on the trunk of the tree and, with no effort, the tree vanished. Not a trace of it remained in their path. Taylor was in a state of awe from the experiences. Every time she caught on, things evolved. It was new, and she had begun to enjoy it.

"Now for the main reason that you are here," said Nicholas, looking at the white dove cooing nearby.

"There's more?" Taylor asked with a naked and vulnerable confusion.

"Oh yes. A million times more," Nicholas said and put out his right-hand motioning to their path. Taylor looked up the path to see a woman approaching. She was beautiful and elegant. Slightly taller than Taylor and with long beautiful hair that went almost to her waist.

The woman approached with a confidence that could only come from a fully actualized being. The odd part was that Taylor felt an immediate connection to the woman. There was something familiar about her, but Taylor couldn't quite put her finger on it.

The woman smiled at Nicholas with an air of intimate familiarity. He bowed and took a few steps backwards, then vanished. Taylor couldn't see him anywhere. Turning back to the woman who now stood in front of her, she looked at the woman's face. It was radiant almost glowing.

"I know you," Taylor said in her mind.

"Of course you do," came a powerful yet gentle reply.

How do I know her? Taylor began to delve deep into her memories. No reply came from the woman across from her, so Taylor searched on. *This woman is so familiar.*

An idea nearly floored Taylor. She knew her, but it wasn't from her past. Taylor looked up, her mouth agape.

The woman smiled gently, raising her right hand and placing her palm on Taylor's forehead. A flash of light blurred into Taylor's mind and a burst of thoughts, memories fragments and emotions erupted into her.

Taylor gasped, and everything went dark.

Chapter 9 – Waking Up

Taylor opened her eyes and looked around frantically. It was dark as she sat up. She quickly realized, though, that she was in her room at the Estate. She had been laying on her bed the whole time. The rock that Nicholas had given her fell to the floor. She inhaled, deeply trying to figure out what had just happened. The faint light of the early morning seeped past the curtains on the east wall of her room. The green letters on her alarm clock glowed 5:55 a.m.

She tried to piece everything together as she swung her feet over the side of the bed and picked up the rock.

But wait, did that really happen? She raced back in her mind, trying to recall the moments before. She remembered Nicholas and the bear and the deer and the familiar stranger. It had been a bizarre encounter and an even crazier dream.

"That was no dream," she heard a voice say quietly.

Looking around the room, she was quite certain she was alone. *Who said that?* She tried to shake the weirdness off as she got up and went into the bathroom. Turning on the light, and, with the door partially open, she allowed the light from the bathroom into her bedroom. She looked. Again, no one was there. She had to prove to herself she wasn't going crazy.

Taylor fought to get her eyes adjusted to the bright light and turned to wash her face. Maybe some cool water would cleanse her mind. She applied it liberally before she grabbed a nearby towel. As she finished drying her face, she looked in the mirror. She had seen her reflection so many times that normally she didn't think twice about it. This time, however, something was different. Something clicked as she peered at herself in the mirror. She knew who that woman was, who had seemed so familiar in her dream.

Excited by her revelation, she dressed quickly. The clock now read past six. She skipped doing her normal morning routine. All she could think of was how much she wanted to find Nicholas. She had so many questions, and knew he would be able to unravel this enigma her dream had presented her.

She had put the experience on repeat in her mind as she finished getting dressed, but in her haste, she knew she was starting to forget the details. In response, she quickened her pace as she headed down the stairs towards the dining area.

"Hey, speedy, where are you off to so early?" a familiar voice said. Taylor didn't have to turn to know it was Sheena. Of course, the woman would be up already in her nicely pressed business casual outfit. Maybe she would be able to help her.

"Sheena, where is Mr. Ryan?" Taylor said as she slowed down to match pace with the austere woman. "I need to speak to him urgently."

Sheena cocked her head slightly to the left. "Mr. Ryan's not at the Institute today. He left yesterday morning and won't be back until this afternoon."

Taylor felt like she had been sucker-punched. "What?" she asked. "How can that be? I saw him last night in the study!"

Sheena looked at her narrowly. "I don't think so. I talked to him over the phone last night. He's in Wyoming."

Taylor looked down at the floor, searching her thoughts. *Maybe it all had been a dream.* She had stopped walking and now Sheena looked at her worriedly.

"Excuse me?" Sheena asked.

Taylor shook it off. Apparently, she had spoken out loud. "Nothing," Taylor said.

Sheena didn't respond.

"Okay, sorry for the trouble," Taylor said ready to go.

"You okay?" said Sheena said with an inquisitive look.

"Huh? Oh yeah," Taylor said. "Yes, I'm fine." She was trying to hide the fact that she was now searching her mind again.

"I'll tell Mr. Ryan you'd like to talk with him as soon as he gets back," Sheena said, and wrote the matter off as closed.

"Yes. Thank you," Taylor said. "I would really appreciate that."

Taylor and Sheena went their separate ways, and Taylor continued to the dining area, all the while pondering the experience. Only a few of the staff were already up and eating. The other students were absent, but then, it was still too early for them. In fact, they probably wouldn't be up until it was almost time for them to be doing their morning routines. The dining area wouldn't see them for probably another hour.

Taylor took advantage of the quiet hour and walked into the dining area only to see Geri having her breakfast. The chef was getting her meal in before the rush when she'd be cooking for everyone else. She was sitting quietly by herself, looking at some papers with her empty plate and a glass of juice beside her.

Taylor carefully approached Geri, not wanting to intrude. She desperately wanted somebody to talk to. She had to focus on something else. Her dream was going to consume her if she didn't.

Geri looked up as Taylor approached. The older woman's face was split by a big smile. "You're up early," she said.

"Can I join you?" Taylor asked.

"Sure," said Geri. "I'll have the rest of breakfast out for you guys in a little bit. I hope you're not in a hurry."

"No. It's alright," Taylor said as she took a seat across from Geri. "I'm not really hungry."

"What's up?" the chef asked, setting the papers aside.

"Can I run something by you?"

"Yeah. Go ahead."

"I had a dream last night," Taylor said. "And I've got a lot of questions about it."

"Was it a bad dream?" Geri asked.

"No. It was actually a good dream, I think."

"You're not sure?"

"No," Taylor said, admitting it to herself as much as she was to Geri. "And I'm not sure that it was a dream."

"Hmm," Geri said. "This one might be out of my league, but I'll listen to you if you want to tell it to me. I mean, it sounds like something for Mr. Ryan."

Taylor nodded. "Yeah, I think so." For the life of her, she could not figure out the meaning of the experience. Geri remained silent for a moment to allow Taylor to further process her thoughts.

When the silence became a little awkward, Geri interrupted Taylor's thoughts. "I've got to go get breakfast for the rest of the crew. Raul and Mani are going to be helping in the kitchen today, and I want to make sure things are ready so they don't mess up my routine more than necessary."

"Mani!" Taylor said as she got up to leave. The idea of that prankster in a kitchen made Taylor shudder. "Thanks, Geri, and good luck with those two," she said and headed for the hallway.

"Thanks, and I don't know what I did, but you're welcome," she said as she picked up her papers and heading to the kitchen.

What Geri didn't know was that the mention of Mani had helped Taylor remember that she had seen Miranda and Mani leave the study after talking to Nicholas late last night. That had been right before she had gone in to talk to him and he had given her the stone. Maybe one of them could help her get in touch with Nicholas.

Taylor didn't know what rooms Miranda and Mani were in, so she decided to try looking on her own first and then to track down Sheena if she had to.

Taylor went to the study where she had last remembered seeing Mani, Miranda, and Nicholas last night. It was empty. *Where would they be?* They were her friends, but they had never been super close. *Maybe they're in the gym.* It was worth a shot.

Taylor quickly headed down the corridor to the west wing, which led to the large workout area where most of the students exercised. It was after seven in the morning now, and several of the other students were appearing. She saw some familiar faces. Pajori was talking to Annie as they casually entered the gym. They were both wearing their workout clothes, and Taylor wasn't sure if Pajori was flirting with Annie or Annie was flirting with him.

Taylor took the opening and hurried up to the couple. They abruptly stopped their conversation.

"Tay!" Pajori said. "Wasuuup?" He said, painfully trying to be funny. In the past two years that Pajori had been going through the different programs at the Institute, his ability with languages had increased tremendously. He could fluently speak six languages now, in addition to his native Russian. If he chose, he could speak without any accent in English, Spanish, Italian, Portuguese, and French. His Mandarin Chinese was fluent, but not polished. He also really enjoyed learning different slang and, outside of class, that was his language of choice.

His goofing around slightly irritated Taylor. She tried to shake it off. "Hey, guys. Have you seen Miranda or Mani this morning?"

Seeing Taylor was not in the mood to play, Annie shook her head and Pajori got a little more serious. "Yeah," he said. "I know where Mani is."

"Where?" asked Taylor urgently.

"He went for a morning run with Talia and Raul. They should be back any time now. I think he's on KP."

Taylor nodded thanks. She turned to leave, but halted as Pajori continued. "Check the west patio."

A few moments Taylor was at the west patio as Talia, Raul and Mani came walking down the path, breathing heavily. They were talking happily as they approached.

"Hi guys," Taylor said. "Have a good workout?"

"Yeah," Talia said. "I smoked them both."

Raul and Mani started piping about how they let her win. Talia was starting to fire back when Taylor interjected.

"Mani?"

They stopped and Mani turned to her. "What's up?"

"You got a second?" she asked.

"Yeah," Mani said. Raul and Talia started to leave. "Hey, I'll catch up with you guys later," he added.

"Did you happen to talk to Mr. Ryan last night?" Taylor asked.

Mani looked like she had hit him with a haymaker. "You know he's in Wyoming, right?"

"Yeah, it's just...I couldn't sleep last night, and I thought I overheard you guys talking with him in the library."

"Eavesdropping?" Mani asked, half-joking, half-serious.

"No, I was just passing by as you guys were leaving," she said. "I was wondering if you guys knew how to contact him. I had a couple of questions for him."

"Nah," Mani said. "Mr. Ryan isn't the sort of guy who you find unless he wants you to. I had a dream that Miranda and I were talking to him, but I was in bed all night. Honest."

"Ahh," Taylor said.

"Shoot, if you saw me in my dreams, are you some kind of mystic now?" Mani said with a twinkle in his eye.

"Hardly," Taylor said and smiled. "Thanks for the chat."

"No worries," Mani said. "If it helps, Sheena said he'd be back later today."

Taylor had already turned to go. She waved a thank you and headed back to her room. When she got there, she noticed that Austin had called and texted her. She ignored it and hopped in the shower. The rest of her morning went in accordance with her average daily routine. With the exception that she ignored five messages and at least four missed calls from Austin. She had to admit he was persistent.

Sitting down to do some reading, her phone buzzed again. She sighed and fought the urge to chuck it out the window. Checking she found a message from Sheena.

"Mr. Ryan is back and will see you in his office."

Taylor didn't waste a moment. She made a beeline for his office. As she approached, Austin tried to call her for what felt like the millionth time. She turned off her phone in frustration before knocking on Nicholas's door.

"Ah, Taylor," he said. "I am glad Sheena was able to get a hold of you. I wanted to have a chat with you about something. Please, come in."

Taylor was a little taken aback by the greeting, but she followed him into his office. Nicholas quietly closed the door. He motioned to Taylor to take a seat by his office table and sat next to her instead of behind his desk.

Taylor swallowed hard, not sure why. "How was your trip?"

Nicholas smiled. "We don't need to make small talk. I know what you are here for."

Taylor's jaw dropped. *He knew?* "The other night. With the bear?"

Nicholas smiled and nodded as he sat back in the chair. "Taylor, what do you know about duality experiences?"

Taylor considered his question. She had learned about duality. "The concept of two or more separate dimensions coexisting at once and the ability to consciously access them?"

"You are not far off," Nicholas said with a smile. "A duality experience is more akin to what people think of as lucid dreaming or an out-of body-experience, for lack of a better term." Nicholas steepled his fingers. "You see, in your dream I mentioned to you that we were on a higher plane in a different dimension, so to speak."

Taylor remembered because, unlike her usual dreams, her memories of this dream had not faded. Nicholas had said something about that. "You said we had entered the seventh dimension, and that that was not the final dimension either."

"You are absolutely correct," Nicholas said, trying to hide his excitement that she was grasping such a complex concept so quickly. "You needed to learn something, Taylor. You were hurting, so I helped arrange a download for you. Something that would help you make some rather difficult choices you are being forced to deal with."

"A download?" Taylor asked.

"Sorry," Nicholas smiled. "I am not trying to lose you. You had a visitor and she gave you some memories."

"Yeah," Taylor said surprised. Searching her conscious mind now, "I saw what Austin would be like in the future."

"Yes," Nicholas nodded. "He has incredible potential, doesn't he? Was that all you saw?" The way he phrased the question made Taylor aware that he knew what she saw, but it was going to be up to her if she wanted to discuss it.

"No," she said. "I also saw myself."

"And?" Nicholas said, inviting her to delve deeper.

"She was me."

Nicholas smiled, his face lit up like a father as his daughter took her first steps. Taylor looked at her hands.

"Or who I can become," Taylor said. "If..." She let her words trail off. The room filled with a pregnant silence. Finally, she sighed. "If Austin and I were to get married."

Nicholas was not all smiles anymore she noted, peering at him. He was contemplative, not saying a word. He was giving Taylor another moment to think, to process her feelings.

She thought about how immature Austin was. It nearly infuriated her. *Why did her becoming her highest self, pivot so much on him? He is so dense and pig-headed.* Then the image of him helping her and her grandmother after her grandfather died flashed through her mind. Her feelings began to soften.

He was rough around the edges, but he had a depth to him. He was compassionate to a fault. She was starting to see a little of what she could learn from him. *Does that mean I'm going to refine him?* She looked at Nicholas.

He nodded. Taylor looked back at her hands. It had been as if Nicholas had been inside her mind as a sort of referee while she fought with her feelings. It had worked. She knew what she needed to do now.

"Thank you," she said, looking up. Nicholas smiled as she gave him a hug and then excused herself. She had been putting this off all day. She knew she had to talk to Austin, but was glad she had waited to sort out her experience first.

Taylor didn't pay much attention to anyone as she quietly slipped outside. She smiled as she made her way to one of the walking trails. She needed the fresh air. She took out her phone and powered it back up. It showed thirty missed calls and over a hundred text messages, all from Austin. She didn't bother to check them as she dialed his number. It rang once.

"Taylor?!" Austin's voice came over the phone frantically hopeful. "I am so sorry! I am such a screw-up! You are the best thing in my life! Please! Please! Please! Forgive me!"

Taylor was blown away by the ferocity of Austin's apology. He wasn't trying to justify himself. That was a step in the right direction.

"Listen," he said, pressing forward. "I want to make things right. Please, tell me what I can do."

Taylor cleared her throat and he quieted down. "First," she said. "I need to apologize to you."

Taylor could almost hear Austin's shock. "I unloaded a lot of stuff on you, and, to be frank, I wanted to be angry at you. I made you suffer, because I wanted to be mad. And *I* am sorry."

"You don't have to—."

"Yes, I do," she said. "For our relationship to go anywhere we need to be honest and open with each other. So I'm sorry."

Austin accepted her apology, and then went back to another bout of pleading for himself. He really wanted to come back, Taylor could tell. She decided now was not the time to tell him about meeting her future self in the seventh dimension or getting a download of future memories. Right now they needed to fix things between them and get Austin back in his programs if at all possible.

"What can I do, Tay?" Austin said, finally.

"Just come back."

"What?"

"Just come back, Austin," Taylor said. "What we need can only be fixed face to face. No amount of Facetime, phone calls, or texts can work this out. Come back to the Estate."

"But I was suspended," he said.

"Then you had better talk with Nicholas," Taylor said. "I am sure he would be willing to work with you. You know he's reasonable."

There was a moment of silence. "Alright," Austin said. "I'll come back and apologize, grovel if I have too, and try to be taken off suspension."

Chapter 10 – Austin Returns

After getting off the phone with Taylor, Austin hastily scribbled down all of his negative emotions. The list took up a couple pages front and back with what he'd been feeling the past few days. The experience with the horse, Incident, and Nicholas expelling him had really sent him into a negative spiral.

Austin found he was tapping on his chest with his left hand and scribbling out the final words with his right hand. There was a lot, and his emotions were supercharged, but he felt he got it all down. Now for the fun part.

Austin tore up the papers instead of burning them, because of the fire ordinance in the building. He dropped the illegible pieces in the wastebasket and washed his hands. He then got a drink of water, like he had been taught the previous summer. He could feel the calm returning to him as he slowly swallowed the liquid.

"Alright," he said to himself. "Time to get on to the rest of it."

"The rest of what?" Collin asked with his face buried in the fridge.

Austin hadn't even heard him come in. "Dude! You startled me!"

"Sorry, bruh," Collin replied. "What are you getting to now, anyway?"

"Right," Austin said with a nod. "I am headed back to the Estate."

"Thought you got kicked out, man."

"Suspended," Austin said.

"Same diff," Collin said and pulled an old pizza box out of the fridge. "You want any?"

"Nah," Austin said. "But thanks for letting me crash here for a couple of days."

"Easy peasy, man," Collin said. "Catch ya on the flipside."

Austin nodded and Collin headed back to his gaming.

It wasn't even twenty minutes later that Austin had his stuff in his car and was on the road.

The long drive allowed Austin to clear his mind. He kept going through what he would say to Nicholas how he would apologize. Somehow straight groveling felt wrong, just about as bad as bargaining. He would have to read Nicholas's mood.

Austin shifted gears and let Taylor know he would be there soon. Maybe she had thought of some sage way to help him get his apology across to Nicholas.

When he arrived at the Estate, Austin found Taylor waiting in the parking annex. He climbed out of the car as she came around to him.

"Tay, I am so sorry," he began.

She answered him with a hug and pulled back. "Thank you," she said simply.

Austin was confused. Everything was hot and cold with Taylor, the hug seemed so lukewarm. It was cordial and intimate. This was a definite grey area.

She smiled seeing his furrowed brow and said, "Just let the bad stuff go. It's in the past and no longer needs to be brought up, at least between us."

"Uh, ok," Austin said. He was so glad to see her. She seemed genuinely glad to see him also. *So far so good.*

Austin made a mental note not to stop being so humble and contrite anytime soon. Meanwhile, Taylor told Austin what she thought would be the best approach to talking to Nicholas as they headed to the main building. Her plan was simple. Grovel, beg and plead with Nicholas, and hope he would be willing to let Austin back in, if he would do whatever he was asked to do.

The plan was an exact copy of what Austin had thought of.

"He's a fair man," Taylor said as they walked into the building. "But don't expect it to be easy." They checked Austin in and walked in silence through the hall towards Nicholas's office. Nobody paid them any mind.

As Austin and Taylor rounded the corner to Nicholas's office, Sheena and Alchesay were coming out. Austin gulped, but Sheena smiled at them. None of them said a word as they passed each other.

Austin exhaled. It was the moment of truth. Taylor reached up and gently kissed him on the cheek.

"You got this," she said as she turned and left. Then, there Austin stood alone, a man ready to face the recompense for his crime. He timidly knocked at the door that was left partially open.

"Enter," Nicholas said in a firm, but distinct voice.

Austin peeked his head inside and then entered cautiously. It felt like he was entering a dangerous animal den or something, but that could just be in his head.

Nicholas's office was immaculate, as usual. Clean and orderly as well as stately and elegant, yet somehow it still had an overall business-like quality to it. Nicholas sat behind his desk opposite the door, looking down. It seemed like he was going over files.

"Sir," said Austin. "I didn't mean to bother you. I can come back later if you like."

Without looking up, Nicholas lifted his arm and pointed to the leather looking couch on his right. He then busied himself typing on the tablet on his desk. Austin sat down, following the nonverbal command obediently. He didn't utter another word.

Moments ticked by in agony. Nicholas continued his work, as Austin sat there. He could actually feel his palms growing sweaty. He hadn't even been this nervous on his first official date with Taylor!

Finally, Nicholas stopped typing and put down the device. He got up from his desk and shut the door that Austin had unintentionally left open. Austin watched Nicholas move back across the room stopping to sit on the front edge of his desk. Austin gulped as Nicholas turned his full attention to him.

"Mr. Davis?" he said with startling formality.

Austin cleared the lump in his throat. "Well, first," Austin said, and then began to vomit out his apology. "First of all, I wanted to apologize for my behavior. To you and to the horse. And anybody else that I need to."

He paused looking at Nicholas' impassive face. There wasn't a single emotion there, which made Austin even more nervous. He hung his head to avert Nicholas's gaze, and said, "I have no excuse for what I did, sir."

Nicholas's silence communicated for him. He didn't move a single muscle, not even blinking. He just watched Austin.

Austin dared a glance up and dropped his head. He sighed. What else was there to say other than, "I'm sorry." He steeled his resolve and met Nicholas's cool, level gaze.

Austin tried to maintain eye contact with him, but had to look away almost immediately. When he looked back, Nicholas was still looking at him, his eyes not moving at all. It was as if he was looking through Austin and placing his soul on some great cosmic scale to judge him. For some strange reason, the image of a white ostrich feather came into his mind. After a long moment, the silence became unbearable. That was when Nicholas chose to speak.

"Is there anything else you wish to say?" he asked.

Austin's eyes looked down at his hands, and then back at Nicholas. "No. I think that's pretty much it."

Nicholas nodded. "All right then," he said. "What are you asking of me?"

Austin had anticipated a generous tongue-lashing. Nicholas's no nonsense demeanor left him floundering. "Uh. Well, um," he said, trying to find the right words. "Well, I guess I'm asking to come back and continue with the Ascension and Genius Training programs. If that's alright with you, of course."

Slowly, Nicholas went back around his desk and sat down. "Have you done all the emotional clearing from this experience?"

Austin wanted to explain how he felt the past twenty four hours, but instead responded with "Yes, sir."

Nicholas nodded. "And are you ready to really apologize to Incident and everyone else involved in the experience?"

This time Austin nodded in an enthusiastic affirmative. "Yes, sir."

Nicholas leaned back in his chair and looked up at the ceiling. He seemed to ponder for a few moments before looking back at Austin.

"Alchesay is waiting in the hall for you," he said. "Go with him to the stables. Apologize to Incident. It's time you completely let go of this. And then, tomorrow morning, you can get on with your next portion of the Genius Training."

Austin felt his heart leap for joy. He got up and extended his hand to Nicholas. "Thank you, sir. I promise I won't let you down."

Nicholas's handshake was firm and decisive, but he said nothing more.

Austin turned to leave and then stopped. Nicholas had said he could do the Genius training, but he had failed to mention the Ascension training. Austin turned tentatively. "Uh," he said. "Will I still be able to do the Ascension training?"

Nicholas shook his head "No. Not at this time."

Austin decided not to press his luck and nodded. "I won't let you down," he said. "Not ever again."

As he left Nicholas's office he was relieved, though mildly disappointed. It seemed like all the other guys were doing the Ascension Training program and had been doing it for some time. They seemed so much more advanced than he was.

Austin looked up and was startled by the massive form of Alchesay.

"You ready, kid?"

"Uh," Austin said and gulped. "Yes?"

Chapter 11 – Apology

Alchesay had him to the stable in no time. The man was all business in such a way that Austin had to admire him. After their brief exchange of words in front of Nicholas's office, there had been a strict silence.

They arrived at the stable and Austin could hear Will and Mani talking.

"Man, why did Sheena need us here anyway?" Mani said. "We didn't do anything wrong."

"Dude," Will said. "Does it even matter?"

Austin saw Alchesay shake his head at the banter. He stopped.

"Alright," he said. "You're up." Alchesay took up a spot in the room by the door and ushered Austin in.

Everyone was silent. Aside from Will and Mani, Austin saw Joseph brushing Incident, and even Taylor was there, most likely at Sheena's request. He looked around, taking it in, and noted a few other ranch hands were also there.

Austin swallowed hard as he approached the paddock where Joseph was brushing Incident down. Joseph gave him a smug smile but didn't say anything.

Austin ignored Joseph for the time being and stood in front of the horse he had delivered a haymaker to. If he was being honest with himself, this was so embarrassing. Here he was, in front of everyone, about to apologize to a horse.

Austin wanted badly to smack that smile off of Joseph's face, or at least try to. He was so smug about all of this. Instead, Austin took a deep breath and focused on the horse. *Get through this and you're back in one of the programs, at least.* He cleared his throat.

"Mrs. horse," Austin said.

"Her name is Incident," Mani said from behind him. He was leaning on the fencepost to the paddock. Will elbowed him sharply in the ribs and Mani made a zipping motion over his lips.

Austin pinched the bridge of his nose and turned back to the horse, who seemed to be eyeing him warily.

"Incident," Austin said trying to keep down his sarcasm. The horse's eyes were locked on him. Austin turned away. *This is so stupid*, he thought.

Austin wanted to slam his fist against the wooden fence. How could he stoop so low? How could he condescend to this level, how could he apologize to a horse, of all things? Was he really doing the equivalent of a hazing ritual to keep his precious spot in the million-dollar Genius program? He looked at Taylor and saw her, almost as if for the first time. Her bottom lip trembled between her teeth, silently urging him on.

Austin knew what he was doing. He was falling back on his old habits, trying to rationalize this away. He realized if he was not careful, one day he might rationalize Taylor away as well, and that was too much.

He turned back to Incident. Joseph wasn't smug anymore, but Austin paid him no mind.

Austin reached out a tentative hand and touched Incident. The horse flinched, but relented. Then Austin brought his head to the horse's. "I'm sorry," he said. "I am sorry for hitting you. I am sorry for hating you and demeaning you."

The horse didn't pull away. It was Austin who pulled back. "I hope you can forgive me."

Everyone was still as Austin let his hand drop away. The horse looked at him, unmoving.

"It will never happen again," Austin said and then paused. "I promise."

The horse sneezed as if to accept the apology, and Austin looked around at the others, who were still speechless. He had done it. He had apologized to a horse. And, oddly, he found it relieving.

Alchesay interrupted the moment by coming up to Austin with a shovel in hand.

"Now that you cleared out all your emotional crap," he said as he handed Austin the square shovel. "It's time to clean the rest of the crap." A sly smile crossed the big man's face.

Austin's cheeks burned red as Alchesay ushered the others out. Only the ranch hands remained while Austin spent the rest of the evening cleaning manure out of all the stalls in the large barn. It was well after 11 p.m. when he finally finished.

Austin sat for the first time in hours, and looked at his phone. There was a text from Taylor. It was two simple emojis: a smiley face and a thumbs up.

Austin smiled. Everything was going to be alright. He was dog-tired, but his heart was reignited as he headed back to his room.

Chapter 12 – Austin's New Deal

By the next morning, Austin had fallen back into the routine as if nothing had changed. He woke up and prepped for the day, including doing some early morning meditation exercises before meeting Taylor in the hall so they could head down to breakfast together.

She smiled up at him as he took her hand. Things were coming back together splendidly. Austin mentally chastised himself for being so pigheaded about the whole situation with the horse. It had been his own fault.

He and Taylor sat down wordlessly to their breakfast. The silence was not awkward, it was more of a silence between lovers, a void into which nothing needed to be said, because they were happy to simply exist near one another. Austin smiled at Taylor and she smiled back.

Before they could begin their meal, Sheena appeared.

"Good morning, you two," she said.

"Morning," they said in unison.

"Austin," Sheena said. "You are to report to Joseph to do some preliminary training."

"Huh?" Austin said. "I thought Mr. Ryan said that even though I couldn't do the Ascension training, I would still be doing the Genius Training."

"Mr. Ryan informed me this morning that he thinks it would be of benefit to you to train under Joseph before continuing on with the Genius Training program with the others."

"You have got to be kidding me!" Austin said. Taylor looked at him pensively. "He took the Ascension Training from me because I screwed up and lashed out at his horse. Now he's taking the Genius Training from me and making me work with Joseph of all people? How much do I have to sacrifice to show him I'm sorry?"

Austin stared at Sheena, who was impassive, then at Taylor. She was biting her lip, and he knew he was still on thin ice. Maybe everything wasn't as back to normal as he had thought.

"Fine," he said, trying to calm down. "I'll do it."

"Right. You have today to prepare, and re-acclimate yourself to the Estate. Tomorrow morning you will start with Joseph," Sheena said. "I suggest you sit in on Mr. Ryan's lecture today." With the clicking of her heels, Sheena walked off.

Austin and Taylor finished their breakfast quickly and headed off to the lecture. They had planned on checking out the class, anyway.

They arrived and sat down in the large, but comfortable classroom. They recognized some of the familiar faces of the other students who were training at the Estate, but also noticed some unfamiliar ones, as well. Many of them looked like business professionals or very impressively dressed executives.

Austin fought back the desire to go up and introduce himself to them and network. These people weren't here to see him. Then again, if they were here, they very well might be looking for a young up-and-comer to begin with them at a plush executive level position. He made up his mind and was about to stand when Nicholas entered from the right side of the room.

The class was beginning. *So much for lost opportunities*, he thought.

Chapter 13- Value of Mentors

Nicholas took center stage at the head of the classroom and let his eyes sweep over all the students. He noticed Taylor and Austin in attendance.

"Pablo Picasso once said, 'Good artists copy, great artists steal,'" Nicholas said and let the murmured laughter teeter away.

"What exactly does that mean?" he said. "It's simple: it means that people want to move forward, but sometimes they don't know how to do it."

A new murmur arose, this one a little more speculative. "Let me pose a two-part question to you and let's see what you think. How did the old masters and modern creative geniuses find the fortitude to move forward when there wasn't a clear path? And, second, what does that Picasso quote we started with have to do with it?"

The students were abuzz with talk amongst themselves, trying to figure out the root of Nicholas's words. He stood still and observed as they drew their own conclusions.

A willowy young girl raised her hand timidly.

"And what do you believe I am getting at?" Nicholas asked.

She stood and cleared her throat. "That we should fake it till we make it?"

The class erupted in laughter and her cheeks went a bright crimson as she sat down. Nicholas nodded his head and smiled.

"You're not wrong," he said, when the group quieted. The girl blushed again. "But it's only half of the answer. Today we are discussing the value of mentors. But, why mentors, you might ask? Why would anyone deem to copy someone else? Well, you need to get rid of the outdated notion of what it means to copy or imitate. Your ability to imitate is one of the biggest predictors of the success you will have in your life."

He had their attention now. "The great minds of the past all had mentors. Alexander the Great had Aristotle. Sir Isaac Newton learned from the works of Galileo. Even famous television personality Oprah Winfrey was inspired by Nelson Mandela and mentored by Maya Angelou. Gandhi was influenced by Leo Tolstoy, and mentored by Gokhale and Raychanbhai. Bill Gates has Warren Buffett and Warren Buffett had Benjamin Graham. The list is endless. Wherever there is brilliance there is a mentor."

Nicholas clasped his hands behind his back now. "It is a three-part formula for success. You should be spending a third of your time helping others move up. Then spend the next third with your peers, learning and growing. And the last third of your time, you should be spending with people who you admire and hope to live up to, preferably people who you feel are five to ten times better than you."

Nicholas paused to take a breath. "Those three things and being willing to let go of your emotional baggage and limiting beliefs. After all, **you are not the thoughts you think or the emotions you feel.** The fact is, for success to occur, you need to be humble, teachable, perseverant, and determined. Are you willing to do what you must to have the life you want?"

Austin sat intently for the duration of the class.

Nicholas reiterated the importance of reading high quality books. "The great mentors of the past have concealed their experiences and knowledge. Reading will open these hidden treasures to you."

Taylor seemed to be soaking it in, and Austin tried to be extra diligent whenever she looked at him. He caught her hidden smile for him, especially when Nicholas stated that people deserve to be happy.

Most of the class was centered on the lessons he had picked up the previous summer. The definition of insanity: doing the same thing repeatedly and expecting a different result and the philosophy that if you're not happy and living with joy in your life, find out why, and change it for the better. It was like a collection of the greatest hits of all the things Austin had already heard with a few extra tidbits.

Nicholas drew everything to a close about sixty minutes in, with a quote by Chief Tecumseh. "**Love your life, perfect your life, beautify all things in your life. Seek to make your life long and its purpose in the service of your people.**"

After Nicholas's presentation, several people flocked to talk to him. Some of the other students headed off for their next class, figuring they would have ample time to talk to him later. Austin motioned to Taylor that they should head out, but before they could turn, Nicholas called out. "Austin, a moment please?"

Austin stopped and nodded. Taylor smiled and hugged his arm. "You're turning into the teacher's pet."

Austin was dismayed. *What does Nicholas want to talk to me about now?*

"Hey," Taylor said before he got a chance to address her teacher's pet comment. "I'll wait for you outside. Come find me when you are done."

Austin followed her with his eyes as she ducked out and turned his gaze back to see that Nicholas had dismissed the rest of the attendees and was now standing in front of him.

"I hope the class was insightful for you," Nicholas said as he shook Austin's hand.

"Uh, yeah. I, uh, mean yes it was, very," Austin said.

"Did I catch you at a bad time?" Nicholas said, raising an eyebrow.

"No, no. No. Just trying to soak it all in," Austin said to cover up for the fact he wasn't sure what was going on.

"I needed to let you know that in order for you to do the Genius Training, you must first complete a preliminary training regimen I have set up with Joseph," Nicholas said.

"Yeah. Sheena told me. Is it punishment for hitting the horse?" Austin asked. He thought he had already apologized. *Wasn't the groveling enough?*

"The experience with Incident is past and gone," Nicholas said. "It's time to move forward. This is about new beginnings, Austin."

Austin stared at the ground and bit his tongue. He had never really cared for Joseph, especially after how he had almost ruined his chances with Taylor the previous summer. Austin was thinking fast. There had to be a way out of this.

Nicholas snapped his fingers. "There is no other way, Austin. It is that or nothing. Your choice."

It was like he had read his mind, thought for thought.

Austin could see Taylor watching from the hall. She was listening. He couldn't blame her.

"You will still do recaps of principles learned occasionally with me," Nicholas said to reassure him. "But you must do this first with Joseph before moving on."

Austin could feel Taylor pleading for him to make the right choice. He didn't even have to look in her direction. He then remembered his words of commitment to Nicholas and Taylor. Dropping his head, he nodded reluctantly. "I'll do it."

Taylor made a high-pitched noise of satisfaction and Nicholas smiled. "I trust it will all work out better than you had hoped," he said and left Austin in his thoughts.

Chapter 14 - Taylor's New Deal

Taylor stood in the hall and listened to Nicholas's footsteps as he came her way. It looked like he had given Austin his last chance. *How would he perform?*

She looked up to see him standing right in front of her. "Ms. Schaffer, can I ask you a question?"

Taylor gulped and nodded. Was he going to discipline her for eavesdropping on his and Austin's conversation? She tried to play it cool. "Of course."

"What would you like from your experience here at the Institute?" he asked. Taylor was a little bit surprised. She wasn't sure if she was an employee working here to earn money or a student going to classes if she had to be honest with herself. She looked down at her feet to escape his piercing gaze.

Austin had made his way to the doorway and stopped there. Nicholas was apparently interrogating Taylor now. He was curious how she would answer that question. After all, her answer could somehow affect him and their relationship.

Taylor took a deep breath. "What are my options?" she asked.

"The sky's the limit," Nicholas said. "You can ask me for anything. You may not get it all right now, but if you could have anything you want here, what would it be?"

Austin strangled a scream and hid inside the doorway. *He just gave her a blank check, and I got the raw end of the deal? How important was that horse?*

Taylor on the other hand had to use the wall to stay steady. "No limitations?" she said.

Nicholas nodded to her. "It doesn't hurt to ask," he said.

Austin's incredulity had quickly evaporated. He had had a similar experience, he recalled, and been given an incredible scholarship for the programs. He was happy Taylor was being given a blank check like that and could not wait to hear what she requested now.

Nicholas waited patiently for her reply.

Taylor's eyes focused and she set her jaw. It was as if Nicholas's permission had allowed her to give her own aspirations permission to awaken inside her. She looked him in the eye and said, "If I can have whatever I want here, I would like to do the Ascension Training and the Genius Training." Nicholas nodded, but she wasn't finished.

"And," she continued, "I'd like to get paid to do it."

Austin gasped at the boldness of Taylor's request. He couldn't help himself. Who was this woman?

Nicholas smiled. "Nice!" he said. "How about we start with the Genius Training for now? Let's see how that goes and then maybe we will work you into the Ascension Training program."

Taylor grinned at Austin. Apparently they had both known he was eavesdropping. He blushed, but couldn't help returning her smile. He was elated for her.

"And if you will commit to it for a full year," Nicholas continued, "and do it wholeheartedly, I will make sure you are compensated very handsomely."

Austin was almost blown away by such a generous offer. A lucrative one-year contract to be a student? *How come he didn't make that offer to me?*

"Thank you so much, Mr. Ryan," Taylor said, resisting the urge to give him a hug.

"Of course," Nicholas said. "But you do know you will still have to help out around the Institute as needed. Are you still good with that?"

"Absolutely!" she responded. "Whatever I need to do."

"Fine, then," he said, extending his hand. "We have a deal."

Taylor shook his hand confidently.

"Sheena will get you the details. You will be working with her and Mrs. Ryan. As for now, I think you two are late for your next classes." He nodded at Austin. "Mr. Davis."

Austin wanted to say something, but he didn't know what. He simply looked at Taylor smiling, so happy for her, maybe even a tad jealous of her deal...until she returned the smile.

The memory of the dream Taylor had had and the experience with her future-self came back to her as

Nicholas left them. She then looked down at her watch. "Crap! We are going to be late for class!"

Chapter 15 - Austin Trains with Joseph

"Austin."

Austin turned to see Sheena approach.

"Mr. Ryan needs you to meet him tomorrow morning at 5:00 to begin your training. He will be waiting for you out front."

She hurried off before Austin even had a chance to acknowledge the instructions.

This has to be punishment for me for hitting that horse, he thought shaking his head.

The next morning, after a quick breakfast, Austin yawned as he wandered out to the front of the Estate. Not knowing exactly what to expect, he still was a little surprised to see Joseph there with Nicholas. A packed horse stood close. He noticed a shovel, pick, and ax and other supplies.

Unaware to Austin, the horse became skittish as he approached. He watched Joseph calm the horse with soft strokes. Hurried footsteps pulled Austin's attention away and he gave Taylor a tired smile as she jogged up.

"I heard you were leaving to start your training today and I wanted to say goodbye," she said.

Austin wondered how she could appear so chipper that early in the morning.

"Thanks," he said.

"Morning, Austin, Taylor," Nicholas said. "Austin, you will be working with Joseph. You'll be rebuilding the upper shaman trail. He's in charge, so make sure you follow his instructions."

Austin could tell by Joseph's glower that he wasn't too pleased with this arrangement, either.

"How long will we be gone?" Austin asked.

"As long as it takes," said Nicholas.

Austin held back the grumble of annoyance and asked if he could go pack. Not knowing what to expect, he had brought nothing for the journey. He only had his phone. Nicholas responded with a shake of his head and held out his hand for the phone. In his other hand he held an unusual looking, straight-blade knife in a sheath. Austin took it and secured it to his belt. He felt the unfamiliar weight of it as it rested against his thigh.

Taylor's soft goodbye kiss lingered on his cheek after she moved away.

Austin smirked when he noticed Joseph's scowl.

With a deep breath, he followed Joseph and the horse across the driveway and off into the woods.

Nicholas smiled at Taylor. *He's up to something*, she thought. *Still, this would be a great experience for Austin if he let it.*

The early morning dew lingered on the underbrush as Austin made his way down the familiar trail. The swish of the tail in front of him was almost hypnotic to his tired eyes. The horse looked familiar. Realization dawned. It was Incident.

"Maybe I should call it 'Dense' for short," he said with a chuckle.

"Don't call her that," said Joseph firmly.

They hiked in stony silence for the next hour. The trail grew steeper and narrowed as it cut through the trees. Austin could see the field where he hauled rocks the previous summer, the place where he learned the difference between thoughts, emotions, and his identity.

"Oh, crap," Austin growled.

"What's the matter?" asked Joseph.

"Nothing." The sight of fresh manure all over his shoe was enough to fire the frustration and fatigue that had been building all morning. He'd tried for hours to use the tools he'd learned for dealing with negative emotions, but obviously there was still more inside just waiting to be cleaned up.

"There's a clearing up ahead," said Joseph. "We'll stop there and take a break."

Austin grunted his approval.

Within minutes, the trees stepped aside and the path widened to let them enter the clearing. Joseph led the horse over to a small stream. Austin sat down and leaned against the nearest tree.

"Here," Joseph said.

A water bottle flew across the space and landed in Austin's outstretched hand.

"Thanks."

A screech of a bird from high overhead pierced the silence. Austin looked up. It didn't look like the black and white birds he had seen last summer, the ones Nicholas had told him represented opportunity. But *maybe there is an opportunity here, anyway.* He continued to watch the bird. It floated on the wind, its wings catching every current to lift it higher.

"It's a hawk." Joseph's voice came from across the clearing.

That's all it took to start the conversation between the two men as they continued on up the trail.

"Why do you get to lead?" asked Austin.

"I know where we're going," said Joseph.

"Well, it sure stinks back here."

"Then why don't you walk in front of the horse?" asked Joseph.

"Why didn't you tell me that earlier?" Austin said.

"You didn't ask."

Austin stepped around the horse through the brush at the side of the trail. Incident shied away slightly, but calmed quickly with Josephs soft touch. The view improved with Austin's new perspective of the trail and the mountains. A small green hummingbird swooped down, almost hitting Joseph before flying off.

"Wow, that was close," Austin said.

"You just noticed. It's been with us the whole time."

The rest of the hike was spent in companionable silence. Austin's shirt stuck to his back by the time they reached the campsite. His stomach growled in protest at the lack of food. Joseph must have heard, because he said

Austin needed to take care of the horse before they had lunch. He begrudgingly headed over to the skittish horse. Joseph appeared on the other side and removed the gear, saddle and blanket while Austin tied the rope to a nearby tree branch. With a tentative hand he reached out and began to stoke the mare's side. The agitation slowly faded from himself and the horse. Incident lowered her head and greedily drank the cold stream water and then gave Austin a shower with a shake of her head when she finished. Austin grinned and went to get his own lunch.

The campsite sat in the middle of a small grove of aspen, their leaves danced in the breeze. Rocks turned black surrounded a small fire pit. The grass on the far side of the clearing lay pressed against the ground in preparation for the tents that would be placed there. Between the trees Austin saw the green fields far below them. The small hummingbird cut across his view, stopped momentarily in front of Joseph and darted off into the trees.

It didn't take long to throw up the two small tents and set up the rest of their primitive camp. His hands inside the soft leather of his work gloves, gripped the shovel and pick that sat on his shoulder. The shaman trail took only minutes to get to. The two worked clearing rocks and debris from the path.

After a while, Austin noticed the hair on the back of his neck standing on end. He glanced around, not seeing anything. Only the hummingbird. Three times he had felt something watching him. It had become a bit creepy. He tried to refocus his mind back to the task at hand.

Austin drug his tired body back to camp well after sunset, ate a quick dinner, and collapsed in his tent, willing sleep to come quickly. Because of the strange sounds in the forest, he tossed and turned late into the night. The heat of the sun filled the tent the next morning and forced Austin out.

"Here's a protein bar and some water," Joseph said. "It's time to head out."

Austin took the food and stared at Joseph. He was dressed in clean clothes and it looked like he had even taken a bath. Austin looked down in disgust at his own dirty, slept-in clothes. Without much of a choice, he retrieved his gloves and tools and followed Joseph out of camp.

Yesterday seemed like a piece of cake compared to that morning. He and Joseph worked with hardly a break. A small mud slide had covered a section with logs, brush, and feet of dirt that needed to be cleared away.

Austin's sore, tired body screamed for a rest. But Joseph still wouldn't let him stop. Anger and frustration churned together in the pit of his empty stomach. Four long, painful hours later, they headed back to camp. He pulled his sweaty shirt off and threw it in the stream, saturating it. The cold water was a welcome shock to his overheated body as he wrung the shirt out over his head.

"I think I'm going to be your brother-in-law," Joseph said abruptly.

Austin stood up, water dripping down his face, and stared at Joseph.

"I've felt that impression more than once."

"You're crazy," Austin said. He turned away, got some lunch out of the pack and sat down next to the nearest tree. "There's no way that will work. I only have one sister and she's already married and there's no way I'm going to marry into *your* family."

Austin could see Joseph bristle with that remark, but he continued. "I want to marry Taylor eventually, and her only sibling is her brother, Connor. So the only way we can be brother-in-laws is if you marry him." Austin paused. "You're not gay, are you?"

Austin realized he had probably gone a little too far when Joseph clenched his jaw and his face began to turn red.

"It's time for some alone time," Joseph said between his teeth.

He strode away farther upstream. Austin grabbed his lunch and followed. When he caught up to Joseph there was a circle in the dirt, only three or four feet in diameter.

"Whatever you do, it has to be done inside this circle," Joseph said. "You have to stay in it, until I say. I would suggest you meditate."

Austin watched Joseph stalk back to camp. *Of course he had to draw the circle in the dirt,* Austin thought as he sat down. *And not in the shade either.*

Meditate, he thought, closing his eyes. They immediately flew open when a bug tried to land on his face. He swatted it away and closed his eyes again. A spot in the middle of his back began to itch. He opened his eyes and looked for a stick he could use to relieve it. He then settled back down to meditate. The hair on the back of his neck again began to rise. Austin's eyes flew open and darted around seeing nothing, but trees, dirt and plants.

"This is stupid," he said to the dirt and stood up. Not wanting Joseph to know he was there, Austin crept quietly towards the camp only to find Joseph sound asleep in the shade. He turned and stomped back to the circle, stirring the dirt as he walked right through it. On the far side, he crashed on some long grass under a copse of trees.

Chapter 16 – Taylor Learns from Vivian

That same morning that Austin and Joseph were working on the Shaman trail, Taylor opened her eyes with more optimism than she'd felt for a long time. As her eyes became accustomed to the room, she caught sight of her Creation Board.

The word "Relationship" stood out a little more than usual and she imagined what she desired most in an ideal relationship.

Forcing herself from her cozy bed, she pulled on her yoga pants and raced down to catch the morning class. Her yoga practice was less peaceful than she liked, given the persistent rumbling of her stomach.

After the final Namaste, Taylor beat a quick path to the dining room, grabbing a smoothie and a plate heaped high with whole wheat pancakes, berries, and syrup.

As she entered the seating area, Taylor heard her name.

"Taylor! Over here."

Taylor scanned the room and spotted Makayla, a friend from last summer, waving Taylor over to her.

Taylor returned Makayla's warm smile and made her way to the table, observing
Makayla's light and happy countenance and the half-eaten stuffed omelet on the plate in front of her.

"I'm almost done here and have to get to the greenhouse, but can you sit for a moment?" Makayla asked.

"Of course. How are you? I can't believe this is the first time I'm seeing you,"

Taylor gave Makayla a quick hug and dropped in the seat beside her.

"I know. They keep me very busy. I'm sure you are, too," Makayla said with a smile.

"What are you working on?" Taylor asked.

"Drought-resistant hybrids. My pet project is a rice hybrid that will grow in arid climates," Makayla said before putting a slightly too large forkful of omelet in her mouth.

"Like Africa?" Taylor quizzed in between syrupy bites.

"Exactly," Makayla said, chewing quickly. "How about you? How are you?"

Taylor could see the genuine care in Makayla's eyes and felt gratitude again for the friendship that had resulted from a vulnerable conversation at the end of a hard summer working together. Makayla had been Taylor's boss at the greenhouse and had been unkind to her for nearly the entire summer. In the last weeks of the summer program, the two bonded over the shared experience of losing their parents too young, and they'd exchanged texts and emails over the past school year.

"I'm good. Mostly. Life has stretched me in ways I didn't expect."

"But with good results?" Makayla asked.

"Yes. Well, sometimes. I can see it will eventually be all good, but it hasn't been easy, for sure. While I'm here, I hope to do the Genius Training program."

"That's awesome."

"I know. I feel so grateful for the personal time Mr. Ryan is willing to invest in me."

Taylor took a long sip of her smoothie. "You didn't answer my question, you know."

"I didn't?"

"I asked how you are," Taylor reminded Makayla with a smile.

Makayla nodded and looked down at her plate. "Well, I think I can say the same thing about the growing I'm doing here at the Institute. It hasn't been easy. It's drawn pretty painful things out of me that are hard to experience, you know?" Makayla gestured to her plate. "I see progress and it feels amazing. But, losing my parents suddenly..." she took a deep breath and let it out slowly. "Well, you know, I was left with so many fears and the feeling of no control over any part of my life," Makayla paused, wiped a tear and looked directly at Taylor. "Bulimia became my coping mechanism."

Taylor put her hand on Makayla's. "I had no idea."

"No one did. I was bottled up pretty tight." Makayla gave Taylor a wry smile. "I feel like the most important idea I internalized last summer was Nicholas' constant refrain: **you are not the thoughts you think or the feelings you feel**. It helped me process my pain and refigure my relationship with food and my appearance." Makayla put another, more manageable bite in her mouth.

"That must have been very hard work," Taylor said sympathetically.

Makayla nodded. "Yes," she said simply. "But now I feel uniquely empowered to help others. That's part of my work here at the Institute this summer. I'm helping to heal the wounds that cause so many people—mostly young women—to starve themselves."

"That's wonderful," Taylor said sincerely. She watched Makayla happily pop the last savory bite in her mouth.

As Makayla gathered up her dishes to take to the kitchen, she looked at Taylor thoughtfully. "You know, the most enlightening thing I've learned from counseling others? The deepest wounds don't necessarily come from big, traumatic events, but rather from a million small negative messages that chip away at a person's sense of worthiness. The less worthy someone feels, the more ashamed, and then the more distant. It's like viewing the whole world through an Instagram filter: one-dimensional snapshots with little connection. From a distance, it's easy to believe everyone else is perfect and has it all figured out. That belief grows resentment and self-hatred. And if that's all you see in the outside world, every interaction is like one more blow to remind you that you're a mess without any value," Makayla downed the last of her grapefruit juice. "You know that's what I did to you last summer – kept you at a distance and hated you because you seemed to have a perfect, easy life."

After a moment, Taylor asked, "What was your breakthrough?"

"You. You worked to get to know me and share some real, human interaction, though I made it so hard. Have I said thank you for that?" Makayla asked.

"You made yourself vulnerable. I didn't do that."

"I think the timing was right for me to change my worldview, between your friendship and what I was learning here," Makayla wiped her mouth and winked at Taylor as she stood to go. "Well, that was a deep dive. I'm so glad to see you. We should hang out again, okay? Sorry for dashing off to the greenhouse. My nights are mostly booked with the body image workshops I'm teaching, but text me." Makayla gave Taylor a quick hug before gathering her things and dashing out the door.

Taylor watched her go and marveled again at the life changing ideas available at the Institute. *I'm so lucky to know this now, to have these tools in my.*

As she slurped the last bit of smoothie from her cup, she heard the distinctive click of Sheena's stilettos behind her. She turned and greeted her.

"Hello Taylor," Sheena said briskly. "Your schedule has been amended," she informed her. "Get cleaned up and then meet with Mrs. Ryan in her office. She has requested for you to start the mentoring program with her," the words were barely out of her mouth before

Sheena turned and was clicking her way out of the dining room.

Taylor was frozen for a moment with surprise. "What?" She felt equal parts thrilled and anxious. Getting paid to do the Genius Training was like a dream come true, but personal time with such an accomplished woman? Taylor knew Vivian Ryan worked with corporate leaders who paid six figures for the mentoring program. She could not believe her good fortune and hoped she could keep up.

Taylor raked up her breakfast tray, then hurried to her room to get showered and changed. She was midway through her speedy shower when her mind became troubled. *Wait, why are the Ryans giving us so much?* She remembered the tireless work Nicholas had offered Austin last summer when he was acting like a complete brat. *Why him?*

Taylor turned this over in her mind as she dressed and made her way to Mrs. Ryan's office. *Why would Mr. Ryan be paying me to do the Genius Training at all? Why would Mrs. Ryan devote her precious time rather than one of the other teachers at the Institute? The other students pay big money to do this training. What do the Ryans want from me?*

A feeling of concern was creeping up within her. Taylor looked at the ceiling as she walked down the hall to the offices, and inquired, *What do they want from us?*

"You will succeed us," came a quiet, but distinct voice in Taylor's mind. A feeling of peace came into her heart, and she remembered the dream of Austin and her future self.

"Hello, Taylor." Taylor jumped slightly at the greeting that interrupted her musings. She turned and saw Vivian Ryan behind her. She was dressed simply in a fitted blouse and pants. Her long dark brown hair fell in loose waves and her face was bright and make-up free. Taylor was tempted to ask Mrs. Ryan for her skincare regimen. *How can she look this good? She has to be north of fifty,* Taylor thought.

"Did I startle you, dear?"

"I'm sorry, I was just thinking," Taylor covered. "Thank you so much for this personal mentoring. I can't believe how lucky I am for this time with you and Mr. Ryan."

"Please call us Vivian and Nicholas," Vivian said generously, ushering Taylor into her office. The fragrance of fresh cut lilacs greeted Taylor as she stepped onto the plush carpet and sat in the offered seat across from Vivian's modern, but elegant desk.

As Vivian made her way to the upholstered chair at the head of her desk she smiled at Taylor and asked, "Are you ready to get started?"

Taylor nodded, realizing she had zero idea what they would be doing.

Vivian sat across from Taylor and gave her a long, probing look. Despite the prolonged eye contact, it wasn't uncomfortable. "You know, Taylor, I think we'll start somewhere else. Will you follow me?"

Vivian rose from behind her desk and walked through the door, waiting for Taylor so they could walk together down the hall. They passed several classrooms before they came to another office with a nameplate on the door that read, "Dr. Mila Johnson." Vivian knocked gently on the door.

Doctor? thought Taylor. *A medical doctor?*

They heard a faint "come in," and Vivian pushed open the door and gestured for Taylor to enter the room first. The office was sparse yet comfortable. The few framed photographs on the walls seemed to be from Australia, with images of kangaroos and desert savannas. A stuffed toy koala sat on the backside of a leather couch, looking out of place in the arty, functional space. Two young women about Taylor's age were seated on a couch facing a long desk and an older woman with short, blonde hair.

"Mila," Vivian said in happy greeting, approaching the woman and kissing the air by her cheek.

"Hello, Vivian," Mila said with an accent that Taylor couldn't quite place.

Vivian put a hand on Taylor's arm and addressed Mila, "This is Taylor Schaffer."

Taylor stepped forward and shook Mila's hand firmly.

"Welcome, Taylor," Mila said personably. "It's very good to finally meet you."

The greeting confused Taylor. She looked to Vivian to explain how Mila might know about her. Vivian turned and gestured towards the young women on the couch who were now standing.

"This is Danielle," Vivian said, pointing to the shorter of the two girls, whose thick brown hair was pulled into a long braid. "She'll be in the room adjacent to yours."

Danielle's face remained expressionless. Taylor awkwardly stepped towards her and extended a hand in greeting. Danielle accepted the handshake with an aggressive turn of her wrist, so that her hand was on top of Taylor's. Taylor dropped her hand and took a step back, taking in Danielle curiously.

Vivian then nodded to the other woman. "And this is Talia Kohen. I believe you remember her from last year. She is in the room across from yours." Talia was a couple inches taller than Taylor. Her dark hair was loose and beautifully complemented her olive complexion. She smiled openly and stepped forward with an outstretched hand.

Taylor smiled in return, gratefully accepting a normal handshake.

Dr. Johnson went around her desk and sat down as Vivian took her place on an overstuffed chair facing the couch. Mila gestured for all three young women to sit, and Taylor took a seat next to Talia.

"Taylor," Vivian began, "I know you've been here for one summer, but this will be your first year in the Genius Training program. Talia has put in two years in Ascension

Training, and has recently been added to the Genius Training program. Danielle here has been with us at the Estate for three years, and is considering doing the Genius Training."

Vivian smiled at all three young women and turned to Mila. "I think everyone would benefit from an overview of the program."

"Certainly," Mila took a moment to look at each young woman in the eyes before speaking to them. "Ladies, the Genius Training program we offer here at the Institute is ground-breaking. We combine all aspects of knowledge and adapt it individually to each student. You will experience a holistic approach to learning unlike anything else in the world. After you've successfully completed this program, you could be among the smartest people on the planet." She smiled ruefully, "I know that is a remarkable claim to make with the billions of people that share our world, but our methods have results that can be measured."

Taylor was afraid to blink. She wondered how she'd ended up on this couch, being offered personal training she knew was incredibly valuable.

After Mila again took a moment to make sure her words had registered with each girl, she continued. "Danielle, you will be working directly with me and some of my team. Talia and Taylor, you two will be mentored by Mrs. Ryan and Ashir..." She stopped abruptly and stole a quick glance at Vivian. Taylor noticed Vivian give Mila a slight shake of her head.

Turning back to the girls, Mila continued, "You will be working with Sheena and Mrs. Ryan," she repeated. "Are you ready to begin?"

The three young women nodded enthusiastically in the affirmative.

Mila stood. "Danielle's family lives nearby, but she will be living at the Estate while she's doing some of the training here." She now looked at Taylor. "Since you two are rooming close together, would you help Danielle get settled?"

"Talia, you can come with me," Vivian said, standing and moving to the door to greet Sheena. Taylor hadn't even heard the door open or Sheena enter the room with her electronic notepad in hand.

Talia followed Vivian and Sheena from the room, leaving Taylor and Danielle standing awkwardly by the couch. Mila smiled and prompted them to leave with a gesture towards the open door, "Off you go."

As the two walked into the hallway, Taylor offered, "Our rooms are this way. Should we get your things first?"

Danielle nodded and reversed their direction, heading out to the parking garages. *Here we go again.* Taylor thought dejectedly, remembering how hard it was the previous summer to navigate Makayla, who made sharing living space a pretty miserable experience. *Well, kindness worked that time. I guess I get to practice it again*, she thought as Danielle silently loaded Taylor's arms with bags to carry up to her room.

Chapter 17 - Back at the Camp

The darkness was smothering him. He couldn't slow the race of his heart or the breath that threatened to explode his chest. Bang! The sound moved over him, wave after wave. Then the incessant knocking began.

"Wake up."

The dream faded, but the irritating knocking continued. Austin opened his eyes to see Joseph kicking his foot.

"What did you do that for?" Austin asked as he slowly got to his feet.

"You aren't taking any of this seriously," said Joseph.

"Me? What about you? I saw you asleep back at camp." Austin was fully awake now.

"What I do, is no concern of yours. You just do what I tell you."

"I don't need your crap right now, let's get this over with and go back."

"We're not leaving here until I say so," said Joseph. "And honestly, I don't know what Nicholas sees in you or why he wastes his valuable time with you!"

Austin had heard enough. Frustration and anger propelled his fist towards Joseph face, hitting nothing, but air. He threw another punch and watched as Joseph dodged it effortlessly and went into a combat stance.

The more Joseph avoided his attempts, the more Austin's anger raged. His punches flew out of control.

Austin's own momentum propelled him to the ground when Joseph slid to one side. Austin rolled into a crouched position, his lungs burning. He lunged at Joseph, missing again, and stopped himself just before hitting the tree. Slowly getting to his feet Austin mirrored Joseph's stance. When Joseph didn't move, Austin stepped in and took a shot at Joseph's head. His blow grazed Joseph's cheek before being deflected. Austin didn't have time to feel any satisfaction when he found himself flipped around and caught in a chokehold.

Joseph, tired of keeping his composure, tightened his arms around Austin's neck.

"You're never going to amount to anything."

Austin heard the hiss of anger in Joseph's words.

The trees in Austin's vision began to blur. He pulled at the arm locked around his throat, choking for air.

"I deserve to be here just as much as you do, if not more!"

"You shouldn't even be here."

Austin moved to one side and slammed his elbow into Joseph's gut.

Joseph gasped.

The hold around Austin's neck quickly released, as Joseph stepped back and fell to the ground.

Austin turned and collapsed to his knees. Coughing, he stared at Joseph across the few feet that separated them.

As they stared at each other, trying to size up their opponent, a green flash swooped between them. They both saw the hummingbird, but turned back, readying their next move.

Austin could tell Joseph was about ready to lunge at him. He also knew that he couldn't beat Joseph.

Just before Joseph leapt, the hummingbird shot in and smacked Joseph on the side of his head. Bouncing off, it flew away. Joseph turned with a slight shake of his head. Austin watched the angry scowl, slowly change to a smile. Austin couldn't help, but smile himself.

He rolled onto his back and breathed in the much-needed oxygen. Joseph crawled over and sat beside him holding his stomach.

"Nice shot," he said. "I wasn't expecting it."

"Thanks," said Austin still breathing heavily. "Where did you learn to fight, anyway?"

"I learned it here at the Institute. In the Ascension Training we do a lot of martial arts. The main one we do is called Aikido."

"You're pretty good at it," said Austin.

"Not as good as I thought," said Joseph as he rubbed his left cheek.

Austin could see the bruise that started to form.

"Yeah, sorry about that," said Austin.

"It's okay. I guess I deserve it," said Joseph. He paused for a moment. "Sorry about the way I've been acting lately. You just seem to really piss me off."

"Me!" exclaimed Austin.

Joseph shook his head and smiled. "No, it's not you. It's me."

Austin tried to decide if he should be upset again or not, but Joseph continued.

"As we were leaving, Mr. Ryan told me what I should do to help you in your journey and that I was supposed to help you. But he also said that I needed to take advantage of this time to work on my own unresolved issues and that you would help me by being a catalyst to churn up my emotional baggage."

Austin, still on his back, looked up at the sky. "Glad I could help." They both started to laugh.

After a few more moments of silence Austin continued. "What's up with that hummingbird?"

"That hummingbird is one of my totems," said Joseph. "It's a messenger and a guide for me. It's been trying to teach me while we're up here."

Austin thought for a moment about what a totem is. "So the message was not to fight?"

"More or less," said Joseph. "I think that it was more than that, though."

"Yeah, it literally had to slap you upside the head to get your attention." They both started laughing again.

"I'm sorry, man," Joseph said.

"Me, too," said Austin. A comfortable silence fell over the clearing until Joseph's stomach began to rumble.

"Want to eat?" Austin asked.

Chapter 18 – How to Think

Sheena messaged Taylor to meet at the garage at 11:45 and to wear comfortable clothing. Taylor arrived to find Danielle, Talia and Sheena already inside Ben's SUV, awaiting a few others.

Taylor climbed in to a clipped greeting from Sheena and a warm smile from Talia. Danielle didn't meet her eyes or acknowledge her. Taylor took the back row of the SUV to avoid sitting beside Danielle. Minutes later, three other young women arrived at the vehicle and were impatiently waved inside the car from the passenger seat by Sheena. They hurried through the open doors, one dropping beside Danielle and Talia in the first row of benches, and the other two sliding in beside Taylor.

Sheena gave a quick nod to Ben, who started the car and drove out of the garage.

"Please meet Meeki, Ching, and Mia," Sheena called over her shoulder to the SUV passengers. "And this is Taylor, Danielle, and Talia." The girls took each other in, not sure which names applied to whom.

Taylor guessed Ching was the beautiful Chinese girl with the cheerful eyes and her thick dark hair pulled up in a bun. Meeki did everyone a favor by gesturing to herself and saying her name.

"I'm Mia," a cute Hispanic girl said, looking at Taylor. "And you are?"

"Taylor," she said, shaking her hand. "Nice to meet you."

Sheena then announced where they were going. "You each need a physical to be enrolled in the Genius Training program," she said, keeping her eyes on her tablet and furiously typing. "It's all very standard and important for us to know where you're starting from a health standpoint. The Estate clinic is down the road."

The rest of the short ride was in silence. Once they arrived, they filed into the clinic quietly and found several of the young men seated in the waiting area. Taylor recognized Pajori, Mani, Demetri, and Will from the previous summer and nodded a hello. There were two other guys that Taylor didn't recognize.

Each chair had a clipboard with neatly stacked medical forms. Sheena gestured for each young woman to take a seat and start filling out forms, as the young men were already doing.

Taylor sailed easily through the first few personal pages, but paused when she began to fill out the family medical history form. Her heart felt tender, as if the wound was still fresh, when she recorded her father's heart attack in his early forties. Taylor even felt tears spring to her eyes. She drew her face closer to her clipboard to hide this sudden emotion. *I thought I had cleared all of this hurt*, Taylor thought. *I wonder if it will ever stop hurting.*

Then Taylor came to the maternal history portion of the form. She felt rage bubble up in her chest. *How the hell do I know her medical history when she never bothered to be a mom or stick around?* Taylor found herself ranting inwardly. All Taylor really knew about her mother was that she was alive as of a year ago, when she dropped in without warning after fourteen years of complete abandonment. Taylor hadn't wanted anything to do with her then and had no idea where she'd gone. There'd been no contact since the summer before. Again, Taylor was able to note her feelings and even where they were in her body. *I have some clearing to do tonight,* she realized.

She breezed through the last pages, signing release forms for the clinic to obtain her health history and another Confidentiality and Nondisclosure Agreement about what she would see and learn at the Institute.

Shortly after Taylor finished her forms, the physician assistant, Kara, called her back to the exam room. Taylor remembered Kara from the previous year. She gathered the usual data—weight and height, blood pressure, pulse, blood oxygen levels, BMI—while catching up on Taylor's life since they last saw each other.

It was during the blood draw that Taylor shared her grandfather's sudden death, and they both teared up in the face of Taylor's grief. After all of the tests were finished and Taylor dried her tears, she asked why they needed blood.

"It's a basic blood panel to establish a baseline of health, check nutrient and hormone levels, and test for genetic deficiencies or anomalies," Kara responded.

"What kind of genetic deficiencies?" Taylor asked.

"Any deficiencies, but we are especially interested in the MTHFR gene."

Taylor didn't know what that meant.

The group returned to the Estate for a late lunch, and after Taylor had gotten a sandwich, she received a message to meet Vivian in her office.

Taylor made her way back through the hall of the Estate and found Vivian Ryan's door open, and Vivian reading at her desk. She had a very focused, almost troubled look on her face. Not wanting to startle her benefactress, Taylor gentle knocked on the door.

Vivian quickly put whatever she was reading in a drawer and a wide smile spread across her face. "Come in, Taylor," she said, beckoning Taylor out of the hall.

Taylor sat on one of the ultra-comfortable chairs facing Vivian's desk.

"How was your physical?" Vivian asked.

"Easy breezy," Taylor said. "But I am curious."

"About what?" asked Vivian.

"Why do we need a physical for the Genius Training program?"

"That is a really good question," said Vivian. "It's to help us know that you are physically fit enough to do this rigorous program. It's also to help us **establish your baseline**."

"A baseline? What do you mean by that?" asked Taylor.

"It's a gauge. We need to know your starting point, and it also helps you see the progress you're making. Some of the other students have been in this program for a while, and each is progressing at a personal pace. We want to quantify your progress, and hopefully it will be motivating for you as well."

"That makes sense," Taylor nodded.

"Shall we begin?"

"Sure," said Taylor. "Let's get this rolling."

Vivian smiled at her enthusiasm. "I'm going to hit you with a lot of training techniques and unfamiliar phrases, but it's helpful to keep in mind that the Genius Training really has two main functions: first, to cleanse out the restricting, inhibiting, or low-frequency elements, and second, to build you up and create new habits and patterns."

"That sounds too easy," said Taylor. "I'll be a genius after I clean out the bad and put in the good?"

"That's oversimplified, but to a small degree, it's true. To keep it all straight, I'll visually map a plan now with you and provide you with more detail and tools about everything we discuss."

Taylor nodded and pulled a notebook and pen out of her bag.

Vivian shook her head. "No notes, dear. Just absorb what you can now." Vivian waved her hand over her head and a three-dimensional screen appeared above her.

Taylor felt herself jump a little in her seat. She'd seen technology like this in movies, but thought it was fictional. Vivian got up from her desk and came around to sit beside Taylor. The screen, which was about the size of a large tablet, moved in front of her. It was divided into two columns. At the top of one column was the word **Cleanse** and at the other, the word **Build**.

As Vivian spoke, words appeared in the two columns. It was distracting at first, and Taylor had to work to focus on the words Vivian was saying, rather than the bizarre technology Vivian had introduced so suddenly.

The first word that appeared in both columns was the word **Physical**. "Your physical health is essential in the Genius Training program. There is a direct correlation between intelligence and physical health," Vivian said.

Other words started forming below the Cleanse category. "We're not doing all of these at once," said Vivian. "But this will give you an idea of our goals. **Nutrition** is one of those essential elements to brain health. Marti and Geri know that you are doing the program, so all your meals—the portion sizes and what goes into them—will be measured out precisely. And this is not a weight control program," she said. "But I think you'll find you will be in the best health of your life while you're doing this program. Even better than last year."

Taylor was very pleased with the physical results of her previous summer at the Estate. She'd left the program at her ideal weight, but with the stress of school and grabbing fast food when she could, she had added on weight and lost muscle mass.

More words appeared in both columns as Vivian continued. "We'll start with a mild colon cleanse and adjust it accordingly. Your nutrition will be high in healthy proteins and fats. No junk food or soda pop, very little sugar and gluten, and no synthetic food."

Taylor knew well Geri and Marti's culinary genius. She felt excitement that she would be upping her nutrition game and gratitude that all of this wonderful food would be prepared and figuratively spoon fed to her.

"Nearly all of our **food** is organic and **high in Prana**," Vivian continued. "We produce as much of it as we can here at the Estate."

"What is Prana?" Taylor asked.

"It's life force energy or the breath of life. It's the universal energy that flows in currents in and around the body. It's in the air, water and soil. Real food has prana in it as well. Non-altered foods grown without pesticides and eaten when fully ripe, hold that energy. When the food is consumed, that life force energy goes into the body," explained Vivian.

Taylor remembered working at the greenhouses the previous year and how much she enjoyed working with the earth. *All of this is starting to make sense*, she thought. She remembered the orchards around the Estate, and the local farms owned by the Ryans, producing more food than everyone here could consume.

Vivian continued, "I would like you to drink at least seventy ounces of **water** a day," she said, handing her a large water bottle with the words "Love" on one side and

"Taylor" on the other. Taylor admired it. It looked like glass, but there was something unusual about it.

"This is a special carbon crystal made specifically for you. Fill it up in the kitchen as often as you can. There is a separate faucet there that has special high alkaline water. Geri or Marti will show you if you haven't seen it already," Vivian said. "Besides what you eat and drink and the cleanses, we have certain nutritional supplements for you."

Taylor saw the words Supplements, Probiotics, and Nootropics appear on the screen.

"Your personal trainer will be Samantha."

Taylor remembered Sam worked with Austin the previous summer. "She's good," Taylor said.

"She is one of our best trainers here," Vivian concurred.

"Will I be working out as hard as she made Austin last year?"

Vivian sighed. "No. Mr. Ryan's intent with Austin last year was to have Samantha help him with emotional release. Samantha will adjust your workouts according to what you need."

The next screen read: **Exercise** five to six days/week. Minimum of fifty minutes in more than one set per day.

"Your **routine** may seem rigid, but it's a guideline. We'd like you to stick to it as much as possible. You'll be meeting with Sheena or myself three times a week for brief accountability sessions, but this program requires your **commitment and action** to do it to be successful. You're the one who has to do the work, to see the results."

Taylor nodded. "I'll do it."

"How about going to bed by 10 p.m. and rising by 7 a.m. six days a week?"

Taylor shrugged her shoulders. "Honestly, Mrs. Ryan that seems like a vacation. At school I would often stay up until two in the morning, and then be back up early to make it to my 7 a.m. classes. I can do this easily." Taylor thought for a moment and posed a question. "Shouldn't we get up earlier to get more done?"

"No. Not for this program," Vivian said. "At your age, your brain is still developing. Ample **sleep** is crucial to brain development. A person deprived of sleep in their adolescence and twenties is more likely to have cognitive issues the rest of their life. It may not seem like it, because you're young and healthy, but you must have adequate sleep at this time in your life for your brain to develop to its highest capacity."

On the screen, the points they'd just gone over became smaller and moved to the top of the screen.

"We will work further on your **emotional health** as well," continued Vivian. "Last summer you worked on clearing your negative emotions. We're going to take that to a higher level this year."

Words like **Emotional Cleansing, Emotional Freedom Technique, Write and Burns, and Affirmations** appeared on the screen.

"There's a lot more to each of these techniques, and I'll give you more information as we go along," Vivian said as the list shrank and rose to the top of the screen.

Taylor was starting to see the pattern.

Mental health was the next phrase to appear. "The same with this one," said Vivian. "I will give you a list of things that need to be released, including false paradigms and common limiting beliefs. And the tools to help you do so."

The words: **Awareness, Yoga, Memorization skills, Music, Languages, Creation Board,** and **Super Exponential Learning** appeared in this category.

Taylor was familiar with a few of these phrases. She pointed out the phrase "Creation Board."

"I did that last year."

"And how were the results?" asked Vivian.

"Impressive, actually" said Taylor.

"Great," continued Vivian. "We'll work together to take that to an even higher level. You should be creating on-demand."

The next phrase appeared: **Etheric**.

"Some people call this the **spiritual category,** but whatever designation you give it, connecting with the other dimensions is essential at the highest levels of training," Vivian said.

A slew of other phrases appeared all at once: **Chakra Clearing, Third Eye Exercise, Meditation**, and **Communication with Higher Self**.

It was a lot of information, but when Taylor saw Higher Self, she smiled, thinking of her dream and her communication with her future self.

As if seeing her thoughts, Vivian gave Taylor a knowing glance, then continued on to the next category.

"**Generational Clearing.** This one is helpful in two directions. We're going to help you release limiting beliefs and false paradigms that you've acquired genetically, culturally, and from your ancestors."

Taylor thought about her mother. "How am I going to do cleansing generationally?"

"We will give you some tools and walk you through it. This can seem painful, but it doesn't have to be. And we will support you along the way."

"Okay," said Taylor. "I may need a lot of help in this category."

"I understand," said Vivian. "You can do it, but I do have a question for you."

"What's that?" asked Taylor.

"Some of the other advanced students doing the Ascension and Genius Training programs are invited to teach different concepts and help their peers. I've asked some of them to help you. Are you okay with that?"

Taylor considered the idea for a moment. "Yes. I would appreciate the extra help."

"Would you have any problems working with Joseph?" asked Vivian. "He's the one that will help teach part of this category."

Taylor smiled ruefully. "I don't have a problem with that, though Austin might."

"Mr. Ryan thought the same thing," Vivian said with a knowing laugh.

The **Generational Category** reduced down and made way for the word Energetic.

"Wait," said Taylor. "Before we continue, I am curious: why Joseph for the generational category?"

"Joseph has a lot of knowledge about family history and genealogical research. He lived in Utah much of his life. The subculture there is very big on this topic. He's done more training since he got here as part of his Ascension Training."

Taylor nodded looking back up at the screen.

"The **Energetic category** has to do with the energies around us that we normally cannot see, hear, taste, touch, or smell."

"Can you give me an example?" asked Taylor.

"Microwaves, gamma waves, radio waves, electromagnetic radiation—they really do exist, but we don't normally think about them. We'll help you with the cleaning and building in this category as well."

Again, several phrases appeared at once: **Tai Chi, Qi Gong, Meditations, Breathing Exercises, Foot Zone Therapy, Reiki,** and others.

"That's the short version of it," concluded Vivian. She waved her hand again at the screen and it disappeared.

"It's a lot," said Taylor. "How am I going to remember it all?"

"You will get the hang of it," said Vivian handing her an electronic device that she had picked up from her desk. It looked like a smart phone and had the initials TS on the top.

"Thank you," said Taylor. "But I already have a phone."

"This is not just a phone. This device has all of the information I shared moments ago. It can answer questions, and will keep you apprised of your daily routine, along with updates and texts with the others involved in these programs, including Mr. Ryan and myself. We can even video-conference your accountability sessions when I'm away."

"Wow," said Taylor looking at the device admiringly. It looked like her smartphone, but there was no brand label on it.

"The last thing," Vivian said, "Have you ever taken any classes on how to think?"

A little surprised, Taylor responded. "I've taken a lot of classes, but never a class on how to think."

"You're going to take a set of tests in a few days, much like an IQ test. The IQ test is not a really accurate test of genius or intelligence, but rather it measures one's ability to take tests. We're going to use the IQ test and several other tests to establish a baseline. You will then take the same test later to quantify and show your progress. Some of these tests might appear unusual and establishing a baseline in the categories we discussed might appear a bit vague, but it's important, and our testing gets accurate readings.

"Then we will take on your **thinking patterns**, and teach you how to think at a higher level. You'll be processing abstract ideas, going from second to third and fourth dimensional learning and beyond. It gets a little more complicated at the fifth dimension." Seeing a slight look of panic on Taylor's face, Vivian added, "But don't worry about that right now."

Taylor pulled up the information she had received on her device and looked over it. It seemed overwhelming, but she was at peace knowing that she'd have help with it.

Chapter 19 – Joseph's Story

"So, what's your story?" Austin asked, content now that his stomach was full.

"I don't know if I should tell you," said Joseph. "Nicholas says that a person needs to earn the right to hear another's story."

"I think I've earned that right," said Austin. "With everything last summer and so far this summer, especially after you kicking my ass like you just did."

Joseph smiled and nodded. "Okay. Okay. I guess you've earned it."

"I'm the third in a family of seven kids. Utah was home for most of my growing up years. My family moved to Cardston, Canada for about three years, but then came back to Utah when I was sixteen. I graduated from high school and later moved to Alaska for a few years."

Austin was curious about this, but didn't want to interrupt.

"When I was twenty," Joseph continued. "I came out here and started going to school at the Institute on a scholarship. This is my third summer."

Austin questioned Joseph about his previous experiences at the Institute. The more he listened, the more he came to like Joseph. *He's actually kind of cool*, Austin thought. *Still a little arrogant and condescending, though.*

The crackle of the logs in the fire was the only sound from the forest. Austin sat patiently mesmerized by the flicker of flames that danced in the falling darkness, as he learned about Joseph's life.

"Ask him about his real story." Austin swore he heard Nicholas's voice. He looked around, expecting to see him standing nearby. Only darkness greeted him as he peered into the trees.

"Ask him." The voice came again.

"So, what's your real story, Joseph?"

Joseph looked up into the night sky, not speaking.

"I really do appreciate all you are doing for me," said Austin, a little surprised at his own words.

"I had an average life growing up," Joseph said quietly. "It was kind of weird having so many kids in the family, but I didn't know anything different. That was the norm, I thought."

"How about your parents?"

Joseph smirked. "My father was the type of guy who put on a great front to everyone outside of the family. And everyone thought that he was the nicest guy in the whole world. When I was around nine or ten-years-old, I realized I didn't like how he treated my mother. It had been that way my whole life, but it was around that time that I began to realize that he was emotionally abusive to her. He verbally manipulated her and made her feel like it was her fault.

"When I was about thirteen, my father got a job assignment that moved us to Canada, and it seemed like it lessened. At least on the surface. But looking back now, I realize that my mother was just stuffing the emotions. It was a big façade. Shortly after my family returned from Canada, my mother got some autoimmune disease. She'd been chronically tired for years, but by then the doctors were able to put a label on it."

"That really sucks," said Austin, trying to be sympathetic. "Is she still alive?"

"Yeah, and still married to my father, but she's not happy."

"Why doesn't she just divorce him?" asked Austin.

"She always told us growing up that she doesn't believe in divorce," said Joseph.

"Why not?" asked Austin puzzled.

"Because she thinks she won't make it to heaven if she divorces him."

"That sounds more like hell to me," said Austin.

Joseph nodded. The glow of the fire illuminated the faraway look in Joseph's face. Austin's mind went to his own parent's relationship, and he wondered if they were truly happy together.

"So how about the rest of your brothers and sisters?" he asked.

Joseph chuckled, shaking his head. "They are okay, more or less," he said unconvincingly. "My oldest sister is married and lives in Virginia. My older brother is still single and going to school in Idaho. Three of my younger siblings are still at home." Joseph paused for a long moment.

"I thought you said you have four younger siblings."

"Yes," said Joseph. "The brother just younger than me..." he paused for a moment, "he's having some struggles and lives in Washington State."

Austin could tell Joseph was very uncomfortable with the conversation so he decided to change the subject.

"So, how did you get out here, I mean working with Nicholas?"

Joseph's countenance changed and he started to brighten up.

"That's a funny story," he said. "When I got back from Alaska, I didn't want to stay around home. I wanted to go to school, so I started applying for a whole bunch of scholarships out-of-state. It was either inspiration or a total accident that I learned about the Institute here in Colorado. When I read about the programs I was excited, but when I found out about the half million dollar tuition per year, I figured it was hopeless.

"But the thought wouldn't leave my mind. A number of synchronistic events happened and I decided to at least apply for a scholarship here."

"And you synchronistically happened to get it, right?" smiled Austin.

"No. I was turned down. I was accepted at several other schools in and out of Utah and was offered several scholarships to those schools," he said.

Austin was a bit surprised, "So how did you get here? Are you paying the full tuition?"

Joseph smiled shaking his head. "I felt prompted to reapply immediately. I fought it, but it wouldn't go away. So a week later I reapplied with a letter of explanation detailing why felt I should receive a scholarship."

"Then you got in," said Austin.

"No. Not then, either. In fact, I got a very nicely phrased letter from Sophie, Mr. Ryan's personal secretary, saying that he had reviewed my application and the letter personally, and for me to consider reapplying the following year."

This time it was Austin who shook his head. "I still don't get it. You've been here for three years now. So what did you do?"

"I gave up," said Joseph. "I accepted a scholarship to a school in Idaho, the same one my brother is at now, and got ready to leave home for good. Besides, I couldn't stay there any longer. Things were getting worse between my parents and with my younger brother."

Austin sent Joseph a puzzled look.

Joseph ignored it and continued.

"Three days before school was to start, I had..." Joseph stopped pausing and looking upward then back at Austin, "a dream. In that dream my deceased grandfather, my dad's dad came to me and told me I needed to go to southwestern Colorado and follow my promptings. He showed me some things about the past and potential future and said that he and many others needed my help. And that I would acquire the knowledge and tools I needed to do this at Mr. Ryan's Institute. I didn't want to try again, but he was very persuasive. That's also when I received my first Native American totem."

Austin followed Joseph's gaze to the branch of a nearby tree, barely able to make out the green hummingbird that was quietly sitting on the branch watching them.

"Hummingbirds are not usually this high up in the mountains," said Joseph. "But he is my buddy, my messenger, and my guide. Symbolically, the hummingbird represents timelessness, healing, messenger, and warriors."

"And sometimes he needs to smack you up the side of the head to get the message across, doesn't he?" Austin said with a laugh.

Joseph smiled and continued. "I left early the next morning after getting the address and got to the main Institute building late after having some synchronistic events in getting there. Everything was closed up by then and I didn't know what I was going to do. I talked to a woman in the parking lot that night. It turned out to be Sheena. She wasn't any help. She told me to go home and email the Institute the next day. I wouldn't give up, though. I had come 386 miles to get there and wasn't going back without giving it my full effort. That night I slept in my car right there in the parking lot."

"I'm surprised Sheena let you off that easy," chuckled Austin.

"It gets better," said Joseph. "I was awakened early by some really old guy saying, 'You no park here. You no park here!'"

"I got out and explained my situation, but he wouldn't listen. He just handed me a pair of grass clippers and told me to come help him. I spent the next two hours with him cutting the lawn with a pair of hand clippers and him asking me about my life. After that, we went around the back of the Institute and he showed me some of the other buildings and talked to me about some of the things that they do there."

"That sounds promising," said Austin. "So did he introduce you to Nicholas after that?"

"No, he took me back to a large soccer field and told me to cut the grass with a pair of hand clippers and then left. You think you having to haul rocks off of that field last summer was a pain, well, this soccer field was over an acre in size. And I had to do it all with a pair of clippers."

Austin started to laugh. "That makes me grateful that I didn't have to do that to get here. I just had to let Mr. Ryan beat me at a race."

"You let him beat you," said Joseph. "He beat you like a drum. Admit it."

Austin nodded. "So how long did you have to cut the grass by hand?"

"I hadn't had anything to eat all day and being in the sun that long was getting hot, but I kept it up. I was really getting ticked by the late afternoon, but I kept going."

"What finally happened?" asked Austin.

"It wasn't funny at the time, but looking back, I can laugh at it now. This hundred-year-old looking guy comes driving onto the field on a massive commercial lawn mower and in minutes mows the entire field, including the area that I had spent hours working on. I was so pissed when he did that, I threw the clippers and headed back to my car. Then a green hummingbird flew right up to my face.

Austin's eyes flew up to the branch. The bird batted its wings before settling back on the branch.

"Seriously, it was an inch off of my nose. It wouldn't let me get back to my car and no matter what I did; it was in front of me. I tried to get away from it, but it was too fast," said Joseph.

Austin watched in amazement as the small bird left the branch and landed on the end of Joseph's outstretched finger. It sat for a moment and then flew off.

"I grabbed a stick from underneath one of the trees and tried to smack it away. It kept diving at my head and was actually leading me back around one of the buildings. When it finally flew off I was so frustrated and exhausted that I just sat down to catch my breath. It was then that I saw the old man kissing this beautiful young woman."

"Who was it?" asked Austin totally surprised.

"Long story short, it was Mr. and Mrs. Ryan. They had been watching me the whole time. Mr. Ryan was wearing a latex mask and costume. They were both laughing their guts out at me.

"Afterwards, Mr. Ryan said anyone with that much determination is worthy of at least one semester's worth of a scholarship. The rest is history. And yes, my first summer I had to haul rocks in the same field that you did last summer. I had to work hard for it, but I'm so grateful that I'm here."

"Have you already done the Genius and the Ascension Trainings?" asked Austin.

"No," said Joseph. "The first summer was pretty much like yours last year. The rest of the year I did classes at the Institute to work towards my bachelor's degree. The second summer I was going to do the Genius Program and did do some of it, but Mr. Ryan allowed me to move into the Ascension Training shortly before you arrived last year. I didn't get it all the way done before classes started again. This summer he's allowing me to do the Genius Training with the rest of you Newbs."

"I've got to hand it to you, Joseph. I don't think I could've done that."

They continued talking late into the night, enjoying the cool evening and the warmth of the fire.

Chapter 20 – The Dream

"So, Joseph, what was it that your grandfather needed you to do?" asked Austin.

"I still don't know. Even after all this time, I'm not sure. I have had a recurring dream, but I don't know what it means. Mr. Ryan said before I came up here that if I would help you with this, that you would be the means of helping me find the answer."

Austin was puzzled at that. "What can I do about it?"

"I don't know, maybe sometime I'll tell you about the dream, but I'm too tired," he said, climbing into his sleeping bag that lay on one side of the fire.

Forgetting his tent, Austin crawled into his bag and lay down. He thought about what Joseph had said as deep sleep crept over him. The last thing he remembered was the rustle of the leaves that swayed in the breeze.

Austin didn't move until early in the morning when he had to relieve himself. A peaceful stillness had settled over the camp. The fire had died down to a pile of deep orange and red embers. Incident stood quietly nearby, her reins lashed to a low branch. Not wanting to linger in only his shorts, Austin hurried back to his warm sleeping bag.

He fell asleep, quickly this time. But not to a restful sleep. Disturbing images filled his head. He awoke to a strange feeling that settled deep in his chest: frustration at not remembering any of the dreams clearly, just vague images and intense emotions. He shook them from his mind. In his half-asleep state, he could see a glimmer of the early morning sunrise begin its journey over the eastern horizon. He pulled the sleeping bag higher and fell asleep.

The dreams moved over him with power. Intense feelings of fear circled him like great prowling monsters. The terror spread over the camp. A horse whinnied. Austin moved restlessly in his sleeping bag. The images became clear. Horses, their hooves pounding on the hard surface of the ground. Loud gunshots followed by the screaming of women and children. People were running and trying to hide. More gunshots, closer this time, and people falling around him. Joseph. *Where was he?* Austin felt compelled to find him, save him, pull him out of this horrible experience. His eyes frantically searched for his friend. There stood before him a young girl, her eyes filled with terror. She looked at Austin, pleading for him to save her. A large man on a black horse rode up. He leapt to the ground and pointed his rifle at the young child, preparing to shoot.

A gunshot and a scream rang through the night air. Austin sat up with a start. His heart felt ready to leap out of his chest and his lungs burned with the effort to breath.

It's a dream. It's only a dream, he told himself trying to regain his awareness. He sat still for a moment and looked around. The morning was still shrouded in darkness as Austin pulled himself out of his bag. Joseph sat near on a log next to the blazing fire, a deeply troubled look on his face. Austin wanted to talk to him about the dream, but stayed silent.

"Hey, man. You okay?" he asked after a long moment. He took a seat next to Joseph on the log. Joseph looked over at him with a blank stare, then turned back to the fire.

He put his hand on Joseph's shoulder. "Are you all right?"

Joseph shook his head. Neither of them spoke as they stared into the leaping flames.

A nervous whinny and a stomping of hooves shattered the darkness of the morning. They spun around and saw a large brown shape move in the brush, not ten feet from where they sat.

"Crap!" said Joseph jumping up. "Get more wood on the fire!" Austin quickly obeyed, not exactly sure why.

Joseph grabbed the non-burning end of one of the sticks in the fire and held it up to create more light.

"That wasn't Ashira!" he said in a panic.

"Then what was it?" exclaimed Austin. "And who's Ashira?"

For the next half-hour, the two paced nervously, staying close to the fire. Joseph had brought the mare closer. He stroked her neck, which calmed him as well.

A nervous silence permeated the camp. It seemed like the sun rose at a snail's pace, but eventually the images of the trees surrounding them became more clear.

Finally, Austin collapsed next to the fire. He looked up when he felt a tap on his arm. Joseph stood there with a bottle of water.

"Thanks," said Austin. He reached out to take it, but Joseph held on, staring at the ground at Austin's feet.

"What?" said Austin. He looked down. His eyes grew wide in surprise. Large paw prints stood out in the dirt. They looked around the fire. Large prints were everywhere. Austin looked closer. He bent down and touched one of them and then looked at his own footprint in the soft dirt, inches from the rocks of their fire ring. Austin watched as Joseph walked over to his sleeping bag. He saw the same large paw prints less than a foot away from where his head had been earlier that morning.

Joseph pointed at them, not saying a word to Austin, who jumped up and came over to look. He looked at his own sleeping bag and saw the same paw prints about six inches from where his head had laid an hour before.

Austin swallowed hard, looking at Joseph then back at the paw prints.

"What would you think if we headed back early?" Joseph asked.

Austin nodded and, without a word, grabbed his sleeping bag.

They had their gear packed and the horse loaded in record time. Austin held a long stick in his sweaty hand as they made their way down the trail. He looked around for Joseph's hummingbird, but didn't see it. Every forest sound caused Austin to almost frantically search around knowing they are being watched.

"There's something out there," Austin said in a hushed voice.

"I know." Joseph paused in the middle of the path, took a few deep breaths, closed his eyes, and tilted his head towards the sky. After a moment, he turned and looked at Austin. "We'll be fine. Just stay on the path."

After some time, Austin asked Joseph who Ashira was.

"She's kind of a pet to Master Ryan. You most likely will see her sometime. She runs in the woods with him," Joseph said. "But that's not the cat we saw."

"Those paw prints so close, really creeped me out. Especially, when I had that awful dream," said Austin.

"You weren't the only one having nightmares this morning," said Joseph. "Mine were probably worse."

The trail narrowed as the two continued their descent down the hairpin turns. Near the bottom of the ravine the path widened allowing Austin to move around the horse next to Joseph again.

"So what was your dream?" asked Joseph.

Austin began to describe his dream. The more details he shared, the greater the look of concern transformed Josephs face.

When Austin got to the final scene, Joseph stopped. He turned and Austin saw the blaring shock and surprise on his face.

"That was the same experience I had," said Joseph. "But mine wasn't a dream. It was a duality experience. And it wasn't the first time."

Austin didn't know what he was referring to. But they had both seen the same thing at the same time. He didn't know how to wrap his mind around that at all.

"I was there," whispered Joseph, looking at his feet. "September 11, 163 years ago. I was there."

"Where?" asked Austin as they continued down the trail, the horse dutifully following behind.

Joseph shook the troubling images from his mind. "A place in southern Utah called Mountain Meadows."

Austin wanted desperately to learn more of what Joseph was referring to. A tremendous feeling of anxiety and fear remained in his soul. Was the experience he'd had more than just a dream?

They didn't say much until they were back in familiar territory. Austin took a deep breath of relief when they emerged through the trees near the house.

"Let's say we not talk about this to the others," said Joseph. "Let's just say we had a fun time and missed everyone, and wanted to come back early."

Chapter 21 - Austin and Joseph Return

Austin returned Dakota's wave as they neared the back of the house, where he sat with Nicholas and Rex on the patio. It was almost as if they were waiting for their return.

Austin was excited to see Nicholas's mentors again. He hadn't seen them since the previous summer.

"Come join us after you've cleaned up," said Nicholas.

The two headed back to the patio forty-five minutes later. Rex and Dakota were the only ones there. Austin was excited to see them again. Nicholas had introduced his mentors to Austin the previous summer.

"Nicholas had to take a call, but have a seat. We can chat until he returns," Dakota said.

"How is the Genius Training going?" asked Rex.

"It's not that easy," said Joseph. "But I am learning a lot."

"What about you, Austin?"

"I'm still waiting for Mr. Ryan's approval to start, but I am trying to be patient, and I've done tons of emotional clearing about it," he said.

Emotional release was not a new concept to Austin and Joseph, but Dakota explained the process in greater detail.

"In order to completely be free of negative emotions," Dakota said, "the person who is holding the negative emotions must release them physically and energetically, even if they did not have the experience where the emotions were formed in the first place. You can acquire emotions either directly through firsthand experience or you can pick them up from somebody else.

"When a person acquires the emotions and chooses to retain them, those emotions are stored in the body, specifically the fascia of the body. Fascia is the fatty covering under the skin and surrounding the organs and tissue inside the body.

"To be completely free of the emotions, specifically the negative emotions, they must be released from the fascia in the physical body and energetically from the etheric body. Some people call the etheric body the spirit," said Dakota.

"Is the soul and spirit the same thing?" asked Austin.

"They are very similar," said Dakota, "but if you get really specific, a person's spirit is the nonphysical portion of that person. The soul is the spirit and body united. Upon death, the spirit of the individual leaves the body. The body is laid to rest in the ground to decompose, and the spirit goes to the fifth dimension and beyond."

Austin had to think about that for a moment.

"Joseph, what are some ways a person can release emotions from the physical body?" asked Rex.

Joseph smiled. This was one of the first principles he was taught when he came to the Institute a few years earlier. "The emotions must be released through some sort of physical exertion."

Rex nodded and looked back to Dakota.

"What are some forms of physical exertion that can release emotions?" asked Dakota.

Joseph continued, "Mr. Ryan usually has us run, specifically parkour in the woods. I have found that's the easiest way for me."

"That is my preferred option as well," said Dakota. "Any other options?"

"I guess anything else that is physically exerting, mostly exercise."

"Yes, a few other ways would be getting a massage especially a deep tissue massage. There are several other forms of physical release such as cleansing the body externally or internally, some people will use a sauna or hot and cold therapy."

"What is hot and cold therapy?" asked Austin.

"Hot and cold therapy is when you transition from very warm to very cold quickly, such as being in a hot tub and then jumping out and rolling in the snow."

Austin was a little surprised at that. *That didn't sound very fun*, he thought.

"I've done that before," said Joseph. "Mr. Ryan had us do that several times last winter."

"Another form of physical release is what's called EFT: Emotional Freedom Technique. That uses a tapping sequence on different points of your body to release emotions. If you don't know specifically which points, just tap your sternum," he said. Dakota tapped on his breastbone showing them how. "Not too hard, but hard enough."

"That is a really good form of release," interjected Rex, "as with all of these techniques, be sure to drink plenty of water when you do so. If you release too fast, you could get flu-like symptoms. Emotion in the fascia is quite often combined with stored toxins in the body. So releasing the emotions also can release toxins, then the liver and kidneys have to clean it out of the blood. Too much can overload them."

"Yeah," said Dakota. "A heavy release of emotions can make you sick," he said, smiling at Rex.

They both paused for a moment, looking at each other.

"It sounds like there's a story behind that one." Austin said.

"As a matter of fact, yes, there is," said Rex. "Do you want to tell that story, Master Kavanaugh, or would you like me to?"

Austin looked at Joseph curiously. Apparently Joseph hadn't heard that story, either.

"Why don't you tell that one," said Dakota.

Rex took a deep breath, looking up, then back to the two young men. "Years before we met Mr. Ryan, I was going through my own learning process of these materials that we are talking to you two about. Master Kavanaugh is a few years ahead of me. During one particular experience I was releasing some very deep seated emotions that were stored in and around my lungs. He had taught me about tapping to release the emotions, but that wasn't enough for these particular emotions." Rex looked at Dakota again.

"So what did you do?" asked Joseph.

"I got a big stick and beat the emotions out of him," said Dakota with a grin.

"Indeed he did," continued Rex. "He got a stick a little bit bigger than your thumb in diameter and started tapping on my back with it. At first it was quite gentle, but as we continued it got harder. He was tapping on my shoulders and upper arms my lower back and sides. I was holding my breath and that was restricting the release of the emotions. He told me to breathe very deeply. After some time it really started to hurt and I started to cough. He would back off and then start again. I knew the emotions were coming out. He would talk with me about what emotions he saw, and I would visualize them leaving my body with every breath. When we finally got down closer to the real roots of the issue, I collapsed on the ground. Coughing and choking.

"That's when I went and got you some water," said Dakota.

"Which I really appreciated at that time," said Rex.

"Didn't that really hurt?" asked Austin.

"Yeah! And it was very effective in helping release the emotions I had pent up for decades, as well."

That wasn't the end of it, though," said Dakota. "After he took a break, we started up all over again."

"The second time rapidly became more intense than the first time, until I was again on the ground coughing up my lungs," said Rex.

"You had to do it twice?" asked Joseph.

"No," said Rex "we did it three times. The third time I was breathing so deeply, I felt like I was going to pass out. However, I could feel the emotion and substance in the lower part of my lungs, coming out."

"His breath smelled like metallic acid," interjected Dakota.

"That and stale carbon dioxide that had been in there for years was finally coming out. It felt like I was coughing out my toenails." Rex paused, "I eventually collapsed and started to vomit. It wasn't pretty, but it worked."

"Wow!" said Joseph. "What emotions were you releasing?"

"That's a great question," said Rex. "I was coughing out toxin, coupled with the emotions of not feeling good enough and not deserving to live. I didn't feel like I deserved life, joy, and love. Holding my breath was a subconscious manifestation of the negative emotions I had stored in my lungs."

"Isn't there an easier way?" asked Austin, somewhat concerned.

"Of course," said Rex. "That was an extreme example. You don't have to do it that way. Some easier ways would be trying not to pick up the emotions in the first place. And if you do, be aware of it quickly and release it to visualization before it can store inside your body."

"What if you've already stored it, though?" asked Joseph.

"An easier way would be to routinely clear any negative emotions that you may feel about any experiences, past, present, or future. Releasing the negative emotions on a periodic basis helps them not to pile up and clears out old ones that might be bubbling up in the present. Also, writing down your emotions on paper and then throwing the paper away while tapping on your sternum works very nicely. You just need to remember to do it consistently."

"Wait," said Austin. "You said past, present, and future? How can you clear emotions from experiences that haven't happened yet?

"Oh, that's a good question," said Rex gesturing to Dakota.

"You can pre-clear the emotions from experiences that haven't happened yet. If you become aware of a potential future experience, think about what emotions you may feel and clear them in the present. The experience may still happen and there may be many negative emotions from that experience, but it won't be nearly as painful as it would be if you hadn't precleared."

"That's cool," said Joseph.

"So let me get this straight," said Austin. "If I proactively clear my emotional baggage, then I wouldn't have to do it the way you did?"

"Right," said Rex. "It's a lot easier."

"So what is the advantage to doing it with a big stick?" asked Joseph.

"The advantage is that it's very fast and deep. It's also very painful physically and emotionally. But it really works," said Rex.

Joseph looked down at the ground.

Austin piped in, "If you would like me to, Joseph, I would love to beat you with a big stick."

"I'll bet you would," said Joseph with a smile.

Rex continued, "You would only want to do that with someone who knows what they're doing, someone who is very intuitive. So they can walk you through the emotions and the release process."

"I think I'm pretty intuitive," said Austin.

His head jerked to one side as something struck him from behind. He quickly turned around to see Nicholas standing behind him with a grin on his face.

"Your intuition needs more intuition," said Nicholas, still smiling.

"Even Master Ryan went through a similar experience, not as extreme as mine," said Rex.

"But pretty close," interjected Nicholas.

"I want to hear about that," said Austin while he rubbed the side of his head.

"Some other time," said Nicholas. "For now, we're going to get you going in the Genius Training program.

A huge grin immediately appeared on Austin's face.

"Joseph, if you would go with the other masters, they have some activities for you."

"Congratulations, man," Joseph said before following Rex and Dakota out the French doors to the patio.

"Let's get you caught up," said Nicholas to Austin.

Austin left with Nicholas out the same French doors, but headed in the opposite direction as the others. Their walk to Dr. Mac's office left him plenty of time to share with Nicholas his experience of the past few days. Nicholas made it difficult to leave anything out, even the reason for their unexpected early return.

Nicholas left Austin with Dr. Mac for the rest of the morning. He was worried about the physical, but it ended up not being that bad. Then Kara came and worked on his feet. This was the second time she had given him a Foot Zone. The massage that came next was the best part of the morning. His body melted on the table under Kara's gifted hands.

Taylor walked Austin to the library after lunch. He ran into her in the gardens on his way back from his massage. The hug and kiss he received rivaled the ninety-minute massage. He could keep his arms around her all day. They parted a few minutes later promising to meet up for dinner and some time at the pool that evening.

Nicholas sat reading in one of the chairs placed strategically by an open window. Austin made his way to the matching chair and sat down. Nicholas walked him through his nutrition plan for the next hour, along with internal cleanses that he would begin that evening. He explained that it requires energy to maintain waste. People, especially older people, have more toxins and waste in their body which require large amounts of energy to maintain. Eventually, their cells literally drown in their own waste because the body can no longer maintain it.

Austin looked forward to beginning the exercise program Nicholas outlined next. He would be spending more time in the gym with weights and doing H.I.I.T. training. He looked forward to running parkour with Joseph and the guys. This program turned out to be more intense than what he had done in the past but, Austin felt excited to prove himself to Nicholas that he hadn't made a mistake in allowing him to do the training.

Chapter 22 – The Test

Exactly five minutes to ten, Taylor met Austin in the large training room where the testing was to be administered. Mrs. Ryan and Dr. Mila Johnson were at the front of the room in quiet discussion. Many of the students were milling around, waiting for class to begin. Taylor noticed that all the windows were covered with heavy dark curtains. The room felt cramped and a little dark, even with all the lights shining. All of the couches, chairs and end tables had been removed. Small, grey cubicles lined the walls and a row ran down the center of the room, instead. Each cubicle held a small table, holding a water bottle and chair. The room felt very different to Taylor, sterile almost.

Everyone moved to the seats set up at the front of the room at Mrs. Ryan's request. After her welcome she introduced the schedule for the day.

"You're going to take a series of tests today." Taylor could hear Austin's moan as well as others in the room.

"This is the first in a series of tests unlike any others you've taken in your previous scholastic experience. Please do not feel pressured, but do the best you can. Don't stress over it. This test is to establish a baseline so you can see how well you're doing in the Genius Training program. We will be taking breaks at various points throughout the test. Snacks and drinks are at the tables in the back of the room," she said.

Turning around, Taylor could see the table laden with soda, candy bars, bags of chips, and containers of cookies. She turned back, wondering why there was only junk food. This was the first time she had ever seen soda at the Estate.

"Now let me introduce you to Dr. Mila Johnson," Vivian said. "She will be doing the research around your testing experience. She has a Master's degree in Psychology and a Ph.D. in Instructional Design. She has been working with us for a number of years. She does research, teaching, and consulting with several of our companies. She helped us develop the Genius Training program. She is also a director at the Institute and will explain more specifically about the tests."

"Mr. Lee will be assisting us with the testing today," Dr. Johnson said, stepping up to address the group.

Joseph strode confidently through the maze of students to join Dr. Johnson at the front of the room.

Taylor noticed Austin scowl.

"There are four components to this test," said Dr. Johnson. Taylor noticed her accent right away. *Probably Australia or New Zealand*, she thought.

"This first section consists of story problems and will test your stream of logic and certain portions of your cognitive function."

The look Austin shot Taylor had concern written all over it.

"The second component will be the conceptual and hands-on portion of the test. It will test your kinesthetic abilities."

Austin leaned over to Taylor "What does kinesthetic mean?" he whispered.

Before Taylor could answer Dr. Johnson continued. "The third component is your general knowledge of a variety of topics. And the fourth will test your problem-solving abilities through what-if scenarios.

"The questions from all three of the first components have definite answers. However the questions from the problem-solving portion of the test may not. In fact, there may not be an answer at all."

Talia, who was sitting on Taylor's right, raised her hand.

"Yes?" said Dr. Johnson.

"If there isn't a definite answer to the question, how will you know if we got it right? she asked.

"That portion of the test is not about getting the right answer as much as for us to see how you think."

Talia nodded.

"Are there any other questions?" she asked.

Taylor noticed a feeling of uncertainty fall over the occupants in the room. No one raised their hand.

"Then with that," said Dr. Johnson, "let's begin."

Joseph handed out packets of papers as everyone headed to their assigned desk. Taylor returned his smile and took her test packet. She noticed Austin's look of displeasure as she did so.

Once everyone was seated and had their packet Vivian began the test, tapping the timer on her phone. "You're forty-five minutes begins now."

Austin and Taylor were assigned booths next to each other at the end of one wall. He could see Taylor dive right into the first question on the test. He quickly wrote his name, but didn't go any further because he heard Joseph and Dr. Johnson talking quietly as they worked at a table near him. They were preparing some small boxes, probably for the next test.

Looking at his test, Austin couldn't help but listen to their quiet conversation.

"I took a similar test last year," Joseph said.

"Yes," replied Dr. Johnson, "But this test is slightly different. We have refined it more and it's taken from Nicholas's training that he does with corporate executives."

"What's different about it?" asked Joseph.

"This is a much more detailed test. More refined," said Dr. Johnson. "We are establishing a baseline for each person taking the test. They're going to take an identical test every day for a total of six days. Each time it will be slightly different."

"This is different. I only took it once at the beginning of the summer and once at the end.

"Yes," said Dr. Johnson. "This is quite a bit different. The test they're doing now is more difficult from beginning to end. If ten is the hardest and zero is the easiest, this test is level six. The difficulty will stay the same for the most part except for the last test on Saturday, but there are other factors that will change every day."

Austin gave up any pretense of starting the test, engrossed in their conversation.

"What other factors?" asked Joseph.

"For example, today the test started at 10 am. Everyone had a regular breakfast, they all have their water bottles so they can be hydrated, they've had a normal full night sleep, they're all sitting in cubicles with no natural lighting, only fluorescent lighting. Between tomorrow and Saturday we're going to administer an identical level of test, same difficulty for the most part, but we're going to change other factors each day."

"Wow, that sounds a lot more complicated than when I took the test," said Joseph. "Why are you making it so hard?" he asked.

"It's not the level of difficulty that we're testing them on, at least until the very last day. We are testing other factors like sleep, diet, hydration, lighting, etc. In about three months we're going to do a similar set of tests after they've gone through our Genius Training program and compare the results."

"This is more elaborate than when I took it," said Joseph. "It sounds like you're using them like lab rats. I'm glad I didn't have to do it this way."

"You did," said Dr. Johnson.

"What!"

"Yes, last year when you and a few of the others took a similar test, we used some of the results in adjusting our Genius program here at the Institute. We are constantly refining it. Now, help me get these boxes ready."

Austin's mind shifted back to the test. *Lab rats?*

The first page of story problems went by easily. He skipped question seven, not sure how to even start it. The remainder of the questions seemed challenging, but Austin felt okay about how he had done. *Wow, Atom is finished already*, he thought as he watched the young man walk to the snack table. He turned back to look at question seven again and hoped this time it would make sense.

During the break, Austin ate a candy bar and had a soda. He stood next to Taylor. He could tell she didn't know what to take. She ended up eating a small bag of cookies and took another water bottle before going back to her desk.

Lining the back of Austin's desk were plastic bags filled with wooden blocks of different shapes and sizes. Dr. Johnson said they were to use the shapes in each bag to create cubes. They would be tested on how quickly they were able to finish them. Austin finished early and felt very proud of himself, but then he noticed the room was almost empty. *I guess I wasn't as fast as I thought.* Taylor, he could see, was having a harder time with this test. He stretched out as best he could in the folding chair to wait for her to finish.

Lunch was a needed break. Austin and Taylor sat at a table on the patio. The warm seats, heated by the summer sun, felt relaxing to Austin. He smiled as Taylor slid down in her seat, resting her head against the back while she soaked up the much needed sun. It did feel different after sitting in the stifling room all morning. They spoke for a few minutes about the tests and how they felt they did, but for the most part they just ate in companionable silence.

The next test looked to Austin like someone had put questions from every topic in college in a big bowl and randomly drew them out and put them on the test. Everything seemed so scattered. Questions about chemistry, followed by cosmology, to geography and then genetics, and that was just the first few pages. It was hard to stay focused when the topics changed so abruptly. Austin's mind struggled to stay on task. And then came the dreaded statistics questions. *Of course that has to be on the test.*

"Times up," said Mrs. Ryan. "Bring your test booklets to the front and take a twenty minute break."

Austin flipped through the last few pages of questions. He finished only part of the test. *Lab rat*, he thought, tossing his packet on the pile on the table. Only a few others were bringing up their test booklets. Everyone else must have finished early.

Austin read and reread the questions for the last exam of the day. None of it made any sense to him. It wasn't a story problem. More like a scenario that he had to explain or fix. He couldn't even figure out what the problem was that he needed to solve. He hoped all the questions weren't like that. He skipped that one and went on. That's how the rest of the exam went: skip a few, try one, skip one, and try two or three. Austin breathed a sigh of relief when Mrs. Ryan concluded that day's testing. He placed his exam on the table and turned to find Taylor. She was waiting by the door. He hurried over, took her hand, and pulled her away from the room.

"Those tests were different than the ones I took in college," said Taylor.

"Yeah," said Austin. "It really doesn't matter anyway. I think they're using us for research, so it doesn't really matter how we do."

Austin could tell his remark puzzled Taylor, but at this point, he was too tired to care.

"Let's go to the pool," he said.

Chapter 23 – More Testing

"What!" said Austin.

He walked away from the kitchen with Taylor, his stomach rumbling. He didn't like this kind of testing: no breakfast! Taylor didn't seem upset by it, so he decided not to complain. The room looked the same as the day before. He and Taylor were assigned desks on opposite sides. Instead of an end cubicle he was crammed between Atom and Mia.

Part way through the first test, Austin reached for the water bottle that wasn't there. They would be given a drink at lunch, but not before. His concentration was fleeting. His mind kept wandering to his empty stomach. The second exam turned out to be pathetic as well.

"Lunch is on the back table," said Vivian at the conclusion of the mornings testing. "You will only have ten minutes before the next test will begin."

Joseph stood at the back handing out bags of lunch. Austin looked inside and saw a bottle of fruit juice and a small bag of potato chips. He rifled through the paper sack, hoping to find anything else, even a carrot or celery stick would be better than just chips. He looked up at Taylor. She grimaced and pulled open her chip bag.

The afternoon's testing dragged on. Austin spent more time looking at the clock on the wall than taking the test. His mind wouldn't focus on the questions, and he struggled with what he thought should have been the easy ones. *I wonder if I'm the only one having an off day today*, he thought, when he saw Atom get up and leave, finishing his last test with half the time still remaining. Twenty agonizing minutes later, Austin stood and took his test packet to Mrs. Ryan, then quietly left the room.

Taylor found him leaning against the wall in the hall. Eyes closed, arms folded across his chest, and feet crossed at the ankles. He looked asleep. She reached out and poked his muscular arm, surprised when all he did was open his eyes and look at her.

"Today's test was awful," Taylor said.

"Don't want to talk yet," said Austin. "My brain is hungry. Until it's fed, I can't guarantee you a coherent conversation."

She took Austin's hand and dragged him off to find some food.

Taylor cleaned her plate and sat back in her seat, her long slender fingers idly wiping the condensation off the side of her glass.

"Something was different about the testing today," she said. "I don't think the questions were more difficult than yesterday, but the answers must have been hiding somewhere in my brain. I left a number of them half-finished or untouched."

"I was distracted," said Austin. "That was my problem. I kept watching the second hand on the clock. I swear it didn't move."

Taylor heard the comments of the others as they made their way to the door. Everyone was complaining about the day's testing.

"How about a movie?" said Taylor.

Austin nodded and slung his arm over Taylor's shoulder as they walked to the lounge.

Taylor felt rested when she got up the next morning. She and Austin cuddled on the couch and watched an Abbott and Costello movie the night before. Her clock read 9:03 when she crawled into bed. She didn't move all night.

She found Austin joking with some of the guys in the dining room. *He seems happier this morning now that he got to eat*, she thought. Curiosity flitted through the conversations that flowed around the breakfast table. No one wanted to venture a guess on what would be different today.

The note on the door directed Taylor and Austin to a different room for the test. It was bright, even with the absence of windows. The tables sat scattered throughout. Water bottles, test packets and pencils filled a long table just inside the door. Taylor picked up one of each and moved further into the room. Austin nudged her.

"Let's sit over there."

They made their way through the labyrinth of seats to the far side of the room. A little before ten Dr. Johnson announced that they could begin as soon as they wanted.

"So what is different about today?" Joseph asked Dr. Johnson, "Besides no cubicles."

Taylor could hear the quiet question. She paused to listen.

"It's the full-spectrum lighting that is in here," she said. "It is more like natural light."

The hours sped by as Taylor worked on the different exams. The answers climbed out of their hiding places in her mind and her pencil flew across the page. *If only the rest of the week could be this easy,* she thought.

Lounging in the pool with Austin that evening, Taylor could tell by the smile on his face that he did much better on the tests today, as well.

"Whatever they changed for today's testing paid off," she said." I did lots better than yesterday."

"Yeah, no stupid cubicles."

"Of course," Taylor said. She jumped on Austin. Surprised, he sunk in the water under her weight. They chased each other around the pool, dunking and splashing each other.

Breathing heavily, Taylor hung onto the edge.

"That's not what I meant," she said. "It was something else, but I'm not sure what. I think it has something to do with the lights. At least, that's what I heard Dr. Johnson tell Joseph."

"Now that you mention it, something did feel different."

They lingered in the pool and hot tub until late. Mrs. Ryan said they were to stay up until at least midnight. Austin didn't mind the late night. He liked spending time with Taylor, but the 7 AM start time bothered him.

He ran into class right at 7:00 the next morning and slid into the seat Taylor saved for him.

"What took you so long?" she asked.

"Snooze, there should be clocks without them."

He saw Taylor's stifled giggle. He smiled, then opened his test and began.

The day went pretty much like the others. Austin found himself getting tired by the last test. Retrieving some water off the back table helped wake up his tired brain. He would be glad when this was over.

Austin carried his plate and Taylor's out the patio that evening. A gentle breeze rustled the leaves of the nearby trees. Butterflies flitted around the patio and landed on bushes covered with pink and red petals.

He filled his lungs with the clean fresh air, basking in the sweet smell of the freshly cut grass. His biceps bulged as he stretched then sat down. He took a long drink of cool water from the glass Taylor handed him.

"Half-way," Taylor said.

"What do you mean?" asked Austin.

"Only three more days of testing," she said.

Austin chewed his bite of lasagna, appreciating the spicy blend of flavors. He pondered the past few days. He knew his scores on these tests would be better than any of his college exams. It still amazed him how different he was now than a year ago.

"I wonder what they will throw at us tomorrow?" he said.

The grass felt cool and damp under Austin's feet. Exams that day were being held out on the grassy field beyond the back patio. Tables spread out under an expansive canopy, like blobs of paint splattered on a canvas of green. Sunlight filtered through the thin, white mesh. The omelet at breakfast satisfied his hunger after an intense workout that morning. He and Taylor parted company relatively early the night before and, after a good night's sleep, he felt more vital and alive than he had all week.

The silver and black fidget spinner swirled between Austin's thumb and finger while he pondered the next question. Dr. Johnson left an assortment of fidget devices on the table along with a small pile of colored stones. The impatient part of him was distracted by the soft whir of the toy in his hand as he moved slowly through the remainder of the questions.

I wouldn't mind taking tests, Austin thought, *if it could be this way all the time.* Even with the distractions outside, Austin could tell he focused better here than inside.

He and Taylor had no desire to go inside once their exams were finished. Austin felt the heat of the late afternoon sun on his back as they strolled across the lawn. Tired after all the sitting, it felt good to stretch his legs for a while. They walked in comfortable silence, neither one feeling the need to talk. Taylor's fingers brushed against his, he took her hand, lacing his fingers with hers. At the far end of the yard sat a small wooden bench. It hugged the edge of the lawn, secluded from the house by a lilac bush in full bloom. Austin stretched out on the grass at Taylor's feet, the stress of the week seeping from his body and into the ground. He idly stroked Taylor's ankle as he watched the cotton clouds move slowly across the sky.

"Today's testing was kind of fun," Taylor said. "Everyone seemed to be in a better mood."

"I think I actually did pretty well today," Austin said. "And that's coming from someone who has never done well taking exams. I hoped we would finish the tests on Monday, but I guess it will be nice to get the last day over with."

Taylor and Austin were up early the next morning and put in some time at the gym together. They ate a delicious and filling breakfast: a protein shake and a large cheese and veggie omelet that Marti and Geri had been told to give to all who were taking the test.

They sat at two small tables on one side of the testing area. The real salt dissolved in Taylor's mouth, causing her lips to pucker. Austin held back the laugh that tried to break free as he watched her and waited for the salt in his mouth to dissolve. They drank some water and washed away the flavor of the salt that lingered on their tongues.

Dr. Johnson came around with their exam packets and a small bottle.

"Would you be okay with taking a supplement today?" she asked Taylor and Austin.

They nodded and took the test and the supplement. Austin looked around and saw the others taking the vitamin and then beginning their test, all except Atom. He just set his on his desk. *We really are lab rats*, thought Austin as he swallowed the capsule.

"What else is different about today?" asked Taylor.

"Well," said Dr. Johnson. "The level of difficulty for the past five tests was a level six. The test today will be a level nine or greater in difficulty. We are also mixing up the order, and you will be given less time to complete the exam."

Taylor thanked Dr. Johnson, pulled her legs up on her seat Indian-style, and gave Austin an uneasy smile as she began her test. Austin rubbed his feet in the wet, cool grass. He felt a little uneasy about the more difficult test, especially if their time was cut. He hoped he would do better than the previous four days of testing, but now he wasn't so sure.

Dr. Johnson announced before the test began, that this would be the last of this type of testing until the end of the summer. A loud cheer burst from the students.

Austin felt pleased with how the first page of questions went. He flipped to the next page.

What is Onychorrhexis? Austin read. His mind went blank. Ony-what? He read the second question. What are the first nine digits of pi? *Pi! What flavor? And these aren't even multiple choice questions!*

He looked at the next three questions. They were each similar in difficulty. Baffled, he returned to the first question. The words seemed to get hazy before his eyes. It reminded him of his business statistics class the previous year in college.

He looked up at Dr. Johnson, who was busily working on her tablet, a stack of tests piled nearby.

"Wow!" came a voice from behind him. He looked to see Mia frantically writing. She was halfway done with the first page.

Austin felt weird. *What's happening?* Shaking his head, he returned to his own test. Then it happened.

The sunlight shining on the grass appeared brighter like it was coming out from behind the clouds. Austin looked around. The grass seemed so much greener. The shrubs and flowers boldly displayed their vibrant colors and patterns. He never realized until now just how beautiful this part of the Estate was.

He could hear the chirping of birds nearby. The moist, dank smell of decaying underbrush mixed with the pungent scent of pines. Looking over at, Taylor he could see the perspiration gleaming on her forehead and smell the soft vanilla scent that was all her. He felt the beat of his pulse in his throat. He took a deep breath and reread the first question.

What is Onychorrhexis?

He put his pen to the paper. Onychorrhexis is the medical term used to describe longitudinal ridges on the nails that often accompany brittle finger and toenails, he wrote.

He stopped writing and read his answer. *Is that really what it is?* Going to the second question, he wrote 3.14159265

The information flowed easily. And he understood the questions better than the previous times he had taken the test. He looked up for a moment and caught Taylor's eye. She had a big smile on her face. She nodded and went back to her test.

Austin returned the smile. He stared across the yard, happy with where he was and who he was with. And even what he was doing.

He brought his focus back to the test and finished with ample time left over. He rechecked a couple of answers but didn't feel the need to change anything.

"How did it go?" asked Vivian when he returned his test at the break.

"A lot easier than I thought it would be," said Austin.

He and Taylor took a quick break, and then hurried back for the next test.

The thirty minutes of the next part went by quickly. The Rubik's cube almost solved itself. Taylor smiled and felt almost giddy this being her first time trying it. She and Austin returned their cubes to the table and left for lunch on the patio.

Marti and Geri outdid themselves with lunch that day. Red, green, and orange peppers streaked black piled on foil sat next to marinated chicken that sizzled on the grill. The roasted cauliflower and broccoli, large bowls of spinach salad were options for those eating vegan. Bright blue ceramic bowls heaped with mouth-watering fruit finished off the lunch. Pitchers of ice water graced the smooth white cloth-covered tables.

Taylor sat quietly eating while she listened to Pajori and Austin's conversation about the morning's testing. The answers came almost effortless to more than just Taylor. The air crackled with a sense of excitement as they made their way back to the shade of the canopy. Her toes curled in the warm grass beneath her feet. Taylor looked around at the others. Some were writing almost frantically on their papers, others were still waiting for their exam and vitamin. Atom had his shoes on. Two capsules lay on the corner of his desk. She saw a look pass from Vivian to Dr. Johnson and then over to Atom.

Taylor's test lay on her desk, daring her to begin. With only seventy minutes left, she picked up her pencil. She moved through page after page of questions. The level of difficulty increased with each page, but the answers flooded her mind. She found herself finished at fifty-two minutes. *Wow*, she thought. She joined Will and Demetri at the front table. They were quietly conversing with Vivian. Austin joined them a few minutes later, after he had handed his paper to Dr. Johnson with a triumphant look. Taylor moved close when he slid his arm around her shoulders. Atom shoved through their small group and threw his paper towards the table. Taylor turned and watched as he stalked off, the test landing near her feet.

Taylor and Austin moved through the tables towards the house for a short break. They passed Grace still at her table, eyes closed, hands clasped in front of her and a big smile on her face.

Taylor munched on some grapes as she and Austin made their way back for the last test. A smile glued to her face.

As Taylor worked through the first few questions she noticed Austin. He sat with a look of concentration. His eyes darted back and forth then closed, then opened and darted back and forth again. She could tell when the answer clicked. His eyes lit up and a small smile curved his lips. She heard the scratch of his pencil when she turned back to her own test. They finished a moment before Vivian ended the session. She stretched and gave Austin a high five.

"Before you get too excited to be on your way there are a few things you need to know," Mrs. Ryan said. "Dr. Johnson will be evaluating the exams. Mr. Ryan and I will then go through them and coordinate your specific schedule for classes and training. We will meet with each of you individually and go over your schedule."

Joseph came around with another stack of papers. Taylor took one and began to look through it. The information was divided into categories.

General:
- ☒ Physical cleanse and build
- ☒ Nutrition
- ☒ Exercise
- ☒ Emotional release
- ☒ Brain enhancement activities
- ☒ Piano and other musical instruments
- ☒ Languages and memorization.

The next section was titled "Genius Training":
- ☒ Visual and spatial games
- ☒ Focus and meditation
- ☒ Logic games
- ☒ Multi-dimensional chess and checkers
- ☒ Idyllic memory
- ☒ Super Exponential Learning
- ☒ Math and problem-solving.
- ☒ Technology/computers.
- ☒ Science: chemistry, physics, biology, astronomy.
- ☒ History

"On your page is a brief sample of the courses you will be studying," Mrs. Ryan said.

"What about things like Extra Sensory Perception and Telepathy Training?" came a voice from the back.

"Eventually, those who go on and do the Ascension Training will learn that, as well as opening the third eye chakra, Awareness exercises, martial arts, breathing and cold showers."

"How do you learn cold showers?" Austin asked.

"You'll have to wait for Ascension Training for that," Vivian said with a smile. "The last group of activities are not part of the Genius Training program, but will be added to your schedule. I think you will enjoy these."

Taylor read the list.

Extra Activities:
- ☒ Martial arts
- ☒ Weapons training: guns, knives and swords.
- ☒ Horseback riding
- ☒ Public speaking
- ☒ Ancient and modern linguistics.
- ☒ Awareness and reflex training
- ☒ Parkour, gymnastics and dance.
- ☒ Weight and endurance training.

"I think I want to be in your gymnastics class," Taylor said. She bumped her hip into Austin as they walked back to the house.

"No gymnastics for me. I'll stick with sword fighting."

Chapter 24 – Rocks Again

The leather of the chair stuck to Austin's calves as he waited for Nicholas to finish typing on his tablet. He willed his hands to relax, the perspiration soaked into his khakis. *Why am I so nervous?* he wondered. *It's not like this is the first time.* It took all of his focus not to fidget. The testing had finished three days previous. Austin wondered all weekend what he would be doing for the Genius Training Program. Taylor had already started hers and it was now his turn.

Nicholas laid the papers aside and looked at Austin, his eyes piercing in their perusal.

"Are you willing to do what it takes?" Nicholas said.

No small talk today, Austin thought.

"Yes," Austin said. "I'll do whatever you say."

"Meet me out front in fifteen minutes in work clothes. And bring some water and a lunch."

Austin nodded.

Fourteen minutes later, Austin found himself in the same small truck from the previous summer. Apprehension closed in when Nicholas parked the truck next to a field covered with rocks.

"This field is 12.76 acres and your responsibility is to have all the rocks the size of a tennis ball or larger moved off," Nicholas said. "When the field is cleared to my satisfaction, you may continue the Genius Training."

Austin swallowed the anger and frustration that began to form within him. He had done the same task in a nearby field the previous summer. He took a deep breath and said, "Okay."

He climbed out of the truck and watched Nicholas drive away.

Austin bent over and picked up the nearest rock. "I am not my emotions, the rocks are my emotions," he chanted. This reverberated in his head with each rock that flew. *This all can't just be about emotions*, Austin thought. No reply came as the morning inched along.

The sun beat down as Austin trudged to the edge of the field. He sat in the welcome shade and wiped the sweat off his brow with his shirt. He stretched his tired muscles and took a long drink of warm water. Not even a bird marred the cloudless sky. He hoped to see a message from Taylor, but when he pulled out his phone, he remembered. No cell service. *Of course.*

With lunch over, he laid down in the tall grass and watched the canopy of branches sway in the warm breeze. *There's got to be an easier way*, he thought. He set the alarm on his phone for fifteen minutes, closed his eyes, relaxed, and searched his mind for an answer. He fell asleep before one came.

The afternoon continued with no change. Rocks flew, piles grew, and Austin was no closer to alleviating the chore. He launched a small rock. The clang of metal got his attention and he sauntered over to investigate. Off in the trees stood a large blue tractor, its immense tires caked in dirt. To one side lay a metal frame on wheels with a rusty scoop attached to the front. *Cool*, he thought as he climbed on the tractor and sat down on the faded leather seat. Levers and dials spread over the dash. Austin shook his head in confusion, climbed down, and walked slowly back to the field.

He didn't say much when Benjamin picked him up later that afternoon, his mind lost in thought about the tractor parked in the trees.

The cool shower ran over his hot, tired body. He stood there until the ache in his muscles began to dissipate. Not long after, dressed in a clean t-shirt, shorts, and shoes, Austin meandered into the kitchen, dished up a plate, and went in search of Taylor, who he hoped would be in the dining room. He spied her getting up from a table on the far side of the room. The distance between them diminished in no time.

"Hey, Taylor, can you stick around for a minute?" he said. "I haven't seen you all day."

Taylor turned and sent her bright smile his way.

"I have a class in ten minutes, so I can't stay long," she said.

Austin listened while she told him about her day. It sounded so much better than his. All too soon, she gave him a quick kiss on the cheek and rushed off.

Austin roamed the halls of the Estate after dinner. He thought about the field and tried to figure out a better way. He pondered the different tools he had been taught when a picture began to form in his mind. After a quick stop in the library, Austin hurried to his room. Blue painters tape and a few punch pins were placed on his desk next to a book. Unsure where it came from, Austin pushed it out of the way and set down the photo from the library. A tic-tac-toe pattern in blue tape divided his bulletin board. Austin arranged the picture of a beautiful, lush, field full of loamy soil on the top middle section, securing it with a pin. Then stood back and looked at it. *Not quite right*, he thought, then moved it to the bottom middle section. *That's it.*

Curious about the book, Austin picked it up. This wasn't a cheap paperback. Tom Sawyer by Mark Twain was imprinted in the dark brown leather cover. He flipped open to the middle of the book and started to read. The story caught his interest, so he got comfortable and began again, this time on page one. The next few hours were spent absorbed in Tom's adventures.

Austin stopped in the middle of the sentence and picked up his buzzing phone to see a message from Taylor. The book lay ignored in his lap. His fingers tapped quickly.

"No, I can't chat," came Taylor's text. "I'm in bed, just wanted to say hi."

Austin tapped his reply.

"Yeah, great day. Fun classes. How was the field?" she replied.

Austin sent back a more positive response than he felt.

"See you tomorrow?" was her last text with a heart emoji.

Austin smiled and went back to his book.

His food and jug of water lay tossed in the shade the next morning. The more rocks Austin threw, the angrier he became. The whole mental game of staying positive wasn't happening. The sweat dripped down his bare chest and back. A rock hurled over the fence into the next field. *Another summer of doing this will probably kill me*, Austin thought.

Lunch came early that day. He didn't bother with the alarm. The breeze, cooled by the shade of the tall trees, lulled him to sleep. Laughter broke through the trees. A startled Austin jerked up and looked around. Across the fence, Taylor and some other girls went running by. She waved, but ran off with the others.

Irritated, Austin went back to work in the field, putting his shirt back on. It stuck to his back as he continued to clear the field. *Better to be hot and sticky than fried*, he thought. The ache in his back reminded him to bend at the knees. The muscles in his legs burned, but he kept at it. Each rock carried with it anger, resentment, irritation, and many other labels.

He stretched his back, not moving as he watched a hawk fly overhead. It soared on the wind high above the trees. Its call echoed over the field. *If only I were that free*, Austin thought.

"You will be," came the words to his mind, as the breeze picked up and gently bent the branches of the trees.

The snap of twigs drew his attention off the bird and to the side of the field. Austin turned, hoping to see Taylor again.

"Anyone want to place a bet?"

Austin heard Will's question before he saw him. Will, Joseph, Demetri, and a few others jogged out of the tree line and onto the field.

"What's the bet?" Austin asked.

"How long you're going to do this," said Will.

"I'm doing this because Mr. Ryan told me to."

"We all had to do it last summer." Will said not able to contain his laughter any longer.

"Why are you laughing?" Austin asked.

"I'm just wondering how long you are going to keep this up." Will said.

"What's the catch?" asked Austin. "Am I missing something?"

"We can't tell you." Will said as he and the others ran back into the trees laughing.

No more rock throwing today, Austin thought. He stormed over to the shade kicking rocks and dirt on the way. He sat against a tree, his arms rested on his bent knees. A long blade of grass twisted in his fingers while in his mind an image of a field free of rocks materialized. *Now if I could just get that image out of my head and onto this field*, he thought.

Benjamin picked him up at the usual time. Back at the Estate, Austin hurriedly showered and dressed, anxious to find Taylor. He caught up with her in the kitchen. They found a secluded table next to a bank of windows. Birds darted across the patio before soaring into the blue of the early evening sky. Butterflies flitted from shrub to shrub, their soft wings fanning the delicate petals of the flowers.

During dinner, Austin shared the conversation he'd had with Will earlier that day with Taylor.

"There's got to be more to this than just clearing emotions," Austin said.

"You're probably right," said Taylor.

"It frustrated me this afternoon when they wouldn't tell me anything. I don't know if I will figure it out and I really don't want to be throwing rocks all summer."

"What if it's not about throwing rocks?" Taylor asked.

"Maybe not, but I still don't know what it has to do with being a genius. I think it's a waste of my genius potential."

"You're not a genius yet," said Taylor. "It's probably some kind of test."

Austin walked Taylor to her class after dinner. The hug and quick kiss she gave him brought a smile to his face, a first for the day. He strode confidently back to his room, resolute in his quest for an answer. With a notebook and pen in hand, he stared at the picture of the field on his creation board. He waited and wrote down any negative thoughts that came to his mind. That paper landed in pieces in the bottom of his garbage. With a clean sheet, he looked at the photo again. What do I need to do to get this? Then he waited. And waited. Determined not to be frustrated, he looked around his room for something else to do. His gaze focused on the brown leather book on his desk. He toed off his shoes, picked up the book, and settled back on his bed as he began to read.

Thoughts formed in Austin's mind as he read. *Tom has to paint a fence. I have to haul rocks. Tom gets his friends to paint the fence for him and they 'want' to do it.* Austin set the book aside and sent Nicholas a text.

"Do I have to get all the rocks off the field by myself?"

Nicholas's response came a moment later. "You are responsible to make sure that all the rocks are cleared off the field before you can move on in your training."

"Do I have to do that all by myself or can I have other people help me?" sent Austin.

"If you can talk other people into helping you, then sure. However, their help cannot take away from their training."

"Thanks," read Austin's reply.

Is there any way to get the others to want to help me clear the field? Austin rolled his eyes. *I think not.*

His sleep was restless that night. His mind not able to shut down. Different ideas and options for clearing the field darted around his head. Early in the morning, he had a strange dream about a field full of blue tractors. All his friends were driving around, laughing and pointing as he threw rocks in the next field.

The next morning at breakfast, Austin asked Pajori if he would help him with the rocks.

"I'd love to man, but I've got a full schedule today."

Austin pushed aside the frustration that begged to be released and approached Joseph with the same question.

Shaking his head, Joseph smiled. "Man, even if I wanted to, the two of us couldn't clear off that field the way you're doing it. It would take over a year. You're heading in the right direction. You haven't got it yet, but you're on the right track."

"What do you mean?" asked Austin.

"I had the same test last year. Don't worry, you'll figure it out."

I think I've been going about this all wrong, Austin thought later that morning as he stood in the middle of the field. The rocks mocked him with their number and size. He had worked for two long days and the only thing to show for it were sore muscles.

What would a genius do? he thought, gazing up at the cloudless sky. He read Tom Sawyer for a reason, he knew that. *Was getting others to help the answer?* He found a comfortable spot in the shade, pulled the notebook and pen out of the backpack he had brought and quickly wrote down his thoughts about the past few days.

Emotional Release:
-I am not my thoughts and emotions.
-Rocks represent emotional baggage, but they're not my identity.
-What would a genius do?

"If I can't get help and one rock at a time is too slow, how about if I moved a lot of rocks at once?" Austin lips moved but no sound came out.

The pen moved across the paper again.

-A big bag or tarp.

That would still take too long, he thought. *There's got to be something better. Maybe I could use the truck.* The more he thought about it, the less he liked the idea.

If only there was something on the truck that would load the rocks while I drove. That would be great, but there's nothing on the truck that would do that.

Tired of sitting, Austin got up with a water bottle and strolled around the edge of the field still deep in thought. One idea after another worked its way to the surface. None of them were quite right. A memory of something Nicholas had said the year before popped into his mind.

"I have equipment that can clear the rocks from these fields much better and faster than any one person ever could."

The tractor! Austin ran over to it and walking around, almost tripped on the metal frame hidden in the grass. Frantically he cleared some of the tall weeds to reveal more of the machine. He pulled out his phone and snapped photos of the tractor and the machine next to it.

Puddles of dust formed under his feet as he jogged over to the truck and took off down the dirt road. As soon as he has cell coverage he pulled over and looked up how to drive a tractor. After watching some tutorials he sped back to the field. He tried to remember what the videos showed as he looked at the dials on the blue tractor. The key sat in the ignition, Austin turned it. Nothing happened. *Oh, ya. I'm supposed to push the pedal at the same time.*

He bent down and looked at the pedals. One sat on the left and there were two on the right. Austin pushed one down and turned the key again. Nothing. The other two gave him the same response. He let out a growl of frustration. Austin sat back, closed his eyes and after a few deep breaths he could feel himself calm down.

"How do I do this?" he whispered to the sky, the trees, anything and everything. *Nicholas said I have a higher power. Now would be a good time to get acquainted.*

His head fell forward and landed on his arms as they rested on the steering wheel. Its support felt almost comforting. Sweat from his forehead blended with the moisture on his arms. He chuckled into the steering wheel as the dream from the night before came back to him. Austin saw Joseph's grin as he bounced across the field in a tractor, a blue one that looked identical to this one.

Austin jumped down from the tractor, gathered his pack, and crossed the field a second time that day to the truck. This time, he didn't stop until he pulled up in front of the Estate. He picked up a sandwich and a drink from Geri and strolled out to the patio. He smiled to himself when he saw Joseph. Austin pulled out a chair and sat down across from him.

"Do you know how to drive a tractor?" he asked.

"Yeah, I've driven one before. Why do you ask?"

"You don't have to, but will you show me how? Or at least show me how to turn it on," Austin said.

"Ok, I guess I could, if we go now."

Austin paid close attention as Joseph outlined all the dials, pedals and parts of the tractor to him and then walked him through how to start it. *This is easier than I thought.*

Austin started up the tractor and, with Joseph's help, backed it up to the equipment; a hopper Joseph called it, which remained half-buried in the grass. Fifteen minutes later, covered in grease and a big smile, Austin maneuvered the tractor onto the field. Joseph had one more piece of advice before leaving.

"Make sure you dump the hopper when it is half-full because the hydraulics can't lift more than that."

Austin threw him a wave farewell as he bounced across the field. Distracted by the new experience, he forgot to keep an eye on the hopper. It took him what felt like an hour to unload enough before the hydraulics worked. He vowed not to let that happen again. The field began to look more and more like the picture on his vision board. Austin grinned, enjoying the music that blared from his phone. *Who knew hauling rocks from a field could be so entertaining.* He'd never felt so ruggedly masculine in his life. Too bad Taylor couldn't see him. It took only a second to send her a selfie.

A little before 5:00, Austin unhooked the hopper and parked the tractor in as close to the exact spots they had been in. For some reason, he hoped Nicholas would think he finished it all by hand. Austin jumped to the ground. Nicholas stood a few feet away from him with a smile on his face. Austin felt a little embarrassed and proud when Nicholas began to clap.

"Three days," he said. "I'm impressed."

Austin wasn't sure how to respond.

"So it was a test, after all?" Austin said.

"More like a learning experience," Nicholas said.

"What did you want me to learn?"

"I wanted to see how long it would take you to figure it out, among other things," said Nicholas.

"Like what other things?"

"Well, how to work with the earth and be in touch with nature, get your hands dirty. I also hoped you would come to understand the difference between smart and hard work. And I wanted to remind you of all you learned last summer about who you really 'Be.'"

Nicholas looked at the rock-free field and smiled. "And I wanted to see if you would take advantage of the opportunity to expand your mind. I also wanted to see how determined you are and if you would quit. The real turning point happened when you put the picture on your creation board."

"How did you know I put that on my board?" Austin asked.

"Let's get you back for dinner," said Nicholas. "It's about time you get started in the Genius Program."

Question avoided in true Nicolas fashion, thought Austin.

Chapter 25 - New Routine

"You now have your routine," said Nicholas. "Do you have any questions?"

"No. I've already started some of it and I'm excited to do more," Austin said the next morning.

"Good," said Nicholas. "I just want to make sure you're clear on what you're doing."

Austin wondered when Nicholas would get to the good stuff.

"What are your goals, Austin?" Nicholas asked.

"I want to become a genius as quickly as possible."

"Even though our Genius Program is finite, becoming a genius isn't. It's a process. So while that's a good goal, I think you need to start with something a little more specific," Nicholas said.

"I want to excel at the training."

"Be more specific," said Nicholas

"I would like to make better use of my Creation Board," Austin said.

After a bit more discussion, Austin had a list of short and mid-term goals. When his classes began, he would add more.

"Remember when we talked last summer about who you 'Be?'" asked Nicholas.

Austin nodded.

"Keep pondering that as well as what your life purpose and mission is. Finding those answers will help lead you to some of your long term goals. We will meet again later and firm them up."

The time Austin had spent with Nicholas went by faster than he expected. He did come away with a detailed list of goals he would focus on each morning. His alarm went off most days at 7:00 and now he would add stretching and a mild workout for two to three minutes along with a grounding exercise before his meditation. Making and using a Creation Board came next on his list.

Austin smiled when he looked at that one, pleased with his first accomplishment that summer and ready to move forward onto bigger and better things. Now he needed to get a binder to collect his Creation Board accomplishments in.

Nicholas had given him a list of books to read, including The Talent Code by Daniel Coyle, The Code of the Extraordinary Mind by Vishen Lakhiani, and Awaken the Genius by Patrick K. Porter. *They seemed interesting.*

Austin also looked forward to his workouts with Sam. He would get to do that every morning. Then time to get cleaned up, eat and be off to his first class by 10:00.

Not having many classes with Taylor was a disappointment, especially when he found out he wouldn't be eating breakfast or lunch with her, either. He would be given a more specific diet than the previous summer. No complaints about that. *The food here tastes better than anything I've ever made*, he thought.

Chapter 26 – Taylor's Training

"Taylor," Vivian began, peering at her protégé from across the desk in her office, "Today we're going to get more specific with your training. And I'm going to let you in on a big secret that few people in the world know."

Taylor nodded, anticipation filling her mind. "Am I allowed to talk with other people about this secret?" she asked.

"To a certain degree, yes," said Vivian. "Though most people won't get it, and even if they do, they won't do anything about it. The majority of people don't understand the severity of what I'm about to tell you."

Vivian seemed very serious. Taylor felt a twinge of concern. *Do I really want the responsibility of this information?* She felt a peaceful feeling come over her the moment she internally verbalized the question.

"Can I share it with Austin, or the other people here at the Institute?" asked Taylor.

"For the most part. Some of the people here at the Institute are mentally and emotionally mature enough to handle this information. But only share to their level. You will have to keep it very basic with most people."

Taylor nodded.

Vivian smiled slightly. "This is not the greatest secret of all time, but it's one of the biggest ones that is affecting the entire planet at this time in history. Nicholas may share an even greater secret with you and Austin, but that's for another day."

Taylor was still on edge, waiting for the anticipated information.

Vivian continued, "This great secret is that there is a pandemic that is affecting the entire world, especially the United States. To one degree or another, this is affecting about 95% of the population of the planet and about 99.9% of the population of the US."

Taylor knew what the word pandemic meant, but didn't understand. A puzzled look on her face. She couldn't imagine what unseen disease could be hurting almost everyone.

"This pandemic is causing starvation," said Vivian. "You see, Taylor, most of the food that is eaten in the United States is not real. It has been hybridized or genetically modified or is simply synthetic.

"Synthetic food?" asked Taylor.

"Yes, fake food," continue Vivian. "It has calories in it, and vitamins and other added nutrients, but it contains little to no pranic life force energy. This means the body is not getting the actual nutrition it needs in a form that can be used to perform basic functions like cellular repair and build, or fuel for performance. If you look at the packaging of most food, it may contain ingredients that look like or once was living food, but in the processing and alteration of it, the food becomes almost unusable for the body. Most Americans get plenty of calories, but their bodies are starving for real, life-giving nutrition."

Taylor was trying to process what she was hearing to make sense in her mind.

"When you go shopping, the middle of the grocery store is primarily full of processed foods. The food is full of preservatives and additives, but the body simply cannot use it. The food is full of chemicals, not real living substance.

"What about the produce that's sold in the stores?"

"It's better, but, then again, much of the produce is grown with chemical fertilizers and in soil that's been depleted from years of over farming. Also, much of it has been hybridized or genetically modified or sprayed with some sort of chemical to make it look appealing, but when it comes right down to it, not even the bugs will eat it because they know it's not good for them. If bugs won't eat it, why should humans?

"The standard American diet or, S.A.D., is so devoid of true nutrition that is usable by the body that most people are literally starving even though they're getting plenty of calories. They eat food that has been heavily processed, like junk food or fast food, but their body doesn't get enough real nutrition. When that happens, the body signals the brain, saying send down more food. So people are continually eating, but not getting enough real nutrition. That's one of several reasons why obesity is such a major issue in the United States."

"When did this happen?" asked Taylor trying to remember her history.

"This is been going on very gradually for some time. Most of it started very simply and quite innocently around a hundred years ago. Before that, the bulk of people raised their own food. But as time went by, more people moved into manufacturing jobs and into the cities and they couldn't produce their own food. There became fewer farms, but more mouths to feed. Companies started altering food in order to feed the growing masses. It was necessary to a certain point, but slowly, for profit's sake, it became malicious. Companies learned that if a person was addicted to their products, they would have to buy them repeatedly. Also the forms of marketing became more specialized and that added to it as well. I could go on for a long time about this, but the gist of it, is that people eat food because of convenience, taste, and addiction. Meanwhile, the body is starving, and there are all these diseases that are popping up that didn't exist a hundred and fifty years ago. The most common health issues from this pandemic of starvation are the big five: obesity, cancer, autoimmune issues, diabetes, and heart disease."

Taylor remembered all the people she knew who had died from one of these diseases or who were currently suffering from them. She thought of her father dying in his early forties from a sudden heart attack. As she remembered that day, the emotions started coming back. Finding him on the floor of their bathroom pale and lifeless. The tears started to form in her eyes.

As if reading her thoughts, Vivian gently put her hand on Taylor's arm. "People shouldn't be dying in their thirties and forties from a heart attack," she said.

Taylor shook the thoughts from her mind. She had done a lot of emotional clearing about her father's death the past year. The memories were still painful, but not nearly as bad as they had been. She wiped the tears from her cheeks with her hand. "I think I need to do some more emotional clearing," she said, trying to regain her composure.

Vivian smiled as she continued. "Anyway, so there's this major pandemic of starvation going on in this country and the world.

Taylor brought her attention back to the conversation. "Yes," she said, thinking of her father and how she'd do anything to save another child from losing their parent at such a young age. "What can I do about it?"

Vivian smiled bigger this time with her question. "I'm glad you asked. Did you notice anything different last summer when you were here at the Estate? Anything different with your physical energy levels or mental abilities?"

Taylor thought for moment. "Yeah, I do remember a few weeks into last summer I felt noticeably better. I seemed to have additional energy, and my mind was more clear. But I don't know what to attribute that to, even though now that you bring it up, it was obvious. The extra energy seemed to fade a few months after I left here, but I am doing better since I got back." Looking at Vivian questioningly. "What is it about this place?"

"A lot of things about this place would help anyone: the routine, the environment, having healthy meals prepared at no cost to you."

Taylor smiled. "That reminds me. I need to thank you and Mr. Ryan for providing the food while I stayed here last summer and now. It is so good. And not having to worry about meals makes the other things I'm doing here so much easier. When I'm not here, I just eat whatever is easy and inexpensive."

"That's normal for most people. Convenience and cost. The value of good nutrition is one of the many things that Nicholas and I have learned the hard way over the past thirty years. You and the others get the benefits of our experiences. And, believe me, it hasn't always been easy," Vivian said. "We don't mean to be overly strict, but we've found that everybody does better when they're eating healthy. More energy, increased mental capacity, and emotionally more stable. Nutrition and brain chemistry go hand-in-hand. People here at the Institute can eat whatever they want; however, we ask that those doing the Genius and Ascension Training programs follow a more strict eating regimen. Would you be okay with that?" she asked.

"Sure," said Taylor. "If I don't have to buy or prepare it, I'm totally game with that."

"Great," said Vivian. "That's what I wanted to hear. As part of the Genius Training, we're going to set up a nutritional program to help facilitate your increased mental capacity. **Nutrition is just one element of the program**, but it has several components that we're going to talk about in greater detail. From today on, you will be eating a more specific diet, a diet that will help increase your mental capacity in a very obvious way."

Taylor was more curious now than she was earlier.

"First, we will start with some cleanses, specifically the large intestine and liver. Then we'll go into the building stage. Geri, Marti, Sheena, and Dr. Johnson have all the details, and they will help you with it." Vivian handed Taylor a half a dozen papers stapled together. She paused as Taylor looked through the papers.

Nutrition and eating **suggestions** – Low or no: processed sugars/sweeteners, refined flour, caffeine, gluten, chemicals, drugs, dyes, or synthetic/artificial food.

- ☒ Appropriate levels of B12
- ☒ Essential fatty acids
- ☒ Herbs and supplements
- ☒ Essential amino acids
- ☒ Minerals
- ☒ Vitamins
- ☒ Brain supplements
- ☒ Healthy fats
- ☒ Healthy protein – quantity/quality
- ☒ High pranic fruits and vegetables
- ☒ Correct Carbohydrates

"I don't think I can remember all this," said Taylor.

"You don't have to," continued Vivian. "Sheena will text you your new nutritional routine two days ahead of time."

"That's great," said Taylor, still looking at the papers. A word caught her attention on the second page. "What is a nootropic?"

"Nootropics are supplements and foods that improve cognitive function, memory, creativity, and motivation," Vivian said, leaning back in her chair.

"Wait," said Taylor, holding up her index finger. "Are you saying that the foods I eat will make me a genius?"

"There is a direct correlation between cognitive function and mental capacity, and diet. If you put poor quality fuel into a car, you're going to have poor performance. The same thing for your brain. By feeding your brain high-quality fuel through nutrition, you will get improved performance."

That made sense to Taylor.

"Nutrition, however, is not the only thing we're going to do in the Genius Training." Vivian handed her a second stack of papers. You will be going to classes and getting more information on all of these principles and you're going to learn some amazing things."

Taylor quickly looked through the list.

Topics to **consider**:

- ☒ Breathing patterns and brain neuroplasticity.
- ☒ Math exercises
- ☒ Memory Palace exercises
- ☒ Challenge taste buds. Knowing the notes/tones of food
- ☒ Dancing/moving body
- ☒ Exercise appropriately
- ☒ Sunbathing correctly
- ☒ Sleep quality/quantity
- ☒ Massage, Foot Zone Therapy, Reiki, Yoga, Tai Chi, Chi Kung
- ☒ Mnemonics
- ☒ Brain games
- ☒ Music - Piano/Other instruments
- ☒ Learning a foreign language
- ☒ In depth emotional clearing
- ☒ Affirmations/Mantras
- ☒ Mental/subconscious programming
- ☒ Gratitude list
- ☒ Super Exponential Learning
- ☒ Mental downloads
- ☒ Reading and acquiring information
- ☒ Mind enhancement games: checkers, multidimensional chess, problem-solving exercises

Taylor felt overwhelmed as she looked down the list. She knew absolutely nothing about a few of these subjects. At the same time, she was a little excited.

"Over at the Institute," said Vivian. "We do the Genius Training for athletes and gifted children. They each have a staff of personal trainers assigned to facilitate their training. You will have some of that, but it will be in more of a classroom format with the other students here at the Estate. There will be some individual training, and I will help assist you with that."

Taylor nodded her eyes still on the list. "What's Super Exponential Learning?"

"That's a very advanced form of learning where you acquire vast amounts of information quickly and are able to process it multidimensional."

A look of bewilderment crossed Taylor's face.

"Don't worry about that now. You'll get there when you're ready."

Somewhat relieved, Taylor continued to read the list.

"You will also be teaching," said Vivian.

Taylor's eyes widened and shot up to meet Vivian's. "I have to teach? Teach what?"

"We'll decide that later. A great way to learn is to teach. So what do you think?" asked Vivian.

"Terrified, but excited as well," she said.

"Great," said Vivian, gathering her things. "This program is truly life-changing, and I know it will help you a lot. But remember, you are already amazing the way you are."

Vivian put her arms around Taylor and gave her a hug. "You'll get a text from Sheena about your routine and diet for the next two days within the hour. Have fun, and if you have any questions, don't hesitate to ask." She turned and walked away.

Taylor watched her, amazed at the energy emanating from this wonderful woman. Gratitude and love grew in Taylor's heart. *I wish I had a mom like her*, she thought.

Chapter 27 – Austin Talks to Vivian

Austin threw his phone on the bed and stomped outside to do his parkour run with some of the other guys. He knew he shouldn't be upset with Taylor, but it felt like he was the only one who wanted a relationship.

He'd started the Genius Training two weeks ago. The classes kept him busy and were surprisingly fun. The breathing meditation classes were his favorite. Unfortunately, he and Taylor seldom had class together. Even their meals were scheduled at different times. When they had a free weekend, Taylor ended up going home to see her brother and grandmother. She was always going somewhere. Her last text frustrated him. It was Friday afternoon and they would both have free time that weekend, but she was off to her grandmother's again. *Is she ignoring me?*

The summer was in full swing in Southwestern Colorado, but the temperatures were still comfortable for the demanding run. Austin slowed to a walk when he reached the patio. He pulled his shirt off and used it to wipe the sweat from his face. He cut through the kitchen to get a water bottle and went on to his room to shower. His phone lay on the bed where he'd tossed it earlier. Curious, he picked it up and checked for a message from Taylor. None. There was a message from Sheena informing Austin that he had an appointment with Vivian the next morning after breakfast. He turned off his phone and it landed back on the bed as he headed to the shower.

Austin ate breakfast the next day a little puzzled by his meeting with Mrs. Ryan. It didn't happen very often. He sat on the edge of his seat, too nervous to sit back and relax. He was taken aback when she informed him that he would be teaching a class the following week to his peers. Mr. Ryan would give him the topic and more details. When she suggested he do some clearing about it, Austin nodded.

"How are you doing with your training?" Vivian asked.

"It's great. I really like my classes."

"How is everything else going?" she asked, almost as if she already knew Austin's thoughts.

Austin decided to tell her about the current status of his relationship with Taylor, the frustration of rarely seeing her and how he felt ignored.

"I think the 'Why' exercise might help you," Vivian said.

"Why exercise? I've never heard of that," said Austin.

"It helps you get to the root of the emotions by asking the question 'Why,'" she said. "Would you like me to walk you through it?"

It made sense, but not quite understanding how it worked, Austin nodded.

"Tell me what you are feeling," Vivian began.

"I feel anger, frustration, annoyance, ticked off, disappointed."

"Why do you feel disappointed?" asked Vivian.

"Because I worked so hard during the school year and I was hoping to spend more time with Taylor this summer."

"Why?" Vivian said.

Austin thought about it for a moment. "I was hoping to take our relationship further, so I figured if I worked really hard during the school year, that would pay off now during the summer."

"Why? Are you expecting something from her?" asked Vivian. "Is it possible that your motive for working hard during the school year was so you could take your relationship further now?"

Austin leaned forward, his arms rested on his legs.

"Yes, I guess so," he said.

"What does taking that relationship further look like now?"

"Spending more time together than we are," he said.

"Is there more to that?"

Austin felt uncomfortable, not sure where this line of questioning would lead.

"Like what?" he asked.

"Like certain expectations that go along with a more in-depth relationship," said Vivian.

Austin didn't understand. "What kind of expectations?"

"You tell me. What would you like to have more in your relationship besides time together?"

"At least more time and taking our relationship to the next level."

"What does taking your relationship to the next level mean?" Vivian asked.

Austin had to think hard about this one.

He looked at Vivian questioningly. "I'm not sure."

"If you did know, what would it be?" she asked.

Austin stared at the floor, not sure what Vivian wanted him to say.

After a moment Vivian prompted, "Maybe something more on a physical level?"

His head shot up. "Well yeah! Of course," he said. "We've been together for more than a year now and we still haven't..." he stopped himself.

Vivian knew full well what he was thinking. She waited a few moments to let him process the thoughts.

"So, tell me this," she said. "And if I'm wrong, please correct me. When you left the Institute at the end of last summer, you had a whole bunch of new tools and you were ready to move forward in a grand way."

Austin nodded.

"You worked really hard, tried your best to stay motivated, and you did very well. You were even supportive when her grandfather passed away."

"She really needed the support. I thought I did a really good job of helping her," Austin said.

Vivian nodded. "Yes, I'm sure you did. And I'm sure you worked very hard the rest of the school year, as well. Then you get back here, and you're hoping that this will be a vacation and you'll have time and opportunity to get into her pants."

Austin felt his face get warm.

"What was your motive for working hard at school last year? Was it for her or for you? A woman can be a great motivator for a man. But have you considered that maybe you're being a little selfish and blaming her for something in you that she knows nothing about? It's something to think about," Vivian said as she got up to leave.

"Wait," said Austin. "That might be the root of the issues, but what should I do about it?"

"Use your tools and then go apologize to her. Let the emotions go and talk to Taylor about your relationship with her. Open communication goes along way."

Austin had plenty of time to think about his conversation with Vivian. The next few days, he spent time clearing the emotions he had been feeling. He sent Taylor a text and set up a date for Sunday when she returned. He felt relieved when she sent back an "okay."

The conversation remained superficial when he and Taylor walked down the driveway. Austin wanted some privacy for his apology. When they were some distance from the house Austin pulled Taylor under the shade of the trees that lined the drive. Once he began, the words flowed easily. He explained why he felt the way he had and told her how sorry he was. It hadn't been his intention to hurt her feelings. He conveniently left out, however, the part about getting into her pants. He wasn't ready to have that conversation with her yet and felt she wasn't, either.

When Austin finished, Taylor gave him a hug, the long, lingering kind. *I guess that means I'm forgiven*, Austin thought. On the walk back, they discussed some things they would like to do to improve their relationship. Spending more time together was first on the list.

Chapter 28 - Relationship with Numbers and Money

Austin missed Taylor. Nothing had changed since their talk three days ago. They tried to have dinner together, but there was always a class to attend or something that needed to be finished. One evening in particular, Austin set aside an hour after dinner to spend with Taylor. He caught up with her in the dining room.

"Hey, Taylor," he said. "How about a walk after dinner?"

Taylor's fork tapped against her now empty plate. Her crumpled napkin landed on the plate as well. Her knee brushed Austin's leg when she turned to face him.

"I would love to, but I can't tonight. I'm running about an hour behind and didn't get my reading finished. I wanted to use this evening to get caught up," she said. "So, how are you doing with all your goals?"

"I'm doing great," he said wanting to impress her. "I do need to do some stuff tonight, anyway. How about tomorrow?"

"Sorry," she said. "I'm scheduled to go on some sort of field trip tomorrow, and won't be back until late."

Austin could tell he failed at hiding his disappointment when Taylor's arm moved around his shoulder in a half-hug.

"We'll figure out a time. Don't worry," she said.

Her lips were soft against his cheek, but all too soon they were gone, and so was she. He watched her walk across the room and disappear into the kitchen.

Life at the Estate was better than he ever could have imagined. *I need to be more grateful*, he thought. But gratitude wasn't what he was feeling. He felt sorry for himself. Not allowing himself to wallow in that emotion, he tried to figure out why he felt that way.

"Are you going to finish your chicken?" asked Pajori. He was sitting near Austin and had been casually listening to their conversation.

"It's all yours, if you want," he said, handing his plate to Pajori.

Pajori gratefully took it and dumped its contents onto his.

"Whatcha thinking?" he asked between big bites.

"Nothing," started Austin. "Just...."

"Just what?" encouraged Pajori.

"Well, I love being here at the Estate and doing these programs. But do you ever wish we didn't have to be so busy and could spend a few days doing whatever we wanted?"

Pajori stopped chewing and swallowed. "Honestly, I am so grateful to just be here. This is more than I ever could have imagined."

Austin paused and turned his full attention to his friend.

"I was born in northern Russia. It's cold all the time and a real struggle for the people that live there. They do well to make it from one day to the next."

Pajori paused, but Austin remained silent.

"When I was very young, I was adopted by a family from the United States. Life is noticeably better here. Up until almost three years ago, I thought it couldn't get any better. Now I'm here in this amazing place, with amazing people, and learning things that most of the world would never even dream of."

Pajori looked at his plate then back to Austin. "If I had my way, I would freeze time and stay in this place forever. I know I can't, but I would sure like to."

Austin's phone alarm went off. He had five minutes to get to his evening class.

Hurriedly, he said goodbye to Pajori and left the room. His friend's last statement stuck in his mind. *If I could freeze time*, he thought.

As Austin went through his classes the next day, he tried to focus on feeling gratitude for his experience. He had several short classes that day in a wide range of topics, including a memorization class, as well as a group piano lesson. Other classes he attended included a nutrition class about fish oil, a history and language class about Portugal, physical geography of northern Japan, the moons of Jupiter and Saturn, and then, before dinner, the group he was with went for a walk with Dr. Johnson in the gardens adjacent to the Estate and she talked with the students about extrasensory perception.

After Dr. Johnson's class, Austin and his group were instructed to run to the upper swimming pools, parkour style, then walk back and get their dinner.

That day, his group consisted of Raul, Mani, Grace, Meeki, and Talia. Austin was looking forward to being able to talk with his friends on the way back after their exercise. However, Dr. Johnson dismissed them one at a time.

Mani and then Meeki left first. Austin took off at a sprint when he heard his name next. He ran through the shade of the trees, exhilarated by the freedom that came with running. The workouts he did had made a noticeable difference in his endurance. The previous summer he couldn't even win a race running downhill on a road. That bet he lost had been the best thing that had ever happened to him. *It totally changed my life*, he thought. *I wonder what would have happened if I won that day?* The idea made him smile.

He slowed to a jog as he came up to the gate to the swimming pool, moving to the side for Meeki to pass on her way back. He took a moment to stretch and could see Grace moving at a slower pace through the trees.

I wonder if I should wait for her? He didn't know anything about Grace other than that she was doing the Genius Training program, but he wanted somebody to talk with.

The growl that emanated from his stomach got his attention. He glanced down at his watch. 6:15 p.m. *If I hurry back now, maybe I can spend some time with Taylor.* Forgetting about Grace, he jogged back to the house.

Austin came into the kitchen at the same time Taylor did. She dropped off her dinner tray and turned to leave when he caught her eye. When she saw him, her beautiful eyes reflected the smile on her face.

"Hey," she said. "How was your run?"

"It was great," he said. He wanted to go and take her in his arms, but decided he better shower first.

"How did you know?"

"Mani told me of your ESP class with Dr. Johnson and that you had to go run after."

"Yeah, I don't know what the connection is, or even if there is one, but it was an interesting class. Are you already done with dinner? I thought we could spend some time together."

"Sorry. I just finished. I have to go help set up a class for Mr. Ryan or I would love to."

Austin didn't even try to hide his disappointment, and he knew Taylor could see it in his face.

"What are you doing at seven tonight?"

Austin looked at his watch phone hopefully. Tapping the screen to bring up his schedule, he could see that he had a class in one of the Institute buildings then. He tapped once more, bringing up the details.

Time/money/energy class. Institute auditorium. 7:00 p.m.

He turned his wrist towards Taylor. "Is this the same class?" he asked.

"I think so," she said. "I have to hurry, but hopefully I'll see you there."

"I'll save you a seat in the back," he said.

With a wave she was gone.

Austin picked up a sandwich and headed back to his room to get showered. He didn't want to be all sweaty for his sort-of date with Taylor. *Even though it's a class, at least I can sit by her,* he thought.

It took him longer than he thought to get to the auditorium. He had been there for classes and seminars before, but in his haste he'd gone in the wrong door. He jogged to get there on time. Outside the auditorium, he raised his arm and sniffed. *I should've put on more cologne,* he thought.

Austin entered from the back. It was 7:12, and the seminar had already started. Five sections of chairs all pointed to a raised platform.

Dr. Mila Johnson stood on the stage with a large screen behind her. She was talking about the mind, the brain, and the difference between the two.

Austin quietly sat down on the back row of one of the sections. The front three fourths of the seats were full. *There must be more than two hundred people here,* he thought, looking around. He recognized some of the others from the Estate, including Ching, Meeki, Mia, and

Grace. Mani sat between a fidgeting Annie and Davi. Next to them was Joseph, with Talia on the end.

He scanned the room, looking for Taylor. Not seeing her, he turned his attention to Dr. Johnson.

"Life is about resources and people," said Dr. Johnson. "Your relationship with people extends far beyond your immediate sphere of influence. The same also goes for resources."

Austin regretted not taking a few minutes to get a notebook and pen. His watch phone was great for many things, but not for taking notes. *I guess now is a good time to practice the memorization tools*, he thought.

"The best thing that you will ever invest in," said Dr. Johnson, "is yourself. Knowledge is a very valuable resource. Money, time, and energy are other forms of resources, but knowledge will always go with you. Getting a good education, whatever that looks like for you in your particular experience, is invaluable. Maybe that is a higher education like college or a trade school. Or maybe it's something less official, such as classes, seminars like this one, mentoring with someone in a particular area who knows more than you, or reading a book. Keep learning. The knowledge you acquire stays in your mind. Even if you don't know it's in there, at a subconscious or deeper level it still exists within you.

"Life is a university that teaches many subjects. What kind of grades are you getting?"

Austin had to think about that one for a minute. "Life is a university." Dr. Johnson's voice faded a bit as he attempted to pull apart the idea.

He swatted his hand on his neck in hopes to shoo away the fly that tried to land. He spun around in his seat when he heard a soft, feminine giggle. Taylor sat behind him, dressed smartly in a black fitted shirt and black slacks. She looked incredible.

Austin moved over to make room for her. He could feel her thigh pressed against his when she sat down. *She's practically sharing my chair*, Austin thought with a smile.

"Hi," he whispered.

"Hi," she whispered back.

"Think of money and time as the same thing. They are manifestations of energy. Energy is a very broad term," said Dr. Johnson.

Austin wanted to talk to Taylor further, but gratefully accepted the notebook and pen she gave him.

He decided to talk to her after the seminar. He felt he needed to listen to what Dr. Johnson was saying, especially when she brought up time and money.

"Changing the way you think about time and money is crucial," she said. "The old paradigms and belief systems around time and money is that of lack. There is never enough time or enough money. If you believe that is true for you and your experience, then it will be your experience. However, if you wish to change your belief systems about money and time, then you will get a different result.

"What are your limiting beliefs about time? What are your false paradigms about money?

"Something to consider: look at your relationship with each of these forms of energy. Take a written inventory of how you think and feel about time and money. You may think that the only issue you have with money, is that you don't have enough of it. If that is the case then I guarantee you have issues with it.

"If you feel like you're living your life in a hurry and are always in a rush, then I promise you, you have issues with time. Are you consistently late to things?" she asked, looking at the back of the room.

Austin and Taylor couldn't help but look back with most of the rest of the audience at the latecomers.

"Sorry," said Will as he came in with Raul, Kay, and Miranda. The others looked down, trying to be discreet. Kay tried not to giggle, but Will seemed to enjoy the attention.

Dr. Johnson didn't seem bothered in the least. She continued on as if the interruption never happened.

"So with this in mind, would you be willing to take a written inventory of your relationship with money and time, in the next twenty-four hours?"

She stopped for a moment, waiting for response. "That was a question," she said.

"Who is willing to do this?" she asked. Her voice carried easily to the back or the room.

Hands slowly began to rise across the room. Austin and Taylor looked at each other and then raised their hands.

"Okay," said Dr. Johnson. "I'm going to hold you to it."

She continued on with her presentation as Austin scribbled a note in the margin. "Are you really going to do it?" He turned the paper to Taylor.

"Of course," she wrote. "Are you?"

A little surprised at her quick response, he nodded.

Dr. Johnson continued on further about the relationship between time, money, energy, and numbers.

"Energetically, there is no difference between the creation of something small or large. Creating one hundred dollars is energetically the same as creating one million dollars. The only difference is your limiting beliefs about them. The same is also true about time."

This surprised Austin. He remembered the previous summer talking to Nicholas about manifesting and creating money. He had done a lot of emotional clearing around the topic of money but never considered his limiting beliefs about time.

"Time is merely another measurement of energy. An hour ago or an hour from now. The past, the future, and the present. If you can't change the past, then it is a waste of energy to worry about it. Regret is a very low frequency emotion, and unless it motivates you to change in the present, it has no value. Sooner or later everyone needs to give up all hope of a better past."

Dr. Johnson paused. "The future isn't here yet. Fear and worry about what may happen in the future is also a waste."

"The ever present 'now' is a gift. That is why it is called the present. Use the past as a teacher and learn from it. But don't stay stuck there. The future has infinite potential because of the choices we make. It is a journey, not a destination. We all live in the now. We might as well make the very best of our now that we can."

"You'll have to excuse me," said Taylor. "The seminar is almost over and I get to help. I'll meet you back here in a bit."

Austin took her notebook and pen and nodded as she left. He turned back to his own notebook and furiously wrote, wanting to get his thoughts down while they were fresh on his mind. Before he realized it, the room filled with applause. He kept writing.

–Time and money are subjects in the University of life. What is the grade that I'm getting? He asked himself on the paper.

–Change your relationship with numbers. Specifically, time and money. Clear out all negative thoughts, patterns, emotions, limiting beliefs about numbers.

Austin began to read the bullet points from the lecture that remained on the screen. He hurriedly jotted them down.

-Numbers, money, and time like order. They are repelled by chaos. Is your bank account in order? Is the schedule of your life in order?

-When clearing emotions, be aware of the freak out point, which is usually three to four periods into the seven periods of creation. Proactively clear limiting beliefs and negative emotions before they can bubble up.

-Money cost value. Is the price worth the value that you're getting from the exercise or the expenditure of energy, time or money?

-Clear rush, hurry, need, want, deadlines, procrastination, when to go to bed, when to get up, number of calories, relationship with food, weight, clutter, debt, balancing your checkbook, money coming in, money going out.

-Diet to lose weight, at three to four days into seven day cycle, watch for emotional outburst, could be parasites and candida dying off.

-The key to success is your awareness of numbers and awareness of your relationship with those numbers. Clearing emotions creates order with numbers.

-Be aware of the numbers, especially in the two dimensional models, but don't be fixated on the numbers.

-Don't allow numbers to control you. The fastest time, the lowest weight. Be aware of your relationship with numbers and let go.

-Thoughts become actions. Actions become behaviors. Behavior becomes your experience.

-Act on your intuition.

Austin paused. *Should I have stopped and talked to Grace earlier?* He shrugged and wrote down the last item on the list.

-What is your story about numbers, money, and time? If you don't like your present relationship with numbers money and time, then change it to get a different result.

Austin paused and looked up when he felt a hand rest lightly on his shoulder.

"You about done?" said Taylor.

Austin looked around the almost empty room.

"Oh yeah, just finished up."

"I don't want to rush you if you have more to do."

"No, I'm good," he said while he gathered their notebooks and pens.

"It's after nine, and I need to..." She stopped. "I'm choosing to get back to the Estate. I don't need to do anything," she said.

Austin smiled, put his arm around her shoulder and pulled her close. They left the building and walked slowly out into the warm summer night. Lights hung from trees and along the path and cast a soft glow over the garden.

Time, Austin thought. *I would love to freeze this moment.*

Chapter 29 – Relationship with the Body

The next day after class, Taylor took the long way through the garden to lunch. The vines and purple blossoms crawled up the wooden fence, creating a mural in their wake. A smattering of shadow and sun played across the grey stones of the patio.

"Taylor." She smiled and waved at Austin as he and Pajori ran past. Her eyes followed him as he disappeared into the trees. *I would love to be with them right now.* Dodging pines, flying over rock formations, and leaping fallen logs sounded fun to her.

The spicy aroma of garlic, onions, and oregano filled her senses when Taylor stepped into the dining room. Thoughts of running, flying, and leaping faded as she followed her nose to the serving area, anxious to see what today's lunch would be.

"Hello, my dear," said Geri with a smile.

"Hi, Geri, what do you have for me today?" she said, returning the smile.

Geri placed a small salad bowl filled with sliced red and green bell peppers, cherry tomatoes, carrot sticks, and small wedges of a white vegetable that looked like a raw potato on Taylor's tray.

"This is just for starters. Martin is putting the finishing touches for the main course," said Geri, handing her a tall glass with a pink liquid in it.

The Genius Training didn't have restrictions on the delicious food. Maybe she would learn some of Geri and Marti's tricks when her turn came up to help in the kitchen as part of a class she was taking. Taylor knew she could have as much to eat as she wanted, but the three meals and two snacks filled her up, even with the smaller portions.

As if on cue, Marti appeared from behind the counter. "Order up for Miss Shaffer."

Geri retrieved the steaming plate from Marti. "Careful, it's still hot."

Taylor breathed in the spicy aroma. "It smells great!" she said. A piece of spiced grilled chicken lay on a pile of what looked like white rice pilaf. Sprigs of asparagus drizzled with a light sauce completed the arrangement.

"Don't forget your dessert," said Geri, handing her a small bowl of what looked like ice cream.

"Thank you," said Taylor.

She turned to find a place where she could enjoy this masterpiece of a meal.

Talia waved and Taylor joined her, Annie, Mia, and Miranda at their table. She'd shared casual conversations with all of them, but had hopes of becoming better friends.

"What do you think about Will, Mia?" asked Annie.

"What do I think? I think Will is an arrogant, self-absorbed, egotistical ass."

"Why don't you mince words?" said Talia.

"I'm not biased," said Mia. "I'm only stating the obvious."

"Oh, yeah, right!" said Annie. "You like him, you know you do."

"That wasn't your question," Mia said with a smile. "Like in Mrs. Ryan's class, there are two parts to judgment. One side is condemnation. The other side is discernment. I'm just discerning a fact."

Miranda cut in. "So what kind of discernment were you having when I saw you check him out this morning when he was working out in the gym? Shirtless, I might add."

"That's a different fact," said Mia. "He may be an ass, but he has a great body."

Taylor listened to their friendly banter while she ate her lunch, still not sure what the white rice-looking food she was eating was. It was very tasty but had some background flavor to it that she recognized, but couldn't quite place.

She looked up as Danielle approached.

"Hi, guys!" she said, pulling out the empty chair next to Annie.

"Wusup, Dani?" said Miranda, not bothered by her interrupting their conversation.

"I was picking up some items for Sheena and didn't think I'd make it back in time for lunch, so I bought something in town."

Taylor watched her pull out a hamburger wrapped in white wax paper. She set it next to her soda, followed by a large order of fries. Danielle wasn't doing any of the training programs at the Institute, so she ate whatever she wanted. Taylor noticed the others also staring at Danielle's lunch.

"What?" Danielle said, noticing the attention.

"How's your burger?" asked Mia.

"It's great. Want a bite?" she said, gesturing with her hamburger towards the others.

The silence that followed answered her question.

"Sucks for you guys. I don't have to eat like a rabbit. I don't even have to take the classes if I don't want. And I still get paid to be here," she said, stuffing three French fries into her mouth.

"I thought you told me that you were worried because you had put on like a hundred pounds since you started working here," said Annie.

"It was only twenty pounds. Working around you skinny butts, I've decided to make some changes," she said, holding up her can. "I'm committed to only drinking diet soda from now on." She took a big drink from the straw. "I'll slim back down in no time at all."

Taylor looked at her half-eaten vegetable salad, not sure what to think of the conversation.

"Besides, I would hate to have to eat like you guys. I like some flavor in my food," Danielle said, taking another bite of her fries. "And think about it. You guys are all eating a high-protein, high-fat diet. I know this is not the best example, but usually I eat low- or no-fat things, like low-fat yogurt and cereal. If you guys keep eating that much fat and protein, you're all gonna balloon out, sooner or later."

The alarm on Taylor's wrist phone buzzed, signaling that she had five minutes to get to her next class. Talia and Annie's did as well.

"This food tastes awesome!" said Annie, getting up with her tray.

"Yeah, Geri and Marti go all out every day, it seems," said Miranda as she cleaned up her lunch and stood up.

"Sure, but think about it. Wouldn't you rather have a nice juicy burger than riced cauliflower?"

That's it, Taylor thought. *Cauliflower.* She knew she recognized the flavor.

The four girls left the table, leaving Danielle to finish her burger and fries.

Taylor hurried to her next class, the conversation with Danielle still fresh on her mind. *Am I getting fat?*

In her next class, Dr. Johnson taught about how to improve one's memory. It was held on the main back patio. Taylor really enjoyed doing classes outside; she seemed to get so much more out of them. Today they talked about a Memory Palace as a tool to help improve the memory. The focused attention and awareness became a great distraction from the lunchtime conversation.

That evening, Taylor skipped dinner and missed out on seeing Austin. She ended up in her room, looking in the mirror and feeling like she was putting on weight. Not liking the emotions, she pulled out her notebook and began to write all the negative thoughts that had been lingering in the back of her mind since lunch.

Keep eating this way and you'll just balloon up. You won't ever be skinny again. You are so frumpy. You're fat.

The longer Taylor wrote, the sloppier her handwriting became. She didn't care. She kept at it until there was nothing left to write. The paper ended up shredded and in the garbage can under her desk.

Her goodnight text from Austin left her feeling a little annoyed. He waited for her at dinner and wanted to know why she hadn't shown up. He wouldn't drop it, so Taylor finally said goodnight and turned her phone off.

The next morning, Taylor came back from her workout hot, sweaty, and sore. After a soothing shower, she caught her image reflected in the bathroom mirror. She twisted around, examining her waist, hips, and thighs. "I'm getting fat," she said with a sigh. *Is being here a good thing? Am I really getting heavier? Would Austin be attracted to other girls, if I'm fat? I'll bet he's already thinking of the other girls here. They are all so much skinnier than I am.*

Taylor growled a little, frustrated at the crazy thoughts that kept plaguing her. She rushed out the door to breakfast, mentally reminding herself to clear again when she had more time. She downed a small protein drink and made it to class on time.

The classes she attended were diverse. About half of them were taught outside. She saw Austin momentarily on her way to astronomy. His class was on metallurgy. *No idea what that is*, thought Taylor.

Austin gave her a hug. He appeared excited to see her, but Taylor wondered if it was genuine.

After class, Taylor pulled on some lounge pants and a tank top. She piled her pillows in the corner of her bed and settled down to read for a while. Before she could finish a page, she heard a quiet knock on her door.

"Come in," she called.

Taylor, surprised to see Sheena walk in, quickly slid off her bed and stood up.

"Is everything ok?" Sheena asked.

"Sure, why do you ask?"

"I was talking with Talia, and she seemed to think that you are upset about something."

Taylor thought about it for a moment. "No, I'm fine,"

Sheena looked her in the eye and said nothing for a moment. Taylor felt a little uncomfortable at the scrutiny, but didn't look away.

"You're sure nothing is bothering you?"

Uncertainty filled Taylor. Maybe she could talk to Sheena. *No, that would be awkward*, she thought. "Positive, I'm totally good."

"Okay," said Sheena. Taylor could see the doubt in Sheena's eyes.

"If you do need to talk, Mrs. Ryan and Kara are in the study. They are both good listeners." Sheena turned and left.

Taylor let out a sigh and flopped back on her bed. *I've never thought about myself as being overweight. Dad always said I was beautiful, maybe he said that because he had to. I keep clearing, but these stupid thoughts keep coming back. This seems so strange. Maybe it would help to talk to someone.*

The walk to the study gave Taylor time to figure out what she would say.

Kara sat alone reading when Taylor came in.

"Do you have a minute?" asked Taylor.

"Of course," Kara said.

Taylor sat down and the words began tumbling out in a jumble of thoughts and emotions. After several minutes, Taylor finally caught herself. "That probably didn't make any sense. I guess I think I'm putting on weight by being here."

"Why don't we find out, and then you'll know for sure," Kara said.

"How do we do that?" asked Taylor.

"Remember when you first got here in May we took all your measurements and your vital signs at the same time you got your physical. I still have all the numbers on my computer back at the office. If you would like, we could see what's happened over the past few weeks."

"I would really like that. Do you have time to go now?"

On the way to the clinic, Taylor turned her phone on silent. The clinic usually teemed with people during the day. A tranquil silence greeted them that evening.

Taylor glanced around the office while Kara pulled up the information on her laptop. Medical journals sat on bookshelves next to bottles of essential oils. A watercolor graced one wall while medical charts hung opposite. The evening sun shone across the desk, falling to the floor and surrounding Taylor in its light.

The tape felt cool against her bare skin while Kara measured her arms, chest, waist, hips, and thighs. Taylor nervously waited for the results.

"How do you want the news?" said Kara looking at Taylor.

"How bad is it?" asked Taylor. Concern shot straight to her heart.

Kara started laughing. "I'm just messing with you," she said. "You're doing great. You're actually healthier now then you were a month ago."

"Are you sure?" asked Taylor.

"Well, here are the numbers so far. Your arms stayed the same. Your waist has gone down by three inches."

"Seriously," said Taylor. A smile began to spread across her face.

"Your chest has gone up by an inch and a half."

"My bra has been fitting tighter than normal," she commented.

"You might want to go up a size," suggested Kara. "But is that a bad thing?"

"No, not at all. Actually, it's kind of nice."

"You're working out more than six days a week," said Kara. "The upper body workouts you're doing are working, unless you want a smaller chest."

Taylor shook her head. "What about my hips?"

"Your thighs have dropped an inch and a half and your hips are down two inches."

"Two inches! Wow."

"Your Basal Metabolic Index has improved, and you've actually gotten almost an inch taller."

"What! That can't be. I stopped growing a few years ago."

"I attribute that to your posture," said Kara. "Have you noticed how you carry yourself lately?"

Taylor looked puzzled.

"You stand taller, more confident. So you may not actually be taller, even though the numbers say you are."

"What about my weight?"

"Keep in mind, you're eating much healthier and doing a lot of weight training and cardio exercise," said Kara.

"So I've gone up, but you're saying it's muscle."

"Yes, you have more muscle mass, but you've actually dropped four pounds."

Relief filled her mind. She felt slimmer already.

"A month ago when we did these initial tests, you had 21% body fat. For a woman, that is really good. The acceptable range is 25-31% body fat. 10-12% is the bare essential. You need to have some fat to be healthy."

"What am I now?" asked Taylor.

"14-20% is considered normal for a woman who is very athletic. You're at 18% now. Some women would kill to have 18% body fat, especially after having children," she said, patting her abdomen. "You're just fine, Taylor. In fact, you're better than fine."

"So why am I having all these thoughts and emotions that I'm putting on weight?"

"I don't know," said Kara. "But is it possible that those thoughts and emotions are not even yours?"

"Not mine? Where would they be coming from, then? I know that those thoughts and emotions are not my identity. Mr. and Mrs. Ryan have been telling me that since last summer. But if I am not generating those thoughts, who is?"

"When did those thoughts and feelings become obvious?" asked Kara.

Then the light went on. "Yesterday at lunch," Taylor said. "I was listening to a conversation with one of the other girls. She was saying how we were all going to get fat because we were eating fat."

"Danielle?" asked Kara.

"Yeah, how did you know?"

"I recently had a conversation with her. She actually has put on a lot of weight and she's very concerned about it. You may have picked up her emotions or the emotions of the other girls in the conversation."

"What do I do about it?"

"Use your tools. I recommend a physical release as well. I think now you know the origin, it will release with no trouble. Also, be open to anyone else you may need to clear for, especially the women in your family. You may also want to write a letter to your body and your body parts, expressing gratitude to it for the way your body serves you. The mind-body connection is very powerful. Be grateful for your body."

"Thank you so much for your time. I feel better already," said Taylor.

She gave Kara a hug thank you and walked out of her office with a spring in her step.

Back in her room, paper littered the floor while she wrote and tapped on her sternum. The sound of paper ripping permeated the room for long moments. She washed her hands with soap and cool water before drinking the remaining water in her glass.

I wonder what Austin is up to, Taylor thought. She checked her phone. Four messages. She started to type a response, but stopped. Instead, she got another paper and wrote him a letter. She shared her thoughts and feelings that she had about him. All the uncertainty, the jealousy of any girls he may like better, not trusting his feelings for her. For a moment she considered giving it to him. It ended up in pieces in the garbage with all the other letters.

Feeling noticeably better, she tapped her phone and waited for Austin to pick up. They spoke for more than an hour.

Now that's the kind of conversation to end a day with, Taylor thought dreamily as she crawled into bed later that night.

Chapter 30 – Taylor Teaches

Taylor had finished her morning routine and looked at her schedule on her watch phone. *The technology that had gone into this device was extraordinary*, she thought. It was the size of a regular watch, but would do so much more. The only disadvantage to it was that it was so small it was hard to take notes with and type on. However, for the training she was doing, it was very helpful. She knew what her daily and weekly schedule would be. Any changes that needed to be made were done instantly. Mrs. Ryan worked with Sheena to make sure that Taylor's personal training was always up-to-date.

Her first appointment after breakfast was a twenty minute accountability session with Mrs. Ryan. Most of their accountability appointments were through email or text, but she met with her in person, once a week. *I wonder what new things we will be going over today?*

Taylor went over her daily goals in her notebook to make sure she had accomplished all of them. The physical category consisted of sleep, exercise, and nutrition. At least 64 ounces of water a day. *I think I need to up that one.* Taking a pencil from her nightstand, she crossed out the 64. She wanted to do at least a hundred twenty eight ounces, but with her busy schedule she didn't want to spend that much time in the bathroom. *84+ ounces*, she wrote.

She made some mental notes while going through the other categories. She felt good about her goals in the etheric, generational, energetic, and emotional areas.

In the goals for the mental category, she read: do all the homework for all the classes and read an additional hour per day. She liked what she had set for this category, but didn't feel it was enough. She knew she could do more.

Thinking about that, she asked herself, *what more should I do?* Often when she asked a question in her mind, the answer would come quickly. She would then write it down and go do it. This time, nothing came. She looked down on the floor, a technique she had learned from Nicholas when you wanted to find the answer within yourself. She waited for a moment searching her mind. Still, nothing came.

When she wanted to find the answers outside of herself, she had learned to look up. Taylor wasn't sure why, but something about this body language activity seemed to really help.

Is there another goal I should put in the mental category? she thought. Looking at the ceiling, she relaxed her mind and listened for an answer. "You will find out today," came the thought.

Okay, we'll see what happens today then. Using her pencil like a stylus, she tapped on the very small keypad of her phone. Under goals for the day, she wrote: look for additional goal for the mental category.

With her notebook in hand, she headed off to breakfast.

She had hoped to see Austin during breakfast so they could eat together, but after talking to Mani, she learned that he had finished his breakfast and left twenty minutes earlier. Instead, she talked with Talia and Davi. Taylor was really starting to enjoy the other people doing the training here at the Estate. For the most part they seemed very upbeat and like-minded.

Taylor had scarcely finished eating when her phone reminder went off. It was a text from Sheena. Meet with Mrs. Ryan in her office when you're done with breakfast. Always direct and efficient: that described Sheena. Taylor excused herself, dropped off her tray, and met with Mrs. Ryan fifteen minutes ahead of schedule.

"Good morning Taylor," said Mrs. Ryan with a smile.

"Hi," said Taylor.

"I hope I didn't cut your breakfast too short," she said.

"No. I was done when I got Sheena's text."

"The reason I moved up our appointment was because I felt we should add something additional to your training today. The prompting came to me about an hour ago."

That was about the same time I was going over my daily goals list, Taylor thought. "What do you want to add to my list?" she asked.

"I know we've talked about you teaching classes before. What would you think about teaching your first of several classes the day after tomorrow?"

Taylor was a bit surprised. They had talked about her teaching a class sometime this summer, but she didn't think she was going to be teaching more than one and so soon. She swallowed hard. "The day after tomorrow? That's soon."

Vivian nodded.

Taylor had done many class presentations while going to school. She didn't like being up in front of people, but it wasn't terrifying for her if she knew what she was talking about. "What will I be teaching about?"

"This," said Vivian. She took a device out of a black case and held it up. It looked like an electric toothbrush with two gray prongs on the end instead of bristles.

"What is it?" asked Taylor.

"This is a body tuner," said Vivian. "Some people call it a Phi tuner."

"It looks like an electric toothbrush," said Taylor.

"It kind of does, doesn't it." Vivian pushed a button on the device. A low vibrating sound emanated from it.

"All matter vibrates. Vibrations are measured in frequency. This tuner vibrates at different frequencies. The human body also has a vibration, usually between about five and ten hertz. When a person is sick or in pain, their vibration drops. When you hold a tuner like this against different points on the body, it can help the body by changing the frequency. It vibrates at a resonance range of between twenty five and fifty five hertz."

Vivian held up the two gray prongs of the device on her forehead. "For example, if someone has a headache or other issues with pain, this can be a tremendous help. It also does several other things, but this is what I would like you to teach the others about."

Taylor felt very inadequate. Other than what Mrs. Ryan had told her, she knew nothing about this device or what it could do. How could she adequately teach a class on it in two days? She was aware of the emotions building up inside her: fear, inadequacy, not wanting to look stupid in front of people.

"Who will I be teaching this class to?" asked Taylor.

"We'll start with one of the four groups that are doing the Genius Training program with you," said Vivian.

That's not quite as scary, she thought. She knew her other friends would be teaching classes as well, and that would hopefully help them be more empathetic. Still, two days was not that far away. And she had her regular routine. How was she going to become a competent teacher of this tuner in two days? Taylor realized she better start now. Turning her notebook to an empty page, she wrote down, Phi tuner. "Okay," she started. "Tell me everything I need to know to be able to teach this thing."

Vivian smiled. "Good. The first person you're going to teach is yourself."

Taylor made several notes on the paper while Vivian waited patiently.

"Frequency, vibration. So what exactly does this do for people?"

"It is different for everyone. But the whole concept is to bring the body to a higher vibrational state or higher frequency. It is called entrainment. When you bring two things of differing frequencies together, the lower one has to either come up or the higher one has to come down to entrain to each other. They want to come into equilibrium. It's much like tuning a violin. If the violin is out of tune, it's uncomfortable to listen to. When it's in tune, it's beautiful and elevating to listen to. The body is the same way. If the body is out of tune, it is more prone to pain and diseases. When it's in tune, it facilitates health and longevity. Physically, the tuner can help ease pain and release tension in the body. It combines resonance and stress-management techniques to relieve chronic pain."

"Physically, I actually feel great," said Taylor.

"You are actually an exception," said Vivian. "Many people in the world suffer from some sort of pain, mild to severe. What can you teach them about using the tuner to help relieve their issues with physical pain? It also helps mentally and emotionally. It can facilitate the creation of new neural pathways in the brain to help people with attention deficit issues, obsessive-compulsive behaviors, anxiety, depression issues, and addictive behaviors."

"Can it help increase focus and awareness?" asked Taylor.

"Why don't you test it and find out?" said Vivian, handing the device to her. Taylor looked at it.

"Take it with you and show the class. Let people try it out. And be sure to try it on yourself first. It also helps with emotional release. In fact, it speeds up the process better than some of the tools you already have. This is an additional tool that you can use for emotional clearing to add to your toolbox."

"Where can I find more details about this?" asked Taylor.

Vivian handed her a paper and a pamphlet. "This pamphlet shows you the maintenance sequence that a person can do on an ongoing basis. It's mainly for physical pain but will affect the whole person, not only the body. The second routine is called the 'Trauma-Down' sequence. That helps more with the mental and emotional aspects, but also helps tremendously with physical issues. It can be used to clear deep-seated emotions, even if those emotions are not yours. You can also use it for generational clearing and clearing of the negative emotions for experiences that have not happened yet."

Taylor was a bit surprised "How can you clear emotions from future events?"

"Simple," said Vivian. "It is done with intention. Think of a possible future event. If that were to happen, what emotions would result from it? Clear those emotions, even though they haven't formed yet. If the event does not happen, you haven't lost anything valuable. If the event does happen, the negative emotions have already been released. The future experience still could be difficult, but not as hard as it would be if you are slammed with all the negative emotions that could potentially be there." Vivian paused. "Trust me, it can make it much easier."

"It was created by a physical therapist in Utah. You can find more information about this online. The websites are on the back," said Vivian.

Taylor looked at the information. The pamphlet showed the tuner being held against different pressure points on the head, for issues such as headaches, migraines, and jaw and neck pain.

"One more thing," said Vivian as she turned in her seat. She picked up a book behind her. Turning back she handed it to Taylor. "This book will be on the reading list for those of you doing the Genius Training program."

Taylor looked at the book. How to Think Like Leonardo da Vinci.

"Do you know what the *Vitruvian Man* by Leonardo da Vinci is?" asked Vivian.

"I think we talked about that in one of the classes," said Taylor.

"Look that up as well," said Vivian. "Especially in conjunction with you teaching about this tuner. The frequency of Phi is very important in nature and to the human body. I know that was a lot of information, do you have any questions?"

Taylor sat still, trying to absorb everything Vivian had said. "Yeah, a hundred questions. Like, how am I going to know this well enough to teach it in two days?"

"You can do it," reassured Vivian. "Don't underestimate yourself. You will do great."

Taylor didn't respond. She wasn't as optimistic as Mrs. Ryan about this whole exercise.

"If there are no further questions, let's get on with your goals for the next week."

"Okay," said Taylor. "I think I have some new goals to add to my list."

Taylor studied up on everything she could about the tuner. She was especially interested in the effects on the Vagus and trigeminal nerve's. The seven general positions were designed to set the autonomic nervous system to a state of healing.

She wanted to talk to Austin about it, but he was gone somewhere with his group. They traded texts in the evening, as much as they could.

The two days leading up to the class went by quickly. *Too quickly*, thought Taylor.

The morning of the class, she found out she would be meeting with some of the other students individually, not as a group.

She had learned as much as she could in the short time. Trying to be optimistic, she reassured herself with the thought that she knew more about the tuner than her fellow classmates. It would be good to get to know some of the others in the program better as well.

Taylor finished her breakfast quickly and arrived thirty minutes early to the room assigned to her. Five rows of six chairs lined the middle of the room. At the front of the room, two chairs sat facing each other a few feet apart.

"Good timing," Sheena said from her seat on the front row. "I was about to text you."

"I wanted to be early since I've never done this before."

Sheena turned to her. "Are you nervous?" she asked.

"A little," Taylor said. "Not as much as I thought I would be, though. I've been using the tuner to clear my fear of public speaking."

"You will do great," said Sheena.

Sheena always seemed so businesslike, but Taylor felt something genuine in her smile. She couldn't help but like her.

"Thanks," said Taylor. "I hope I'm ready."

"Everything is all set up for you. You will be up front with the person you're working with."

"I thought I would be working with one person."

"Yes, that is correct," said Sheena.

"Then why so many chairs?" she asked.

"You never know who may show up to observe," said Sheena with a smile. "Don't worry about it. Visualize that they're not even there. It's just you and the person you are teaching."

Taylor nodded her head, but she still wasn't convinced.

Sheena could see some apprehension in Taylor. "Can I give you a little advice?

"Please," said Taylor.

"You will want to take notes." Sheena gestured to the bag that Taylor carried.

Taylor pulled out her notepad and sat down. She wanted all the help she could get.

"When you're in the role of a teacher, try to convey confidence. Eye contact is very important. Not so much that it's creepy, but try to look people in the eye. When you're working one-on-one in a teaching or mentor role, do not be judgmental. And when I say judgmental, I mean condemning. Discerning is fine. In fact, you want that. You want to discern what the person you're talking to is thinking and feeling. Don't condemn them for their thoughts or feelings, but be aware of them."

Taylor wrote quickly as Sheena continued.

"As you teach about the tuner today, you are also acting in the role as a mentor. You will notice something about emotional clearing with the tuner. That is, at a certain point, the person using the tuner will start to release their negative emotions. That's good. That's what you want. Make sure you as the mentor don't pick up those emotions. You are just a sounding board. You don't have to fix their problems or pick them up and carry them. Let the person release their emotions. Visualize a shield as a barrier between you and the negative emotions that are being dumped off. Be compassionate and empathetic, but remember, you don't have to be their savior.

"Another thing about emotional release which you probably already know: be sure to replace the negative emotions with positive ones. Especially when using the tuner. The tuner allows for this clearing and replacing process to happen much faster than the other tools you have learned to use so far."

"That's good to know in all relationships," said Taylor.

"Yes," said Sheena. "And one more thing: If you are asked a question that you don't know the answer to, refer them to a professional. You can give suggestions, then it's the responsibility of the person you're working with to decide what they want to do. Don't take away someone's agency to choose, even if they want to give it to you.

"Any questions?" asked Sheena.

Taylor finished writing, took in a deep breath and let it out. "No, not yet. But I'm sure I'll have a bunch after I'm done."

"Great. Your first victim, I mean your first student, is here," said Sheena, smiling and pointing to the entrance at the back of the room.

Annie stood by the door, a little unsure of herself. "Am I my early?" she asked.

"No," said Sheena, gesturing to her. "Come right up and have a seat."

"I'm okay sitting at the back," she said.

"Actually," said Sheena. "It's just you and Taylor for this training."

Annie walked up the center aisle. "Why did you invite so many empty chairs?"

"You never know who may show up," smiled Sheena.

She sat down in one of the chairs, still uncertain about what was going to happen.

"Taylor, you have forty minutes with each student," said Sheena. "Go ahead and start your presentation. I'm going to go sit over there. Act like I'm not here." Sheena walked to the far row and sat down on the front seat. Pulling out her electronic notepad, she looked at the two girls.

"Um, okay. Well, let's get started," said Taylor. *Convey confidence*, she thought.

Taylor pulled out the tuner and began to describe it and what it did.

The time went by quickly and before they knew it, Sheena interrupted. "You have two minutes left Taylor. Start to wrap it up."

She had shown Annie how to use the tuner, but hadn't given her time to actually use it. The last twenty minutes was spent by Annie talking about issues she had with depression and anxiety.

"Do you think the tuner would help get rid of my anxiety?" asked Annie.

"Maybe," said Taylor. "It's worth a try."

"Can I try it out?" asked Annie.

Taylor looked at Sheena, who was quietly watching. "I don't know," she said.

Sheena stood up and walked over to the girls. "Yes. Take this one and get it back to Taylor when you're done with it."

"Thanks," said Annie, taking the tuner. "That was really good, Taylor. I appreciate you teaching me about this. I'll tell you how it works for me." She gave Taylor a hug and walked to the door at the back of the room.

"How was that?" asked Sheena, after Annie had left.

"I was going to ask you the same question," said Taylor a little apprehensively.

"It was great. You presented the material well, but I would leave about twenty minutes at the end for them to practice using the tuner."

A knock on the wall at the back of the room signaled Taylor's next student.

Kaiulani was next. Two sessions later, Grace left the room.

"Very good," said Sheena. "You're starting to get the hang of it."

"Honestly, it's not as scary as I thought," said Taylor looking back at her notes. "The time goes by so quickly."

"Do you feel better about your presentation now?" asked Sheena.

"Now that I've been through it, I am starting to get the bugs out."

"Good," nodded Sheena. "Keep it up. You've got forty five minutes to take a break and have lunch. We'll see how you do with Akihiko when you get back."

Later that night, Taylor sent Austin a text. "Can you talk?"

A moment later, her phone rang. After a quick hello, Taylor spent the next thirty minutes listening to Austin share his day. She snuggled into her pile of pillows and just let him talk. He sounded so excited about the day he'd spent snowshoeing, skiing, and rock climbing in Wyoming. The helicopter ride to Gannett Peak appeared to be another highlight of the day.

"Sounds like you're having a blast," said Taylor when Austin's narration ended.

"I wish you could have experienced it too," Austin said. "That would have made my day."

The silence stretched while Taylor waited for Austin to continue.

"So how did teaching go today?" The question spilled through the phone.

The excitement in Taylor's day in no way compared to Austin's. Even so, she wanted to share with him what she had experienced.

"It was good," she said. "Not perfect, but I learned a lot of things. You do learn so much more when you teach someone else."

"Who was in your class?" asked Austin.

"It wasn't a group thing like I thought it would be. It ended up being one-on-one."

"Oh. Who did you work with?" said Austin.

"There was Annie and Grace and Kay in the morning. They're all really nice. It was good to get to know them a little better. Kay didn't take it seriously, but that's her choice. Grace seemed really genuine. I'd like to get to know her better. I think Annie is dealing with a lot of issues."

"Like what?" asked Austin.

"She has a gene deficiency that is causing her problems. It's called the MTHFR gene. It has something to do with depression and anxiety. Sometimes she even has panic attacks."

"Wow, I'm glad I don't have that."

"Apparently it is pretty common. More than most people think. But she's doing pretty well here at the Estate. She said diet and supplements are helping."

"Were there any guys in your class?" asked Austin.

Taylor could hear the uncertainty in the question. She smiled at the realization that Austin was a bit jealous.

"Yeah, in the afternoon, I taught Aki about the tuner. It went okay, but I really got the feeling he wanted to be somewhere else. I think the only reason he was doing it is because Mr. Ryan told him he had to. I think he doesn't like the idea of learning something from a girl."

"That's interesting," said Austin. "Aki seems okay around me."

"It's probably because you're a guy," Taylor paused. "He didn't seem to have a problem with Sheena though, so maybe it's not all females."

Taylor continued. "After that, Yi-Mee Ki came in and I did the training with her."

"Yi-Mee Ki?" said Austin. "Who's that?"

"Oh, Meeki. Yi-Mee Ki is her full name. Meeki is easier to pronounce. She has had an interesting life. She told me all about it. Her father is an American. Her mother is Korean. They were never married and she has issues with her stepfather who is from Korea."

"Wow," said Austin. "I'll bet there's more of a story there."

"Yeah," said Taylor. "When people start to do emotional release work, it's amazing the things that start coming out."

"What other juicy tidbits did you learn about?" asked Austin playfully.

"Honestly, I probably shouldn't be telling you all the things that I learned," said Taylor.

"Okay, how about the non-juicy tidbits then?"

"I can't tell you everything, but I worked with a really neat girl from Taiwan named Tzu-Ching. Ching for short. She's got a story, too. After that, I worked with Alex. Then Nathan. Had to take a break after that one. That boy's got some issues," she said.

"Like what?" asked Austin pushing her boundaries a bit.

"Nope, can't tell ya."

"That's all right, I understand."

"It really wouldn't surprise you. You probably already know," said Taylor.

"He seems nice enough," said Austin. "Maybe a little shy, especially around girls. But that's pretty obvious."

"You guessed it," said Taylor. "He wouldn't make eye contact with me the whole time."

"Well you are kind of intimidating to an immature man," said Austin with a chuckle.

"Excuse me," said Taylor.

They both laughed.

"Sorry," said Austin. "Keep going."

"After that, I worked with Logan Roth. He seems really cool once you get to know him."

"Yeah, I know Logan. Great guy. I think his family is German. Or, at least, his ancestors are from Germany."

"Yes," said Taylor. "He told me about his ancestors and some of their experiences. He recommended a book to me about Irena Sendler. I guess she had something to do with getting Jews out of Poland during World War II. Apparently some of his ancestors were involved in that somehow."

"Cool," said Austin. "Did you know that he is a pilot?"

"Yeah, he did mention that. I guess Mr. Ryan is having him trained to fly helicopters."

"Apparently he is pretty good," said Austin.

"Well, maybe if my group gets a chance, he'll fly us up to some ski resort in the mountains of Wyoming," said Taylor.

"I'll bet Mr. Ryan has each group do all the activities. So you won't get left out," said Austin.

"You know what that means don't you?" said Taylor.

"What's that?" asked Austin.

"That means I'll be skiing when you have to teach the members of your group how to bottle peaches."

They both laughed at her comment, but Austin knew he would be teaching some topics in the near future.

"I hope it's not bottling peaches. I don't even like to eat them," he said.

"Maybe not that, then," she continued to tease. "How about teaching on how to play the nose flute."

They both laughed again.

"The last one in my group was Talia Kohen," continued Taylor. "Did you know before she came to the U.S. she was in her country's military?"

"No," said Austin, a little surprised.

"After the tuner training was over, we went and had dinner. She told me about how she taught tactics and small arms use for over a year."

"I'll bet she's a pretty good shot, then," said Austin. "I noticed one of my classes next week was marksmanship at the gun range. Kinda glad she's not in my group."

"Why?" asked Taylor.

"She'll probably out shoot me," said Austin.

"Are you afraid you will get beat by a girl?" said Taylor.

"I'm not afraid," said Austin. "I've just never fired a real gun before."

"Then it wouldn't take much," replied Taylor.

"Have you ever shot a gun?" asked Austin.

"Years ago, before my dad died, he took my brother and I to a shooting range a few times with a little .22 caliber pistol."

Austin didn't respond. He just made a mental note to look up exactly how big a .22 caliber pistol really was.

"So how was dinner?"

"It was great. Marti outdid himself, as usual. We had vegan chicken Primavera."

"Vegan chicken Primavera?" asked Austin "How does that work?"

"Don't know," said Taylor. "But it was really good. Marti wouldn't tell us what the chicken was."

Austin chuckled.

"Talia and I had a good conversation. It was great to get to know her and the others better." Taylor was going to say more about what she learned about Talia and her preferences, but decided against it.

"So, now it's done," said Austin. "Are you glad you did it?"

"What do you mean? The teaching part?"

"Yes," said Austin. "As scary as teaching is, are you glad you did it?"

"Honestly, it was kind of fun. I did a lot of clearing beforehand." Taylor paused. "I would do it again."

Chapter 31 – Ancestors

"What exactly is generation clearing?" Taylor asked.

She and Joseph were in one of the small rooms on the second floor. Tall, open windows overlooked the long drive that dissolved into layer upon layer of dense trees, as it wound away from the Estate.

Taylor leaned back in her seat and waited for Joseph's explanation. He gave her a brief description, including some general information about the short course. Still unsure about the purpose of the class, Taylor moved her chair closer to the table so she could see what Joseph had pulled up on his laptop.

"I bet you've cleared a lot of emotions since you've been here," Joseph said.

Taylor nodded.

"What if I told you that some of those emotions weren't even yours?"

Taylor's eyes widened at the thought.

"Then who's are they?" she asked.

"That's what we are going to talk about," Joseph said.

Joseph told her that most people carry at least some of their ancestor's unresolved issues within their physical body. "When we have an experience that triggers our emotions, they often come to the surface, regardless of who or where, they initially originated from."

"So is it similar to picking up someone else's emotion?" asked Taylor.

"Similar, but not quite the same. Your ancestor's emotions are actually stuck within the strands of your DNA."

Joseph showed her some images of DNA strands on his computer. He then went on to share what he had learned from Mr. Ryan. "Instead of just two strands of DNA, there are actually thirteen: two physical strands and eleven others that exist in other dimensions.

"The energies of negative emotions, limiting beliefs, false paradigms, and baggage from trauma, real or perceived, get absorbed into the fascia and imprint themselves on the physical DNA. Those same energies will often get stuck in the other eleven etheric strands. When they die, those energies will go with the spirit of that person to the other dimensions. These energies have a low frequency, and the person's spirit will be stuck in a place of low frequency until they are released. Because the origins of these low frequency energies were trapped in the physical body, they need to be released with a physical body. The body allows us to release emotions, theirs or ours, significantly easier."

"Is that why we've been told to do tapping and other physical release techniques?" asked Taylor.

"Yes," said Joseph. "It helps in the release of the emotions that are stuck in those other dimensions as well as in the physical strands."

Joseph went on to explain that, at this time in history of the world, the backlog of unresolved issues has really piled up both for mortals, and for non-mortals in the other dimensions. There is a growing urgency among the world's dead ancestors that they must be free of their emotional baggage soon or they're going to have to wait a long time before they will have another opportunity. The earth is in a transition time, quickly moving to the next age. If the dead are not freed soon, they will have to wait until the end of the next age. "That's a long time to be stuck under the weight of one's own baggage," he said.

"At conception, and as a person is growing up, mortals have and often acquire more of the unresolved issues from their parents and further generations back. So a person can be born with unresolved generational issues, issues which didn't start with them, but they could feel that they are part of them.

"If a mortal doesn't realize that their issues started in their ancestors, then they can go through life thinking and feeling these emotions began within themselves. They can get tossed around, not realizing that the emotions they are experiencing are not their own.

"We need to know about our ancestors," said Joseph, "and their issues so we can be free of them. In so doing, our ancestors are freed as well. This is where genealogical research and family history comes in."

Joseph asked Taylor about her parents.

Taylor could feel her hands clench to the seat of her chair. Her private life was just that, private, and Joseph had no right to ask about it.

"I don't want to talk about them," Taylor said.

"Can you give me their names?"

"I'd rather not."

"Just your mom's, then?"

She turned to tell him to lay off when she stopped. "That's what this training is all about," she said.

One side of Joseph's mouth tipped up in a small smile and he nodded.

Taylor apologized, and then gave him the information about her parents that he requested. She watched him pull up a "find your ancestry" website and type in her father's name. To Taylor's surprise, they found a lot of information about his family back to his great-grandparents. Her interest was piqued as she continued to read the names and information of the screen.

Her curiosity waned when Joseph asked about her mother.

She knew little about her mother's parents. Joseph typed in what information Taylor could tell him, but not much came up. She was mildly surprised when the more she spoke about her mother; the more she felt her negative emotions fade. *I think all the clearing I've been doing is really working*, she thought.

After Joseph wrapped up his presentation, Taylor thanked him and hurried off to her next class.

Joseph continued to research Taylor's family history. He found that Taylor's mom had two more children besides Taylor and her brother Connor. The first child said "live birth" on the birth certificate and "father unknown." The baby had been born eighteen months after Taylor's birth. The second child, a boy, was born about twenty-one years later, father also unknown.

Chapter 32 – Feminine and Masculine Energy

With her routine finished, Taylor stood by the window. The scent of flowers filled the air, carried in by the gentle breeze. With closed eyes, she soaked in the warm July sun and breathed in the aroma of summer. She thought about her first class of the day, out in the garden pavilion. She loved being out the gardens. Class or free time, it didn't matter. So much of last summer had been spent in those gardens. She knew and loved almost every inch of them.

It took some effort to get herself to move away from the window and prepare for the day. *I wonder if Austin will be in my class*, she thought. It did say a group class. The alarm clock on her dresser read 9:15. *Plenty of time for breakfast*, she thought as she walked out of her room. "I'm grateful for my relationship with time," she said to herself. Her mantras came more naturally this morning than in previous mornings. *I have plenty of time. I use time efficiently and it always works for me.*

She still found herself hurrying down the hall. Not because she was late, but because she had hopes of seeing Austin before class. Their conversation the night before left her wanting more time with him.

The crowded dining room looked different today. The tables were arranged in long rows instead of scattered around. The girls tended to be all at one row and the guys on another. Some Institute employees sat at the other two rows of tables.

A hum of conversation followed her as she crossed the room. She picked up her breakfast and looked around for Austin. *I guess I missed him*, Taylor thought. Joseph and Demetri caught her eye and smiled when she walked past on her way to the 'girls' table.

"Sit here," Annie said. The chair slid away from the table easily.

"Thanks," said Taylor. "So what are you talking about this morning?" she asked. She felt more comfortable with these girls now that she had taught most of them in her class on the tuner.

"We got our teaching assignments this morning and they're really messed up. I mean, some of them are kind of cool, but I'm not sure who came up with them," said Mia. "Like what?" asked Taylor.

"For example," interrupted Miranda. "I have to talk on the history of Native Americans, which I'm totally fine with, but they only gave me a half-hour to talk about it. I could go on about that for a week.

"That doesn't sound too bad," said Taylor.
"Well, that one is okay, but I have two classes."

"What's the other one?" asked Taylor.

"Horticulture," she replied. Exasperation filled her voice. "They seriously want me to speak about the culture of prostitutes?"

Laughter burst from the girls.

"That's not what it means," said Katja. "Horticulture has to do with plants. There are no whores in horticulture. Unless Mia's been working in the garden again."

"Ohhh," said several of the girls at her scathing remark. Mia glared at Katja.

"At least I can get a guy," said Mia. "You're probably still a virgin, aren't you?" she quipped back.

That conversation sure got out of hand fast, thought Taylor.

"Miranda, I'm sure you'll do great at it."

"I hope so."

"Annie, do you have to teach two classes, too?" asked Taylor.

"Yeah."

Taylor could tell by the look on her face that she wasn't pleased, either.

"I get to talk on photography, which I really like. I know a lot about that and it should be fun. But in my second class I have to teach about refined sugar and its effect on the body. It seems like forever since I've had sugar. I would kill for some chocolate or a glazed donut."

"Sucks for you!" said Katja. "I've got a stash of chocolate that I brought with me."

"Can you have chocolate while you're doing the Genius Training program?" asked Davi.

"Sure," said Katja. "But it has to be the good stuff. Not the fake waxy crap. Mrs. Ryan gave a class on the tones of chocolate. It was way cool."

"Sign me up for that one," said Annie.

"So, what do you get to speak on Katja?" asked Taylor.

"Oh, get this," she said. "I have to teach on the country of Finland's history between 1935 in 1947. Some of my ancestors are from Finland, but that was like the worst time in that country's history. And if that wasn't hard enough, I also have to speak on the Koran."

"Isn't the Koran like the Bible for Islam?" asked Grace.

"Yes," said Annie. "It's the Muslim holy book. What about you, Grace? What do you get to teach?"

Taylor looked to the end of the table where Grace sat, curious to hear her classes. Grace wasn't shy, but she wasn't an extravert, either.

"It seems like everyone is getting two very opposite topics. I am supposed to teach on the book of Isaiah from the Old Testament. I think I can do that. I've never actually read the entire Old Testament. I've read the New Testament a bunch, but the book of Isaiah is kinda deep."

Taylor could tell by Katja's body language that she was uncomfortable with the topic. "What's your other class going to be on?"

"I don't think I can do the second one. It's on Darwinist evolution."

"Whoa!" said Annie. "Didn't you tell me you were a Southern Baptist, or born again Christian or something like that?"

"Yeah," said Grace. "I'm going to tell Mrs. Ryan I can't do that one."

"Why not?" said Mia.

"I just can't. I don't feel right about teaching something I don't believe in."

Taylor thought for a moment. "Wait a minute," she said. "Davi what are you speaking on?"

Davi sat quietly next to Grace. She was obviously listening to the conversation as well. She gave a contorted smile. "I have to teach on the caste system of India and what eye movements have to do with body language." She shrugged her shoulders. "I don't know the first thing about what eye movements have to do with body language."

"Girls," said Miranda. "I think I'm seeing a pattern here. Let's see if we can figure this out." She sat up tall in her chair, and turned to the nearby table.

"Hey, Mani," she said.

The guys stopped talking and turned around.

"Are you guys talking about the new teaching assignments?"

Some of the guys at the table looked at each other nervously.

"Yeah," said Mani. "Why? Are you too?"

"Yeah," said Miranda. "What's your topics?"

Mani smiled a big grin, "Peruvian cooking and time management skills. You guys are all in for a big treat. I'm a better cook than my mom, and she's, like, the best cook in all of Lima."

Miranda looked back at the other girls, a puzzled expression on her face.

Taylor began to see a pattern. "Will," she said. "What are your topics?"

He laughed. "You're gonna love this. I'm teaching on the dialects of the United Kingdom. And try not to hurt yourself laughing at this one, but nutrition and colon health."

"That's a real bummer," said Mia. "Glad I'm not teaching that one."
Laughter bounced between the tables.

The familiar click of Sheena's heels alerted the group to her arrival.

"Those of you doing the group class at Pavilion number two, head out there as soon as you can. We're going to start in less than ten minutes."

Taylor looked at her watch. 9:52! The time had gone by so quickly. She finished her half eaten bowl of granola, stood up and left the dining hall.

Most of the seats in the pavilion were occupied by the time Taylor arrived. Austin sat on the back row. She caught his eye and smiled.

"Thanks for saving me a seat," said Taylor.

The pavilion stood in the middle of a beautifully tiered garden. Paths led away from it, one to the house and others to the pool and other gardens.

Everyone quieted down when Nicholas escorted Vivian to the front, then took a seat on the front row.

Vivian's relaxed, pale blue skirt and white, silk blouse stood out against the green shrubs behind her.

"Good morning everyone," Vivian said.

She always put together: attractive, yet still so professional, thought Taylor. She knew Vivian was probably in her early fifties, but still looked thirty-five.

"The topic for today is feminine and masculine energy."

Taylor looked over at Austin. He shrugged.

Sheena made her way from the front of the pavilion and handed out some papers to each row. Taylor took the small pile, kept one, and passed the rest to Austin. It listed feminine traits and masculine traits. She glanced at a few of the traits on each list.

Feminine Energy:
  -Creating
  -Intuitive
  -Yin
  -Heart chakra
  -Flowing

Masculine Energy:
  -Building
  -Action-Oriented
  -Yang
  -Solar Plexus chakra
  -Stability

Taylor noticed that Austin didn't have a notebook, but he did pull a pen out of his back pocket. He turned the handout over and put the date and time of the class at the top of the page. Turning it back to the front, he looked at Taylor and winked. She smiled and turned her attention back to Mrs. Ryan.

"We're not talking about men and women with this class, even though that's part of feminine and masculine energy. Masculine and feminine energy is only that: energy in somewhat different forms.

"Every male has masculine and feminine energy. Every female has feminine and masculine energy. And the balance of that is not always fifty–fifty. No female is one hundred percent in feminine energy all of the time. The same with men and masculine energy. The balance often changes for both men and women. Today, the balance might be eighty/twenty. Tomorrow it could be different, but still be balanced. Balance changes according to needs.

"Also, with this class, I'm not talking about anatomy. That does play a role in the feminine and masculine balance, but gender is not the same as masculine and feminine energy."

Notes filled Taylor's paper as Vivian continued to share the different aspects and characteristics of masculine energy. The masculine tends to go alone and stand out. It is out to achieve a purpose. It sees conflict as a road to growth and it is inspired by a feeling of freedom. She recognized in herself some of the traits on the list.

A quiet mumbling could be heard as the class progressed. Taylor glanced around and could see that not everyone felt comfortable with the information. *It's good we have the tools to clear emotions.*

"In creation, the masculine brings in less refined energy through thoughts, and the feminine holds space for it with emotions and forms it into the final product," Vivian said.

"You need to allow yourself to dream, fantasize, visualize and create in your brain the ideas that you want to create in your life. Then infuse these ideas with positive, high frequency emotions. It takes both forms of energy to create, whether it's a new car or better health," Vivian said.

After a short break, Mr. Ryan began his portion of the presentation. He spent a few minutes going over the traits of feminine energy. "Feminine energy is inspired by the emotion of love. A connection with others is a feminine trait. Togetherness and fitting in are, as well. It sees conflict as a threat, especially in relationships. The feminine wants to be held and protected. Feminine energy is receiving while masculine is giving.

"Too many males are out of balance and fall into a receiving role. I mean sucking and taking energy. That's not healthy. There are women who are in the giving role, which is good, but not when it's out of balance with their receiving energy. All too often, a wounded male tries to find a feminine energy source that he can take from to heal his wound. Sometimes women are willing to give their energy to heal the wounded masculine energy out of compassion. That's also okay, to a point. The problem comes in when the masculine energy only takes and the feminine energy only gives. Eventually, the feminine energy runs out, and there's nothing left for either party. In a different class we are going to talk about this in more depth."

Nicholas continued to explain that, for thousands of years, the world has been in an unbalanced masculine energy. The energy of the mass consciousness and the earth itself has been, that of force, compulsion, and domination. It has been male-dominated, and the feminine energy being suppressed.

He went on to illustrate how that was changing. "There is an increase in feminine energy, which is good in most ways. But one of the problems is that masculine energy is being used to increase it. That is the energy of force, push and resistance. It's been one way for so long and now it is swinging hard in the opposite direction. Eventually it will come into a balance. This mass consciousness energy shift can be soft and easy if we choose it to be. If not, it will happen, with the masses kicking and screaming. The difference is between choice and compulsion. This is happening, ready or not," Nicholas said. "So why not make it easy?"

Absorbed in information, Taylor didn't notice Austin raise his hand.

"How can we do that?" he asked.

"It starts with awareness of self. Be the change that you want to see in the world. As you change, those in your sphere change. That will eventually spread to the entire world. Here are a few questions to start with," Nicholas said. "What is your relationship with masculine and feminine energy? Regardless if you're male or female or how you feel about your own gender and the opposite gender, do you feel judgment or condemnation in those relationships? Now remember, we're not talking about sexual preference here, either.

"Here's another question to think about. What is your relationship with yourself and your body, in relation to today's discussion? What is the feminine or masculine energy that you are giving and receiving?

"Next, clear out the low-frequency energy of lies, limiting beliefs, false paradigms and perceptions. This can also include cultural and social beliefs and issues that hold you back. If you're not sure what these are, look outside of yourself. When you have children, those children will act as a mirror to you. They will take your unresolved issues, magnifying them, and blow them back in your face. Just like I'm sure you have done to your parents.

"For those of you who do not have children, look at others around you. A good example of this is social media and the mainstream news. The intention of the news media is to churn up your emotions. The stories that they report on have been partially fabricated and intentionally twisted to induce an emotional response in the masses. Whether it's in marketing, politics, cultures and societies, or economics, it's primarily for the manipulation of one group over another. A significant example of that is advertising and marketing. Commercials on TV have been created to manipulate consumers into buying certain products and services.

"Social media does this as well. However, it's more exaggerated: invoking emotions into the masses to get them to act in a certain way. It's like emotionally vomiting all over the Internet.

"The reason I'm bringing this up is because examining social media and mainstream news is a good gauge to help you see what your unresolved issues are. Use those two sources as a mirror. As you watch them, what do you see in yourself? Do you see or hear something in those two sources that churns up your emotions? If so, be aware of it and clear it. Now I know doing the training here at the Estate you are somewhat shielded from it. But once you get back to the real world, be aware of it.

"After you are aware of it and have cleared the negative energies, be sure to replace them with higher frequency truths. That which is uplifting and edifying. However, you need to know what those truths are before you clear out the negative so you'll know what you're going to replace them with. That requires knowledge, either from your own experience or someone else's.

"One lifetime is not long enough for you to experience everything. That's okay. you can learn from others. You don't have to live through what they did, but you can still gain the knowledge from their experience."

Nicholas briefly glanced at his wristband.

"So, here is the homework for this class. Journal about what we talked about today. Then take a written inventory about how you feel about masculine and feminine energy, gender, and the opposite gender."

"Clear out any negative emotions and issues, energetically and physically. Also, be sure to clear your ancestors, descendants, even unborn descendants, your sphere of influence, and the entire world. This is done with intention. And, on a side note, it's better to over clear than under-clear as long as it doesn't make you physically sick. There is a limit to how much emotion the body can release in one session. Be gentle, but persistent. If you find it's too much, take a break, get a glass of water, and resume at a later time. You've recently learned about other tools that will be valuable to you in this process."

Wondering at the long pause, Taylor looked up from her notes to find Nicholas looking at her. *The tuner*, she thought. He gave her a slight nod and then continued.

"It is imperative that you replace the energy. If you don't know exactly what to replace it with, put in joy, peace, or gratitude. Also, use higher frequency thought forms like positive affirmations or 'I am' statements."

"Does anyone have any questions before we wrap up?" Nicholas looked around at the audience.

Taylor noticed no hands go up, but still Nicholas stood there in the growing uncomfortable silence. A hand finally shot up.

"How do we best do that while we're here?" Mia asked.

"You have more than twenty-four mirror holders here at the Estate, all with diverse issues. I'm sure you'll find any number of them willing to push your buttons."

"So to conclude, take a written inventory of how you feel about the topics Mrs. Ryan and I presented today. Be aware of when emotions come up and use your tools to let them go. Then replace them with the higher truths."

Nicholas excused the students, but Taylor remained, her mind in a whirl. *That's a lot to process*, she thought. *Where do I begin?*

Some of the others mingled in small groups, their heated discussions carrying through the pavilion. Taylor noticed some couldn't get out fast enough. She leaned her head on Austin's shoulder. His arm moved around her and she relaxed into his embrace.

"What do you think about all that?" she asked.

"There sure is a lot to take in. All the talk about masculine and feminine energy... I'm not sure how balanced I am."

"I know," said Taylor. "How do you know when too much of one or the other is too much?"

"I don't want to be too girly, you know," Austin said with a laugh and a squeeze of her arm.

Taylor playfully punched him in the chest. "I'll let you know if it gets out of hand," she said.

"What about the whole parent-child thing?" Taylor asked. "I thought I was a pretty well-behaved kid for my dad, but now I'm wondering what I was throwing at him."

"I feel like I should apologize to my dad or something," said Austin.

With most of the others gone Taylor stayed and talked with Austin. He opened up about things in his life he had never shared. She felt she understood him better and because of that, had a greater respect and love for him.

Chapter 33 - Intimacy

The morning began pretty much the same as every other day for Taylor. She and Austin even had a few minutes to text before their first class started. Taylor smiled when she read his text about class that morning. All the single guys doing the Genius Training were to meet for a class about sexuality, physiology, and intimacy. Austin had stuck a smiley emoji at the end of that text.

With a notebook and pen in her shoulder bag, Taylor left her first class and headed down the hall.

"Hey, Taylor, can I walk to class with you?"

Taylor turned to see Grace coming towards her.

"What do you think about the class topic for today?" Grace asked.

"I don't know. I hope it isn't too uncomfortable."

"I'm concerned about going," said Grace.

"I think Mr. and Mrs. Ryan will handle it in a respectful way," said Taylor. "I am sure you have nothing to worry about. They probably will be stirring up our emotions, though. I guess knowing that should help make the class easier. If we are prepared for it we can recognize it and get rid of it."

Taylor and Grace met the other girls on the back patio. A few minutes later, they were following Vivian and Nicholas to a small pavilion at the edge of one of the gardens. Patio furniture had been carefully arranged. Grace and Taylor shared one of the soft covered couches.

On one side of the pavilion hung a beautiful charcoal drawing of a couple holding each other in a tender embrace.

The discussion wasn't anything like Taylor imagined it would be. The information was tastefully shared, but even so, Taylor felt the blush come and go on her face. She could tell Grace would rather be somewhere else. The girl rarely took her eyes off her notebook.

"You okay?" Taylor whispered.

"Yes." Grace said. "It feels a little weird having Mr. Ryan leading so much of the discussion."

"Well, I did hear that Mrs. Ryan taught the guys class this morning."

After a few questions, the girls were excused to go to lunch. Taylor said goodbye to Grace and stepped out into the early afternoon sun. She took her time getting to the dining hall.

Someone sure is having fun rearranging the tables every other day, thought Taylor when she arrived for lunch. The girls were congregated at a set of tables on the far side of the room. Taylor picked up her lunch and circumnavigated the rows of chairs that were lined down the middle and found an empty seat. She paid little attention to the conversations around her while she ate.

Boisterous male conversation announced the guys' arrival. Most of them were wearing board shorts and tanks. It looked to Taylor that they had been at the pool. Wet towels still hung around their necks. The room quickly filled with an uncomfortable silence when they noticed the girls seated at the far tables. Austin, Taylor saw, stood in the middle of the group. She watched him run his fingers through his hair. He laughed when water flipped on some of his companions. Taylor continued to stare at him. His attention stayed on his buddies. He got his lunch and ended up sitting with his back to her. Little by little conversations could be heard around the room again. It felt almost like high school, boys looking at girls and vice versa, then awkward laughter.

After about thirty minutes, the chairs in the middle of the room began to fill up. Taylor saw the security guard, Jake, and his wife take a seat near the middle. A young couple, probably in their mid-thirties stood inside the door. Taylor tried to figure out where she had seen them before. The woman smiled and waved at her before she sat down on the back row. Marti, Geri, and a gentleman Taylor was unfamiliar with took seats near her table. Marti sent her a smile before he sat down.

The room became quiet when Nicholas and Vivian walked in, holding hands like usual. Taylor smiled when she saw Nicholas' thumb stroke Vivian's wrist while they made their way to the front of the room. She was surprised to see Rex and Angelica Houston and Dakota and Kelly Kavanaugh follow them in. She met them briefly the previous summer here at the Estate. The four moved to the back of the room at the conclusion of their conversation. They greeted the young couple like dear friends.

Still puzzled at the couple's identity, Taylor pushed the thought and her lunch tray aside, and retrieved her notebook and pen out of her bag.

Vivian got right to the heart of the discussion within a few minutes. This class dove into topics about intimacy, sexuality, and relationships even more than the morning class had. Vivian and Nicholas took turns discussing the differences between men and women and masculine and feminine. Questions were asked and answered in a non-judgmental way. There was a great deal of talk about emotional responsibility in sexual relationships.

Chairs scraped on the floor as their occupants struggled to get comfortable. A nervous cough or giggle could be heard coming from the sides of the room.

The longer Mr. and Mrs. Ryan spoke, the more butterflies took flight in Taylor's stomach. Her thoughts kept turning to Austin. *What if I end up marrying Austin? What would our relationship be like? What if it ends up like my parents or grandparents? My grandparents seemed happy,* she thought.

They'd been married over forty years and she'd lived with them for so long Taylor thought their relationship was better than most. Each of them knew where they fit and what their responsibilities and duties were in their marriage. The more Taylor considered it, the more she realized that they were really just roommates. They lived in the same house and worked well with each other. *Did they truly love each other?* Taylor wondered if their love was nothing more than a comfortable pattern they had fallen into after being together for so long. *Where was the passion, the excitement?* That's what she wanted in a relationship.

Mr. and Mrs. Ryan appear to be very much in love. Taylor didn't know how long they had been married, but they were constantly holding hands when they were together. Their eyes lit up whenever Taylor saw them look at each other. They looked excited to be together every day and seemed to feed off each other's energy.

Taylor remembered seeing Vivian and Nicholas together at the pool. When they were not acting in the role of mentors or teachers, they seemed to be passionately attracted to each other. Taylor wondered then if it was only an act. Now she realized how genuine it was. *They honestly seem so in love with each other. Almost like newlyweds. I wonder if that is what keeps them so young and vibrant looking?* Taylor knew their oldest, Alaina, was probably close to thirty. That would put Nicholas and Vivian around fifty years old. It felt like her eyes were playing tricks on her as she looked at them at the front of the room. She could've sworn they could pass for thirty-something.

Yes, Taylor thought. *That's the kind of relationship I want in my marriage.*

Taylor tried to focus on Mrs. Ryan's words, but her mind shifted to her parents and life before she lived with her grandparents. Her father always seemed so busy, but tried to make time for her. He looked happy most of the time, but now, looking back, Taylor wondered if it was more of a forced happiness. Her mother had always been distant, like she was somewhere else. After the birth of her brother Connor her mother became more aloof. Her parents were never affectionate and acted more like roommates who barely tolerated each other.

And then there was the yelling. It seemed like her mother only had two modes. One was sullen and silent. The other was yelling and out of control. Taylor never remembered her father raising his voice. It was like he buried all the hurt deep in his heart. A wave of sorrow came over Taylor. *That's probably why he died of a heart attack*, she thought. *Death by a broken heart.*

Taylor slipped her hands in her lap and began tapping the side of her left hand. She took a deep breath and continued tapping, bringing her attention back to the class. But as she listened about how intimacy can bring people together, she also wondered if it could also be the cause of pain in a relationship?

Her eyes moved across the room to Austin. He had told her the previous summer that he loved her and that he wanted her to be his girlfriend. In the moment, she said she loved him back. *But what did that really mean?*

I love chocolate, she thought, *but that's not the same thing. What is love? And what does that mean in our relationship? If things continue, would it mean that we'll eventually get married? Is that what I really want? And what type of marriage would we have? Would it be like my grandparents, being together for fifty years? Being comfortable just growing old together?*

Taylor's eyes kept moving back to Austin during the course of the class. He tended to get angry easily. She still could remember when he hit the horse earlier that summer. *Would staying with him be a repeat of my parent's relationship?*

Images of the dream she'd had about Austin floated into her mind. She knew some of his potential and wasn't about to give up on their relationship over that one experience. *That still doesn't mean I have to marry him, though.*

Taylor watched Nicholas look at his wife as she addressed the group. His expression was of total adoration. She looked over at Austin. *Would he look at me that way after being married for thirty years? Does he see me that way now?* As if on cue, Austin glanced at her. Their eyes held.

Austin smiled and silently mouthed, "What?"

Taylor returned his smile. "Later," she said silently.

Thomas and Elsie Campbell! The thought came out of nowhere like a thunderbolt. She spun around and looked at the couple she'd met at the cemetery the previous summer. Nicholas, the year before, had shared their unbelievable story of success with her and Austin. Thomas and Elsie smiled and nodded.

Giddy with excitement, Taylor tried to focus on the remainder of the class. All she wanted to do was get Austin and go talk to Thomas and Elsie. Austin was so completely involved in Vivian's description of energetically connecting to another person through intimacy that Taylor gave up trying to get his attention.

The class finally came to a close as Nicholas reminded them to be aware of their thoughts and emotions and use their emotional release tools when needed. They were given an hour break to do any clearing and, as soon as she was dismissed, Taylor searched for Thomas and Elsie. They were gone.

Unfortunately, Taylor missed seeing Austin for the rest of the day as well. *I guess it is probably a good thing*, she thought. *I do have a lot of emotions to work through because of the class.* When she finished that evening, she sent Austin a "goodnight" text and fell into a deep sleep.

Chapter 34 - Relationships

The next morning Taylor and Austin went busily through their separate routines, which meant not having breakfast together. She sent Austin a text and found out they had the same first class that morning.

The murmur of voices spilled from the open doorway as Taylor made her way into the room. Plenty of seats remained empty, so she sat near the side in the middle and saved a spot for Austin. She nodded a hello to Miranda and Mia, who sat a few seats down the row. Her bag slid from her shoulder as she pulled out her notebook and pen.

"Can you believe it?" Miranda said. "I went to use the restroom after my evening meditation last night and didn't bother with turning on the light. Someone had stretched saran wrap over the toilet bowl."

"That's awful, I just walked into my room full of balloons," said Mia. "It took me over an hour to pop them all and get them cleaned up. I did hear that Talia had purple food coloring in the shower head. She was lucky she turned on the shower before she got in."

I wonder what that's all about? thought Taylor. She couldn't help, but overhear the other girl's conversation. *I'm sure glad that hasn't happened to me.*

Austin plopped down, breathless next to her. "Did I miss anything?"

"Yeah, but I'll tell you later."

Dr. Mila Johnson moved to the front of the room and began. Her class that day would be on relationships and their issues.

These relationships could be: parents, siblings, culture, subculture, humanity, animals, nature/earth, God/higher power, self/higher self, past and future self, spouse, children, friends, food, clothing, music, cars, school, job/occupation, etc.

"What is your relationship with each one of these?" she asked. "Your homework for this class has two parts. First, you are to honestly think about each of these and write down the thoughts and emotions that come up. Think of past experiences, real or perceived, but only focus on the negative thoughts and feelings. Pour it all out onto the paper, even if you don't know where they are coming from. They may not even be your experience. It doesn't matter. And if you can't isolate the particular emotion or thought, then scribble on the paper. When you are done and it's all down on the page, tear up the paper and throw it away. Then wash your hands and drink some water. If you need to take a break and go for a walk or do something else physical, that's a good time to do it"

Taylor quickly wrote the list in her notebook to refer to later.

"Then get out your thought journal, which I know you all have, and think about the same relationships again: your parents, your siblings, the culture, etc. Write down only the positive thoughts and emotions about them. You may want to keep these thoughts. Refer back to them often. Are there any questions?" she asked.

"Yes," said Danielle, who sat in front of Taylor. "What if you can't think of anything good about your family or culture?"

"That's a great question," said Dr. Johnson. "A person's external relationships are a reflection of their own internal relationship. What you see in others is directly correlated to what you see in yourself. Do you see the world outside of yourself as hostile? Or do you see that world generally in a kind way? Your relationships mirror back to you what's really going on inside you, so what do you see in that mirror? A good place to begin this exercise, for anyone feeling this way, would be to start on your relationship with self."

"Are you saying that we create our experiences and that they are mirrored back to us?" asked Mia.

"No," said Dr. Johnson. "We don't necessarily create the experiences, but we can, however, choose how we perceive those experiences. Two people can have an identical experience, but perceive it completely different. One can see it as horrible, which holds them bound in a toxic relationship, while the other can gain knowledge from the experience, see it with gratitude, and be proactive to change it."

"But, like, what if you grew up in an abusive situation? What if you can't control what other people are doing around you?" asked Mia, obviously churned up by the discussion.

"You can't control what other people choose," said Dr. Johnson. "But you can change them. You do it by changing yourself."

She then went on to talk about the martial art form called aikido. "When using force to deal with an opponent, the one with the greatest amount of force wins. And the other loses. But both of the combatants use a tremendous amount of energy in the fight. This does not create effective change. The results of this form of interaction create physical and emotional pain for both parties.

"In the martial art aikido, you treat your opponent with softness. This redirects your opponent and uses very little of your own energy. This is done by you moving, and that facilitates your opponent having to move. If two people are pushing on each other, the strongest one wins. But if you are pushing on someone and they are pushing back, then you move sideways. Your opponent then has to adjust. They can either back off or fall forward on their face. But either way, if you move, they have to move."

"That's really interesting," Taylor whispered to Austin.

"Yeah," he whispered back. "Joseph tried it on me and it really works. I'll have to tell you about it sometime."

Taylor nodded and turned her attention back to Dr. Johnson.

She had Talia and Miranda up at the front of the room. They stood facing each other and were pushing against each other with only their hands. They were instructed to push harder, which they did. Neither one moved.

Dr. Johnson then moved next to Miranda. "Now, ladies, keep pushing on each other as hard as you can."

They did so, applying great force to each other's hands, but still neither one made any progress.

After a moment Talia, took a quick step sideways. Her sudden shift sent Miranda forward. Dr. Johnson had anticipated the move and caught her before she fell to the floor. Helping her regain her balance, she thanked both women.

"This same thing is true in relationships. You can change someone else by first changing yourself."

Dr. Johnson then transitioned the class into a discussion about the **belief of separateness.**

"The belief of separateness insulates you from that which you believe is outside of yourself. When you believe you are separate from everything, including nature and everyone outside of you, that belief allows for isms. Think of the word chasm. A chasm is a gap between. The suffix *ism* means separateness: chauvinism, racism, sexism, selfism. Belief of separateness is what allows for all the atrocities in history. When a person or group believes they're separate from another person or group, then it's easier to justify harming others. But when you realize that you are not separate from your outside experience, you will be less inclined to harm anyone or anything."

"That being said, let me give you another example," said Dr. Johnson. "Does everyone know what a sociopath is?"

Most of the students nodded. Not convinced, Dr. Johnson asked. "Does anyone not know what a sociopath is?"

A few hands rose.

"A sociopath," she explained, "Is a person that feels little to no emotion. They can appear to express emotions, especially low frequency emotions like anger and rage in order to manipulate and coerce others for their selfish motives. Sociopaths and narcissism often go hand in hand."

"What's narcissism?" asked Davi.

Dr. Johnson went on to explain in greater detail that a Narcissist has exaggerated feelings of self-importance, excessive need for admiration, and a lack of empathy for others. They are very self-centered and can be very manipulative. The word narcissism comes from Greek mythology. Narcissus was a hunter from Thespiae in Boeotia who saw his own reflection and fell in love with himself.

"A narcissistic sociopath has a compulsive disregard for the emotions of others especially empaths. They also have a lack of remorse, guilt, shame. They behave manipulatively and have antisocial tendencies, unchecked egocentricity, and the ability to lie in order to achieve their own motives."

"Why is this especially harmful to an empath?" Taylor asked.

"For the most part, a sociopath is the opposite of an empath, who is someone who feels and often takes on themselves the emotions of others. They have the ability to comprehend the mental or emotional state of another. An empath can literally feel what another person is feeling. Depending on the intensity, the empath may feel this emotionally, mentally, even physically."

"Wow," said Austin. "That could be really intense. Why would someone do that?"

"The empath does this for various reasons," said Dr. Johnson. "Sometimes, it's because part of the brain is more active than another. Other times it's out of compassion, with the hope that by doing so, it will relieve the emotions from another. This is like a savior complex. It's very kind of the empath, but it doesn't work. It doesn't relieve the other person of the negative emotions. They still feel those emotions, and now the empath does as well.

"So both people are feeling the same negative emotions. It didn't even fix the problem?" Austin asked, a little stunned.

"It actually made it worse," Dr. Johnson said. "Sometimes an empath tries to be the other persons' savior. This means they have a subconscious desire to take on themselves the emotional baggage of another in the hopes it will somehow atone for a wrongdoing in their own life, actual or perceived. The more guilt and self–

loathing an empath feels from their own experience, the more suffering they are willing to accept.

"Whether they are absorbing the negative energy of others to be a savior or to self-atone, it doesn't work. No amount of self-suffering is ever enough. The pattern continues endlessly. It forms deep synaptic ruts in the brain until it becomes a habit that is very difficult to break. Most of the time, the empath is not even aware that they are even doing it because, in most cases, it is at a subconscious level. They have no idea that there are other options. They actually become addicted to the mental and emotional pain and anguish. Biochemically, it releases hormones in the brain that mimic a runner's high. This is where the addiction comes from. It is very challenging to stop this addiction to painful emotions, but it is possible."

Dr. Johnson paused. "Are you still with me?"

"Is there a connection between a sociopath and an empath?" asked Talia.

"Yes," said Dr. Johnson. "Very much so. Even though they seem very opposite, they usually attract each other on an energetic level especially."

"A sociopath does not want to feel the pain of the emotions of their experience, so they look for someone to dump them on. The empath is subconsciously looking for someone with a lot of emotional baggage that they can be the savior for. The more the negative emotion, the greater the attraction.

"Now, an Educated Empath Is a Sociopath's Worst Nightmare. Because an educated empath is emotionally and often intellectually grounded in reality and are very capable of abstract thought, and are often quite creative, they have boundaries and won't allow themselves to be taken advantage of."

"However, an unknowing empath's worst nightmare is a narcissistic sociopath. The unknowing empath is looking for someone to save and the narcissistic sociopath is looking for someone to dump their emotional and energetic baggage on. They attract each other, and it makes for a very abusive relationship. Usually it's emotional abuse, but often goes further than that. It has varying degrees of severity and is often triggered by stress."

"This was very common in marital relationships in previous generations. Usually the male in the relationship was acting as a narcissistic sociopath and the woman was the empath. Many older men were wounded in their youth and were looking for healing in the feminine energy of a woman. A wounded woman would act as an empath in hopes of saving the wounded man. This could go on for years until the relationship ended or the woman dies an emotional death well before her physical death. She's a doormat, living out years of painful and quiet desperation."

"Is that still going on today?" asked Talia.

"This pattern has begun to change in the past twenty years. There now is about an equal number of men and women that play each role. This is because of a rise in the number of women that have sociopathic tendencies and some men are becoming more empathic."

"Why is this happening?" asked Mani.

"For different reasons," said Dr. Johnson. "The main one is because of a rise in the mass consciousness energy of the planet. More people are beginning to wake up and become aware outside of themselves. When a person becomes aware like that, they begin to see the effects of their behavior and that of others. The individual chooses to change themselves because of what they see. And when they change themselves, they start to change the world outside of them. The more individuals that do this, the more it changes the mass consciousness for everyone."

Taylor glanced around the room and could tell some students were really affected by Dr. Johnson's words. Danielle sat very quiet and stared at the floor, not looking at anyone.

Will looks bored, she thought. He stared out the window for a moment, then looked aimlessly around the room.

"I wonder what he's thinking?" she asked silently. The impression came to her mind, "he's somewhere else. This topic is too painful for him, so he's checked out."

"Do you know anyone here that is a narcissistic sociopath?" asked Mia.

Her question cut into Taylor's thoughts and pulled her back to the class.

"I'm not even going to touch that can of worms," Dr. Johnson said. "Now, a recap on your homework before you are dismissed. First, write down and do the clearing on all the negative thoughts and feelings about everyone and everything on the list. Then write down only the positive thoughts and emotions about the same items. And remember, if you want to change someone, first change yourself. In so doing, you will change the world. The more individuals that do this, the faster the world will ascend. Be the change you want to see in the world."

Chapter 35 – Issues Among Students

Austin and Taylor were enjoying some time together in the dining area when a loud conversation interrupted them. A group of students jostled and crowded through the doorway, too focused on the heated discussion to be polite.

"I think they came from Talia's class out at the shooting range," said Austin. "I don't get what their problem is. When I attended her first class this morning I learned a lot."

"I'm impressed," said Taylor. "Maybe you should teach me what you learned."

One side of Austin's lips curved when he saw the teasing twinkle in her eyes.

"Yeah, sure, I know you would just..."

"I can't believe you took the last one," Mia's voice carried easily across the large room.

"I wonder what has her so upset?" asked Taylor as she looked over her shoulder. She saw Mia and Will arguing in front of the serving table. Will shook his head, walked to the far side of the room, and sat down at an empty table.

Taylor turned back to Austin with a shrug and asked what he learned in Talia's class. It was hard to focus on each other and their conversation because Mia, Miranda, and the others sat behind them at a nearby table, arguing. Snippets of conversation shot by Austin and Taylor: guns, dangerous, government, control, no one is being responsible. You weren't very responsible in the Grand Canyon, your fault, failed.

"They're talking all over each other," Taylor whispered. "I don't think they're even listening."

"This is beyond annoying," said Austin. "Let's get out of here."

"I'm glad you are all here," Vivian said as the last few students filed into the room. "You will only have two hours to complete this training, so let's get to it."

Austin leaned close to Taylor, who sat next to him on the couch.

"This sounds interesting." The soft squeeze on his thigh was her only response.

"You will be using the skills you have learned in the Genius program to help in solving tonight's mystery," said Vivian.

She then proceeded to hand out one name tag to everyone along with a handout of questions to use as a guide.

"One among you will be playing the part of a murderer, and the rest are characters who need to find out who that is and how they killed a fictional character. You must stay in the four rooms on this floor. Part of the exercise is to talk about the mystery with others, check out the other rooms, and then meet back here at 8:00 for a wrap up.

"Are there any questions? Okay, I will be giving you your character bio and a description of the body when it was found. See you in two hours."

It was 7:55 when Austin found Taylor and they headed back, hand in hand. The room felt peaceful and quiet when they entered. Taylor sunk into the soft leather of the couch close to Austin.

"So what did you think?" Taylor asked.

"I think the lunch conversation never ended. At least, the people I spoke to were more focused on venting their frustration about their day than answering my questions about the mystery," said Austin.

"I experienced some of that as well," said Taylor. "The contentious atmosphere had me really annoyed. Katja even ended up leaving early."

"It sounds like it's still going on," said Austin.

Mia stormed into the room and took a chair by the window. As Will and Talia entered, they glanced around the room. Upon seeing Mia, they headed in the opposite direction, continuing their discussion in low, angry tones. The remaining seats filled up a few minutes before 8:00.

Taylor nudged Austin in the side and nodded towards the door where Nicholas stood. No one else was even aware that he was there, their conversations held all their attention. The tension in the room rose with the volume.

Nicholas took a step into the room only to be stopped by Kay.

"Are you going to do anything about this?" she asked.

"Absolutely not," said Nicholas. "They are grown-ups. They need to learn how to deal with their emotions and interact with others in a mature way."

"But aren't you going to set them straight?"

"No, why should I?" said Nicholas.

"Because they're wrong and they know it," Kay said.

"Everyone is entitled to their own opinion and they can choose to feel whatever emotions they want. It's not right for any individual or group to superimpose their belief system onto another. Force and compulsion never created effective change for individuals or the world."

Nicholas began to move to the center of the room. The closer he got, the quieter the room became.

"I recommend you all spend the remainder of your evening clearing emotions and writing down what you have learned tonight. That's all," he said and strode out.

Chapter 36 – Write and Burn

"So, how did your teaching go today?" asked Taylor, grateful for a free evening and a chance to talk to Austin. They agreed earlier to meet on an upper terrace after dinner. Conversations drifted down from the swimming pools further up the path. Water ran from a small upper pond behind Taylor and burbled over the rocks as it made its way down into the lower pond. Their table sat secluded, tucked in next to the rocks that made up the large waterfall.

"You know, I wasn't too excited to teach anything, but it went good," he said, eager to talk to her about it.

"When I went to see Mr. Ryan a few days ago for my accountability meeting, he taught me a more productive way to clear emotions. He said that if I used the tapping sequence in the Emotional Freedom Technique, it would be more effective. I've been practicing that so I could teach it today. Now he says I have to teach about manifesting money."

"What did you tell him?"

"I said that he should be the one teaching it because he does it so well. He told me that I had to because then I would learn it better. I did learn a lot about clearing negative emotions by writing them down. Probably more than anyone I taught."

"Did you have a big class?" asked Taylor.

"We actually met individually, like you did. I was assigned an hour to teach each person. I thought that was a long time, so I prepared a lot of information."

"Did you have enough material?" asked Taylor.

"Actually, I had too much," said Austin.

"I started with the material I had planned, and then finished up by talking about their story with most of them. Mr. Ryan made it pretty clear that if they wanted to talk, I needed to listen. If they finished, I should share my information."

Wow, thought Taylor, *a whole hour of Austin just listening. That would be impressive to see. He has made a lot of progress since last year.*

"So who did you meet with?" she asked before taking a bite of the cashew faux cheesecake that dripped with raspberry sauce.

"First I met with Mani. He seems really cool. Did you know his real name is Emanuel Castille?"

"No," said Taylor.

"His dad is from Peru and his mother is from New Mexico. He can speak seven languages. Four of those languages he learned to speak while here at the Institute. I could hang out with him."

"He's a good dancer, too," said Taylor, realizing what she had said too late. Mani and Joseph had been her dance partners the previous summer. Taylor wished she had not brought that up for fear that it would make Austin jealous again, like it did last year. Her toes curled tightly under her chair.

Austin remembered the experience. He had thought at the time that Taylor and Joseph had a thing going. But he had processed that event quite thoroughly. Thoughts of the experience now didn't bring up any negative emotions.

"He's had an interesting life. I feel a lot of compassion for him."

Taylor relaxed when Austin didn't mention her comment.

"Miranda Adair was next. Of all the ones I taught, I think she will use the emotional clearing technique the most. And she really needs it, too. After hearing her story, I have a greater respect for her. I wouldn't want to have had her life."

Taylor didn't know anything about Miranda other than she seemed very determined.

"After that, it kind of went downhill for a bit. I met with Atom after lunch. I found out that he is Alex's twin brother."

Taylor had never made that connection, either. They seemed to always be together, but he was so dominating. Alex seemed so quiet, especially when she was around Atom. She seemed nice on her own, maybe a little shy, though.

"Why did you say it went downhill with Atom?"

"Because he wouldn't do any of the exercise that I talked about. He says emotions are for the weak and he doesn't have any issues that he needs to be free of. He likes himself the way he is. He's only here to do the

Genius Training program. But he says he's already a genius. Can you believe the arrogance?"

"Did it get better after that?"

"No, not really," said Austin. "The next one was Katja. She's almost as arrogant as Atom. She thinks she knows everything, and doesn't have a problem telling you so. I actually had to do some emotional clearing myself after the time I spent with her."

"I haven't talked with her much, but from what I've heard from the other girls, she can be a little challenging to get along with. I'm glad she doesn't room too close to me," said Taylor.

"It did get better after that," said Austin. "I met with Will Hastings. We've done a lot of stuff in the group training, but I've never actually had an extended one-on-one conversation with him. He seems really fun. We've done some workouts together. I got the impression that he might be a little insecure, though."

Taylor thought about Will. "He seems really outgoing and usually nice, unless he was in an argument with Mia or Katja."

"Actually, I think he has a thing for Mia. Either her or Talia," said Austin.

Taylor didn't want to respond about Talia. "Will and Mia? Wow! That would be an opposites attract relationship."

"Yeah," said Austin. "I've noticed even when they're arguing there is some sort of sexual tension between them."

"Now that you say that," said Taylor, "I could see that being the case. Was Will your last student for the day?"

"No. The one I just finished with was Talia," said Austin. "Wow, does she have a story to tell. She usually seems not very talkative and kind of businesslike, but I learned all kinds of things about her."

"Like what?" asked Taylor. She wondered how much he knew.

"She served in the Israeli military for three years. Her father passed away years ago and her mother got remarried to her late husband's brother. I guess it's called Levirate marriage. It's something that used to happen a lot in her culture years ago, but not so much nowadays. I guess she has some serious mom issues," said Austin.

"Can't say that I blame her," said Taylor.

Austin realized the topic of mother issues might be bothersome to Taylor, so he decided to change the subject.

"She seems really cool. I could talk with her all night. In fact, our session went longer than an hour. But I figure since she was the last one, I could take the time."

Taylor could tell that Austin was still thinking about her. *Maybe a little too much*, she thought.

"Did you learn anything else about her?" she asked.

Austin glanced at her, not fooled by her casual tone.

"Mostly superficial stuff. We talked about the emotional release technique and she said she would do it." Not wanting Taylor to get jealous, he shifted the conversation. "I think I can see a little bit why Nicholas wants us to teach classes. It's a good learning experience. I learned a lot from preparing the materials, let alone presenting it."

Taylor sat back and relaxed in her chair. *If Austin starts to like Talia...boy, will he be surprised,* she thought.

Chapter 37 – A Kiss

Taylor felt her eyelids begin to fall. *I hope class ends soon,* she thought. The classes she attended that day were more intense than usual and even her brain felt the strain. As soon as the students were excused, she headed to the dining hall to get a late dinner. Her eyes fell on Austin almost immediately. He seemed to be in an intimate conversation with Talia. He was leaning with his elbows on the table, his chair tipped forward on two legs. *I think he really might like her.*

She picked up some dinner and turned around. Seeing Talia motion to her, she made her way across the room to their table.

"Thank you," Talia silently mouthed to her as she stood up. "Nice visiting with you Austin. See you around."

Taylor slid into the empty chair and eagerly took a bite of her chicken wrap.

"Hey, Taylor," said Austin. She stared at the grin on his face. *Was he still thinking of Talia?*

"How was your day?" he said.

"Long," Taylor said, as she took a drink of ice water. She looked down and wiped the condensation off her fingers.

"What were you guys talking about?" she asked. Her eyes rose and held Austin's.

"Nothing important," he said. "Mostly just stuff from the classes. I'm amazed at how many different things we learn about here."

Was he shifting the topic of conversation? she thought.

"Like what?" asked Taylor.

"Like how to play the ocarina."

"That's a random one, for sure," said Taylor. "I had to look it up. I had no idea what it was."

They lingered in the dining hall until Geri came out and began to clean up. Taylor took her dishes to the kitchen and led the way to the back patio where they spent the rest of the evening.

The heat of the sun soaked into Taylor and dried the water from her dip in the pool. She and Talia decided to spend their free hour after lunch there. They had spent most of the morning sitting next to each other in class. She enjoyed their discussions. Talia wasn't self-absorbed or arrogant. She was smart and considerate and also very aware. It felt like she had taken a genuine interest in Taylor and their conversation.

"Isn't Austin your boyfriend?"

"Yes, but you couldn't tell by the conversation he had with you yesterday," said Taylor.

"I know, that was so awkward," laughed Talia, "I wasn't sure what to do with all of his flirting. You have no idea how glad I was to see you walk in."

"He just doesn't know," said Taylor.

"He doesn't?" asked Talia. Her puzzled expression turned to a smile. "Maybe we should help him figure it out."

On the way back from the pool, Taylor spied Austin walking across the patio. She pretended to laugh just before Talia leaned in and kissed her hard on the lips.

Taylor could see Austin's eyes almost bugged out of his head when Talia pulled back. The two girls walked off in the opposite direction and pretended not to see him. Once out of sight, they hurried into the house. Taylor lost it. Laughter spilled out, it splattered on the walls and floor and filled the hallway with mirth.

Austin practically ran to the dining hall, his eyes wide in astonishment and shock. He pulled out the empty chair next to Pajori, spun it backwards, and sat down. No one even turned his way.

"Hey, guys, you'll never believe what I saw," interrupted Austin.

Joseph glanced at him across the table and then went back to his conversation with Logan and Demetri.

Austin leaned forward and almost tipped his chair over. "They were kissing!" he practically yelled.

The table went quiet, as all eyes turned to him.

"Who was kissing?" asked Joseph.

"Talia and Taylor!"

Austin looked around the table at the reaction to his announcement. Mani looked about as shocked and uncomfortable as Austin felt. *Why is Demetri smiling?* he thought, more than a little confused.

"That kind of turns me on!" Austin's eyes flew to Will in disbelief as laughter burst from the occupants at the table.

"What did you see?" asked Demetri.

Austin told him what he had witnessed out on the patio moments before. He could see Joseph shift uncomfortably out of the corner of his eye as the story unfolded.

"Does that bother you?" Pajori asked Austin.

"Of course, isn't it supposed to?"

Pajori grabbed Austin's face and planted a kiss right on his lips and then turned back to his lunch, as if nothing out of the ordinary had happened.

Austin couldn't move. His mouth hung open. The laughter exploded again, greater this time. Even Joseph, uncomfortable as he was, lost it.

Chapter 38 – Denial and Boots

Austin was glad Taylor could meet him early to walk to their evening class together. Everyone was expected to attend, and Austin wanted to make sure he had a seat next to her. She kept asking about his day, even with the great detail he shared. It felt as if she were fishing for something. Of course he skipped the whole kissing episode, the picture still too vivid in his mind. It felt awkward thinking about it. No way would he say anything. *What if she knows I saw?*

Austin pulled Joseph into conversation when he overtook them on their way into class. That was better than the embarrassment of Taylor knowing he saw the kiss.

Mrs. Ryan began the class by talking about some of the dynamics in relationships. She was standing in front of the group with a large white board on her left.

"These principles apply to the relationship you have with yourself, another person, a group of people, or any relationship you have with anyone or anything. The principles are pretty much the same in any relationship.

"The example I'm going to use to show these principles is the experience in the Grand Canyon that some of you participated in a couple of months ago. Those of you that participated, I would like you to think back about it. Those of you that did not participate, I would like you to think about what you heard from the others who did."

Members of the group started looking at each other. Taylor could tell the energy in the room was shifting, and not in a good way. She remembered her dream. *Is what I saw, what really happened that day?*

Vivian continued, "When you think about that experience, what emotions come up?"

Demetri was the first to raise his hand. "The whole experience was a fiasco." he said, his voice already emotionally charged. "Certain members of the group wouldn't…"

Vivian cut him off. "I just want you to list the emotions that you felt during and after the experience."

Demetri thought quickly, "Selfishness. Certain members of a certain team are very selfish," he said, looking over his shoulder.

Taylor wasn't sure who he was referring to specifically, but if what she had seen in her dream was accurate, it probably could have been anyone.

"Okay, selfishness," said Vivian. She wrote the word in big red letters on the whiteboard beside her. "Thank you, Mr. Smith. That is a thought. Can you give me an emotion that it triggers?"

Others began to raise their hands, caused by the emotions that were stirred up by the discussion. Austin was fascinated by Vivian's ability to lead such an emotionally charged conversation without stepping into the emotion herself. She permitted each student a chance to express their opinion but wouldn't allow them to hijack the conversation.

He realized, as she listed the emotions on the whiteboard, that he had felt a lot of negative emotions about the experience at first. This surprised him, since he had not even been there. *I wonder if these emotions are mine.* As he became aware of those highly charged external emotions, he tried to visualize himself as an unbiased, third-party observer. *In a strange sort of way, this is actually fun*, he thought as he watched his classmates, charged in their emotions.

On one side of the board, Vivian wrote emotions such as frustration, blame, and anger.

The other side filled up with triggers that related to the emotions. Ego, self-centered, passive-aggressive behavior, irresponsibility, and not taking the situation seriously were all part of this list.

Taylor noticed that Talia, who sat beside her, gently and discreetly tapped the side of her left hand with the fingers of her right. While the other members of the class vented, she remained quiet. Taylor could sense the emotion in her friend, but knew it was being released. They looked at each other knowingly, but didn't say a word.

Finally, when there was a lull in the venting session, Talia raised her hand.

"Yes, Miss Kohen," said Vivian.

"Denial," she said matter-of-factly.

Vivian stopped. "Denial, you say." She looked at Nicholas. He nodded back at her.

"I'm glad you brought that up," she said. "Let's talk about denial. What is denial?"

Miranda's hand shot up. "Denial is saying no. Contradiction. Refusal of a request or claim. Disavowing, or to reject or disown."

"Precisely. Thank you, Miss Adair," said Vivian. "Is it possible that some of you, then, in the experience and even now, are still acting in a state of denial?" she asked. There appeared to be no sign of judgment or condemnation in her voice. Even her body language seemed to convey an unconditional love, while still retaining authority and power.

No one moved.

"Let's talk about some of the forms of denial," she said.

Austin looked over at Taylor when she bumped his arm and took the papers she held. He scanned the title absentmindedly and handed the rest of the stack to Pajori.

Forms of Denial. *How convenient,* thought Austin. *I wonder if Mrs. Ryan had told Talia to bring up that topic before the class started? Is denial such a big issue in relationships that we need to spend an entire class on it?*

After everyone received a handout, Vivian continued. "Let's talk about some of the forms that denial can take."

Taylor looked at her papers as Mrs. Ryan began to discuss each point in detail.

1. **Manipulation** - Attempting to exploit and dominate others by lying, telling secrets, intimidating, creating guilt, and making your love and attention conditional according to one's self-serving desires.

2. **Rationalizing** - Giving what appears to be good reason for unacceptable/irrational behavior. The excuses may seem so reasonable that you honestly believe the excuses are true yourself.

3. **Minimizing** - Reducing serious problems/behaviors to make them seem less important so they become insignificant and unworthy of any real attention.

4. **Comparing** - Shifting attention to someone else in order to avoid any responsibility or blame and to justify behavior.

5. **Uniqueness** - Making up reasons why you are special or different from others, thereby absolving yourself from responsibility. Some addicts demonstrate uniqueness by acknowledging that therapy is fine for others, but they feel it won't work for them.

6. **Distraction** - Avoiding responsibility by being the center of attention or by clowning around, making others laugh; using anger or violence to intimidate and frighten; shocking others with outrageous language or stories.

7. **Omitting** – Avoiding attention by manipulating a conversation as to change or ignore an uncomfortable subject. Intentionally leaving out important pieces of information that would be incriminating.

8. **Blaming** – Taking away responsibilities from yourself and placing it on others. Convincing yourself that it's not your fault and making up elaborate reasons to blame others and circumstances.

9. **Compliance** – Pretending to do what others want or expect, to get them off your back. This is also a form of distraction. Going through the motions of "getting help" with no real intention of changing the behavior. By pretending to be submissive, apologizing for your lack of success, and then claiming to "recommit" in order to keep from actually addressing the issues.

10. **Intellectualizing** – Avoiding the issues by intellectualizing the conversation; getting lost in irrelevant questions and meaningless details; creating an air of intellectual superiority to distance yourself from the situation or person.

11. **Hopelessness/Helplessness** – Acting like a victim of circumstances with no choices or ability to affect your environment. You are sure that nothing will work, so why try? Thus absolving yourself from responsibility or effort.

12. **Compartmentalizing** – Placing various activities, roles and individuals and parts of your life into separate "compartments" in your mind, in order to keep them apart from each other. Compartmentalizing makes it easier to forget and avoid your partner, family, job, and other responsibilities when acting out.

Without mentioning any names, Vivian brought up certain experiences that Austin assumed happened during the mission to the Grand Canyon. He could tell that her words affected some members in the class very deeply.

Vivian didn't ask for questions during the rest of the class. She also didn't call on anyone for comments, either.

At the end of her presentation, she concluded with the recommendation that all the members of the class use their emotional release tools in conjunction with the experience.

"Even if the emotions you feel are not your own, I still recommend you address them, as if they were. Ideally, by first validating those emotions and then expressing them in a physical and energetic form, such as writing them out on paper while tapping or any other form that works for you. Third, completely releasing those emotions by tearing up the paper or visualizing the emotion leaving you and going into an inert object. And fourth and most important, replacing the emotion with something positive, such as gratitude, love, or peace."

Vivian paused, looking at the group. "Now. Do you have any questions?" she asked.

Austin could tell that Joseph and Demetri were bursting to say something. But it was Will who raised his hand.

"Yes, Mr. Hastings?"

"What if a person is honestly not in denial and that person's negative emotions are actually a result of someone else's actions?" he asked confidently.

Taylor swallowed hard. *How would Mrs. Ryan handle this question without this becoming a full-blown argument?*

Vivian didn't skip a beat. "Other people's actions are actually irrelevant. The emotions you feel are your choice. There is no one on the planet that can make you feel a certain way unless you allow them to. It's your choice."

Austin could tell by the look on Will's face that that was not the answer he wanted or expected.

"Everyone, sooner or later, needs to take accountability for his or her own emotions and not be in denial by blaming someone else in hopes of absolving his or herself from responsibility." said Vivian. "Now, do remember that the emotions you feel are not your identity, but don't use that as an excuse, either. Use your awareness to separate who you Be from the emotions you are feeling, regardless of the person or experience that generated the emotion in the first place. Then you can use your tools to release them. Does that answer your question, Mr. Hastings?" she said.

"Yes, mum," he said respectfully.

"Any other questions?" she asked, scanning the audience.

Taylor wondered if anyone honestly dared ask a question.

No one spoke.

I guess not, she thought.

"With that then, we would like you to take the next thirty minutes and, using your tools, release any negative thoughts or emotions from the canyon experience, the topic of denial, this class, or anything else that may be on your mind at this time," she said.

Nicholas stood up before anyone could move and turned to the group. "There is one stipulation with this exercise. You are not allowed to vent or dump any of your emotional refuse on anyone else. If you need to be alone to do this exercise, I recommend you go out in the gardens. That's a good place for it. Nature has the ability to transmute that negative energy."

The members of the class remained quiet as they began to disperse. Austin looked at Taylor. "Do you need to do any clearing about any of this?" he asked.

Taylor shook her head. "No, not really. I could sure feel the emotions from the others, but I don't feel them anymore."

"Me, too," said Austin. "I could feel anger coming from Demetri and Joseph, but it was more of awareness than actually being angry myself."

He reached over and took Taylor's hand and moved towards the door.

"Wait a minute. I do have a question before we go."

Austin followed Taylor as she walked to the front to where Vivian and Nicholas still stood.

Vivian smiled. "Hello, you two," she said. "Did you find this material useful?"

"Yes," responded Taylor. "Very much so. But I do have a question that I'm hoping one of you can answer." Her eyes fell to Nicholas as she spoke.

"What is your question?" he asked.

"The canyon experience took place before Austin and I got here, right?"

"Yes," nodded Nicholas. "It was the day before you arrived."

"I am a little curious," said Taylor. "Was it raining in the morning as they began the mission?"

"Yes, it was," said Nicholas. "Why do you ask?"

"It's just...I had a dream that morning. And it seemed like I was actually there watching the others going through the experience. I heard their conversations. It seemed so real."

Nicholas looked at Vivian. She said something to him, but it wasn't in English.

The language she used sounded foreign to Taylor. She looked at Austin, who shrugged, apparently as puzzled as she felt.

Nicholas responded in the same language then turned back to Taylor. "In your dream, what were you wearing on your feet?"

Without thinking about it, Taylor responded, "I was wearing my regular shoes, I guess."

"Think about it deeper," said Vivian. "Try to remember specifically."

Taylor closed her eyes, trying to take herself back to the dream. Her mind was empty. She honestly couldn't remember.

"Hold your head still," said Vivian. "And move your eyes from side to side."

Taylor did as she was instructed. For a moment, her mind remained empty. Then, in a flash, she recalled. She had her boots on, the same ones she had worn the previous summer, while working in the gardens around the Estate. They were boxed up and sat in the back of her closet in case she needed them here.

"I was wearing my hiking boots," she said.

"And where are those boots now?" asked Vivian.

"I think they're still packed in a box in my room," she said, puzzled.

Vivian and Nicholas exchanged a brief conversation in the unknown language.

"Taylor. Some people have the gift of dreams," said Nicholas, smiling adoringly at his wife. Vivian returned the smile. He turned back to Taylor. "Those dreams can be of the past, present, or future. Most of those types of dreams are observation dreams, when you observe an experience that appears to be outside of yourself. But, some dreams are not dreams at all. They are actually a duality experience."

"What's a duality experience?" asked Austin. He vaguely remembered the conversation about duality the previous summer but he was curious what that had to do with Taylor and her dream.

"Like I said, some of the experiences are merely observations. As if you are watching an experience on a monitor. But some of those experiences can actually be real or at least appear to be very real. Like you are physically there. All of your senses are engaged. You smell the air. You hear the sounds. You feel the experience. And usually your senses are heightened beyond their normal ability."

"So are you saying that I was there?" asked Taylor.

Nicholas turned back to Vivian. After a moment she smiled and nodded.

"It rained that morning," said Nicholas. "At least there around the canyon where the two teams were. I recommend you go to your room now and ponder and meditate on your question. See what you come up with."

Nicholas draped his arm over his wife's shoulder as they left the room.

Austin idly caressed Taylor's hand that still sat cradled in his. Gently trying to massage the uncertainty from her.

"You never told me about the dream".

"The morning after the dream is when you came to pick me up. I was so busy with packing and getting ready to come here, that it slipped my mind."

"I wonder what language they were speaking and what they said?" asked Austin.

"Since being here doing the Genius Training program, I've studied about twelve languages," said Taylor pondering out loud. "It wasn't any of those."

"Yeah, it didn't sound like any of the languages that I've gone over in my classes, either."

"Hey, I have an idea," she said. Her grip on Austin's hand tightened as she pulled him down the hall to her room.

Austin's hand fell to his side when Taylor let go and hurried to her closet. He watched her stretch up and check the shelves, but came up empty. She fell to her knees and shoes began to pile up behind her as she dug further into the closet. A black pair of strappy, high-heeled shoes caught Austin's attention. They dangled from his fingers.

"Why don't you wear these?"

Taylor slid out of the closet and sat back on her heels.

"You don't remember?" she asked tugging at a medium size box in the back of her closet.

Austin shook his head.

She smiled. "Those are my dance shoes," she said. "I wore those when we danced last year at Mrs. Ryan's birthday party."

A flood of memories returned to Austin: the party, his stupid jealousy over Taylor's dance lessons with Joseph, and his own dance lessons, set up by Marti and Geri to help him impress Taylor. He skipped quickly past the assumptions on his part and the argument that almost destroyed their relationship to the end of the evening, when things were so much better.

"Yeah. I remember that night. I asked you if you would be my girlfriend."

Taylor remained silent. Austin glanced over at her and saw her working on the tape that was wrapped tightly around the shoe box that sat in her lap.

Austin wasn't sure if he should be annoyed, but seeing her struggles, he pulled his knife from his pocket, opened it and handed it to her, handle first.

"Do you remember that night?"

The box was only partially open when she stopped and peered inside. Her eyes never moved from the contents as she returned the knife to Austin.

"Do you remember what I said to you that night?" Austin said crouching down next to her. "And what you said to me?"

Taylor seemed to be in another world, one without him. Slowly the boots emerged from their hiding place and stopped suspended in midair. Thick, red mud caked the soles.

The words were an excited whisper on the air as they passed Taylor's lips. "I was there, I was really there."

Chapter 39 – Emotional Children or Adults

Austin and Taylor showed up for Nicholas' class only to be witness to a heated conversation between Katja and Will.

"You are so arrogant and egotistical that you're constantly choking on your own sperm," she yelled.

"So says Cleopatra," Will retorted, "the Queen of denial."

"This is so not going to be good," Taylor said to Austin. They stood across the room, quietly observing the commotion.

The argument intensified and Katja went to slap Will, but her hand only met air. Mia and Pajori simultaneously jumped between them.

"It's a good thing you stopped her," said Will to Mia. "I would hate to have to hit a girl."

"It's a good thing that Pajori stepped in!" replied Mia angrily. "I was about to help Katja kick your ass."

Will stepped towards the girls, his chest out and fists clenched. Pajori tried to push him back, but Will didn't move. Raul quickly moved between them and motioned towards the door. The room fell silent as Nicholas entered.

"Wow, can you feel that?" Taylor said almost silently to Austin.

Nicholas walked decisively to the front of the room. "Sit down!"

Everyone quickly found a seat.

"It is obvious," he said, calm but powerful, "that some of you children still haven't learned to play nice."

"Those of you here, who are doing the Genius and Ascension Trainings are supposed to be among the best in the world, the spiritual, mental, and emotional elite! You're not required to be here. This is your choice." Nicholas paused to let his words sink in. "If you want to be like the masses, then go ahead. But you're not going to do that here. Don't waste my time." Nicholas paused again. "And don't waste the time of others who do want to do this."

Taylor noticed that he looked at Talia, who was sitting between Joseph and Demetri, when he said it.

"None of you can even begin to really understand what I have to share with you!" Nicholas's eyes turned to Austin and Taylor. They could both feel the intense power coming from their mentor. "What I want, and am supposed to share with you."

Nicholas's intense energy started to soften.

"Life eternal," he said, quietly looking down.

After a second his head shot up. He glanced at the ceiling for a moment, took in a big breath, blew it out, then continued.

"You all have a lot of unresolved baggage," he said more calmly. "Whether that emotional baggage started with you or not, you still have to deal with it. No matter where it came from, it still is not your identity.

"The main part of the training for the Genius program and in all we do here is to help you move forward with your life purpose and mission. A big part of that is your relationship with yourself, others, and other things. What is your relationship with emotions? You have to know you are not the emotions. That is a must. Be aware so you can separate yourself from them so they will not control your life. You cannot allow yourself to be acted upon by them, no matter where they originated.

"Lately some of you have been acting like emotional children. **Emotional children** can be any age and are controlled by emotions, brain chemistry like hormones, generational or ancestral issues that have not been resolved, limiting belief patterns, cultural traditions and paradigms, societies programing, etc. Because emotional children are not aware outside of themselves, they get tossed about by these things.

"**Emotional adolescence** of any age, are beginning to wake up to the world beyond themselves. They are learning to be aware of relationships with themselves, their body, mind, soul, other people, masses, groups, money, nature, environment, and world, the whole universe beyond themselves and within them.

"**Emotional adults** are able to control and direct their emotions the way they choose. They act out of choice and logic and are not acted upon. They still have emotions, but they choose what they would like to feel and they feel it: joy, gratitude, love, etc.

"Don't let anything or anyone, including yourself, dictate how you feel. Don't let others control you. Several of you in the first training scenario at the Grand Canyon acted like emotional children. A few of you were at the level of emotional adolescence, but you can all do better. You are so much more than what you've become."

Taylor tried to process Nicholas's words, but couldn't help but feel the intensity coming from him.

"When are you going to grow up?" he asked.

No one moved when he left, neither did the uncomfortable silence.

Chapter 40 – Preparation for Second Mission

It was later that afternoon before Joseph, Talia, and some others had a chance to speak with Nicholas. Austin stood near the door with Taylor and watched the proceedings. Talia spoke for the group when she asked if Nicholas would allow them a second chance.

"Give us another opportunity to prove ourselves," she said.

"I don't know if it is even worth doing again," Nicholas responded after listening to their request. "If I allow you another opportunity, there will be no compensation this time."

"That's fine," said Joseph. "We wouldn't expect any."

"Alright, then. Anyone interested in having a second try at it, meet me in the library this evening at 7:00, and I will give you my answer."

Austin's arm made its way around Taylor as they exited the room.

"What do you think?" he asked.

"I'm not sure. Knowing I was there last time, but not really, makes me kind of want to be there this time. See what it's really like."

"I'm curious to see what it's all about."

The last class of the day ended at 6:00 p.m. Austin

met Taylor, and the two went to dinner before heading to the library. Joseph and Talia were seated around a dark, polished table set off to one side. They invited Austin and Taylor to join them.

"I think we can be successful this time around," said Joseph. "That is, if everyone decides to cooperate."

"In your opinion, what went wrong the first time?" Austin said.

"I feel there were some who wouldn't admit that they had made wrong decisions, or that they simply didn't know what to do," Talia said.

"I agree," said Joseph. "I also felt that no one was willing to work together. Everyone wanted to be in charge and do it their own way."

Their conversation continued uninterrupted until the others showed up. Nervous anticipation spread through the room while they waited for Nicholas to arrive.

"I've made my decision."

Austin turned towards the door and watched Nicholas walk to one end of the room.

"You can try again, but this time it will be more challenging. The purpose of this mission will be to retrieve a specific artifact that has been hidden somewhere in the continental U.S. It's been hidden by Rex and Dakota, and has been energetically charged to amplify its resonant signature. This will allow you to find it more easily," he said.

He divided the participants into two groups. When Nicholas was finished, Austin realized he and Taylor were on separate teams. Setting aside his disappointed, Austin tried to focus.

They would have clues to solve, many of which would be at the Estate. The team members would be allowed to ask anyone, including Nicholas, questions to help them in their quest. They would be required to figure out if the clues were necessary or a diversion.

"If one team figures out the location of the artifact and is ready to go before the other team, the second team will be given the information, but will have up to a six-hour handicap. You may begin immediately," Nicholas said.

Austin caught Taylor's eye and motioned to Nicholas. Instead of leaving the room with everyone else they went up to him.

"Mr. Ryan?"

"Yes, Austin?"

"How did you get this set up in such short notice?"

"I had a feeling those who went before would want to try again. I contacted Dakota and Rex, and they helped set it up. They are in northern Arizona today, working along the Colorado River."

Austin noticed Talia still sitting at the table when he and Taylor thanked Nicholas and left.

"Too bad we're on different teams," Taylor said.

"Yeah, well, good luck," Austin said as they parted out on the patio. He watched Taylor head across the grass to where her team sat, then turned and entered the dining hall. He took a seat next to Mani. Katja, Miranda, and

Atom were already complaining.

"What's up with them?" asked Austin.

"I don't know, something about not wanting to be on the same team or something. They better cut it out. If Mr. Ryan hears about it, I wouldn't be surprised if he scrapped the whole thing."

"Hey, you guys, a question?" Austin said getting the groups attention. "Is this different than your Grand Canyon mission?"

"No, not really," said Demetri. "We were given a bunch of different clues as well that would lead us to what we were after. To this day, we still don't know what we were after, though."

"Maybe it's the same thing," said Mani.

"Where in the Grand Canyon did you end up?" asked Austin.

"Up on the north rim, and that's as far as we made it," said Ching.

"Well, let's see if we can go all the way this time and find this thing," said Raul.

"Here's your first clue." Sophie's well-manicured hand appeared out of nowhere and dropped a paper on the table. "Have fun," she said as she turned to go.

Raul opened the sheet.

"**The One To Try For, Sum are king for ten thousand years tried, For Try To find the One**," he said.

He laid the paper on the table and pointed to the word 'tried'. It was in smaller font and was raised halfway above the word 'years'.

"I wonder what that means?" asked Austin.

"It's probably a typo," Katja said. "That and some pretty bad grammar."

"I think we should go ask Mr. Ryan," Miranda said. "He did say we could ask anyone questions."

"Fine, then, you go," said Atom.

"Fine, I will." She smirked at him and left the room.

Five minutes later, she returned with a confused look on her face.

"He said it was correct. I ran into Taylor on the way. Her team sent her to ask a question, as well."

Shen took the paper and wrote the clue on a whiteboard that had been left sitting against the wall after class that day. It still didn't make any sense.

"What if 'kings for thousands of years' means Hitler?" Meeki asked. "Like a thousand year Reich."

"That doesn't make sense, Hitler was never a king," said Atom.

"We're brainstorming. Any idea is welcome at this point," said Shen.

"Who made you in charge?"

"We have a clue to solve, can we quit this stupid arguing?" said Mani.

"Mr. Ryan said something about Rex and Dakota hiding the artifact. What if we ask Sophie if she knows where they are?" asked Ching.

"They're in Arizona," Austin said.

"And you know this how?" asked Atom.

"I asked him before I left the library. He said they were in Northern Arizona working on the Colorado River."

"Do you think he would've hid it somewhere in the Grand Canyon again?" asked Ching.

"I've figured out the clue," came Atom's smug voice.

"What does it mean?" asked Miranda.

"You figure it out if you're so smart."

"We're supposed to be doing this together," said Mani. "What does it mean?"

"Okay, I cut a hole in the paper and looked at each word on its own. It isn't a phrase it's numbers. The 'one to try for' is 1,2,3,4."

"That's a chiasmus," said Ching. "The beginning is 1,2,3,4. And it's the same at the end. 'For try to find the one is the opposite, 4,3,2,1,'"

"Okay, but what does that mean?" asked Austin.

"A chiasmus is a literary technique in narrative motifs in which two or more clauses are balanced against each other by the reversal of their structures in order to produce a literary, even poetic effect." Ching smiled. "I learned that in class. The beginning and end of a chiasmus are the same except that the end is opposite of the beginning. It points to what's in between. That's the important part. We need to focus on 'Sum are kings for thousands of years tried'. And sum spelled S–U–M means adding all the parts together. 'Tried' could also mean 'three.'"

"Like an exponent," said Raul.

"Yeah," said Shen. "Like this." He wrote a number three next to the word "years" and erased the word "tried."

"So does that mean three kings?" asked Miranda. "Like the three wise men that brought gifts to the Christ child?"

"No one knows for sure how many wise people actually came to the Christ child. Nicholas would know that. That can't be the clue," said Katja.

Further discussion didn't uncover any more understanding of the clue.

"Maybe this has to do with what was found last year," said Austin. "Didn't Mr. Ryan say they found something?"

"If I remember, it was a cube or tablet or something," said Mani. "It had some genealogy of some kings or something on it."

"That wasn't too difficult, we're after the cube," Atom said.

"But what about the other clues?" Meeki said.

"Let's divide up and see if we can find any and then meet back here in an hour," suggested Demetri.

Austin and Mani headed to the kitchen.

"Hey, Marti, did anyone give you or Geri clues for this mission?" Mani asked.

"As a matter of fact I have one here on the counter. I was wondering how long it would take for you to get it." He handed them on of two small framed photos that lay next to the toaster.

"Thanks," said Austin.

He and Mani examined the picture. It looked like it had been taken in some sort of cave. There were what looked like Native American drawings.

"This could be pointing to our Grand Canyon idea," Mani said.

"Yeah, let's see if we can find anymore."

The two asked everyone they encountered as they walked through the building. They found a couple more clues, but couldn't make sense of them, including the one from Austin's trainer, Sam.

The U2 the U seek - Joseph Campbell.

They ended up back in the dining hall and spread what they had found on the table in front of the others. There were about ten more clues that littered the table. After going through them one at a time they decided that over half were probably not useful and set them aside.

"We found a poem," Ching said.

In a land of many towers
Water used its carving powers
Tore asunder earth and sod
Carving scars in the work of God
But left a desert land of heat and fury
Treasure hidden 'neath the one called Mercury.

"Well, there's water in the Grand Canyon and some would call it a desert. We should put this in the pile to look at closer," Raul said. "Did anyone find anything else?"

"Sheena gave us this rock," Meeki said.

Shen picked up the rock and passed it around.

It fit in the palm of Austin's hand. The square shaped rock was a deep reddish-orange color. It was smooth on one side and the edges were rounded. He turned it over and rubbed his thumb over the engravings that were etched into it.

"So we have the photo of Indian drawings, a poem, and a rock. Is there anything else that seems to fit with these clues?" asked Demetri.

"We got a paper from one of the gardeners, and all it says is 'Dakota' and 'Native Americans' on it," said Katja. "It should go with the others."

"I know we put this photo in the distraction pile, but the more I've been looking at it the more I think there is something more to it." Miranda pushed the picture of a pond into the center of the table. It had rings moving across the water, like it had been taken just after a rock had been tossed in. "I think this could be an example of concentric rings."

"I think we should call it a night and see what we come up with in the morning," Meeki said, yawning.

Austin ended up being the one to take all the clues. He set them on his dresser and then sent a text to Taylor. It was late, but he knew he wouldn't be able to sleep. His mind kept going over all the clues they had found. She called a few moments later. He wasn't too surprised when she told him about the clues they had found. They were all very similar or exactly the same as the ones his team had found. They discussed their ideas of what they meant and came to the conclusion that what they were looking for was probably at the Grand Canyon.

Showered and dressed in khaki shorts and a black t-shirt, Austin hurried to the back lawn. He found Taylor reclining in the shade of the large, white tent that had been set up. The grass felt cool under his legs when he stretched out beside her.

"Do you think Mr. Ryan will let us leave?" Taylor asked.

"I don't know, it did seem like all the clues were pointing to Arizona. I would like to get there and start really looking."

"I know what you mean. I don't know if there is much more we can do from here. I think we've found all the clues."

Nicholas walked among the students and stopped in the center of the group.

"I think you have enough information. And both teams are heading in the right direction. I have to congratulate you on solving the first set of clues. Yes, what you are after is in a certain cave near the southern side of the Grand Canyon. The specific area is tribal lands to the indigenous people. You have permission to go, but be very respectful of the place. Don't harm or damage anything while you're there."

"Really, we have to go back *there* again," said Katja under her breath.

Ignoring her comment, Nicholas continued. "Be prepared to leave in two days. Mrs. Ryan has planned an evening of swimming and food up at the pool to celebrate. You all have the rest of the day to relax. Dinner is at 7:00."

"That sounds like heaven." Taylor said as she lay back on the grass.

That does sound like heaven, Austin thought. *Spending the rest of the day lounging around with Taylor. Nothing could be better.*

Chapter 41 – Second Grand Canyon Experience

"Talia, do you have a minute?" Taylor had stopped by her room on the way to bed. The teams were leaving for Arizona the next morning and Taylor wanted to make sure she was ready. "Is there anything specific I need to take?" she asked.

"I don't think so," said Talia, "just the usual."

"I think I'll check the weather. Wasn't there an awful storm when you went last time?"

"Yeah, there was. Text me what you find out."

Once Taylor was back in her room, she checked the weather for the following days, sunny and hot. She sent a quick text to Talia, finished packing, and headed to bed.

Taylor was a little leery the next morning when it came time to go. Nicholas said they would be flying in on two Sikorsky UH 60 Black Hawk helicopters. She could sense Austin's exuberance as they watched the choppers land at the Ryan's airfield. The wind from the blades whipped her hair across her face. He tucked it behind her ear.

"This is going to be so cool," he said. His eyes twinkled with excitement. He turned and headed to the other helicopter.

Taylor noticed Alchesay and Logan in the cockpit when she climbed on board. It would have been comforting to have Austin's arm around her. Even with the clearing she'd done before she left her room that morning, she still couldn't shake the nervousness that her dreams the night before had caused. It had been a twisted mix of what she'd witnessed the last time she'd been at the Grand Canyon and random images about the clues they'd spent so much time on.

She leaned her head against the cool pane of the window and focused on the scenery far below. The green forested mountains gave way to dry deserts and plateaus. *I might as well be on Mars,* she thought as red cliffs began to rise from the desert floor. A large green river came into view, cutting its way through the towering cliffs.

The steep terrain and heat were getting to everyone. The bickering began right after the helicopters had dropped them off. Al told the team that they were about four miles from their destination, but no one could decide which way to go to begin their search.

"Let's head towards those cliffs," Talia said, pointing down river.

Taylor adjusted the straps of her small pack and set off behind her. She passed Austin and smiled. Two strong hands gripped her shoulders and turned her around. She gazed into Austin's handsome face.

"Be careful," he said, releasing her with a quick kiss.

"You, too," she said, then turned and hurried after her team.

The next few hours, Taylor climbed over and

around rock formations into small caves and along dry dusty trails. Progress was slow and tedious because of the danger from the steep cliffs and the deep, swift moving river below. She was surprised she could hear Austin and his team. They were searching some caves above her. Bits and pieces of conversation bounced off the walls of the canyon, and Taylor could tell they were frustrated. Her own group complained regularly about the heat and wanted to quit.

"I didn't think this could be worse than last time," Talia said. "No one wants to be here, and this place is a lot more dangerous than it appears. I'm afraid someone could get seriously injured."

"How about we all take a break for a while and see if we can figure out a better way to go about this?" Taylor said. She went in a shallow cave nearby, removed her pack, and sat down. The temperature was noticeably cooler. The wet bandana she'd pulled from her pack felt good on her face. The long drink of warm water quenched her thirst.

The mood of the group lifted a little once everyone had eaten what little they had brought, but Kay and Grace still were ready to leave. Taylor stayed out of the conversation and focused instead on what the clues had told them about this place.

"Hey, you guys," she said, "We need to find this tower. Maybe we are too close and can't see it. If we go back down to the river and look around, maybe something will look like this Tower of Hermes."

Pajori, Talia, and Joseph joined Taylor in the short hike down the narrow trail to the river. Rocks and dirt tumble down the hillside. A frantic Austin slid down with them.

"Atom fell and hurt himself," he said. "We've got to call the helicopters back in to get him."

Talia pulled her radio from her pack and contacted Al. There was an open area below and not too far from them where it could land safely. With the help of Pajori and Joseph, they were able to get Atom bandaged up and into the helicopter. When the chopper took off, some of the members of both teams were on it.

"I guess it's up to us now," Demetri said. Only eleven of them remained.

"Hey, do you see that guy over there?" Taylor suddenly asked.

"No, where are you looking?" asked Austin.

Taylor pointed to a large rock formation further down the canyon. A young man stood in the sun at the bottom of the towering rocks. It seemed to transform the longer Taylor gazed at the mountain, exposing an opening in the rocks. The man turned and disappeared into the shadows.

"Could that be it?" said Mani.

It was harder to get there than they thought. There was a small creek they had to cross. It cut across the bottom of the canyon and flowed into the river. No one thought to bring dry socks. They climbed up the steep hillside to the entrance. A large boulder seemed to have been rolled aside allowing access into the cave. Deep gouges in the cliff behind were evident. The darkness faded when the three flashlights clicked on. Passageways split off calling the group to explore, only to find dead ends and no signs of what they were looking for.

"Everyone is in too big of a hurry," Taylor said, pulling Austin aside as they exited another dead end. "I think if we slow down and try to be more aware of what is here we have a better chance of finding it."

"I think this is a waste of time," said Kay.

"We've come this far. It would be stupid to quit now," responded Talia.

"Let's try one more and then decide," said Demetri.

Austin led the way, his light shone down the long tunnel.

"I think we are getting close," said Taylor. "See the writing on the walls? We haven't encountered these in any of the other caves."

The walls closed in the further they went. They had to turn sideways to slide through the tight gap in the rocks. The passageway opened to reveal a sizable cavern.

Shining their lights around the room, they could see a variety of images painted on the walls. Intermingled with them were indentations that seemed like natural shelves formed into the stone. In the center of the room was a single granite column that stood on a square plinth.

"Is this it?" asked Demetri still searching around with his light. "Is this what we're after?"

Austin examined the wall. "Wow. This is cool," he said touching the drawings. "These are so clear. Like they were drawn yesterday."

"Another dead end?" said Kay.

"I think someone else got here before us," said Mani.

"Maybe this is what we're supposed to find," said Joseph as he flashed pictures with his phone.

"This is ridiculous," said Kay. "I'm leaving."

Standing in the center of the room Taylor shook her head. "I don't understand. There should be something here." She touched the short column. It's rough form had been carved into what seemed like a pedestal.

"Get out of my way," said Kay. She was standing behind Raul by the entrance. Raul had tried to leave, but his broad shoulders had momentarily halted his progress through the narrow opening.

"Why don't you move him," goaded Demetri.

"Hey, you guys, calm down," said Joseph.

"I'm going right now," said Kay. Her voice raising.

Austin put his hand gently on Taylors shoulder. "I think we better go with the others."

"It's just..." Taylor struggled to process her thoughts and impressions.

"Come on, Taylor. You can do this," she heard quietly.

All the others had left except Talia and Austin. Taylor could still hear the arguing of the others as they proceeded away from the room.

"I don't understand, either," said Talia. "Maybe this is a test that Mr. Ryan wanted us to go through," as she slid into the narrow exit followed by Austin.

Taylor took one last look around the room. *What did we miss?* She thought out loud.

No one noticed the two men who sat high above them on a ledge overlooking the room. From the darkness Dakota and Azaac watched as the kids left. They could still hear them arguing.

In his hands, Azaac held a stone tablet covered with cuneiform characters. A genealogy of the ancient Samarian god/kings.

Dakota shook his head. "They almost had it."

As soon as the choppers landed Talia, Austin, and Taylor went to see how Atom was. He was still in Dr. Mac's office. They ran into Nicholas on their way back and he requested that they join him on the west patio for a recap of their experience. Joseph, Pajori, Raul, Miranda and Ching sat at one of the tables waiting for them. The remainder of the teams were spread throughout the other tables. The contentious conversations ceased when Nicholas arrived.

"I've discussed Atom's injury with Dr. Mac and Kara. He will make a full recovery," Nicholas said.

"He wouldn't have gotten hurt if you would have done your part, Katja," said Demetri.

"It's not my fault. He shouldn't have left on his own in the first place. Anyway, this is not what I signed up for," said Katja heatedly. "I'm here to do the Genius Training program, and be a genius not waiting on a..."

Nicholas silenced her with a piercing gaze. "There's more to genius than facts. Atom knows more facts than all of you, but personal and social skills are also part of genius."

"From what I've gathered from speaking with some of the team members this afternoon, you are still reacting out of emotion. You're acting like emotional children. Many of you are still carrying your baggage right in front of your own eyes and will not allow yourselves to see beyond it." Nicholas stood and surveyed the group. "I expected more out of you this time."

Chapter 42 – Drama Triangle

After faithfully doing her routine the next morning, Taylor proceeded off to her classes. The first two were the same as usual. A memorization class and an inter-spatial learning class. She really enjoyed them. The classes pushed her, but she didn't feel pressured by the teachers, including Dr. Johnson. On the contrary, the lack of force or compulsion to learn the material actually allowed the information to come easier.

Taking apart ideas and concepts and putting them back together again is really kind of fun, she thought.

The third class period of the day was always different. It was often held outside, and the topic usually varied.

Today she had received word to meet in one of the larger classrooms for instruction. That didn't surprise her. However, she was surprised to see almost all of the other students gathering for this particular class.

The room was filling fast. She stood in the doorway deciding where to sit when she saw Austin's wave and smile. No matter how she felt, his smile always made her feel even better. She slid into the seat next to him. His arm lay casually on the back of her chair. She could feel Austin playing with her hair as they chatted for the few minutes they had before class began. *He seems more at peace with himself lately.*

In contrast to that, she noticed that many of the others in the group were acting quite sullen and moody. She tried to tune out the loud, harsh conversations around her. She had spent some time writing her feelings down about the Grand Canyon experience, but obviously others hadn't. After the initial meeting with Nicholas on their return and all the tools she used, she felt pretty good.

Mrs. Ryan walked purposefully to the stage at the front of the room. Taylor noticed an unusual tension in the way she carried herself. Her normal gentle yet professional demeanor was replaced with a determination that Taylor could sense. *Something is up,* she thought.

"Good morning, everyone," said Vivian. "We are going to dispense with the pleasantries and get right down into the topic of today's instructions, of which some of you are not aware of, but desperately need to learn.

"She seems pretty serious about this," whispered Austin.

Taylor nodded, her eyes not leaving Vivian.

Vivian began by talking about **The Drama Triangle**. It was fairly academic. She went over the three players in the drama game: the **victim**, the **persecutor** or bully, and the **savior** or rescuer.

"The victim," she said, "feels oppressed, hopeless, helpless, powerless, and incapable.

"The persecutor is critical and driven by anger or resentment. They are rigid, bossy, and dominating, and continue to put others down and cast all blame away from themselves. One common thought for the persecutor is 'you're not okay, but I am, so do what I tell you.'"

Taylor's pen flew across the page, not wanting to miss anything.

Number three – **savior.**

-**Provides support even when they don't want to.**
-**Feels guilty and anxious if they're not rescuing someone.**
-**Feels capable and worthy when victim is dependent on them.**

She stopped writing and listened as Vivian continued to explain that the savior expects to fail and because of that they are motivated to do even more. Their inner dialogue would go something like, "you're not okay but I'm nice and will fix you."

"This is a common form of interaction," said Vivian, "especially for one or two dimensional thinkers. It's also present in emotional children of any age."

An uncomfortable murmur spread through the room. Taylor could tell this topic meant a great deal to Mrs. Ryan and was stirring up emotions in some of the students. There was an intensity that seemed to flow from Vivian. *I wonder if the others notice,* thought Taylor.

Vivian continued to explain the interactions between the three players. "The bully persecutes the victim, so the victim looks for a rescuer to save them. The bully feels empowered that they have control and can force and manipulate another. This actually gives them the perception of strength and courage. It fulfills their ego and enhances their perceived identity.

"The savior feels inadequate within themselves, but if they can save another, then they feel that they have fulfilled their purpose. It's like a compulsory obligation. Being a savior is usually based in feelings of not being good enough. It feeds their ego and they receive fulfillment by helping another, even at their own expense. This often creates resentment in the savior and an enabling of the victim. It also doesn't solve the problem and keeps the victim in a state of helplessness.

"The players rarely stay in the same role, however. Quite often two people will play all three roles in the same conversation."

Talia raised her hand.

"Yes, Talia?" said Vivian.

"How can two people play three roles at the same time?"

"Good question," said Vivian. "They actually change roles throughout their interaction. Often times the persecutor will become the victim in order to manipulate the victim into becoming the rescuer. When this happens the persecutor shifts back to their role as the bully and makes the savior the victim.

Vivian stopped to make sure everyone was listening. "And on the other hand, the savior may go after the bully in order to save the victim, and then the bully becomes the victim being persecuted by the savior. So the players of this game can change roles very quickly and often do."

Vivian continued for the next twenty minutes, describing in more detail the interactions between the participants in Drama Triangle.

With a deep breath, she stopped. "So how do you win at this game?"

The room was silent. Vivian's energy was poignant and determined. It almost seemed that no one dare to speak.

Taylor watched Vivian scan the room as if speaking to someone in particular.

"The only way to win this game," she said, "is not to play it." She then went on and talked about suggestions on how to make the savior into an unbiased coach. The helpless victim can become a problem-solving survivor, even thriving amidst challenges. The persecutor must change to a nonjudgmental motivator, providing choices without interjecting their own emotional agenda into the interaction.

After fifteen more minutes of explanation, the topic came to an abrupt end. "It's now 12:30," she said. "Many of you have other classes or lunch at this time. I recommend you consider your recent past experiences and the emotions resulting from it. Are you playing one or more of the roles in the drama triangle? If not, that's great, keep it up. Do be aware of it, but stay out of it. If you are in the midst of this pointless game, then I recommend you use your tools and get out of it. You're now dismissed."

The reason behind Mrs. Ryan's intense lecture lingered in the back of Taylor's mind for the next few hours. But by the next morning, she had mostly forgotten the Drama Triangle and was busily occupied with studying the fingering chart for her French horn.

The broad range of topics that she had been studying during the Genius Training program was almost overwhelming to her. She wanted to excel in each of these categories, but it seemed there were so many different ones. How could she become proficient in any of them?

Lost in her thoughts, she didn't notice Austin sit down until he bumped her.

"Sorry, I was somewhere else," she said.

"Where?" asked Austin

"Back in the music room. The French horn is a twisted puzzle I haven't figured out yet."

Austin chuckled.

"What do you think Mrs. Ryan is going to talk about today?" Taylor asked.

"Most likely more of the same thing," said Austin, motioning with his head toward to Katja, Mia, Miranda, and Will who, along with Demetri, were arguing about something in the back of the room.

Taylor couldn't quite tell what they were saying, but it was getting quite contentious. It seemed like they were throwing blame and accusations all over each other.

The noise in the room continued to escalate as Taylor sat quietly on the front row next to Austin, waiting for class to begin.

Vivian's usually soft voice was heard bursting over the speaker system, "Enough!"

The room went immediately silent.

Taylor watched as Vivian and Nicholas made their way to the small stage at the front of the room. She placed her hand over the microphone that was clipped to her blouse and quietly spoke to Nicholas. "I think we should do the Authenticity exercise. What do you think?"

Taylor could still hear them.

"Do you really think they can handle it?" asked Nicholas.

"Maybe, maybe not. But one thing is for sure: they need it."

I wonder what that is? thought Taylor.

Turning to the group, Vivian announced. "We are going to be doing what we call the Authenticity Training. It will be held at the upper pool and is by invitation only. You are all invited."

Taylor glanced over to see the concern and curiosity on Austin's face.

Vivian continued, "It's going to be the entire day. Everyone there will be over eighteen. The experience is completely voluntary, except for some of you," she said. "Those required to be there will be notified personally by Mr. Ryan."

"However, once you get there, you must stay the entire time. It will conclude at 5:00 p.m. Meals will be taken care of. Towels and anything else you may need will also be there. This experience is intended to bring up your emotions in a safe place. You will need to use your tools and clear out any emotions that will surface before you make your decision. Also, be prepared to do plenty of emotional clearing during and after the experience.

"Everyone who decides to participate will need to be there by 10:00 a.m. sharp. If you show up late you will not be allowed to enter the pool area. The training will be held in two days."

A nervous chatter spread through the room.

"One more item," Vivian said. "The training is clothing optional."

The chatter ceased then began gaining momentum and volume in seconds.

"Wait! What was that last part?" asked Austin.

As the others in the room began to leave, he stayed in his seat wondering what had just happened. Joseph leapt from his seat next to Austin and caught up with Nicholas on his way to the door. He left the room with him after a short exchange.

Taylor pulled her feet up in the overstuffed chair. Danielle and Talia sat on the couch on the other side of the black coffee table. Their eyes were fixed on Vivian as she spoke.

"Anciently, in some cultures, there is a story of our original parents, Eve and Adam. As the story goes, they were placed in a beautiful garden in a state where they would never get old and never die. They were naked. And in their innocence, they didn't know any different. Everything in this paradise was provided for them. The atmosphere was such and their bodies were in a state such that they never felt discomfort. All of their nourishment was provided by the garden. They didn't have to work and everyday was the same. This went on for a long time. Maybe even hundreds of years.

"If the story is true, apparently Adam was totally fine with the situation. It was Eve that eventually realized that they were going nowhere. There was no opposition. No contrast. And no opportunity for growth, except one.

"The only variance that she was aware of was a certain fruit that grew near where they lived. They could consume anything else around them and still stay in this innocent, immortal state. However, the seed of this particular fruit would cause a biochemical change in their imperishable bodies that introduced small amounts of blood into their circulatory systems. Prior to that, their bodies were filled with a white fluid that continually recharged all the cells in their bodies. That's why they would never get sick, age, or die. There was absolutely no cellular break down."

Trying to be respectful, Talia asked, "What does this have to do with the Authenticity Training?"

"Eve wanted to move forward. She wanted to progress," said Vivian. "Even if that meant contrast."

"Or being uncomfortable," said Taylor at the exact same moment the thought came to her mind.

"Exactly," said Vivian. "The Authenticity Training, along with all the other training we do here at the Institute, is intended to give you contrast. To push you a little. Not so much, to break you. But enough to get you out of your comfort zone and allow for growth."

Vivian waited to allow her words to settle in. "Adam didn't want to leave the garden. He was fine with the status quo."

"She was willing to experience contrast in order to progress," said Talia.

"It didn't bother them before to be naked because of their innocence, but after they became aware outside of themselves, they began experiencing opposition. They started acquiring negative emotions. The emotion of shame is one of the lowest frequency emotions a person can feel.

"How's that for extremes? They go from feeling no emotions to about the worst emotion that humans can feel."

Taylor was starting to understand. "So in the Authenticity Training, the shedding of clothing represents the removal of the layers of emotional baggage?"

"Yes," nodded Vivian. "The discomfort brings up the unresolved issues and, with the tools you have, you can address and clear those emotions in a safe and effective way."

"Is there any other way to do it?" asked Danielle.

"Yes, there are other ways. But the process of removing all your clothing and being there physically for everyone to see leaves one feeling that everything in your life is open, especially emotions, fears, thoughts, etc. This puts a person in a very vulnerable place where issues and emotions are brought to the surface in a fast and all-encompassing way.

"There are different levels. One of the levels is hiding in the corner while undressing and being very discreet. The other extreme is when a person just drops all their clothing out in the open. Everyone's a little different. But eventually it all works out the same. You're naked in front of other people. And it's not so much about being physically naked in front of other people, it's more about feeling emotionally exposed and how you deal with your emotions because of it. It's more about you having a personal experience."

Taylor felt better about the training now that she understood why they were doing it.

"Watch and see, because you will notice that certain people aren't going to be there. And there's no judgment in that. Not everyone needs this type of experience. That's why there are so many emotional clearing tools: different situations and experiences need different tools. Different people also need different tools."

The soft chime of the clock placed a pause in the conversation while the girls thought about what Vivian was saying.

"Did you notice that Nicholas was a little surprised when I brought this up to the group?" Vivian said.

"Yeah," said Taylor. "It's not often that I see Mr. Ryan surprised."

Vivian smiled.

"Why was he?" Talia asked.

"Because he isn't sure if this group is advanced enough to have the experience in a mature and nonjudgmental way. He didn't think that they had processed enough of their baggage. And, honestly, he's concerned."

Taylor thought for a moment as Vivian continued, "I feel it will be a good experience for Austin. It'll be challenging and emotionally inducing, but still really good for him after he's had a chance to process everything that goes with it."

"Do you think it would be good for me?" asked Taylor.

"Only you can answer that one," said Vivian as she stood and got ready to leave, Danielle with her. "If you feel this experience will be beneficial for you in some way, then by all means do it. And if not, don't feel obligated to attend. You make the choice."

"What do you think?" asked Talia.

Taylor shook her head. "I don't know."

"Me, neither," said Talia. "Normally I would say absolutely not, but this doesn't seem like a normal situation."

"Yeah," said Taylor "I've never had an experience like this before. Not even close."

Talia looked at Taylor questioningly. "Never even...?"

Taylor paused, looking at Talia.

"I thought you and Austin have been going out for a long time."

Taylor's face turned pink. "Well, yes, we've been sort of going out for over a year now, but I haven't seen him without his clothes on." She paused. "We haven't had sex yet. I never have."

"You're still a virgin?" asked Talia.

"Yes," replied Taylor unashamedly.

Talia looked down for a moment at the necklace she was wearing, pondering her past. "Can I ask why? And if you don't want to tell me, that's okay."

Taylor smiled. "It's okay. I've just chosen to wait."

"For the right person?" asked Talia.

"And the right experience," replied Taylor. "I've dated a lot of guys and been close with three or four of them, but never had the right experience. I've had plenty of offers, but never felt that the time was right."

"Even with Austin?" asked Talia. "Never had the time or opportunity with him? Or is he just not into that?"

"Oh, I know he would when I'm ready, but..."

"But?"

Taylor took in a deep breath. "When I was growing up, I watched my parents. My father was so in love with my mother. He would do and did anything for her. But she had a lot of issues. She had postpartum depression after my younger brother was born. I was ten years old then and had to pretty much raise my brother because my dad had to work and my mother just stayed in her room with the curtains shut. She was so emotionally unavailable and broken. I found out later that she had had several affairs before my brother was born. Each time my father forgave her and welcomed her back. But I could see what it was doing to him."

Taylor forced a smile. "When I was eleven, I came home from school and found my dad with tears running down his face. He told me my mom was going to be away for a little while. She just needed some time for herself. I wouldn't see her again for another ten-and-a-half years."

"Wow," said Talia.

"Yeah," Taylor said. "She showed up at my grandparents' last summer and took my brother for the day. She wanted money and figured that was the easiest way to do it."

"What about your dad?" asked Talia.

"He died when I was fifteen," said Taylor stoically. "They said it was an aneurysm, but I know it was actually a broken heart. He was still in love with her."

"I'm so sorry, Taylor," said Talia.

"That's why I haven't slept with Austin or any other guy yet. When I do, it will be a full commitment. Not a one-sided relationship like my parents. I could see the pain it caused both of them. I don't want that for me or my future husband."

"How is your relationship with your mother now?" asked Talia.

"It's better because I've done a lot of emotional clearing. But I still don't trust her."

Talia was quiet for a moment. Taylor watched her rub the pendant on her necklace, wondering what she was thinking. It seemed as if their conversation had released some deep seated memories in both of them.

Looking back up at Taylor, "Do you know why I wear this?" asked Talia, holding out her necklace.

"It's beautiful." The pendant on a silver chain had a broad tree inside a circle that lay over an almost symmetrical labyrinth. "Why?"

"To remind me who I am. Who I *Be*."

Taylor examined it closer. The red, green and blue tree over the silver image was exquisite. "What do you mean?"

"It's a Shechinah over a Native American Tapuat."

Talia smiled at Taylor's confused expression. "To the Hopi Indians of America the Tapuat is a symbol of a mother and child's connection. My relationship with my mother was terrible as well. When I turned twelve, a stranger came to me. She said her name was Ashira. That means 'wealthy' or 'rich one' in Hebrew. She gave this to me." Talia gazed at it admiringly. "In Arabic it's 'Sakinah,' which means peace and calm. I so needed that in my life then. In Hebrew, 'Shechinah' means the dwelling place of the divine presence of God. I wear it over my heart to remind me of my relationship with my feminine Higher Power." She turned her attention back to Taylor. "With the way my life has been, I have to admire your decision about not having sex until you're really ready."

Taylor felt a sense of closeness with Talia for sharing this with her.

"I know the Authenticity Training has nothing to do with sex, but it still blows my mind thinking about it," said Taylor.

"So do you think you'll go?" asked Talia.

"Maybe, but I can tell you this: if I do go, Austin is going to be blown away by this hot body of mine."

They both laughed.

Chapter 43 – Joseph's Issue

"Mr. Ryan. Can I speak with you privately for a moment?" asked Joseph. He had waited until most of the others had left before approaching.

"Can it wait until tomorrow?" asked Nicholas.

"Sure," said Joseph, not wanting to impose. If he could procrastinate long enough, maybe Nicholas would change his mind and Joseph would not have to deal with the emotions that were rising within him.

Nicholas turned to leave, then stopped and turned back to Joseph. He had planned to leave with Mrs. Ryan, but felt impressed to speak with Joseph right then. He asked Vivian to excuse them, which she did, smiling at Joseph.

"Let's talk now, Joseph," said Nicholas, walking to a more secluded place. "What's on your mind?"

"I would like your permission to be excused from doing the Authenticity exercise."

"You were actually one of the ones Mrs. Ryan was talking about. We feel you need to have this experience."

"Why?"

"There are things you need to learn."

"I feel really uncomfortable with this, though."

"That's understandable, but that is part of why we are doing this training. We give you a safe place to push you beyond your comfort zone," said Nicholas.

Joseph didn't respond. He folded his arms, a look of apprehension crossed his face.

"Before I excuse you from this exercise, how about you tell me why I should."

Joseph glanced at the ground. "The religion I belong to prohibits sexual relationships before marriage." Nicholas didn't respond. He waited for Joseph to continue, which he didn't.

"And your point is?"

"That is my point. I'm not allowed to have sex before I'm married. And since I'm not married, I feel I should not attend the exercise."

"There will be absolutely no sexual contact or anything like it whatsoever in this exercise. Even consensually. And if anyone does or even tries to, they will have to leave immediately and possibly get expelled from the Institute. So rest assured that won't be an issue."

Joseph looked down in thought.

"Is there anything else?" asked Nicholas.

"Well, yes. In the church I belong to, we are not allowed to look at a naked woman. Pornography is strictly forbidden."

"I respect that," said Nicholas. "And your dedication to your church. But I want you to tell me why you personally feel this way."

Joseph had to think about that one. "I don't know. That's what I've always been taught."

"Have you ever considered how you personally feel about what you were taught?"

"I've never thought about it. I just did what I was told without questioning it."

"You went with what you were taught by your family and culture, correct?"

"Yeah," responded Joseph sounding unsure.

"I want you to think about it now. I know this is bringing up some significant emotions and belief patterns. I will even walk you through it if you want my assistance," responded Nicholas.

"I would really appreciate your help."

"Okay, then. Why is it bad to look at the female body?"

"Because I was taught that if I looked at a woman's body it would lead to lustful thoughts and premature sex."

"Have you ever seen a female and found her attractive?"

"Well sure. All the time," said Joseph. "I'm not gay."

"Did you ever have sex with any of them?"

Shocked, Joseph replied, "No! Of course not. I've never been married, so that's not allowed."

"But you did have those feelings didn't you?" asked Nicholas.

"Yeah. I think all guys have those feelings. Don't they?"

"Yes." responded Nicholas. "And females have those thoughts and feelings as well. My question to you is, are these feelings evil or are they good?"

"I've never thought about it that way. I was always told those feelings were dirty and wrong."

"What about after marriage. Are those feelings still bad?"

"No, it's okay then. In fact, you're supposed to have those feelings after your married, so a married couple can have children."

"So the feeling is the same before and after marriage. It's evil and wrong before, but good and expected after you get a piece of paper, from the government, saying it's okay?"

"When you put it that way, I'm not so sure."

"I'm not saying that you should go and have sexual relations with just anyone," said Nicholas. "Sexuality is a very sacred and powerful energy, not to be used flippantly. But you shouldn't be afraid of it either. Think about that, Joseph. You've been doing very well at the Genius Training and have even started some of the Ascension Training. You have the tools and knowledge to deal with this concern."

Neither one spoke for a minute. Joseph was clearly trying to process what Nicholas had said.

"What was the number one principle I taught you when you first got here?"

Joseph seemed puzzled. "I don't remember."

"The field and your shoes?"

The light came on in Joseph's mind. "I remember you knocked me on my back the second day I was hauling rocks in the field, tore off my shoe and threw it into the trees."

They both said in unison "I'm not the thoughts I think or the emotions I feel."

"Right," said Nicholas. "They are not your identity."

Joseph nodded.

"So here's what you're going to do, Joseph. Don't eat anymore tonight. Get your stuff and go up to the training circle. Take plenty of water and if you need to, spend the night up there. I'm giving you tomorrow off from your routine and classes. I will tell Sheena so you don't have to worry about your responsibilities."

"What am I going to do while I'm up there?" asked Joseph.

"You're going to talk to your higher power. Your God. I know a lot about your church. Some of my close friends are associated with it. Vivian's grandparents also belong to it. I even had an in-depth conversation with her father about intimacy in marriage before she and I got married. That was very revealing coming from him."

Joseph had a puzzled and curious expression on his face.

"I want you to go and meditate on this. Inquire of your higher power about it." "What do you mean? What am I going to ask?"

"In your belief system, you believe God is the Father of your spirit. Right?"

"Yes," said Joseph.

"And that God is the Father of all spirits?"

Joseph nodded again.

"Then, if God is the Father of all those spirits, he must know about procreation, reproduction, and sexuality, having created all those children."

Joseph was shocked.

Nicholas continued, "You're going to ask your God about sexuality. In its truest form."

"What! I can't do that," said Joseph.

"Why not?" asked Nicholas.

"There are certain things you don't talk to God about. You don't question authority and you don't talk about dirty things. You just don't," Joseph said matter-of-factly.

"Really," said Nicholas. "Is your God so fragile that you can't have an open and honest conversation with him about something that affects everyone on this entire planet?"

Joseph was clearly upset. This had struck a nerve deep within him.

Nicholas waited to let him calm down. "You can do this, Joseph. Talk to your God openly and honestly in a conversation like we're having now. Take your notebook and pen. Write down your questions, then ask, and write down whatever comes to your mind without thinking about it."

Joseph didn't know what to think. Nicholas put his hand on Joseph's shoulder and looked him straight in the eye. "I don't think you're giving your God enough credit. I think he can handle the subject better than you think he can. Give it a chance. I think this experience will surprise you."

Joseph still didn't respond. He didn't know what to say.

"I'll tell you what," Nicholas said. "You go up and do this, and if by tomorrow night you honestly feel you shouldn't do the Authenticity Training because your God told you that you shouldn't, then you will not be required to attend Friday's exercise. There will be no dishonor in it. I'll tell the others you were assigned to help Rex and Dakota that day. They're close by in Durango now, anyway. However, if your God tells you that you need to do this exercise, will you attend and participate fully?"

Joseph looked down, then back up at the sky. "I don't think he will, but if he does, I will. I guess."

"You are going to have to be truly honest with yourself and with your higher power. And I will honor whatever you decide." Nicholas turned to leave.

"Wait a minute. One more thing," asked Joseph.

Nicholas turned back to him.

"What did Mrs. Ryan's father say to you about sex before you married her?"

Nicholas smiled, "He sat me down and told me his version of the birds and the bees."

"Which is?" asked Joseph curiously.

"Men have to have sex because they are weak and can't control themselves. Women are obligated to have sex with their husbands because of the belief that the original mother of the human race made a mistake. He also said that women shouldn't enjoy it. If they do, they are carnal, sensual, and devilish."

Nicholas chuckled "And that you should only have sex at night, in the dark, with as many clothes on as possible, and only when you want to conceive a child."

Nicholas's expression changed, his smile faded. "Vivian's grandparents had thirteen children. Her grandmother died from breast cancer when their youngest child was only a year old."

Nicholas paused for a long moment, then began to smile again. "Vivian's father also told me that if I had sex with his daughter before we were married, he would shoot me."

Surprised, Joseph smiled. "He didn't really mean that, did he?"

"Yes. I think he really meant it," said Nicholas. "He said it while cleaning his 12-gauge, Browning double-barreled, over-under shotgun. He was very serious about it." With that, Nicholas turned and left.

Chapter 44 – Austin's Authenticity

Austin found Nicholas walking to the kitchen.

"Can we talk for a minute?" he asked.

"Sure," said Nicholas.

Austin caught the apple Nicholas pulled out of the blue ceramic bowl on the counter and tossed to him. The glass double doors that led out to the patio stood open, the outdoors beckoning.

"It's about Friday. I don't have a problem with doing the clothing optional experience," said Austin, not wanting to make eye contact with Nicholas and feeling embarrassed. "Seeing other people without their clothes on doesn't bother me, but …"

"But what?" asked Nicholas.

Austin didn't answer right away. His eyes followed the patterns of moss between the slate stone of the patio, searching for the root of what he was thinking.

"I'm not sure," he said.

"Would you feel condemning or judgmental, seeing your peers how they truly are?" asked Nicholas. "No façades whatsoever?"

"No!" said Austin. Startled, his eyes flew to meet Nicholas's. "I'm not judgmental at all."

Nicholas's eyes narrowed skeptically. "Are you concerned that your peers may judge you?"

"No," said Austin emphatically.

A hawk called and the breeze picked up, stirring the silence that had fallen while Austin tried to disassemble his jumbled thoughts.

"Well, maybe a little bit. I just don't know what the point of this exercise is."

"The point of the Authenticity Training," said Nicholas, "is to provide a safe environment to be vulnerable, to be completely open. You and the others have been doing the Genius Training program for several weeks now. You've done well with the memorization techniques. And because of your increased memory capacity, you are able to recall a large number of facts. That is a major part of the Genius Training, but it's not all. A true genius has an increased capacity in all aspects of their being. It includes your physical health, hence the emphasis on nutrition and exercise. It also includes your mental, emotional, and etheric health. Letting go of limiting beliefs and emotional baggage allows a person greater capacity at a higher frequency."

Nicholas paused for a moment, catching Austin's eye. "The limitations of ego, pride, selfishness, and jealousy are significant blocks to reaching your greater potential."

"Yeah, I get that," said Austin, "but how does being naked in front of other people help with that?"

Nicholas shook his head. "To get through the experiences of this mortality, people create barriers to the world outside of them. These blocks are created to protect you. And that's a good thing. We need to have those boundaries or else we could easily be harmed. We need to be shielded from the low-frequency energies that would bring us down. However, these barriers to the outside world also create limitations that hold us back. These limiting beliefs influence the story that we create about our lives. It becomes our reality."

It took Austin a moment for his eyes to adjust to the dim light as he and Nicholas entered the forest at the edge of the manicured lawn. The air smelled moist and cool. Decaying leaves and brush littered the narrow trail that cut through the pines.

"Is that a bad thing?" asked Austin.

"No, not necessarily," said Nicholas. "If you like your life the way you have created it to be, then it's fine. However, if you or others around you have subconsciously created a story for you that you don't like, you're stuck in it. You will continue to live the story of your life unless you change that story.

"So how do you change that?" asked Austin.

"You create a new story," said Nicholas.

A new story, thought Austin. *What would my story be if I could go back and write a new one?*

"When you first came here last year," continued Nicholas. "You were living the story of the wounded victim. The issues you received genetically at conception and then through your experience as you were growing up became the basis for your story. The experiences with your parents, especially your father, your relationship with money, school, and people...your perception from all these experiences facilitated the creation of the story of your life. That's what you created and you're getting the results of that.

"But now, looking back at my life," interjected Austin. "It wasn't so bad. If anything, it was probably pretty average. I like how my life is now."

"Yes," said Nicholas. "But could you say the same thing fifteen months ago?"

Austin considered Nicholas' words. *Fifteen months would've been just before I met Nicholas. That was also right before I met Taylor.* Thinking further, that was the time when his parents stopped paying his bills. Financially, it was the lowest moment in Austin's life. His lowest point in school as well. More and more examples flooded his mind.

"Things were a lot different then," said Austin

"Yes," nodded Nicholas. "Think of the story that you were living then, the experiences you had leading up to that point were what helped you create that story."

"Yeah, that was a really sucky time in my life. I was dealing with a lot of issues." He looked over at Nicholas. Now that the trail was a bit wider Austin was able to move up next to him. "I'm glad that I was able to find you, then. You changed my life."

"I didn't change your life," said Nicholas "You did. I presented you with the tools and ideas, which you strongly resisted at first, but eventually you were the one who chose to apply them and change your story."

It was beginning to make more sense now. The days he had spent hauling rocks out of the field last summer, all the emotional clearing and release he had done. Using his creation board and working on his relationship with money and other people.

"I did do it, didn't I?" said Austin.

"Yes, and you did very well," said Nicholas. "But you're not done yet. Those experiences and your choices have brought you where you are now. You are changing your story, and your life is changing accordingly. But now, to move you and the others to a higher level, you need to let go of the limiting belief of separateness."

"**Separateness**?" asked Austin.

"Yes, **the belief that you are separate from that which is outside of you**."

The scratch of pine needles across his neck and face drew his attention away from Nicholas. He moved to push the branch out of the way. With a soft snap the branch fell to the ground. Austin kicked it aside and continued on after Nicholas.

"Explain," he said.

"Everything and everyone are all part of a much greater oneness. However, humankind has been taught for eons that we are separate from the world around us. History is full of experiences that perpetuate this great lie. In the Judeo-Christian belief of Eve and Adam being expelled from paradise because of sin, they were separated from God, which resulted in many negative thoughts and emotions. Emotions like guilt, shame, regret, and the need to regain that which was lost. At least, that's the story that we are told in the Old Testament and Torah."

In one of Austin's classes on memory techniques, he had learned to speed read with a great deal of accuracy and retention. Between that and his super exponential learning class on how to download information, he was able to get information from books very quickly. Part of his homework had been to read many classical works, including the Koran, Torah, Bhagavad-Gita, Apocryphal records, Old and New Testament, along with other religious and secular texts.

What Nicholas was saying made sense. Thinking of many other stories, Austin put together the pieces.

"The belief of separateness permeates all of mortal experience," said Nicholas. "The belief that you are separate from your environment, separate from wealth, separate in your relationships. The list goes on and on."

Deep laughter and the pounding of feet on the pavement rushed by as Austin and Nicholas stepped onto the road. Austin watched his friends, losing sight as they went around the bend. He jogged over to the other side of the road where Nicholas stood waiting. They continued down the trail, following it as it wound under the canopy of branches and leaves.

"Why do the Authenticity Training? Because the belief of separateness has created barriers in all aspects of one's life. Seeing others how they truly are brings up the emotional baggage that reinforces the belief of separateness. Emotions such as ego and pride, vanity and conceit, shame and guilt. Those are all emotions that have resulted from the belief of separateness."

"I think I'm starting to understand," said Austin. He was lost in thought for a moment, thankful for Nicholas's patience.

"How about this," said Austin. "I'm okay seeing others as they truly are, but what if I just wear my swimsuit? Mrs. Ryan said this is clothing optional. That means we all have the option to choose, right?"

"Yes," said Nicholas. "You have the option to come to the experience or not."

"Don't you mean go to the experience," said Austin. "You're not going to be there are you?"

"I mean come to the experience. And yes, Mrs. Ryan and I will both be there." Nicholas paused. "The experience is optional because it's not part of the Genius Training program that you've chosen to do. However, it will be ineffective for you if you don't attend and participate fully."

Austin knew what Nicholas meant. He swallowed hard "So, it's not optional for me then. I'm required to come?"

"That's not what I'm saying. You still have the choice. But if you really want to up your game by changing the story you tell yourself, you will at least consider participating in the experience.

"Go spend a few hours with Joseph up at the train circle tonight," said Nicholas. "You need to learn something about this from him."

Chapter 45 - Joseph's Question

Austin's afternoon wasn't turning out like he had planned. He was hoping to spend some time with Taylor but hadn't been able to find her.

Curious, he ran up the trail. *What can Joseph possibly teach me?* Slowing to a walk, Austin entered the clearing to find Joseph sitting in the center circle.

The training circle or 'Masters Wheel' was actually several circles. A shallow ditch in the ground outlined the almost forty foot circle. Inside this circle rested four smaller ones, about three feet in diameter. Another circle sat centered between these four, about twenty-four feet in diameter. In this circle, four straight lines were drawn on the hard, packed earth fanning out from the northern circle. Centered between these lines rested the circle where Joseph sat. Some other unusual geometric patterns were placed systematically around the inside of the greater circle.

"What are you doing here?" Joseph asked.

"Mr. Ryan said I need to come up here and think about Friday's experience."

"You, too?" said Joseph.

"Yeah," said Austin. "I mean, like, it's really no big deal getting naked with a bunch of people."

"Riiight," said Joseph nervously. "I don't have a problem with that, either," he said with a shrug of his shoulders.

I thought I was the only one dealing with issues about this, Austin thought. He knelt down, aware of the discomfort that hung in the air, and traced one of the patterns painted on the ground inside the largest circle.

Joseph spoke up. "Then why are we both here?"

Austin could hear the laughter in his voice. He stood and looked Joseph in the eye.

"Actually, Mr. Ryan said I needed to learn something from you."

Surprise and then annoyance flashed across Joseph's face.

"So what are you doing?" asked Austin.

"It's actually kind of personal," said Joseph.

"Okay. I don't mean to interrupt. Do whatever you were doing and act like I'm not even here. I won't say a word." Austin sat on one of the split logs surrounding the nearby fire pit, pulled out his pocket knife, and started to whittle a piece of wood he'd found lying on the ground. He ran up here often, but had never taken the time to really appreciate the beauty that surrounded him. *I'll bet there is some sort of symbolism in all this.*

A rope course of sorts, The Challenge Tower, sat in its own circle about thirty feet from the Masters Wheel. A tall pole stood in the center with eight thick ropes attached near the top. The ends of the ropes were evenly secured in the ground around the perimeter of the circle. *I wonder what that's for?*

Austin caught Joseph's eye when he looked back at the Masters Wheel. Joseph was sitting cross-legged in the dirt. He looked down and began to whittle. He tried to ignore Joseph, but was curious. He watched him out of the corner of his eye. Joseph glanced over a few times and Austin tried to appear uninterested. The next time Austin looked up, Joseph was sitting with his eyes closed, his lips moving slightly. *It seems like he's talking to someone.*

"He is," came a voice in his mind.

Startled for a moment, Austin sat still thinking about who or what Joseph was talking to.

"His higher power," came the voice again.

The conversation going on in his head and what he was observing from Joseph puzzled Austin. With a shake of his head, he went back to the piece of wood in his hand.

"Why don't you make yourself useful and make a small fire?" Joseph said a while later. "I have some things to burn."

Austin nodded and took some wood shavings, newspaper, and a few small sticks from the nearby firebox. Austin watched the pen in Joseph's hand move quickly across the page. He tore it out of the notebook, ripped it up, and threw it in the fire pit.

"What is..." Austin started to speak but catching Joseph's eye, stopped himself.

Joseph stood silently by Austin and they watched the paper turn black. Austin watched Joseph repeat this, but couldn't stay quiet any longer.

"I know I said I wouldn't talk, but can I make a suggestion?"

"What would you recommend?" Joseph asked.

Austin could see the annoyance on his face, but continued.

"If you are releasing negative emotions by writing them down, it will go faster if you do a little tapping."

"Thanks," responded Joseph genuinely.

"Anytime," said Austin. Glad that he could make a useful contribution to Joseph experience.

Austin sat and stared at the fire, listening to Joseph's quiet tapping. Another paper was ripped and burnt. Austin watched Joseph return to sit at the table for a moment before picking up a nice leather bound book that lay on the other side of the table. He stood, unable to look away as Joseph sat both arms on the table with the palms of his hands open and facing upward. Austin observed him staring up at the sky. *It seems like he's having a conversation again.*

A feeling of jealousy began to fill Austin as he observed Joseph's experience. *Spiritual jealousy: how can he get answers so clearly and I can't? Interesting emotion*, Austin thought. It changed to envy, then inadequacy, and then admiration. Austin felt a greater amount of respect for Joseph after watching the communication.

The clearing was quiet when Austin left and started back to the house. *I learned more about Joseph this afternoon than the whole time I've been here*, Austin thought.

Chapter 46 – Demetri

"I'm going to do it," Joseph said.

"I thought that would be the answer," said Nicholas. "I suggest you spend some more time today actively clearing any remaining emotions, thought patterns, or limiting beliefs about tomorrow."

Austin walked into the middle of the conversation. Unsure what to do, he slowed down, intending to take a different path, away from Nicholas and Joseph.

"Austin," said Nicholas. "Join us."

With a slight nod, Austin fell into step behind Nicholas.

Joseph looked back at Austin cautiously. "I think I've already cleaned out everything that I can."

"Then let's see how well you have done," said Nicholas. "The next level is helping others."

From where he stood, Austin could see the questioning look Joseph gave Nicholas.

"I would like you to talk to Demetri. He is having some struggles with tomorrow. Maybe you can help him and also help yourself," said Nicholas. "Austin, go with him. Watch, listen, and learn."

Austin began to speak, but before he could, Joseph turned and headed back to the house, leaving Austin to follow.

They found Demetri in the gym. Trails of sweat dripped down his back, soaking the band of his shorts, a red t-shirt carelessly tossed aside on the floor. The punching bag swung haphazardly from the chain that held it securely to the ceiling.

Austin and Joseph stood inside the door watching the physical release of emotions on display.

Demetri wiped the sweat off his chest and turned to get his water bottle, sitting on the floor next to his shirt.

"Sup," he said casually when he noticed Joseph and Austin walk over to some chairs that lined the wall.

"How's it goin'?" said Joseph.

Demetri took the chair next to Joseph, stretched out his legs, crossing them at the ankles. Austin could tell there was a lot going on in his head. He sat and waited to see what Joseph would do.

"I'm assuming that display we walked in on had something to do with tomorrow?" Joseph said.

That question opened a door for Demetri. Concerns and issues came rambling out.

Demetri must think a lot of Joseph to open up that easily, thought Austin. He continued to watch in amazement as Joseph seemed to know what Demetri was thinking. It was a combination of genuine validation and active listening, mixed with incredible intuition that was almost as good as Nicholas's.

Austin was concerned for a moment that his presence may inhibit Demetri, but it didn't appear to. As Joseph helped Demetri work through the layers towards the root issue, Austin began to feel his own concerns about the next day were quite trivial.

Demetri explained how his grandfather was very rigid in his belief system, especially when it came to women. His grandmother and seven-year-old father had escaped the controlling and abusive man and fled their country. When Demetri was fifteen, he found out his father's only sibling, a younger sister, had been left behind as a means of control by her father.

"I know that's why my grandmother died an early death. The heartbreak at having left her only daughter behind to become the property of another. Alive, but better off dead. I can't help but think that's what screwed up my biological father, too."

Demetri continued with hardly a word from Joseph, describing the mental and emotional abuse he had suffered until the age of eight, when his father died and mother got remarried shortly after. His stepfather had been an improvement, but only slightly. When his mother died three years later, his stepfather's girlfriend had raised him through his teenage years until he was seventeen.

"Honestly, in retrospect, she was the best thing that ever happened to me. At least, until I met the Ryans. If it wasn't for her and them, I'd be dead by now."

Demetri stopped speaking for a moment, took a big drink from his water bottle, and nodded towards the door. Austin could see the emotions turning behind his eyes. He turned and saw Katja, Grace, and Raul walk in and sit down.

"So what does this have to do with the clothing optional exercise tomorrow?" interjected Austin.

Joseph scowled at him for his abruptness.

Not bothered by the question or the growing group around them, Demetri continued, "Growing up, I was taught some things about women that I just can't reconcile with what's going to happen tomorrow."

Austin was surprised as Demetri began talking about extreme promiscuity and extreme celibacy. And that it's a woman's fault if a man has lustful thoughts and feelings. Austin could tell the conversation bothered Grace, who was nearby listening. She kept moving about as if trying to get comfortable and couldn't.

"Wow! I thought I had issues with this," said Joseph. "You're more screwed up about this than I am."

"Thanks, man. That makes me feel sooo much better." They both laughed.

"I don't know what to do. Should I go tomorrow or not?"

"You get to figure that one out on your own," said Joseph.

"Are you going to go?" asked Demetri.

"Yeah. Nicholas says I have to." They both laughed again.

"I don't necessarily agree or disagree with the things I was taught growing up, but it still really bothers me."

Austin continued to listen until Demetri started talking about women and the atrocities in some parts of the world.

"Why is it a woman's fault?" Katja said.

"Some people think that if a woman raises her kids right, then there wouldn't be so many problems in the world."

"Well, maybe if the fathers would stay home and be a responsible parent, these problems wouldn't happen," she said.

Things got more heated when Mia and Miranda showed up.

Austin could feel the contention growing. He watched Joseph, wondering what he was going to say.

"Hey, guys, wait a minute," he started, but Katja cut him off.

I am out of here, thought Austin, exiting the room. *I've spent enough time cleaning my own emotions, I don't want to pick up any of theirs.*

Chapter 47 – Authenticity Experience

Friday morning came in clear and beautiful, not a cloud in the sky. The air was warm but not uncomfortable. It seemed like the day was perfectly tailored for the upcoming experience.

Taylor did her morning routine as usual, with an extra emphasis on releasing anxiety and uncertainty about the day ahead.

She didn't see Austin during her workout or later at breakfast. That wasn't surprising because their schedules were slightly off. *I wonder if Vivian and Nicholas intentionally set up our schedules that way.*

The dining hall was unusually subdued that morning. Quiet laughter came from a corner table where two girls sat chatting while they ate. A small group of guys were quietly talking at a table across the room, very different than their usual boisterous conversations. Taylor chose a seat somewhere in the middle.

"So, are you going today?" Talia asked, sitting down with her tray next to Taylor.

"I'm going," she said. "But I don't know what I'm going to do when I get there."

Talia nodded as she started into her breakfast. "I guess Annie was having a breakdown. I heard her talking to Mia."

"What was she saying?" asked Taylor as she worked on her breakfast.

"She was saying things like it was stupid and a waste of her time and money. I think that was actually a cover for what she was really going through. Mrs. Ryan said that if the Authenticity Training doesn't bring up a person's emotions, then it's not working."

"Well, it's sure brought up my emotions. I burned up eight pages this morning," said Taylor.

"Eight? You're better than I am. I only did six." Talia laughed. Taylor joined her.

Logan, who was sitting with Pajori and Mani at a far table, looked over at the girls, making eye contact with Talia. He swallowed hard and turned back to his conversation with the other guys.

Taylor saw the exchange and looked at Talia. "Is there something going on between you two that I don't know about?"

"No. We're just friends, but I can't help but wonder what our ancestors would be thinking about us doing this exercise today."

"What do you mean?" asked Taylor between bites.

"Logan and I are from a similar culture. There are a lot of customs and traditions that go back thousands of years. I think if they were here today, they would be freaking out."

"I don't know what my ancestors would be thinking, but probably the same thing," said Taylor.

They continued eating in silence.

After a moment, Talia looked back at Logan. "But I can't help but think if a few of them, probably the women, might actually be proud of this."

Taylor smiled at her. "Yeah. I think so, too."

Walking in with Raul, Joseph made eye contact with Taylor. He gave her a nervous smile as he got in line for breakfast.

"I wonder who else is not going to be there today besides Annie?"

"I don't know, but either way, it's going to be interesting," said Taylor, finishing her last bite of gluten-free pancakes. "I actually got the impression that this might be life-changing for some of us."

Austin's alarm went off just as he was tying his shoes. He hadn't been able to sleep much with so many concerns flying through his head. The thought of Taylor being seen naked by other guys really bothered him. *I'm feeling jealous of all these guys and they haven't even seen her yet.*

He had been so occupied with getting his grades up and keeping his scholarship that he hadn't been able to spend much time with her. What free time they did have was spent with her grandparents and brother. They had never actually had sex. He had seen Taylor change her shirt before, but it was from the back. That was the extent of what he had seen of Taylor.

The book he had hoped would distract him wasn't helping, so he decided to spend some extra time working out.

Sam, his personal trainer, wasn't around when he got to the gym, but he went ahead and warmed up before hitting the weights. Still feeling restless and a little agitated, he headed outside for a run on the upper trail through the woods. He was somewhat surprised that he didn't pass anyone.

Taking a break at the training circle, his thoughts jumped back to Taylor. He desperately wanted to talk with her that morning, or at least text, but he didn't know what to say. *Am I the only one concerned about today, or is she, too?* He ended up putting his phone in his pocket and ran back to the house.

He stopped by the kitchen to pick up some breakfast before heading back to his room to get cleaned up. The doors to the dining area were opened, so he glanced in, hoping to see Taylor. Joseph, Raul, and Demetri were at one table, and a few girls were at another, but Taylor wasn't with them. Somewhat disappointed, he took his plateful of scrambled eggs and continued to his room.

Austin started to panic when he realized it was 9:52. Wearing a T-shirt and board shorts, he slipped on his sandals. As he started to leave, he checked his phone. *Better not take this*, he thought, tossing it back onto his bed before shutting the door behind him. Starting down the hall quickly, he glanced back at the bedroom door beside his. *I wonder what Joseph is going through right now?*

It didn't take long to get to the upper pool area. On his way, he looked for Taylor. He saw Mani and Mia up ahead of him and fell in behind them. Not wanting to interrupt their conversation. In spite of his anxiety, he became aware of the beauty of his surroundings. It was so surreal. The grass, the trees and shrubs. *This place is so beautiful*, he thought, *a veritable Garden of Eden*. Not realizing the irony of his own thoughts, he saw Sheena up ahead of them. There were others passing through the open gate to the pool area. He saw Grace and Miranda, but still no Taylor.

"Good morning, Mr. Davis," said Sheena with a smile on her face. "Glad you could make it."

Sheena was dressed smartly in a two piece swimsuit under a very attractive sundress. *Even in a swimsuit, she is still so professional*, thought Austin.

As Austin entered the pool area as he had done so many times before, he admired the beauty of the place. The large main pool in the center was more than fifty yards long and at least twenty-five yards wide. Five waterfalls from rock cliffs on the far side filled the pool. To the far right were three medium-sized hot tub-pools surrounded by a lazy river that connected to the main body of water. Two beautiful Oriental-style bridges allowed passage over the river and to the far side. A large, grassy area on the far left went around the cliffs to a wooded area behind it.

The large rock cliffs that the waterfalls came off of had trees and shrubs on top and appeared completely natural, even though it was man-made. The interior was honeycombed with caves and tunnels that were carved and stained to seem like real rock. There were all sorts of secret nooks and crannies, even a hidden grotto where they could peer out from behind one of the waterfalls. There was a full size kitchen, bathrooms, and meditation room, along with a machine room that housed the pumps and equipment for all the pools. A larger room inside also acted as a gathering area and theater. Austin often wanted to spend some time there alone, pondering and thinking because of the tranquility and peace he felt there. The sound of the flowing water was so soothing, but all too often someone else had the same idea.

Austin snapped out of his observation when he realized how many people were actually there. At 9:58, it seemed like he was the last one to arrive.

The other students were clustered around tables in two areas. One on the south side close to a grassy area where the other guys were, and the other on the north side by some long banquet tables where three groups of girls sat near the roundtables of the patio area. Farther to the north by the banquet tables was a smaller hot tub and covered pagoda with the sides open.

Trying to decide where he should sit, Austin saw Taylor. She was sitting with her back to him talking to some of the other girls.

"You made it just in time, Joseph," said Sheena. Turning around, Austin saw Sheena close the tall gates through which he had entered.

"Hey, man," nodded Joseph as he passed, heading towards where the rest of the guys sat.

Unsure of himself, Austin followed. He sat down next to Logan and Raul. Mani was talking to Raul about his morning workout. The white lounge chairs and tables were set up loosely on the east side of the pool. Austin tried to act casual and confident. Looking around, Austin noticed that Will and Demetri weren't there. In fact, including himself, there were only six of the other guys there: Pajori, Joseph, Mani, Raul, and Logan.

Glancing over to where the girls sat, he noticed there were a lot more girls here than he had expected. Besides Taylor and Danielle, Talia was there, along with Kay, Meeki, Ching, Mia, Grace, and Miranda. Farther over by the pagoda, sat Alex and Davi, away from the main group of girls.

There are almost twice as many girls here as there are guys, thought Austin, surprised. For some reason, he thought it would be the other way around.

With the gate doors shut securely, Sheena passed between the two groups over to the entrance to the pool house and changing building. Nicholas and Vivian emerged, both wearing white bathrobes. Austin couldn't tell what they were talking about, but noticed that Sheena nodded as Nicholas and Vivian came forward to address the groups.

With the pool behind them, Vivian stepped forward between the two groups, Nicholas standing confidently behind her.

"Hello, everyone. We're glad you could all make it today," said Vivian. "We couldn't have picked a better day to do this. So, without further ado, let's get started. The purpose of this exercise is to help you learn who your authentic self is, who are you really. No facade, nothing phony or fake.

"The first years of life, humans are very real. As we grow older, we begin to acquire baggage, limiting beliefs, and negative emotions. We create barriers to protect ourselves from the outside world to keep us safe from emotional harm. That's needed to keep us safe. You don't want to wear your emotions on your sleeve, but in most people, this covering we create to protect us from others also hides us from ourselves. We don't know who we truly are.

"Like when we have talked about clearing chakras, certain emotions get stuck in certain places in the body. For example, the throat chakra is associated with truth and is blocked by lies, specifically the lies we tell ourselves. This usually happens over time, reinforced by negative experiences where we create stories, real or imagined, about our experiences. It gets embedded at a subconscious level, so most people aren't even aware of it. You cannot lie about who you really are. Who you really Be. To truly be successful and happy in life, **you need to know who you really Be**."

Vivian paused to make sure she still had everyone's attention. Her audience was completely silent and captive. Some because of her words, most because of anxiety and tension for the upcoming experience.

"Another block in almost everyone on the planet has to do with the third eye chakra, located in the center of the forehead. This is the chakra of light or truth, and deals with insight. It's blocked by illusion. All the illusions of the mortal experience. The illusion that we are programmed with through our culture and upbringing. The greatest illusion is the belief of separateness or isms. Things you think are separate and different are actually one and the same."

Talia was bold enough to raise her hand. "Can you give us an example of that?"

"Yes," replied Vivian, obviously pleased with the request. "An example is all the isms in the world. Racism, chauvinism, sexism, classism, ableism, ageism, culturalism. The belief that one group or person is separate than another for whatever reason. This is the basis of all the atrocities in the history of this world, collectively or individually."

"When people believe in isms, they can feel justified, even compelled to harm another person who they perceive as different than themselves."

"It's like your right arm attacking your left foot because it's different than the arm. But, in the end, it's actually hurting itself."

"We are all actually one and the same, yet we live as if divided. We are all one people. It's called collective consciousness. Everything is connected."

Taylor was still feeling anxious about the experience, but still listened intently to Vivian's words. She truly wanted to understand the meaning of this experience. Not sure exactly what she was asking, she raised her hand.

Vivian paused, "Yes, Taylor?"

"You said everything is connected. Does that mean more than just people?"

"Great question," said Vivian. "Yes. It's not only people who are connected to each other. It's everything on, under, and above the earth. It's all the plants, animals, insects, even the elements. Even the belief of the separation of the elements is an illusion. Air, water, fire, earth: it's all the same thing, just organized differently at an atomic or molecular level. So, when the environment is harmed, it's actually hurting everyone. Another example is if someone were to harm an animal. Since everything is connected, then everything is harmed. Even the person doing the harm."

Austin thought about striking the horse, Incident. He suddenly felt shame and wondered if Vivian was referring to him. He didn't look at the others, in fear that they were all looking at him.

"Hence the nature of this experience," continued Vivian. "You not only have the opportunity to see yourself as you truly are, but you can see others as they truly are.

By so doing, you can see the truth in you. Who you truly Be."

Becoming more serious, Vivian surveyed the group. "So here are the rules of this exercise. If you feel you cannot abide by all of these rules, you are welcome to leave before we begin. In fact, we actually request you leave, so as not to take away from the experience for the others. We do not want this to be a negative experience for anyone. If you will truly allow yourself to participate in the exercise fully, I feel it can really be one of the most significant experiences of your life. I know it was for me the first time I did it."

Taylor made a mental note to ask Vivian about her first experience doing this.

"I will explain the rules, then you will be given time to leave before we begin if you so choose.

"Number one. And this is absolute. This is not a sexual experience in any way, shape, or form. Even if you feel it's consensual, it's not during this exercise. There will be no sexual contact, even if both parties agree to it. Is that completely understood?"

Taylor could tell Vivian took this very seriously. She wondered if the others realized as much.

"Number two. There is to be absolutely no pointing, gawking, staring, or making judgmental or negative remarks in any way. Or anything like it. Is that clearly understood?" Taylor had never seen her this way.

Nicholas, who had been standing to the side and behind Vivian, now stepped forward. "This will be a very personal and powerful experience you're about to have. Please don't ruin it for the others. If you feel you may not be able to keep these two rules completely, we're asking that you excuse yourself. There is nothing dishonorable about it. You're free to spend the day elsewhere. I would hate to have to expel any of you from the Institute over this."

Taylor could see that he was as serious about this as Vivian was.

The other students looked at each other, but no one got up to leave.

"Okay, then," said Vivian, the smile returning to her face. "Please respect each other and take advantage of the experience. This will be a once in a lifetime opportunity for most of you. And remember, this is a safe place.

"Marti and Geri have brought us up plenty of food for the day," she said, pointing to the long banquet tables on her left. "Also, there are some books to read if you would like. You know where the restrooms are if you need them. There are also paper and pencils available for doing emotional clearing. I highly recommend you each do that while you're here. Whether your own thoughts or emotions or anyone else's, please address them quickly as they surface. And they will.

"You're welcome to go anywhere in the fenced area of the pools. The hot tubs are all available." Vivian thought for a moment. "There are plenty of towels available also. For hygienic reasons, we request you use them when you sit down. Also, for you men. Obviously this experience may cause certain physiological responses. That's totally understandable and to be expected."

Taylor noticed that some of the guys were blushing at Vivian's comments, including Austin and especially Joseph.

"That's another reason to have a towel close by. It's going to happen, just try to be as discreet as possible. Remember, no judgment of yourself or others.

"We will be having lunch at 1:00, then there will be an activity after. We'll finish at 5:00. Are there any questions?" Taylor looked at Danielle, who shrugged her shoulders, not knowing what to ask in this situation.

Vivian looked at Nicholas, wondering if she had forgotten anything. Nicholas shook his head. "You're welcome to disrobe to your level of comfort. Don't feel obligated or pressured either way. 'Optional' means just that. As much or little as you prefer." She paused again as if to ask if there were any questions or concerns.

"Okay then. Have fun." She and Nicholas turned and walked to the far north side of the largest pool.

Taylor looked at Danielle again, then Talia. They both seemed uncertain what to do next.

To her left, Taylor noticed that the guys were sitting there looking at each other without a word. She wondered who was going to go first. Then she realized that Vivian and Nicholas had placed their robes and towels on two lounge chairs and were now in the pool.

"They seem like they do this all the time," said Talia, who was also watching.

Taylor turned back to the guys. They were talking quietly amongst themselves, not daring to look in the direction of the girls.

"Well," said Danielle, "I'm not going to if nobody else is."

Taylor was about to speak when she was interrupted by a loud yell.

"Cannonball!"

Pajori had discarded his swimsuit and hit the water with as big of a splash as he could create. No sooner than he had done so, Mani and Raul followed.

"Fine, then," said Talia, getting up to get a towel.

"Okay," Taylor said to Danielle. "Let's do this." She gave her a high-five.

"Yeah!" they said in unison.

Leaving their towels and swimsuits on the lounge chairs, they walked confidently to the edge of the pool.

Taylor made eye contact with Austin. "Nice shorts," she said as she jumped into the pool, followed quickly by Danielle and Talia.

Seeing Taylor naked for the first time, Austin didn't know what to think. Even with the emotional clearing he had done earlier and his conversation with Nicholas and Joseph, he still didn't know what to expect. While listening to Vivian's instructions at the beginning, he wasn't sure if he was feeling excitement or terror. *What was Taylor thinking about it? What's she going to do? What am I going to do? What's everyone going to think of me if I don't?* The questions kept coming.

He hadn't seen Nicholas and Vivian get in the pool, but he could see them now. His brain felt like it was short circuiting. It's like it had no idea what was happening. Searching for context for the experience, but finding none.

It wasn't until Taylor walked by that Austin snapped back to the reality of the situation. He had no response to her nice shorts comment.

Not wanting to be outdone, he took in a deep breath and got up. Taking off his shirt and throwing it onto the chair, he noticed Joseph had a look of almost panic on his face.

Resisting the urge to make a smart remark, Austin said, "Hey, man. You okay?"

Not making eye contact with Austin, Joseph replied, "Yeah. I'm fine. I'll be in, in a minute."

Austin was about to speak when a torrent of water smacked him from behind. He turned and saw Mani and Taylor neck deep in the water, laughing.

"Oh, yeah," he said jumping into the water behind them, his shorts still on. He went all the way under. When he came up, Taylor was swimming one way and Mani the other. All of the other guys except Joseph were in the pool now, to the left of Austin. The girls that were in the pool were all clustered to his right. Nicholas and Vivian were on the far side in the middle, across from Austin.

Trying to decide which way to go, he pulled off his shorts and threw them in a wet pile by his chair. He wanted to talk to Taylor, but had no idea what he would say to her in this situation.

He was about to go over, when he noticed Sheena walking by with a towel to give to Joseph. She was fully participating in the exercise. At that moment Austin turned and joined the other guys.

It didn't take long before they were all laughing and enjoying their experience. The guys started to mingle with the girls, with Mani being the first to swim to the girl's side of the pool.

Austin was actually starting to enjoy himself. He had never felt so free. But even then, he wasn't sure if he should swim over and talk with Taylor. He could see her enjoying herself while swimming and talking to some of the others. He casually avoided her, but wasn't exactly sure why, not intentionally staying away from her, but secretly wanting her to approach him.

Surprised, Austin saw Joseph in the water. He hadn't seen Joseph get in, but nonetheless, he had disrobed and was talking and joking with Raul. It actually seemed like he was having a good time. Austin smiled. *I hope this is good for him*, he thought.

After that much time in the pool, Taylor was starting to feel waterlogged. Climbing out of the pool she walked confidently to her chair and picked up a large white towel that she had placed there. She decided to go to the grassy area and dry in the warm sunlight.

Talia, Danielle, and Taylor were in the shade of a broad maple tree. Danielle had a towel draped over her and appeared to be taking a nap. Talia was writing in a leather-bound notebook.

After the initial shock at the beginning of the exercise, Taylor found that she was actually having fun. She thought she was going to need to do some more emotional clearing during the exercise, but with pen and paper in hand, she found that she had very little left to clear. So, she allowed herself to enjoy the experience. The sunlight felt like it was giving her a new life that she had never before realized.

After almost an hour, she became a little concerned about getting too much sun. Earlier, she had gone to the tables with different materials on them for the participants. From one of the three large Kintsugi bowls she picked up a container of lotion specifically made by Geri for this occasion. While she was there, she noticed a few books on the table. One of them caught her eye, so she picked it up. Knowing You, by Camile R. Rigby. *That looks interesting*, she thought, taking it with her.

The next hour passed quickly as Taylor was totally engrossed in the story. When Vivian and Sheena approached, Taylor was surprised and a little disappointed.

"Ladies, would you like to join us for lunch?" asked Vivian. Wearing a beautifully elegant sheer sundress, she and Sheena, who was still completely in a natural state, were going to different parts of the garden where everyone had spread out to enjoy the day. Some were still laying in the sun, others were in the shade, not wanting to get sunburned.

"Yeah. We'll be right there," she said.

"We are eating back at the main pool," said Vivian as they continued on.

Taylor placed a folded blank paper to mark her page and got up. A cool breeze blew in, so she wrapped her towel around herself. Talia and Danielle were also getting up.

Taylor bent down to pick up her book and when she got back up, she was surprised. She had seen the others, including Danielle and Talia, but this was the first time that she actually got a clear and close-up picture of Danielle. Not looking at Taylor, Danielle had gotten up without her towel. Taylor could see the many scars on her arms and legs and other places on the front of her body. A little startled, Taylor turned away, not wanting Danielle to know that she was staring at her.

"Ready to go?" said Talia, putting her towel over her shoulders.

"Yes!" said Danielle. "I'm famished. I don't know why, but I'm really hungry right now."

As the three of them walked back to the main pool Taylor thought, *I wonder what that's all about? There has to be a story behind those scars.*

Chapter 48 – Lunch

When they got back to the pool area, they found some of the white tables and chairs removed. Only three empty tables remained with six chairs around each table.

Taylor and her group were almost the last ones to arrive. She saw Austin sitting at the far table with a white towel wrapped around his waist. He smiled at her generously. She returned his smile, wondering what he was thinking.

Most of the others were already sitting down and there were only a few places left to. As Taylor approached, she could see name tags on each chair. She would be sitting between Talia and Pajori. *I wonder what Nicholas and Vivian are up to.*

As if on cue, they came up behind her, Vivian still wearing her sheer sundress, while Nicholas had a towel wrapped around his waist. *They seemed so relaxed and comfortable in this experience*, thought Taylor. *I wonder how many times they've done this before.*

"Will everyone please find their places and have a seat?" said Vivian.

Sitting down in her assigned chair at the far opposite table from where Austin was sitting, Taylor noticed Davi coming in from the garden, a towel wrapped around her body, another one over her shoulders, and a third one on her head. She nervously found her seat between Mia and Meeki at the center table.

"How is everyone enjoying their experience today?" asked Vivian.

A general murmur of approval came from the group.

"Make sure you're all using plenty of sunscreen," she said. "Or you will pay dearly tomorrow. Marti and Geri have provided us with a culinary masterpiece for lunch today. Feel free now to help yourselves to whatever we have here," she said pointing to three long banquet tables to her left. "After everyone is done we have an activity planned for you."

Wonder what that means, thought Taylor. She noticed a stack of papers in the center of the table and some pencils.

"Dig in," said Vivian, pointing to the tables.

Danielle was the first to get up, followed by the others at the middle table. Not feeling shy, Taylor joined them. Still wrapped in a towel, she talked freely with the others.

Returning with her plate full of food, she passed Austin. He still had a white towel wrapped around his waist.

"Hey, Taylor. How's it going?" he asked a little awkwardly.

Though she was very comfortable, she realized that Austin probably wasn't. "It's great," she said. "It's really fun being here."

Talia had come up behind Taylor with her plate of food.

"Can we talk later?" asked Austin.

"Yeah, whenever you want," she said.

As she passed, Austin got up to get himself a plateful of the delicious cuisine.

When Taylor sat down at her own table, she noticed Pajori. He hadn't gotten up to get himself any food.

"Hey, bud," she said. "You okay?"

He had slid his chair up as close to the table as he could. The edge of the table against his stomach. "Yeah, I'm fine."

Taylor had never had an in-depth conversation with Pajori, only the cordial greetings and passing. *He seems really nervous*, she thought.

"So, tell me about yourself," she said trying to lighten the mood.

"Huh?" he asked.

"Yeah, like where are you from? And what do you like to do?"

Taken a little off guard, Pajori started to open up to Taylor. It didn't take long before he was telling everyone at the table about himself. Taylor and Talia especially listened intently while eating their lunch.

After about ten minutes of the others eating, and him not, he decided to get up. "I'll be right back," he said. Leaving his towel on the chair, he walked over to the serving area and began loading up a plate full of food. Taylor couldn't help but look over at him.

The Ryans were sitting on lounge chairs near the banquet tables. After Pajori had filled his plate, he started to return to the table. Then he turned around and walked back to Nicholas and Vivian.

Taylor couldn't hear what they were saying, but noticed that Nicholas had nodded in approval of whatever it was that Pajori was talking about.

Nicholas got up and followed Pajori as he came back to the table.

"You guys want to see something really cool?" he said, putting his plate on the table next to Taylor.

Taylor wasn't quite sure how to answer that, so she just nodded.

Nicholas, still wearing a towel, cleared his throat to get everyone's attention. The chatter from the different tables calmed quickly. Pajori stood next to Nicholas. He began to breathe quite heavily.

"If I could have your attention please," began Nicholas. "You are all in for a little entertainment during our lunch. Mr. Orlov here has some amazing abilities that he has agreed to share with us." Turning to Pajori, he said, "I don't have a watch, but whenever you're ready, go for it." Nicholas put his arm out towards Pajori and backed up to stand next to Vivian, who had gotten up to join them.

Everyone was quiet as they watched Pajori breathing deeply. "What's he doing?" asked Talia.

Taylor wasn't sure. It seemed like he was panting but it was more of a belly breathing, a similar type that they had learned in their meditation exercises.

After about a minute of this type of breathing, Pajori took in a very deep breath and plunged into the pool.

Taylor gazed into the watery depths. It appeared that Pajori was sitting on the bottom of the pool. The group was silent as they watched and waited. And waited. And waited.

After what seemed like an eternity, Taylor looked at Nicholas nervously. A feeling of almost panic was growing within her. He smiled, an expression of peaceful confidence on his face. She shrugged her shoulders questioningly, and he nodded to her.

The silence was becoming unbearable. With so much tension, Mia couldn't help but speak. "Did he drown?" she asked, a fearful expression on her face.

Vivian walked over to Taylor and picked up Pajori's towel. "No he didn't. He's a fish," she said with a grin.

Coming to the edge of the pool, Pajori burst from the water. Almost, but not quite choking he gasped for air. Nicholas came over and helped him out of the pool. Vivian handed him the towel, which he wrapped around his waist and with a big smile on his face he raised his hands high in the air and yelled, "Yeah, baby!"

They all began clapping and cheering as he returned to his table, taking a bow along the way.

He sat down hard next to Taylor, water still dripping off of him. "How was that?" he said triumphantly.

"Wow!" she said. "How did you do that?"

"I was born in the water," he said still breathing heavily. "I think I'm half-dolphin."

"That must be a record," said Talia.

"Not my best time. That wasn't even eight minutes," said Pajori picking up his fork. "When I'm not nervous and have prepped for a while, I can almost double that."

Taylor looked at Talia in astonishment.

They spent the rest of their lunch listening to Pajori answer a barrage of questions. Between bites, he told about how back in Russia, his mother had been part of a group of women who had done Hydro-birthing. There was even talk about dolphin midwives.

Taylor was totally surprised. Even though she had first met him a year earlier, she had no idea he had such a story.

Everyone at the table continued to talk and listen as they finished their lunch. Even for a while after everyone had finished, they continued on. Taylor noticed that a similar thing was happening at the other two tables. She realized that, for the most part, everyone seemed to be really enjoying their conversations and interactions. The fact that they were all partially or completely naked didn't seem to bother any of them.

This is really fun, she thought. *I've never had this type of experience with anyone. Ever!* Listening to her friends, she felt that everyone at her table was having a great time.

After a while Taylor noticed Sheena heading toward Nicholas and Vivian. Turning from the conversation, Taylor saw Sheena hand Nicholas an old school flip phone.

Nicholas stood up and left to take the call. After a few moments, Taylor saw him return and talk to Vivian. She got a big smile on her face as the two of them stood and came over to the rest of the group.

"Is everyone done with their lunch?" asked Vivian when she finally got everyone's attention. "Because if you are, you're in for another treat. First, if any of you ladies are getting too much sun, we have some cover-ups and sundresses for you, if you would like. And all of you, please remember the sunscreen."

Vivian came over to Taylor's table and took one of the papers stacked smartly in a pile. "The next thing for today's lesson is an assignment."

Taylor smiled when she heard Mani give an audible groan of displeasure.

Vivian continued. "It won't be too painful, I promise. On each table you will find eight packets. One for each of you. It is a list of twenty questions and space for the answers. It's 2:38 now. Your assignment is to talk to everyone here and ask them at least three of the questions on the list. Make notes of the answers. You have until 5:00 p.m. sharp. Any questions?"

Talia raised her hand. "Does that include you and Mr. Ryan?"

"Yes. You are to ask us the questions as well." Vivian paused. "And one more thing before you begin. We are going to be having some guests join us for the rest of this exercise. Please feel free to ask them the questions, as well."

"Wonder who that is?" whispered Talia to Taylor.

Taylor thought about who it was, but honestly, had no idea.

Before Vivian could excuse them to begin the assignment, Mani raised his hand.

"Yes?"

"Do we have to talk to each other while we're naked?" he asked.

The others at his table looked at him, a bit startled. They were thinking the same thing, but didn't dare ask.

Unphased, Vivian continued, "Whatever your comfort level. But do remember what the purpose of this exercise is. It's to be truly authentic with yourself and others, even if it's uncomfortable. How you do that is up to you. If there are no further questions, each of you take a packet and begin."

Taylor took one of the packets and a pencil. She opened it and looked at the list of questions. Some of them were pretty general, like *where are you from or what is your favorite food*, to the more personal questions like *what do you think your ancestors would think about you doing this Authenticity Training*, or, *what's one of the hardest things you've ever done.*

Talia was looking at her list as well. "Should we start with each other?" she asked.

"Sure," said Taylor, her eyes falling on question number three. "What is something significant that most people don't know about you?"

The answer to that question would totally shock Taylor.

Austin thought it was kind of strange that for lunch he was assigned to sit between Joseph and Alex. And as far away from Taylor as possible.

Maybe that's just random, he thought, looking at the other tables. The other two tables each had two guys evenly seated between four girls. Austin didn't mind sitting by Joseph, but he seemed a little distant, like his mind was elsewhere. *Which was fine*, he thought, but on Austin's other side was Alex.

Austin had never talked to her before and didn't know anything about her. He tried to strike up a conversation, but all her answers were either yes or no. And to make things more challenging, she hadn't worn a towel or her swimsuit the entire day. This was too much for Austin, having her so close and yet so distant. So he turned his attention across the table to Mia and Miranda. Talking with them was fun, though he kept glancing over at Taylor's table, wishing he could trade places with Pajori. *Especially after Pajori's showing off*, he thought, jealousy rising within him.

He had wanted to say more when he passed her during lunch, but didn't know how to convey what he felt.

Joseph had put on his swim shorts and shirt. "I'm getting too much sun," he said. He opened up a lot more after that.

With Joseph more dressed than all of them, Austin wasn't sure what he should do. The girls at his table all seemed very comfortable with themselves. Austin decided it best to keep the towel wrapped firmly around his waist.

The lunch and conversation after was great. When Vivian gave them their assignment, Austin was hopeful he could spend some time with Taylor, though three questions wouldn't give them much time.

Joseph had started asking questions to Miranda, who was obviously flirting with him.

Austin looked at the list, then to Alex, making sure to keep eye contact or higher. "So, tell me something interesting about you," he said.

Without any hesitation she replied, "I was conceived and born on the continent of Antarctica."

Austin wasn't sure if she was joking or not. She then proceeded to go on for twenty minutes, telling more about herself than Austin really wanted to know.

When she finally stopped talking, Austin politely thanked her and asked what questions she wanted to ask him.

"I don't have any questions for you," she replied matter-of-factly.

Austin realized she hadn't picked up one of the packets. Without another word, she got up and, leaving her towel on the chair, walked to the grassy area on the far side of the pool. He tried to make sense of what she had said.

Still wearing a towel, he got up with his papers and searched for someone who might actually be interested in asking him some questions. Davi came hurrying over. He was relieved to have someone eager to talk to him.

After his conversation with her, she thanked him and went to talk with Mia. As she did, Austin realized how little he really knew about the people here. *Everyone here has a story*, he thought. *Something unique and special about them.*

He went looking for Taylor, wondering if now was the best time to talk with her. Seeing her by the pool talking to Raul, he took a deep breath. She had left her towel on the chair.

He was about to go over and talk with her when he noticed four fully clothed people walking towards Nicholas and Vivian. Drawing his attention away from Taylor he realized who they were. It was Dakota and Rex and their wives.

Austin saw Nicholas, who had been talking to Mani get up, wrap a towel around himself and he and Vivian welcomed their four guests, each with a hug.

"Oh. You're doing the Authenticity Training. That's wonderful," said Kelly. "I don't suppose we could join in?"

"Of course," said Vivian. "Please do."

"Well, Dakota didn't bring his swim trunks. Do you think he could borrow a pair from Nicholas?" said Kelly with a grin.

"Sure," replied Vivian. "He's not using them."

The three couples laughed.

Taylor also noticed the arrival of the two couples.

"If I could please have everyone's attention for a moment," stated Vivian loudly. "These are our dear friends Kelly and Dakota Kavanaugh and Angelica and Rex Houston."

They have a similar energy as Nicholas and Vivian, thought Taylor.

Kelly Kavanaugh was slender and slightly taller than Taylor. She had long blond hair and carried herself with a strong yet feminine form.

Angelica had a similar presence. She had straight, light brown hair and was about an inch shorter than Taylor. If Taylor were to guess by her appearance, Angelica appeared to be in her mid-thirties. *I'll bet she's almost fifty,* thought Taylor.

Even though they were each quite different, both women seemed to radiate confidence and capability in a very graceful and beautifully feminine way. *I hope I look that good when I get their age.*

"They are going to join us in this activity," continued Vivian as the two couples excused themselves. "Please include our new guests in the question exercise.

Feel free to ask them anything you wish. Don't be shy. They're not."

As feminine as Kelly and Angelica were, Dakota and Rex were equally as masculine. Dakota was slender yet muscular, about five foot nine with short, straight dark hair and chiseled features. He walked with a powerful confidence and ease.

Rex radiated the same type of energy. Quiet yet confident, at almost six feet tall his presence was as commanding as Nicholas's. His long curly, dark blond hair reached almost to his shoulders. His deep blue eyes reminded Taylor of Nicholas. *They look so different, but they might as well be brothers*, she thought.

It didn't take long for the two couples to return, ready to participate completely. *They don't seem fazed at all by this*, thought Austin.

He couldn't help but watch them. They each seemed to almost glow. Austin looked away, feeling awkward in his thoughts. How can guys that old be so ripped? The emotion of inadequacy emerged in his awareness.

Acknowledging the emotion, he shook it from his mind. As he looked back, the four of them were beginning to disperse to other areas around the pool.

Austin's awareness shifted when he noticed that each of them was wearing a necklace. They were simple yet beautiful. Kelly's was identical to the one Angelica wore and was a little more elegant than the ones worn by Rex and Dakota. Focusing on them, he realized he had seen something similar before. Nicholas and Vivian each had a similar necklace but didn't have them on.

Austin's mind searched back to the previous year when he first met the Ryans at a business seminar at his school. They each wore a black ring on their right hands when he saw them on stage for the first time. They were almost exactly the same, but Mrs. Ryan's had a single vibrant blue stone inlaid, while Nicholas's ring had a deep red solitaire. The stones on the necklaces and the rings seemed to be made of the same black material.

Scanning the new guests, Austin noticed that each of the four of them wore a similar ring on the fourth finger of their right hands. The only significant difference was the color of the single stones in each ring.

Kelly's ring had a purple stone while Angelica's was dark green. *An Emerald, maybe?* Rex's was deep blue and Dakota's was clear. I'll bet that's diamond or crystal.

Each of them seemed very vibrant, even at a distance. But it wasn't the stones in the rings that had his attention. It was something about the black bands themselves. *I've got to ask Nicholas about the ring thing*, he thought.

Taylor watched Angelica join a group of guys in one of the hot tubs. She had also noticed the necklaces. *They are so beautiful*, she thought.

Wanting to talk with the older couples, she decided to join a group of girls in one of the pools with Kelly.

Grace and Miranda were listening intently while Mia asked Kelly about her first Authenticity experience.

"Don't forget the lotion." said Kelly. "My first experience was amazing. Life-changing, but I didn't use any lotion and burnt my chest. That took some of the fun out of the experience."

"So you've done it more than once?" asked Mia.

"Yes," replied Kelly. "With no regrets, except the lotion thing. It's very cathartic, even when you've done it before."

"Any suggestions for us newbie's?" asked Miranda.

"Yes," said Kelly. "Two things. One. Do the emotional clearing that you've been taught. Do it before, during, and after the experience. It makes all the difference in the world."

"And two," she said smiling. "The lotion thing. Making sure you use it. You may also need help in applying it to the hard to reach places. And this is a big part of that. Who would you ask to help with the lotion? Sometimes in life, you can't do it all on your own. You need someone outside of yourself, who sees you from a different perspective, to help you. That's where mentors and genuine friends come in. They may be able to see something about you that you don't see in yourself. The lotion represents the healing tools, knowledge, and modalities that allow us to deal with our experience in a much easier way. Even enjoyable. Life doesn't have to be hard. Our resistance is what makes it difficult."

Kelly paused, looking at the small group. "So here is my question for you. Who would you ask for help to apply the lotion of life to those hard to reach places of your experience?"

Taylor had to think hard about that one. After her mother left, she felt abandoned. Years later, when her father died, those feelings had gotten worse. Now she felt she had to take care of her younger brother and grandparents. It seemed like she had lost the innocence of her childhood because she had to be the responsible adult at such a young age. Maybe that's another reason I'm enjoying this experience so much. *I can be innocent again*, she thought. *But I still don't have an answer to Kelly's question.*

All these months at the Estate, Austin hadn't realized that the farthest hot tub was actually a mineral pool. Rex was in it talking with Joseph, Pajori, and Logan.

Wanting to join the conversation, Austin approached the pool trying to be confident yet casual. The water was the perfect temperature as he lowered himself in, trying not to disturb them.

Joseph had been asking Rex questions about religious cultures. Austin was amazed at Rex's wisdom and non-judgmental kindness, especially when Logan asked his thoughts about extremely rigid and controlling organizations.

Pajori was quiet, but listened intently.

When there was a break in the conversation, Austin wanted to pose a question to Rex. But unsure what exactly to ask, he said "Ah, Mr. Houston?"

Rex turned his attention to Austin. "You can call me Rex. Do you have a question for me?"

"Yeah. But I don't know what it is."

Rex smiled a disarming smile. "Then let me ask you a question."

Austin was a little surprised. "Okay."

Rex looked up for a moment, then back at Austin. "Have you ever seen yourself?"

"I'm not sure if I know what you mean?"

"I mean, have you ever truly seen yourself, who you really are?"

"Um, I'm not really sure. I've talked with Nicholas about who I Be. Is that what you're asking?"

"Almost. My question is, have you ever seen who you truly are or, with what Nicholas has been teaching you, have you ever experienced who you really Be?"

Austin had to think about that. "I meditate a lot about who I Be, but I'm not quite sure if I've seen who I really am."

Rex nodded "That's an authentic answer. No blame, no excuses. Just the truth."

"So I'm curious," asked Austin. "Why of all the questions, especially with what we're doing here today, did you ask me that?"

Rex smiled. "Do you understand the nature of this exercise?"

Austin didn't respond.

Rex continued. "The real nature of this exercise is to see past all the barriers, all the coverings to the real authentic, genuine self. By seeing it in others, you can more clearly be aware of it within yourself.

"You see, Austin, you are so much more than what you've become. Yes. You've made great strides, especially in the past year. But you have more to do. And the more you do, the more you'll realize just who you really Be."

Austin thought for a moment. *How does Rex know so much about me? Has he been talking to Nicholas?*

None of the others listening spoke, grateful that Rex was posing these questions to Austin and not to them.

"Okay, I understand what you're saying, but I don't know what I don't know. Can you give me something more specific?

"Yes. This experience today. Tell me honestly, when was the last time you thought of being sexually intimate with anyone?"

Austin was a bit surprised. *What does sex have to do with who I Be?* he thought. "Uh, I'm not sure?"

"Think about it," said Rex. "Go back in your memory and find that most recent thought."

"Honestly," Austin said, "it was at the beginning of lunch today."

"Precisely my point. That was almost three hours ago."

Austin didn't understand. "Is that good or bad?"

"You are a healthy young male. Even more healthy being here doing the training at the Institute. Most guys your age, in the world, think about sex all the time, unless they are focused on something particular."

Austin furrowed his brow, still not understanding.

"You are surrounded here by some very healthy and beautiful women doing this exercise and you haven't thought about sex for three hours. That's impressive."

"Okay, but what does that mean?"

"It means that you're making progress. It shows that you're moving forward and ascending. You're starting to wake up to who you really Be. You weren't mature enough to engage in this type of exercise a year ago. But with everything you're learning, all the emotional and mental clearing you're doing. You're growing, and ascending to a much higher level of consciousness." Rex stopped to let his words sink in.

Austin had to think about it. He's right, if I did this last year, I probably would have died with all these girls around, especially Taylor in this situation.

"Thinking about sexuality and having those feelings and desires is normal and healthy. But you're learning to see that there is so much more to life and to who you Be. You're getting more to the point where you can see deeper inside yourself and others. For example, your relationship with your friend Taylor. Has it become more because of today's experience? Is there more to her than what's on the outside? The same thing with everyone else here and the entire world. Everyone has a story.

Everyone wants to be heard, to be validated, to be loved. But so many people are so covered in the lower frequency burdens of life that no one, including and especially themselves, can see who they truly Be."

Out of the corner of his eye Austin could see Taylor with Kelly. Knowing how distracting she was, he quickly turned back to Rex, trying to concentrate on what he was saying.

"To really see yourself clearly on the inside, it may help to see yourself reflected back by others."

Austin wanted to write that down, but he had left his packet on the table so it wouldn't get wet.

"So how can I apply that?" asked Austin.

Rex nodded in Taylor's direction. "Go talk to the girl."

Austin could hear the quiet laughter of his friends as he got out of the pool. With a towel over his shoulders he strode confidently across the grass. He could hear their voices on the other side of the dogwood bushes. His step began to falter the closer he got.

Pajori's deep Russian accent came bellowing from the pool, "Where ya going, Austin?"

Austin swung around and gave him the middle finger.

As he started to turn back, he felt the warm skin of a woman bump up against the back of his arm. He found himself looking into Taylor's surprised eyes. Startled himself, he jumped back.

"I am sooo sorry," he said, trying desperately to maintain eye contact. His face flushing, he abruptly flipped the towel off, threw it around his waist and left without another word.

Breathing heavily, Austin hurried to the main pool. Dakota and a few others were there. The towel remained tight around his waist as he jumped in and submerged himself in the cool water.

Coming back up he tossed the soaking wet towel onto the edge. He swam half a lap across the pool then back to his starting point.

After a few moments Austin realized how many people were in the pool. They were starting to congregate there as the exercise was coming to a close. Joseph had put his shorts on and was sitting by the edge talking with Grace. A growing group was gathering at one side of the pool, listening to Dakota. Austin swam over to join in on the conversation.

Mani had asked Dakota about Nichols's first authenticity experience. Dakota smiled slyly as he saw Nicholas and Angelica approach and jumped into the pool.

"Nicholas had a challenging time with his first experience," said Dakota. "This exercise is not for the faint of heart or the emotionally immature. I don't mean to be judgmental. but not many people can do this in the spirit that it is intended."

Austin watched Nicholas who was nearby listening.

"It really brings up unresolved issues. It's not always easy." Dakota chuckled. "You should have seen

Nicholas the first time he was doing this. He was an emotional mess. Vivian, on the other hand, sailed right through it."

Unabashed, Nicholas interjected, "Yes, but you and Master Houston threw me into the deep end of the pool, as it were. And that's after an emotional beating, literally with a big stick."

Dakota laughed. "We only did that because we love you and that's what you needed the most. Besides, it changed your life."

"That it did," replied Nicholas confidently.

Austin was surprised at watching the comfortable interaction between these two great men. They could tease and have fun, but there was nothing condescending or egotistical about either of them. *I wish I could be like them*, he thought.

Talia had joined the group. "Did you and Mrs. Ryan do the training together?" she asked Nicholas.

"Not the first time," he replied. "I did most of my emotional clearing after my first experience. Vivian watched me and pre-cleared her emotions before her first experience about a year after mine."

Austin thought about Taylor. Would she still have done this experience if I wasn't here? Would I do this if she wasn't here?

Five p.m. came too quickly. Vivian was wearing a beautifully flowing wrap around her waist and her bikini top. Nicholas stood beside her wearing shorts and a T-shirt.

"Thank you all for your participation. We really hope you enjoyed it. Everyone should have at least their swimsuit on now," said Vivian. "You're welcome to stay as long as you want. And please be aware that emotions may continue to surface for the next few days. Keep using your tools and you'll be fine."

Taylor noticed Alex get up and leave in a hurry. Ching, Kay, and Raul followed soon after. The others still mulled around, talking and eating.

Vivian came over to sit by Taylor. "So, are you glad you came today?" she asked.

"Yeah," said Taylor. "Thank you for providing this opportunity for us."

"You're so welcome. I hope you benefited greatly from it," said Vivian.

"I have."

"Did you have a chance to talk to Austin much?"

"Not hardly at all."

"Now's your chance," said Vivian with a smile when Austin walked up.

Chapter 49 – Takeaways from the Authenticity Training

The table sat in the shade of the trees over in a corner of the patio, far enough away to offer privacy but close enough to hear quiet conversation drifting around them.

"If only our ancestors could see us now," Talia said to Logan while they sat chatting by the pool.

Taylor pulled her attention away from the others and sat back and relaxed in the cool shade. It felt comfortable to her after being in the sun for most of the day. She and Austin sat and ate in silence for a few moments, neither one of them knowing quite what to say.

"You seem more relaxed now," Taylor said. "Are you glad the training is over?"

"Yeah, a little," said Austin. He was more comfortable around Taylor now that he was wearing his swimsuit again.

"Can I ask you a question?" Taylor said.

"Sure," he said after swallowing a bite of sandwich. He didn't know why, but the Authenticity Training had really made him hungry.

"Earlier today when we were out in the garden and we literally bumped into each other, why did you run off so quickly?"

Austin swallowed the lump in his throat. He didn't want to tell her the real reason. *Should I make up a story? No, she would see right through that.* "Ah... well, you see," he started nervously. "Something came..." Austin stopped. "I couldn't talk to you then. I just couldn't."

A knowing smile filled Taylor's face as they both started to laugh.

After a few moments, Taylor continued. "You haven't asked me any questions from the list."

"Sorry, I just figured that we already knew the answers for most of them."

Taylor picked up a copy of the questions. Austin watched her eyes as they moved over the page.

"Do you know the answers to all these questions about me?" she asked, turning the paper towards Austin. "Because I don't know them all about you."

He looked at the list. "Okay, you want to talk about it right now?"

"Sure," said Taylor, scooting her chair around the table beside Austin's.

"Do you want to go first or should I?" he asked.

Taylor ran her finger down the list of questions.

"We don't need to ask each other all of them," she said, "just the pertinent ones. You go first."

"Okay," said Austin, checking the top of the page. "Where are your ancestors from?"

"Not exactly sure," said Taylor. "As far as I know, they're all from the United States. But when I was doing some family history research with Joseph, he seemed to think my ancestors were from England or Scotland. Pick another one."

Austin got the impression she didn't want to talk about it, so he quickly went on to another question on the list.

"What are your thoughts and feelings when you first took off your swimsuit this morning?"

Taylor sat there for a moment not saying anything. Her mind wandered back to earlier in the day when she had asked the others the same question.

"Honestly, it was very surreal. I was kind of freaking out about it when Mrs. Ryan announced it on Wednesday. Last night even more so. I had to do a bunch of emotional clearing yesterday and even this morning. I was talking to Danielle right before it all started and I still wasn't sure if I was going to do it completely."

"So what was going on in your mind when you finally did it?" he asked.

"It was really weird. I was almost terrified to take off my suit. But after seeing Talia do it, I decided, why not? I think it was easier to give myself permission than it was to actually follow through with it though. I started to freak out a little, but then I did it. Just to get it over with, I guess."

Taylor paused for a moment, searching for the words. "Standing there without anything on felt so freeing and liberating. I felt very real," she said. "I understand more now why they call it the Authenticity Training, because for the first time in my life I was actually me."

Mesmerized by her words, it took Austin a moment to say anything. "Wow, when I did it, I was terrified, panicked, and terrified."

"How long were you scared?" asked Taylor with a quiet snicker.

"Kind of the whole time," said Austin.

"After I got into the pool, I was kind of distracted."

Austin gazed over at the pool remembering. "I guess I tried to distract myself from the reality of it for most of the day."

"Really," said Taylor. "You didn't feel a sense of peace or relief the entire day?"

"Maybe," he said, leaning back in his chair and flexing his arms behind his head. "Don't get me wrong. I would do it again in a minute, but it was way out of my comfort zone."

"I think that was the whole point of the experience." said Taylor. "That and being genuinely real."

"Well, if that was the purpose, I would say it worked."

"My turn now," said Taylor, picking up the list.

"Here's an interesting one. What are your thoughts about the people who were invited, but chose not to come?"

"I'm not sure," Austin said. "I think I was a little too judgmental at first, like they were so insecure or too arrogant that they wouldn't come, as if the experience was somehow beneath them. But now, looking back at it and talking to the other guys, I think it's fine if they choose not to come. They missed out on a great experience, but I don't feel any judgment towards them. How about you?"

"Honestly, there were some people that I thought would stay away, like Grace and Mia. But they came and I think they had a good experience. Others that I expected to come, didn't."

"Like who?"

"Demetri and Will," said Taylor. "I thought for sure they would be here."

"Oh, did you want to see them here?" asked Austin not liking the jealous sound of his question.

Austin caught the fleeting look of frustration in Taylor's eyes before she answered his question.

"I just thought they would come, that's all. I don't think any less of them for not participating. If anything, I think I respect them a little more if that's what being authentic was for them. Being true to yourself can manifest very differently for everyone.

Glancing down at the paper, Taylor said, "What's your full name?"

"You don't know?"

"You've never told me."

"It's Curtis. Austin Curtis Davis. Curtis is the name of my mom's dad. I was named after him."

Taylor sat back in her chair and eyed Austin. He was a little leery of what she would say next.

"Are you going to tell your parents what you did today?"

"Wait a minute," said Austin. "What about you? Do you have a middle name?"

Taylor smiled. "Do you think I have a middle name?"

"Now that we're talking about it, I assumed your name was Taylor Schaffer." Austin paused. "Well, do you?"

"Eve. Taylor Eve Schaffer. You don't need to ask where it came from because I don't know," she said as the smile faded from her face. "Before my mom left, my dad would call me Evie. I asked him once where that name came from and all he said was that my mom picked it out."

Austin knew that talking about her mother was still a sensitive subject even with all the emotional release that Taylor had done. "Cool," he said hoping to lighten the mood. "Eve is a really pretty name. Do you want me to call you that?" he said smiling.

"No," she said, returning the smile. "You can call me Taylor or Tay."

The sun spread its rays over the small table under the trees, the occupants oblivious to everything except each other, deep in conversation. There were so many things they thought they knew about each other but didn't. Even simple things like favorite foods or colors. The conversation had moved to deeper and more meaningful topics, as well. Austin soaked in the time with Taylor. They hadn't shared moments at this level before. He loved the serious side of her and appreciated how she wasn't afraid to be emotional and passionate about what she believed. He loved how her sense of humor would just pop out of nowhere, causing laughter to surround their little corner of the world. He couldn't remember when he felt so relaxed and comfortable, especially around Taylor. He never wanted this conversation to end.

The noise of clattering dishes startled Austin and Taylor out of their little world. Marti smiled apologetically and winked at them as he went back to cleaning up the dishes.

"Did you get enough to eat?" Marti asked as Taylor and Austin came up to him.

"Yeah," said Taylor, setting her plate on a tray of dirty dishes.

As she and Austin helped stack the dishes on one of the carts Marti had left sitting by the table, she thought about her conversation with Austin. It had been something she had been wanting for a long time. He had finally opened up and talked. For the first time, she felt like she was actually getting to know who he really was without the facade.

As they were working, Taylor noticed Kelly and some of the girls talking on the grass nearby.

"If you want to go chat with the girls, I'll help Marti finish up," Austin said.

"Thanks."

Austin watched her walk away, wishing he was going with her.

"You've got it bad," Marti chuckled. "Help me get this back to the house."

Not wanting to interrupt the conversation Taylor sank quietly to the grass next to Davi.

"So why did you decide to come today?" Kelly asked Danielle.

"I couldn't stop thinking about it. I couldn't concentrate on my job, and Dr. Johnson sent me over to see Mrs. Ryan. She said I was having a hard time because there were emotions that were trying to get out and it was causing me anxiety. I spent the afternoon writing and burning papers. I haven't really done that seriously before, and I wasn't sure if it would even help. I felt better this morning, so I came."

"How do you feel about what happened?" Kelly went on to ask.

"I was still worried about what people were going to think when they saw me, but that's just me. No one has even looked at me weird today. I've lived so long being concerned that my scars are all that people see, but today I noticed that people wanted to be with me and it had nothing to do with my appearance. I still kept the towel close, though."

Kelly reached out her right hand and pointed to the three parallel scars on her left wrist. She then leaned back and gestured to a grove of majestic quaking aspen trees that provided shade to the far side of the lawn. "What do you see when you look at those trees?"

Taylor focused her attention on them. It was as if she had never seen them before. They all appeared similar, but the trunks of each were covered with their own unique blemish. The wind blew through them like a cellist drawing her bow and the rain drum leaves became the winds' larynx. The white sound was exquisite; delicate, yet deep.

Quieting her mind, Taylor stretched out further with her awareness. She was cognizant of the conversation between the grove and Danielle. The scarred trees seemed to speak to her. "*It's okay. It's okay.*"

Looking over at Danielle, Taylor watched the awareness light up in her tear filled eyes as she gazed at the trees.

"They're covered with scars," said Danielle.

"Yet, each one is still so magnificent," responded Kelly. "Everyone has scars. Not all are visible on the outside, but we all have them. We are all beautiful no matter where they are."

Kelly and Danielle continued to talk as Taylor excused herself. She started back to the house, lost in thought about what Danielle's true scars really were.

She pushed open the tall wooden gate, the path naturally flowing from the patio. Her flip flops slapped the ground as she walked. Her wrap fluttered around her, caressing her legs in the warm evening breeze.

The path dropped down a short flight of stairs before disappearing around a stately pine. Taylor could hear Mrs. Ryan's quiet voice somewhere in the distance. Coming around the tree she saw her sitting on an iron bench covered with a light blue cushion the color of the early morning sky. Grace and Meeki were with her.

"I'm sorry. I didn't mean to interrupt," said Taylor.

"You're not. We were just going to the house," Vivian said as she stood. "Would you like to join us?"

Taylor nodded and the four of them leisurely walked through the garden.

"As I mentioned before, I was doing really well with the whole experience," Grace began. "But the longer I was there, the worse I felt."

Everyone's experience is so unique, Taylor thought. *Mine, Danielle's, and now Grace's.*

"What was going through your mind before the Authenticity Training?" Vivian asked Grace.

"When you first announced it, I was shocked. Because of my religious upbringing I couldn't bring myself to do it."

"What changed that?" asked Vivian.

"I cleared a bunch of emotions that I really believe were not mine. After that, I decided to go. In fact, I was actually excited about it."

Vivian was silent, waiting for Grace to continue.

"Then, last night I was talking to Katja. Or rather, I was listening to Katja, Atom, and Demetri have an argument...I mean discussion."

Taylor was puzzled. Why would that have changed her mind?

"What were they saying?" asked Vivian.

"A lot of things. Things about men and women. Things about different religions. Evolution versus the Bible. And things that I believe happened anciently." Grace's usual confident manner was now replaced with uncertainty.

Taylor noticed she was looking at the ground while she walked.

"It sounds like you believe something they said," suggested Vivian.

"Usually that type of thing doesn't bother me. I figure everyone is entitled to their own beliefs, as long as they allow me the same courtesy. But this time it kind of messed with my brain."

"How so?"

"Katja is an atheist and Atom is a staunch agnostic, and I'm totally fine with them being that way. I don't think any less of them because of that." Grace paused. "I guess Demetri's grandparents were very devout in their faith. They aren't Christian, but I'm okay with that, too. He put up a strong argument with them."

"Is that what bothered you?"

"Demetri was saying some things about women that I didn't agree with. Things that he said his grandfather taught him."

"Let me guess," ventured Vivian. "That women are less than men. Not as good, not as strong, not as capable."

"Yeah, that and all the world's problems are because of women."

"There's something more, isn't there?" asked Vivian.

"Demetri said he was taught that it's a woman's fault that men sin. He doesn't personally believe that. But it really made me wonder."

"That belief system has been around for a long time." Vivian paused, making sure the girls were listening. "The truth is that females and males are all equal. Different but equal. That's what brings balance. That women are inferior to men is an archaic thought form that, even now, is giving way to the higher consciousness," said Vivian.

"I did a lot of clearing on that last night and this morning, and was determined to do the training, anyway. Everything was great until this afternoon."

Taylor couldn't help but interject. "What happened then?"

"I was watching poor Joseph. He seemed to be having such a struggle with the experience. I started to feel guilty that I was causing him to feel that way."

"Whoa, whoa, whoa!" said Vivian. "First of all, those were not your emotions. Second, even if they were, they are not your identity. It's not your fault what other people feel. What others think and feel about you is none of your business."

"You can't go through life trying to make sure everyone is perfect. That's like taking away their ability to choose. You can't do that, even for someone you care about. I happen to know today was a very cathartic experience for Joseph. He is a better person for it. Don't take his emotions or anyone else's. You're not a savior. Stop trying to be."

"I've always felt that way though, for as long as I can remember."

"And how's that working for you?"

"Not very well, I guess. If I'm not feeling one person's emotion, I'm feeling someone else's. It seems like no matter what I do it's never enough."

"That's because you can't do it. They have to."

Grace nodded. "That makes so much sense. Thank you, Mrs. Ryan."

As they continued silently to the house, Taylor noticed Grace seemed to be so much more at peace that earlier that day.

Meeki stumbled and bumped Taylor's arm.

"Are you ok?" she asked.

Meeki nodded her head.

"Taylor, would you mind making sure Meeki gets back to her room okay?" Vivian asked.

"Of course not," Taylor said.

"Stop by the kitchen first and get some real salt and some water. Ground yourself and get to bed," Vivian suggested. "You should feel better in the morning."

"I will," Meeki replied.

Mrs. Ryan and Grace headed down a smaller path while Taylor and Meeki went on to the house.

"What's wrong?" Taylor asked.

"Mrs. Ryan said I did too much emotional clearing yesterday and my body is having a hard time processing all of it."

Austin arrived back at the house just in time to see Marti unloading bins of plates and utensils from the back of a four wheeled utility vehicle.

"You gonna give me a hand with these?" he asked.

"Sure," said Austin.

They both proceeded to move the large bins into the kitchen through the service door. Joseph was already in the kitchen helping Geri do the dishes and clean things up from the day's activities. It didn't take long with the four of them.

"Thanks, guys," said Geri when they finished. "We really appreciate your help."

"Hey, Joseph," said Marti. "Would you mind taking the four wheeler back to the garage?"

"No problem," said Joseph, heading for the door. "You want to join me?" he asked Austin.

Austin had never driven any of the four or six wheeled utility vehicles at the Estate. He was a little surprised at how accustomed Joseph was to them. The engines were relatively quiet, and so was the conversation as they drove around to the main underground parking area.

When Joseph turned off the engine Austin realized how quiet the vast underground parking area really was. Austin started to get out, but Joseph hadn't moved.

After a long and almost awkward pause, Austin sat back down and said, "Hey, man, what are you thinking?"

Joseph leaned back in his seat. With everything that had happened the past two years, he had grown to respect Austin. He didn't want to because of his competitive nature, but with all their experiences, positive and negative, he couldn't help it.

"I was just thinking about today. And the past few days," said Joseph.

Austin could understand why he had been thinking about that day. "What are you thinking about the past few days?"

Joseph took in a long deep breath. "This is my third year here. When Mrs. Ryan announced the Authenticity Training, I didn't know what to think of it. I had heard the Masters had experienced it before, but I didn't think we would actually do it."

Curious to see Joseph opened up, Austin listened quietly.

"I've got to admit, of all the training that I have done here, that one was the most difficult and yet most rewarding."

Austin smiled, impressed to see that even Joseph was still learning after being here for so long. "How so?"

"All growing up, there were certain thought forms and stigmas that I was taught. And they were good. I needed to have them when I did. They kept me from making bad choices when I wasn't mature enough to understand. So I'm grateful for what I was taught."

"Is that why today was so hard?" asked Austin.

"Yeah," said Joseph. "I did so much clearing, but I still wasn't going to go. The Authenticity Training seemed to go against everything that I had been taught."

"So what changed it?" asked Austin.

"You did." said Joseph, turning to Austin.

"I did?"

"Well, it was actually Mr. Ryan and my higher power. But you played a part in it."

Austin was still puzzled.

"Mr. Ryan requested that I inquire with my higher power before making the decision to go or not. But even before you came up to the training circle, I had already made my decision. All I was going to do is take my decision to my higher power then go back to Mr. Ryan and tell him that I had done as he had instructed, and wasn't going to go."

"How did I change that?" asked Austin.

"With you there, I realized I needed to give it an honest effort. Maybe it was ego or pride, but I wanted to prove something to you."

Austin felt a bit of competition and his own ego, but decided to remain quiet as Joseph continued.

"In trying to prove it to you, I actually had to prove it to myself. I used to think that I was better than you. Then I realized I was being arrogant and taking great pride in my humility. I realized I was seeing myself in you. Last year with the dancing lessons and Taylor, this spring when you hit Mr. Ryan's horse and your relationship with

Taylor." Joseph looked at Austin. "Then when we spent those two nights in the upper training area. I so wanted to hate you. All those emotions I felt in seeing you were actually what I saw in myself. So, when you came up to the training circle yesterday, I was determined to prove that I was better than you. More spiritual. More powerful. That's when I realized that I was being fake. Phony. Even before the training today, I saw that it was you who is really being authentic." Joseph looked down.

A flood of thoughts and feelings went through Austin. He wanted to be insulted. He wanted to fire back at Joseph, but none of the negative feelings took hold. Instead, a feeling of peace and admiration towards his friend for being truly authentic.

"That's when I honestly asked my higher power if I should do the training. And I got an answer that I couldn't deny."

Austin put his hand on Joseph's shoulder. "Thanks for telling me that," he said.

After a moment Austin tried to lighten the mood. "So now, looking back, are you glad you went?"

Joseph smiled, "Dude, that was awesome. I would do it again."

"Would you be as nervous the next time?"

"I don't think so," he said. "I still have to do some more clearing because of the way I was brought up, but for the first time in my life I actually feel real. Thanks for your help in that."

After leaving the parking area and his conversation with Joseph, Austin felt a feeling that he couldn't describe. It wasn't fake or forced. Rather, it was a feeling of peaceful confidence, a power within him that he had never felt before. He liked feeling that way.

As Austin headed back to his room he felt a strong impression to stop by and talk to Will. He didn't know why, but feeling the prompting, his feet took him passed his own room, down the hall to Wills.

He was a little surprised to see Davi leaving Will's room. As she passed Austin, she smiled at him, an expression of confident resolve on her face.

I wonder what that was about, he thought. Reaching Will's room, he saw the door partially opened. He heard a thud from inside. Pushing the door open, he saw a stack of books scattered in disarray on the floor. Will stood there without his shirt on, His fists clenched as he stared at the pile on the floor.

"Hey, man, you okay?" he asked.

Will looked at Austin, his face red. The anger and frustration seemed to drip from him. "What?" he said, turning his back to Austin.

Not sure if he should, Austin entered the room anyway. "We missed you at the Authenticity Training today."

"What of it?" he said, picking up a rolled up sock from a pile of laundry and throwing it against the wall. It made a soft thud when it hit the ground.

Wanting to lighten the mood, Austin smiled. "So, how's Davi?"

Will's eyes flashed. "Not that it's any of your business, but terrible!" he said, sitting down hard on the side of his bed.

Realizing he had struck a nerve, Austin wanted to speak, but felt it better that he didn't. Instead, he sat down on the floor almost directly across from Will and waited.

Will fell backward on his bed. "The Authenticity Training was supposed to make things better between us," he said, putting his hand over his eyes. "Instead, it ruined it."

"Do you want to talk about it?"

"No, I don't want to talk about it."

Austin waited for a long moment, trying to decide if he should leave and let Will process this on his own. Still feeling compelled that he should stay, Austin remained silent.

"She's so infuriating!" Will started.

"Why?" asked Austin calmly. That opened the floodgates.

"We've been sleeping together for over a month. And now because of this training thing she thinks she can just leave? She doesn't realize how good she had it. She doesn't appreciate me. I gave her my time and attention and she thinks *she* can just end it," said Will. The anger and frustration radiated from him.

Austin remained mostly quiet, other than the occasional question, as Will broke down and began dumping his emotions, venting all over. Intentionally trying to stay out of judgment, Austin had to remember not to take any of Will's emotional baggage on himself.

After almost an hour, Austin finally had to cut in. "Will, are you even listening to yourself? You're talking like she's your possession."

"Is that what I'm saying?" His eyes widened in realization. "That's the way the men in my family have always treated their women."

"Do you really believe that, though?"

Austin then shared some of the things he had learned from the training that day. Things like seeing a person's inner beauty and what true value really is. "These emotions and beliefs may not even be yours."

"You may be right. I'm going to have to do some generational clearing on this, I guess."

Before Austin left, he made Will promise that he would use the emotional release techniques that evening to let go of the feelings and beliefs that he was experiencing and replace them with positive, uplifting emotions like gratitude and appreciation.

"Remember to honestly see people how they truly are, including yourself." Austin paused, more serious than he had been in a long time. "The thoughts you think and the emotions you feel are not your identity."

He looked at Will straight in the eyes. "Who Be you, Will Hastings? Who Be you?"

As Austin left the room, he was amazed at how much he had matured over the past few weeks. *Wow, I really am wise*, he thought, as he walked down the hall. When he turned the knob to his own room, the words came to his mind, "Those were not your words that you spoke to William." For a moment, the impression got Austin's attention. He shook it from his mind. *Of course they're my thoughts.*

Chapter 50 – A New Mission

"I wonder why we're all here," asked Taylor.

Nicholas had called a meeting of everyone that had participated the day before in the Authenticity Training, and even the students who had not.

"I don't know," said Austin, "but it's probably a recap of what we learned from yesterday's experience."

They were sitting in the dining area with all of the chairs facing the same direction. A large screen had been set up at the front of the room. Austin and Taylor sat in the middle section with Talia, Mia, Pajori, and Joseph. Nicholas and Dakota entered the dining area and moved to the front of the room. Dakota took a seat on the front row.

Nicholas waited for the group to quiet down before speaking.

"Good morning, everyone, thank you for coming. The reason I've called you here is to give you some information and get your input on something that is very important. Last summer a few of you participated in some exploration that was done in northern Arizona. At that time, some caves were discovered which contained some very interesting artifacts in them. Recently, Masters Kavanaugh and Houston have made some additional findings near that same area."

The lights in the room dimmed and the screen on the wall lit up. The picture of a canyon appeared. Red tiered cliffs towered above a large green river.

"That looks a lot like the canyon where we did the training a few weeks ago," whispered Austin to Taylor.

She nodded, her attention firmly on the image in front of them.

"You may recognize this area, since you've been there before," said Nicholas.

The image changed to an overhead map. A red dot appeared on the screen. "You may recognize some of the landmarks: "Confucius Temple, Dragon head, Shiva and Mencius Temple, and the Osiris tower. Over here we have the Buddha Temple and Sumner Butte."

The image magnified. "And here we have what is called the Osiris Tower. This is not the same area that we did the training two weeks ago. This is further north. On the other side of the Colorado River," he said.

The image moved and magnified further. "This is the area that I'm talking about," he said, directing everyone's attention to a mesa with a pointed top. "Roughly here, the Masters found the entrance to a very well-hidden cave."

Nicholas stopped for a moment, looking at Dakota as if he was mentally seeking permission to continue. Dakota nodded.

"Their findings there confirmed the information we obtained the previous year."

The image on the screen changed to show a picture of a very old scroll that had been unwrapped.

Taylor strained to see the writing on the scroll. She had seen the writing before, but wasn't exactly sure what language it was.

"This is a picture of a scroll from a Gnostic library at Nag Hammadi. It's from the fourth century A.D. and is called the Corpus Hermeticum, or at least part of it. I was able to obtain this photograph before the original disappeared." "The Corpus Hermeticum talks of many things but one of the specific things that we are interested in is the same information that is found on a Smaragdine tablets."

The image of a thick green tablet appeared on the screen. The tablet was less than an inch thick by about eighteen inches wide and about twenty four inches long. It was a beautiful green, lighter around the edges and darker, and more vibrant in the center. It appeared to be made out of stone, but unlike any other Taylor had seen. She could see characters engraved on its surface, but didn't recognize them.

The next image was a black and white photograph of six of the tablets stacked neatly on top of each other, connected together by two metal bands looped through holes on the right side.

"This is an image taken back in the 1930s of similar tablets found in Southeast Asia. Even though the photograph is in black and white, the tablets seem to be made of a similar green material with almost identical markings on them."

"This next image is of a similar tablet," the screen changed to show a colored photograph of a single green tablet in a stone box. "Found in a very remote place of Australia."

Nicholas continued to click through the images more quickly. They were all similar tablets found throughout the world: The Swiss Alps, the Andes Mountains of Peru, near the Great Lakes in North America, the Caucasus mountains near the Baltic Sea, the Isle of Man in the UK, and a number of them found between Egypt and India. He finally stopped on an image of Dakota standing in a cave in front of a large green stone. It was taller than he was and appeared to be made out of the same material.

Nicholas turned to the group. "I need to remind you and make sure that you're each very clear on something before we continue. This information we're talking about right now is not to be shared with anyone outside of this group. You will not talk about this material through emails, texts, or phone calls, even between each other. This information is very classified. Do you each understand that clearly?" he said, making eye contact with everyone individually. "If anyone has a problem with this, please tell me now."

The group was silent as they looked at each other. Nicholas waited for a moment, then looked at Dakota, who nodded.

"That being said," said Nicholas, "let's continue."

"To our knowledge, these original tablets have all disappeared. Except this one," he said, turning to the screen. "This one you see behind Master Kavanaugh is over eight feet tall by about six feet wide, and we're not sure how thick it is. The characters engraven into it are identical to the other photographed tablets Multiple witnesses saying the same thing. After the Authenticity Training, we started translating the engravings. Master Houston is still doing the final touches as we speak."

Talia cautiously raised her hand. Nicholas turned his attention to her.

"If I may," she said, "What does it say?"

"It seems to be a record written by a priest-king a long time ago named Thoth. In the ancient Greek translation, his name is Hermes of Tyana or Hermes Trismegistus. Trismegistus means 'thrice-greatest' or something like that. I believe it means 'thrice-born.'"

Nicholas magnified the image. "The tablet seems to speak of a transformation process, something akin to alchemy. We should know more within the hour."

Will raised his hand. "Excuse me, sir. This is really cool," he said. "But what does this have to do with us?"

"Good question, Mr. Hastings," said Nicholas. "What this has to do with you is this image here," he said pointing to the screen. The image magnified several times. It showed a picture of a circle about six inches across.

"Can I take this one?" interjected Dakota, getting up from his chair.

"Please," said Nicholas. He stepped away and sat in Dakota's seat.

"The tunnel we had to pass through to get into this part of the cave where we found this large tablet was very small, only about two to three feet in diameter. We could tell that the passageway had been carved out of the solid rock by some sort of mechanical means. But it was not chiseled. It was perfectly formed, uniform the entire distance of roughly one hundred and twenty feet off of the main passageway. The chamber where we found the large tablet is a rectangular room roughly forty feet long by about twenty five feet wide by about sixteen feet high. As far as we could tell, there was no other way in or out of this large room. The tablet itself seemed to be fused into the solid granite wall behind it. There was no way to detach the tablet from the wall. And even if we could have, there is no way you could get such a large single tablet in or out of there to the passageway. And there were no seams on the tablet."

Austin had to think about that for a moment. Not realizing what he was asking, he raised his hand.

Dakota stopped, turning to Austin. "Yes, Mr. Davis?"

"Then how did they get the tablet in there in the first place?

"That's what I'm alluding to," said Dakota. "We're not sure. But it almost seems like the tablet was created in the room, as part of the wall."

Taylor wondered how that could be.

"And that is one of the many questions that we have about this ancient record: not only how it got there, but who put it there. It seems incredibly old. And we find it very curious that it's so similar to smaller versions of the same type of material. Of greatest interest to us, is this image on the top right," he said pointing to the image. It magnified and became very clear.

It looks like a doughnut, thought Austin, *with an elongated hole in the middle.*

"If you closely examine all of the characters, you'll notice they all seem to be engraven into the surface, except this one."

Taylor did as he said. Instead of the image being carved down into the material, the circle with a faint center circle, was raised, convex, jutting out slightly about a half an inch above the surface of the tablet.

Dakota panned the image back slightly. "We find this image particularly interesting. The writing around this particular image speaks of a worldwide flood which is very similar to that of Gilgamesh in the cuneiform texts of the ancient Sumerian culture. It also speaks of a time in history when there was only one continent on earth, not several. We would call that single continent Pangaea. This raised circle inside of a circle we believe is a map of the pre-diluvian continent of Pangaea. If you look closely, it appears to have names of what we believe are cities or significant points of interest on this map."

"I still don't understand what that has to do with us," said Will.

Dakota continued, "The text on this part of the tablet describes how very advanced the inhabitants of this world were at that time. Even more advanced than we are today. The priest king Thoth knew that a major flood was imminent and that it would set the entire world back a very long way. So he created fourteen sets of records that would not be destroyed by a cataclysm and placed them in different areas of the world so that someday that knowledge could be restored. Each set of records consists of six tablets."

Austin looked down. What does that really mean? He glanced over at Taylor, who he could tell was trying to process the implications of what she was hearing. His attention then went back to Dakota.

"Thoth didn't put the exact information on each set of tablets. It's like each set was an intricate part of the whole picture. We have modern translations of some of these tablets, but not all of them."

Dakota looked at Will. "It's not only what's written on the tablets that are important. It's the actual tablets themselves. Whatever material these tablets are made of, it's like some kind of recording device. Like a very powerful hard drive in a computer. The engravings on the surface of the tablets can be translated onto a single sheet of paper, but the real treasure is what is actually embedded into the material. Think of a memory device with a quadrillion terabytes of information embedded into it. Both embed a vast amount of knowledge and information in the tablets. But a compact disc won't do much for you if you don't have a way of reading information off of it. This is where you guys come in. Thoth speaks of two keys that he would leave behind to allow future generation's access to this knowledge. One of those keys he would leave in his place of residence, the place where he had ruled for tens of thousands of years. We have strong reason to believe that today that place is buried deep under the water. Realistically, it's unattainable at this time.

"Thoth would have the second key left in a place called Antium. It would have survived the great flood by being carried by his great-grandson on a boat. A very large boat."

Nicholas step forward, "Thank you, master Dakota." He turned to the group. "This is where you guys come in. You don't have to do this, but if you're willing, I'm asking for your assistance in helping us retrieve this key. With what was found last summer in Arizona, we now have one complete set of tablets. We know what's written on the surface of these tablets, but we need the key to access the knowledge embedded inside it."

Austin thought of what that might entail.

"If you know where the key is," interrupted Will. "Why don't you just go get it?"

"It's not that simple," said Nicholas. "The second key was to be left in a place called Antium. That would be in modern-day Egypt. We happen to know it hasn't been there since a great flood covered that land. The last record that we know of suggests that it made it to Eastern Turkey."

Nicholas turned back and gestured to the picture of Rex and Dakota standing by a tall rectangular rock with a hole near the top. The rock seemed to be about a foot thick, four feet wide and about eight feet tall and made of dark gray stone.

"This is called an anchor stone," said Nicholas. "We believe this and many others were used to keep a large vessel stable in turbulent waters. All of the eight that we have photographs of have engravings on them. Some of those engravings are as recent as 400 years ago, Christian symbols alongside other more ancient engravings. The oldest one that we found describes a vessel created to carry the Key of Knowledge to a new world. Many more things are engraven on the stones which seem to support this idea. We have reason to believe that the key still remains hidden in the mountains of eastern Turkey."

Nicholas stopped and folded his arms. He didn't speak for nearly thirty seconds. Unfolding his arms he continued, "This is not part of the Genius Training program. However, I'm asking for your assistance in retrieving this key. I would like each of you to consider this. At this time, I'm not exactly sure how this would be done, but we're working on it. Do any emotional clearing that you need to and, if you choose to help in this endeavor, please meet with us back here on Tuesday morning. You are all dismissed."

Everyone took their time leaving the room. Austin could tell the others were processing this new information. He wasn't sure what he thought himself.

He could hear Nicholas and Dakota continue to discuss the retrieval as they slowly walked towards the door.

"I think we need more information," said Dakota.

"I agree," said Nicholas. "We're not exactly sure what we hope to find there, or even if it's still there after all these years. Also, if we do go to such a place, we would have to do it soon before we start getting into the autumn months."

"Agreed," said Dakota. "Even though we're already into August, it would take some time to prepare for such an expedition."

"Let's ponder on this further before we make a final decision. We could really use some higher help," said Nicholas.

"I will consult with the other Masters and get more details by then," said Dakota as he exited the room.

Chapter 51 – Austin's Dream

Two days later, Austin awoke with a start. *Where am I?* His mind was swimming. Powerful images flowed through his mind: a great mountain, water, wood, air, fire...No, not fire. Light! A great white light. Blue sky. Then it was gone.

It was a dream. But it was more than a dream. It was in color, intense colors, and all of his senses were involved. The smell of the air. The sound of birds calling. He could even feel the wind on his skin and the great expanse.

He searched his mind, his eyes still closed but moving from side to side like he had been taught when wanting to recall a memory. Focusing on his breathing, the images started to return. A high mountain peak loomed large and barren in the distance. And something else. Something greater.

He opened his eyes slowly. A beautiful canopy of stars shown with vivid detail above him. He lay on his back in a sleeping bag under that beautiful night sky. He turned his head slightly to the right.

On the eastern horizon, the outline of light creeping over the mountains told him that dawn was not far away. *It must be around four or five*, he thought.

He searched his mind again, trying to bring back the dream and the experience in it, but he was distracted, and the image was gone.

His attention was drawn to his left, where he could hear, not far from him, the crackling of a fire.

That's weird for this time in the morning, he thought.

He heard the quiet sound of voices and was aware of movement nearby. After a moment, he began to remember the night before, sitting around the campfire with Nicholas, Dakota, and some of the other students. They had stayed up late into the night, talking about many things, including: ancient world history, the nature of the earth and higher laws of the universe.

Austin had been pondering their conversations as he drifted off to sleep the night before. His dreams had been fascinating, revealing, and powerful.

Nicholas had gotten up moments before Austin had opened his eyes and walked over to Dakota, who was meditating in the lotus position by the fire he had restarted earlier. Nicholas sat down beside Dakota, trying not to disturb his mentor.

After a long moment, Dakota spoke without opening his eyes. "What did you see?" Austin strained to hear the conversation of these two men that he had grown to respect greatly.

"It's not what I thought," said Nicholas.

"It rarely is," said Dakota, his eyes still closed. "Tell me what you saw."

"I saw three men in a large room. Very tall men, probably six-and-a-half to seven feet tall. They were in a large room more than twice their height. Two of the men seemed younger, the third was their father, I think."

"Keep going," said Dakota.

"All three men wore a necklace with some sort of pendant or amulet. A stone that glowed with light. The room did not have any windows or other forms of light that I could see, but the stones they wore gave off enough light that it filled the entire room."

Dakota nodded. "What were the men doing?"

"One of the younger men and the older man were looking at the wall. It had carvings on it...images more than words."

"What was the other young man doing?" asked Dakota.

Nicholas paused. "He was holding an object...a block or cube of some sort. It was green and somewhat translucent. Probably about ten inches thick, but it wasn't a perfect cube. The young man had his left hand on it."

"What did you see next?" asked Dakota.

"Another younger man came in, probably in his late teens or early twenties. All four of them had long beards." mused Nicholas.

Dakota smiled and nodded.

"The younger man wanted the other three to come with him."

"Where?" asked Dakota.

"All four of them went through a very small passageway and through some dark halls. The necklaces they wore gave them light, the only light in the passageways."

"Did the youngest man have a glowing stone like the others?" questioned Dakota.

"Yes, they each had a necklace with a stone that glowed brightly on it, like an LED light bulb.

Dakota nodded, his eyes still closed, "And where did they go from there?"

"They traveled through hallways, up some stairs, and even up a ladder. Eventually they emerged on top of a vessel. A large wooden vessel. An ark," said Nicholas with surprise. He paused, processing the thought that he had just perceived. "It was massive," he exclaimed.

"So they came out on top of this vessel, describe the vessel." continued Dakota, who was not surprised.

"It seemed very long. The roof was mostly flat, but slightly sloped to each side. There was a raised section about six feet wide that extended along the length of the ship. It was moving...floating. I saw water all the way around it, except..."

"Wait." interrupted Dakota "Was anyone else there?"

Nicholas paused for a moment, "Yes. There were other people there. Women. Two or three women and some children. A small baby and at least one child."

"Keep going," said Dakota.

"The four men went over to stand by the women and children."

"What were the women doing?" asked Dakota.

"They were looking at something," said Nicholas.

"What?" Nicholas thought out loud for a moment. "A mountain. A very large mountain. Not far from them. Actually, the mountain was an island, and they seemed to be moving towards it. Propelled by some unknown means."

"Keep going," urged Dakota.

"That was it," said Nicholas.

Dakota was silent. Nicholas waited on his younger mentor.

After a few moments, "What does it mean?" asked Nicholas.

Dakota took in a deep breath held it for a moment then blew it out his mouth. "Go back to the image. There's one more piece at the end what else did you see."

Nicholas closed his eyes. "That's it. The boat. The water. The mountains." Nicholas paused again. "There were birds flying around. I remember seeing that."

"The island," said Dakota. "The mountain. What was above it?"

Nicholas paused again, breathing deeply, his eyes closed. "Color. Light. A rainbow."

"Yes," said Dakota. "Not just any rainbow. The first rainbow ever to appear on this planet."

Dakota and Nicholas were some twenty feet away, but in the great stillness of that early morning, Austin had heard every word. The images forming in his mind. He had seen it, exactly as Nicholas had described it, and more. The birds. Many white birds. Gulls, doves and more. He'd felt the movement of the ship as if he had been standing on it. He could smell the air, but it didn't smell salty like the ocean, even though he could feel the expanse of the water in every direction. He remembered feeling the wind as it blew the great vessel towards the island. And yet, it was no island. It was the top of a great mountain.

He reached out with his mind further. In the far distance, he was aware of other mountaintops sticking out of the water. Beautiful white, fluffy clouds, and the rainbow. The great rainbow. Vivid and beautiful. The word "covenant" came into his mind. Covenant? What does that mean?

His attention shifted back to the image as he remembered the ship very near the island. The barren peak looming above him. He remembered the great vessel heaving to one side as if some great anchor had caught and pulled the vessel to a stop, less than a hundred yards from the exposed rock of the mountain.

He moved slightly in his sleeping bag, realizing there was a heaviness on his chest. He wasn't cold or uncomfortable. He moved his hand to his chest. To his great surprise, he felt what seemed like a medium size rock on the center of his chest by his heart.

*What the...*The rock was oval, a little smaller than a tennis ball. Austin opened his eyes to reveal a glowing crystal in his hand. The light growing stronger. He wasn't sure if it was because his eyes were more open or if the light was getting stronger, but it was definitely getting brighter. The growing light almost hurt his eyes. He closed them again, but he could still tell the light was getting more intense.

Dakota and Nicholas had stopped talking and came over to Austin. Austin watched out of the corner of one eye as they stood over him. He covered the stone to block the light the best he could.

Austin opened both eyes wide, gazing up at Nicholas and Dakota. They looked at him questioningly. Each mentor brought a hand out and opened it to him. For a brief moment, Austin and his teachers saw the light. Austin smiled.

A very powerful feeling had come over each of them. The moment slowed to last almost a thousand years, until it stopped completely. Then the light began to fade. The feeling subsided. Austin opened his fist slowly, the weight of the object lifting off his chest. When he looked into his hand, the rock was gone.

Chapter 52 – Preparation

Taylor forced her burning muscles to continue the last few yards through the snow. Sweat soaked into the t-shirt that she wore under her coat. Climbing over ice flows had been a new challenge for her, especially at that altitude.

Exhilaration and adrenaline had coursed through her veins that morning when she, Austin, and a few of the others boarded one of the two Agusta-Westland AW109 helicopters for their ride to Torreys and Grays Peak, west of Denver. Their group would spend the day hiking and rock climbing around the Dead Dog Couloir snow field. At an altitude of around 14,000 feet, Nicholas wanted both teams acquainted with the low air pressure and other conditions of that environment.

The experience was more challenging than Taylor expected. Now she just wanted to successfully finish the course. For the past few days, the workouts and training had increased in intensity. Alchesay put them through exercises and scenarios that pushed their bodies to the limits. She could still feel where the harness and ropes had dug into her thighs and hips from her rock climb the day before.

The helicopters and Austin came into sight as she crested the ridge. It was good motivation to have the end in sight.

Smiling, Austin silently helped her take off her pack and load it onto the helicopter. Mia was already on board, breathing heavily.

The blades of the chopper slowly started to turn as Logan began to warm the engines. Taylor's muscles throbbed as she climbed aboard to sit next to Mia. Joseph and Talia joined them from the other side, after waiting for Will, who has the last to arrive. Austin slid the door shut behind him as the engines kicked in and they began to lift off the icy field.

As they began to rise, Taylor peered through the side window to see members of A-team loading on to their helicopter. Something was odd. The other group was loading their gear, which wasn't unusual. The strange thing was that Dakota Kavanaugh was there helping. She hadn't seen him board the helicopters that morning to join them. Another curious thing was the way he was dressed: jeans, boots and a short sleeve t-shirt.

"Here," said Talia, pulling Taylors attention away from the other team. She handed her a capsule of real salt and other minerals and a bottle of water. "This will help with your electrolytes."

Austin's shoulder was better than a pillow on the hour long helicopter ride back to the Estate. She felt exhausted, but satisfied with her efforts.

"Hey, beautiful," Austin whispered in her ear. "We're almost back."

Taylor opened her eyes to see the airfield near the Estate grow larger in the window.

"After you get cleaned up, meet Mr. Ryan in the dining hall to get your teams assignments." Alchesay voice came from the co-pilots seat of the helicopter.

Austin waited for Taylor at the bottom of the stairs. He could see Nicholas's office door from where he stood.

"Mr. Ryan, could I talk to you a moment?" he asked when Nicholas exited his office.

"What can I do for you?" asked Nicholas.

"I was wondering if Taylor and I could be on the same team."

"Tell me why you feel that way."

"We already know each other pretty well and we can work together," said Austin.

"Are you sure it's not because she's your girlfriend?" asked Nicholas.

"No, It's not ...well, maybe that's part of it. But there are other reasons as well. I like her and want to be with her as much as possible, and we've both done a lot of clearing about our relationship. I feel we can work very well together to accomplish this mission."

"I already have you assigned to opposite teams, but because of your honest request, I will consider making a change."

"Thank you," said Austin "I really appreciate it. I will do my best, whatever you decide."

Nicholas walked down the hall, tablet in hand, and entered the double doors leading to the dining room.

"What was that all about?" asked Taylor, as she joined Austin.

"Oh, nothing much, I just had a question."

They joined the others entering the spacious room and took seats at a table near the front.

Nicholas began as soon as everyone was seated and the doors were closed. He spoke of the time he'd spent discussing the mission with Dakota and Rex and the pondering and meditation he'd done before making the decision to move forward with this mission.

"This decision is not one that I've made lightly. It could even be a life or death situation for you. This is not some fictional scenario we are doing. It is the real thing. If everyone does their job correctly, I feel we will obtain our objective. You must all take this very seriously for the safety of everyone involved. Everyone's safe return is my first concern and highest priority.

"You will be divided into two teams, some will go on the expedition and the rest will remain behind to help with communications and support. And a reminder: this is all voluntary. If, after learning your assignments, this is something you choose not to do, I need to know as soon as we are concluded here. If you would like a change in what team you're on, I am open to that option."

A screen descended from the ceiling behind Nicholas and a list appeared.

Austin glanced quickly through the list of Team-A, scanning for his and Taylor's name. They were both absent. He breathed a small sigh of relief and sat back in his chair. His arm curved around Taylor's shoulder and he smiled when their eyes met.

A – Team:
Stephen - pilot. Pajori - copilot.
Demetri – Team Leader
Meeki, Raul, Mani, Ching, Miranda

Support for A - Team
Aki – Base Communications
Annie - 2nd Comm.
Davi, Grace, Alex

The next list appeared a few moments later.

B -Team:
Alchesay - pilot. Logan - copilot.
Talia – Team Leader
Joseph, Will, Austin, Taylor, Mia

Support for B - Team
Shen – Base Communications
Danielle - 2nd Comm.
Kay, Nathan

"That will be all for now," said Nicholas. "I would like A–Team to stay in your seats and B–Team go wait outside, and I will join you shortly."

Miranda hopped up from her seat next to Taylor and hurried over to Nicholas. Austin could hear her excited conversation.

"Grace told me she asked you to change her assignment. I'm grateful that you chose me to go in her stead. I promise I'll make you proud," said Miranda.

"You have nothing to prove to me. I'm already proud of you," said Nicholas. "Work with the others and do your best. That's all I'm asking."

She gave Nicholas a quick hug and hurried back to her seat.

Austin kept his arm around Taylor's shoulder as they followed the rest of their team out the side door. They caught up with the others and sat in a shady area in the grass at the far end of the patio.

"How do you feel about being the team leader, Talia?" asked Taylor.

"I'm a little hesitant, but if Mr. Ryan feels I'm capable, I am willing to do it."

She didn't get a chance to say more as Nicholas joined them.

"I hope you're okay with this team configuration," he said. "I met with Talia and Demetri this morning and they agreed to be the team leaders. We put together the members of each team. I hope the choice of who is on which team has not caused any of you a large amount of consternation. If it has, I recommend you do some emotional clearing on it. If you still have issues with someone on your team that you can't get over, I recommend you bring it to the attention of Talia or myself. At this time, is there any one of you that has strong feelings against being on this team?"

Mia immediately raised her hand.

"Yes," said Nicholas.

"I'm totally fine with being on this team as long as everything is fair."

Nicholas folded his arms and looked at Talia.

"What do you mean by that?" asked Talia.

"I mean, everyone must pull their fair share of the weight," said Mia.

"Are you thinking that some of us may not?" asked Joseph.

Austin could see where this was going fast. He watched Nicholas, who was intentionally staying out of the conversation, waiting to see how the members of the team would work this out.

"I'm saying that when it comes right down to it, some people may be a little selfish," she said, her eyes darting toward Will.

Will bristled and opened his mouth to respond, but Taylor stepped in.

"Mia. I think we can all work well together if we can set our differences aside. We've all been here long enough and have the tools and training. We can do this," she said as she looked from her to Talia.

Austin could tell that Will was bothered by Mia's comment, but impressed that he held his tongue.

"Mr. Ryan," said Talia. "I think we can all work together and make this happen."

Nicholas smiled, "All right, then. One more thing: do any of you have an issue with Talia being the leader?"

The members of the team turned to Will.

"Why are you all looking at me?" he said, spreading his hands. "I don't have a problem taking orders from a girl."

Nicholas turned away. From his spot on the ground Austin could see Nicholas trying not to laugh.

Joseph spoke up. "Talia, we'll support you as our leader for this mission. Right, guys?" he said.

"Sure."

"Of course."

Mia and Will agreed as well, albeit reluctantly.

"You have one hour, and I recommend you choose a second-in-command and talk out any differences you may still have with each other."

Nicholas got to his feet.

"One more thing," he said. "Just so you know, I appreciate all of you doing this. You don't have to. If you feel you can't or don't want to, tell me. You are all the best. Compared to others in the world your age, you are far superior. Not just because of what you've learned here doing the Genius Training program, but because of who you truly are. I employ others here, and elsewhere, that could probably do this mission better than you. And in all honesty, I would actually rather have them do it because of their experience. But you are the ones that are supposed to do this, for your own sake and for mine. Thank you."

Nicholas left the group to ponder his words.

Silence hung over the group until Will spoke up.

"So, who's second-in-command, chief?" he asked.

Talia looked down for a moment and then back to the group. "First of all, I have to tell you, I didn't ask to be the team leader. Mr. Ryan approached me about it. I wouldn't have chosen this on my own, but he asked me to."

"Second, along with Demetri, we discussed all of you and the members of the other team. This group configuration is what we thought would be best to accomplish this mission. To be honest, I had some issues with some of you, but I used my tools, and at this time, I'm good with every member of this team. I promise I will do my best for all of us and for Mr. Ryan."

"We will, too," said Taylor. "Won't we?" she said, looking at the others.

"Yeah," said Austin. "Let's do this."

"Thanks, you guys," said Talia. "Who do you feel should be the second in command for this mission?"

"Who do you want?" asked Taylor.

"I would like the five of you to pick," said Talia.

Austin considered the group and wondered who he would want to be in charge.

"Who would like to be?" asked Taylor.

Will started to raise his hand, but quickly put it back down.

"It may not be very fun," said Talia. "But I'm going to need all of your help with this. We all need to work together. So, here's what I'm going to do. I'm going to say each of your names. You each have one vote. Whoever gets the most votes will be it."

"That seems fair," said Mia. "Who are you going to start with?"

"How about ladies before gentlemen," said Will.

"We'll start with Taylor," said Talia.

"Do you want to be the second-in-command?" Austin said to Taylor.

"I would rather not. But if the rest of you decide that way, I'll do it."

"Who wants Taylor?" said Talia.

No one raised their hand. Austin waited hesitantly, watching Taylor to see what she would do. He was about to raise his hand if she did.

"Okay, then," said Talia. "Who wants Mia?"

Mia's hand shot up, but no one else's.

"Well, thanks a lot," she said, lowering her hand.

"Who wants Austin?" said Talia.

Austin wanted to raise his own hand, but didn't want to be too presumptuous. He wanted to be in a leadership role, but when he really thought about it, it was more for the accolades, not the responsibility. He was a little surprised, though, when Joseph raised his hand.

"That's one vote for Austin," said Talia. "How about Joseph?" she continued.

Taylor and Austin both raised their hands simultaneously.

"Fine," said Will raising his hand.

"That makes it Joseph, then," said Talia. "Are you okay with that then, Mia?"

"I guess, if I have to be," she said, rolling her eyes.

"I really want us to be united in this," said Talia.

Mia sighed. "I'll have to do some clearing on it, but yes, I'll be good with Joseph."

"Are you okay with this, Joseph?" Talia asked.

"Honestly, I may have to do some clearing, myself, but I will do my best."

"That's all I ask," said Talia. "That's all I ask from all of you."

"Are you finished here?" Alchesay said upon joining their group.

"Yes,'' said Talia.

"Mr. Ryan has set up a team building exercise before dinner. This is the first of several that you will be doing the next few days. Your team is scheduled to be down at the lake in forty-five minutes."

The walk to the lake took about twenty minutes. Austin used the time to practice awareness. He scanned the foliage around them and was surprised that it remained quite green this late in the summer. There were areas of grass around the lake and tall trees, their branches casting shadows far into the water. The lake was crescent-shaped and about fifty yards across at the widest point and about eighty yards at its longest. Cattails grew in abundance around the edges on the far side.

They passed A-Team returning to the house on their way from the lake.

"They don't look very happy," said Austin quietly to Taylor. "I wonder what happened."

Alchesay stood waiting for them near the water's edge.

"Here's what you need to do. There are some materials and equipment stacked in the grass over there. You may use anything you find to help you retrieve the chest that is floating on a buoy anchored out in the water."

That doesn't seem too difficult, Austin thought.

"There are a few stipulations before you start. All team members must touch the chest while it is still attached to the buoy and you must get the chest back without it or yourselves getting wet. You will also be timed. Now, let's see if you can do better than the last group," he said with a grin on his face.

Abruptly, Alchesay clicked his watch. "Time starts now." He stepped back and sat down on the grass to watch.

Will left immediately to examine the pile. He tossed a rope, rake and an ax out of the tall grass.

The others headed over, following Talia. Austin saw four large wooden barrels with openings on one end and a small stack of wood as well as various other items.

"Let's see if we can lash these planks together and to the barrels," said Talia.

"A raft," said Joseph.

Austin looked back across the water to the buoy. The chest floated about a foot above the water. *How is the best way to do this?* he thought.

Joseph and Austin pulled the barrels out to a clear area and laid them on their sides and began to lash the planks to them.

"This will never work," said Mia.

"Right," said Talia, "the water's going to run in."

"Even if we just use the two barrels that aren't open, it's still not going to be big enough for all of us," said Will. "What if we made a smaller raft and one of us goes over and retrieves the chest?"

"Everyone has to touch the chest first before we can bring it back," said Joseph.

"Then we could make a smaller raft and go over one at a time and then the last one can bring it back."

"Good idea," said Taylor.

Austin and Joseph went back to tying the planks to two of the barrels. It was still kind of shoddy when they were done.

"We have to go over on this little thing," said Mia. "It'll never work."

"Sure it will," said Will. "Watch. Joe, help me get this in the water."

They each picked up an end and dragged it into the water.

"Guys, she's right." said Talia, "Even one at a time, you'll never get there and back without falling in."

"Have you got a better option?" said Will. He carefully put his weight on the now floating raft, but jumped off when it started to slip off the barrels.

Mia began unraveling the rope, and with Austin's help, bound the planks more securely. This time they used all four barrels and had them on their ends with the open sides up.

Using the rake as an ore and the ax as a rudder, Will and Joseph began to row out to the buoy.

Austin laughed and poked Taylor when she covered her eyes.

"I just know they are going to fall in. Even with your hard work, it still looks really unstable."

Austin caught the smile that hid behind her hands.

Joseph and Will succeeded in touching the chest and made a very precarious trip back. But when Will began to rock the small raft, he and Joseph tipped off.

Laughter rang from the trees.

"You two are out."

"What?" said Will. He stood in the knee high water and glared at Alchesay.

"One of the rules stated that you don't get wet."

"Sorry, man," Austin said to Joseph as he and Will sloshed past him. Joseph shook his head.

"Austin and Mia, you're next," said Talia.

Austin knelt carefully on one side of the raft next to Mia. They worked to balance their weight and row at the same time and made it safely to the buoy. After they both touched the chest, Mia tried to pull it off the buoy.

"Wait, let me untie the rope on this side," Austin said.

Mia didn't wait and pulled on the chest again. Austin tried to counterbalance her movement, but was too late and they both went in. Austin stood up and felt a bit foolish at being totally soaked. He and Mia dragged the raft to shore.

"I know, we're out, too," he said, as he dropped to the ground next to Joseph.

"It's up to us, I guess," said Taylor to Talia.

Using the ax and the rake like oars, they made their way carefully to the buoy.

Austin could see the conversation and concentration as the two girls worked to get the rope untied. The chest stayed attached despite their efforts.

"There's got to be a better way," said Taylor. She glanced around at the shore and some thirty yards from where they had left, she saw something unusual in the grass.

"The axe," said Talia. Taylor held onto her side of the chest while Talia chopped at the rope. A moment later, the chest was free. Together, they slid it onto the raft and headed back to shore. The applause started as soon as they arrived on the beach. That was when they noticed Nicholas sitting in the shade next to Alchesay.

Taylor and Talia carried the chest to where everyone waited and sat down.

"We did it," said Will.

"You took a lot longer than the other team," said Nicholas, "but they didn't completely obtain the objective."

"What happened to them?"

"They built their raft in half the time. They all got on their raft at once and made it over, but on their way back they dropped the chest into the water."

"So, they didn't actually obtain their objective even though they were faster."

Nicholas said. "Taylor, what are your thoughts?"

"Is the raft the only way over there?" she asked.

"What do you think?" asked Nicholas.

Taylor got up and went over to where the pile of tools had been. Austin watched her step further into the tall grass.

"Austin, could you come here for a moment, please?" she called.

He hurried over to where she stood. There, in the grass and underbrush, lay a large canoe. Together, they pulled it out and up into the shade by Nicholas.

"You didn't consider all your options," said Nicholas. "Always be aware of your surroundings and look for other options."

Chapter 53 – Graphene Wristbands

The trip to Nicholas's secret underground office was a new one for Taylor. Nicholas's main office was familiar to her, but she never thought there was a secret room with an elevator behind the large bookcase that lined one wall. Alchesay said he was to escort them to a meeting with Mr. Ryan.

"Did you know about this?" she asked Austin as the elevator continued its rapid descent.

"Yes. Mr. Ryan showed me last year, but made me promise not to tell anyone. Sorry."

The elevator slowed to a stop, and the door slid quietly open to reveal a small room that was adjacent to another larger room. Going through it, they entered Nicholas's second lower office. A large glass topped desk sat off to the side. Suspended on one wall hung a wide flat screen computer monitor and a built in bookcase covered the other wall. Alchesay led them to a steel door opposite the desk. He touched his palm to a pad on one side, and the door silently slid open.

They followed him silently down the concrete hallway to another steel door that was already open, as if waiting for them. The massive room they entered reminded Taylor of something she would see in a movie, like some enormous underground spy center. An imposing table filled the middle of the room and all the seats were taken except two. She and Austin hurried to the empty seats and sat down. A quick glance told Taylor that every person there was intentionally invited. Out of everyone who attended the last meeting, only Atom and Katja were missing.

Nicholas stood as Alchesay took the seat beside him. The lights above them dimmed and the screens behind them lit up.

"When you began the Genius Training program here at the Institute, each of you signed a contract. In that contract, you committed that you would not divulge certain information that you acquire directly or indirectly. Most of the things you have learned here are not a secret. You can share them with the whole world. Eventually, you're going to want to, when the time is right."

"However, what I'm about to show you, you are not allowed to communicate about with anyone besides the people in this room. The only exceptions to that rule are Mrs. Ryan, Sheena, Master Kavanaugh, and Master Houston. Other than them and those in this room, you will not communicate in any way, verbally, in written form, or any other means, including and especially electronic form, about the information I'm about to disclose to you. Is that very clearly understood?" asked Nicholas. "You would not like the consequences of breaking that contract."

The occupants at the table shared a nervous look, as Nicholas continued.

"If you feel you cannot abide by the terms of that contract, now is the time to say. Just raise your hand, and Alchesay will be happy to escort you out. There is no dishonor if you choose not to be here. You will still be able to continue on with the training programs here at the Estate, but not participate in our upcoming endeavors."

Nicholas paused, looking around the room. All hands remained down.

"The microphones in this room are recording this meeting. I am assuming that the answer for each of you then is that you will abide by the terms of this contract?"

They started to nod. Nicholas interrupted, "Everyone say 'yes' out loud."

Taylor and Austin both said out loud "yes" along with the rest of their peers.

"Alright, then," said Nicholas. "Let us begin." The word "Graphene" appeared on the large screen behind Nicholas.

"One of the companies I own has been working on a substance called Graphene for some time now. It's quite an amazing substance." Different images formed on the screen behind him. A pencil, a glass of water, medical equipment, and an elevator rising so high into the sky that the upper levels reached the lower orbit of the earth.

"Graphene is a very light, strong, and flexible substance. It resists corrosion and conducts electricity with very little resistance."

The images on the screen continue to change as Nicholas spoke. "It is quite different from most other materials in many ways. It expands when it is cooled and contracts when heated."

Austin thought about that for a moment. *That's the opposite for most materials.*

"Its molecular configuration is so incredibly strong that a layer one molecule thick is difficult to penetrate. Several layers of the substance are almost impenetrable. Almost," said Nicholas. A picture of body armor appeared on the screen behind him.

"Because of this substance, we have developed microprocessors for computers that are indescribably faster than silicone-based microchips. They can process on a quantum level. Graphene has also allowed us to create batteries with an incredible capacity." All the lights in the room began to fade. The room went almost completely dark, then the lights gradually came back on.

Nicholas continued, "This amazing substance also allows for very efficient light conductivity. You may have noticed there are no light fixtures in this room. It's because the walls actually give off light."

Taylor examined the walls and ceiling. They literally glowed. It was lighter towards the front of the room than the back. Taylor could see the light fade from the walls when the room darkened again for a brief moment.

A picture of the world appeared on the screen behind Nicholas. "The earth itself has an electromagnetic field that surrounds it. It actually has several fields surrounding it, depending on the dimensions you observe. Our bodies also produce electromagnetic fields. There are many fields within and emanating from the physical body.

The main field surrounding the outside of the body is called the primary or purpose field. On most people it extends an eighth of an inch to about three to four inches from the skin."

An image of a human body with a field surrounding it appeared on the screen.

"This field is primarily associated with your life purpose. The secondary field is the emotion field." Nicholas extended his arms out to his side. "It extends roughly three to four feet around you, like you're in a big ball. This field adjusts to your emotions. Some schools of thought call this your aura. If you could visually see this field, it may appear as different colors. Each color in the light spectrum represents a different set of emotions. If someone feels sad or depressed, that field will turn a pale blue. If a person is feeling rage or anger, it will turn an ugly red. Fear is a dull yellow. Each color of the visual spectrum represents a certain set of emotions, positive or negative. All colors except gray have a positive and negative aspect to them. Even the color black has a light side and the color white has a dark side. The positive emotion of gray is actually silver.

"Another field that emanates from a person is called the thought field. This field changes as fast as your thoughts do. In this way, humans are like radios. They transmit and receive energy. When the energy is in the form of thoughts, this third field will transmit your thoughts out infinitely into the universe. Because these thoughts are being transmitted in other dimensions, it happens instantaneously in all space. The thoughts you are having right now are transmitted to other galaxies as fast as you think them.

"We have multiple other fields, but those three are the main ones. The earth itself also has multiple electromagnetic fields, much like the human body does. Every plant and animal also has these fields surrounding and emanating from them. It's very much like being in an ocean of constantly moving water. We are surrounded by, and are part of this energy.

"If you were to drop a rock into a pond, the ripples that emanate from the surface impact, expand outward until they come in contact with resistance that stops or redirects the wave. I call these ripples concentric rings. Our thoughts, our emotions, and our very presence create concentric rings. They are always emanating from us. When the waves of these concentric rings come in contact with waves from something or someone else, the frequency of the waves change.

"Humans have the ability to transmit and receive vibrational frequencies using these concentric rings, very much like a radio. If you tune your receiver to the correct frequency, you tap into what's being played on that station.

"An empath is a person who has the ability to feel other people's emotions. That ability could be a blessing or a curse, depending on how you view it. Empaths have the ability to tap into the emotion field. Whether they're aware of it or not, they can feel an individual's or group's emotion. If they don't know it's not another person's emotions, they may feel that it is their own. An empath in a large group can feel all their emotions and it's like listening to a hundred loud radio stations on at once. A similar thing can happen with the thought field. You can pick up the thoughts of someone else or they can pick up your thoughts. That's one reason why controlling your thoughts is important."

Austin raised his hand.

Nicholas stopped in his presentation. No one had dared ask any questions up to this point. They all were listening very attentively. "Yes, Mr. Davis?" he said. "You have a question?"

"Is it possible to put a thought into another person's mind?" he asked.

Without Nicholas saying a word, Austin heard very distinctly in his mind the word "absolutely."

Austin was shocked. He watched Nicholas closely. His mouth had not moved, but Austin had heard the answer very clearly in his mind.

Austin held eye contact with Nicholas, not wanting to turn away. Not understanding what he was experiencing, he wasn't sure if he had created that thought or that it truly was from Nicholas.

"Test me." Came another thought to his mind.

Austin looked away from Nicholas to Taylor, "Did you hear that?" he asked her.

"Hear what?" she said, watching the silent interchange between the two.

"You didn't hear that?"

Taylor was very curious about what was going on, but hadn't audibly heard anything.

Without a word from Nicholas, Alchesay got up and went to a nearby table. He pulled out a small pad of paper and two pens. He walked over to Austin and tore off the top sheet and handed the rest to Austin along with a pen. "Let's see how good you are, kid," he said with a smile.

Returning to the front of the room Al handed Nicholas the other pen and a single blank piece of paper.

Sitting back in his chair Al looked smugly at Austin.

"Austin," said Nicholas. "I want you to write down the next phrase that comes into your mind. Will you do that?"

Austin's puzzled concern was quickly replaced by curiosity.

"Okay," he said nodding. Tearing off the first sheet of paper from the pad he put the pen on the paper.

"Don't think of a pink elephant doing 875,214 push-ups, green apple tree." The thought came clear and pronounced into his mind. Emotions he couldn't describe moved within him. *Could this really be?* He shielded the paper with his hand and began to write, he paused, not remembering the exact number. 875,214 entered his mind again. He wrote it down and finished the phrase.

Smiling curiously he folded the paper so no one can see, not even Taylor or Joseph, who sat on each side of him.

"Okay, now what?" he said, covering the paper on the table with both hands.

"Now, hand the paper to Miss Shaffer," said Nicholas, still standing confidently at the head of the table.

Taylor received the folded paper questioningly.

"Taylor, would you please stand up," said Nicholas.

With the piece of paper in her hand, she cautiously rose.

Nicholas didn't move, but behind him on the screen came the phrase, "don't think of a pink elephant doing 875,214 push-ups, green apple tree."

"Please read what Mr. Davis wrote," said Nicholas.

Taylor hesitantly unfolded the paper. To her astonishment she saw the words. Smiling she read out loud, "don't think of a pink elephant doing 875,214 push-ups, green apple tree."

There was an audible gasp from the others in the room. Talia and Joseph leaned forward as Taylor placed the paper on the table. The other students leaned forward as well, peering at the writing on the paper.

Nicholas continued, "Yes, Mr. Davis," he said. "It is possible to place a thought in someone else's mind. It takes practice, but yes. It's doable. Most of the time, the person receiving the thought thinks that the thought was generated within themselves. Austin stared at Nicholas, his eyes wide in disbelief.

"We are digressing though," said Nicholas. The group settled back to their seats as he continued.

"A person has multiple magnetic fields emanating from and surrounding them. The earth also has many fields emanating from different points, above, below, and on the surface. In humans these energy fields are produced from more than seven points in the body. These "power plants" within the body are called chakras. The transmission lines between the chakras and the rest of the body, are called meridians. There are concentrated points where these meridians come to the surface. Places like the eyes, earlobes, hands, feet, colon, teeth and genitals are examples of this. Acupuncture and acupressure work along these Meridian points. Foot Zone Therapy is another modality that accesses the body through these Meridian points.

"The energy produced by the chakras is stored in and retrieved from the fascia surrounding the different organs of the body and the entire body itself just below the surface of the skin. It is possible to store high concentrations of energy in the chakras, but it's not advisable to do that, especially in the upper chakras. It's okay to store large quantities of built-up energy in the sacral chakra, but it can be problematic if you try to store it in your heart or your head. I wouldn't advise it." Nicholas flashed a knowing smile.

"The human body has seven main chakras, six secondary chakras, and 72,000 tertiary chakras. There are other chakras outside of the body. Some of them are above the head and some are below the feet. These chakras and the energy fields they produce extend into the other dimensions.

"The earth also has chakras and meridians. The meridians are sometimes called Ley lines. Each of the seven continents has a chakra. All of these chakras are not currently active. The earth has many secondary and tertiary chakras, as well."

Talia raised her hand, "I don't mean any disrespect, sir, but some of us already know about chakras."

Nicholas nodded and continued, "As the earth rotates on its axis, the Earth's magnetic field is constantly charged, especially at sunrise and sunset."

The picture of a battery appeared on the screen behind Nicholas. "The graphene technology that we have now allows us an unlimited supply of clean electromagnetic energy."

A picture of a car and boat appeared on the screen. "We have developed engines that do not require fossil fuels and will run indefinitely using the energy created by mother Earth."

He stopped allowing the implication of his words to sink in.

This time it was Mia who raised her hand.

"Question?" said Nicholas pointing at her.

"Are you saying you can make a car that doesn't run on gasoline?"

"Not only cars, but trucks, trains, boats, airplanes, and satellites."

Taylor saw the shock on Mia's face.

"Wow!" said Mia. "That is so cool."

Nicholas got very serious for a moment. "Remember, you can talk to people outside this room about chakras and meridians all you want, but this information about the graphene technology and accessing an unlimited supply of energy from the earth, you cannot. This is the type of thing that gets people killed."

"Why?" asked Mia.

"Because of money and power. There are dark forces out there that make hundreds of billions of dollars a year off oil and the military industrial complex. This technology would put them all out of business."

"I still don't understand," said Mia.

"Thanks to Nikola Tesla and graphene technology, my companies have created inexpensive devices that can harness the Earth's energy and power pretty much anything. A device the size of a shoebox and costing less than $100 would create all the electricity to power a home. The same for your car or a semi-truck that ships food and materials for consumers and producers. Neither would ever have to be refueled. The engines would draw energy from the earth."

"And this is a bad thing?" said Mia, her hands out.

"The struggle for the control of power has been going on since the dawn of humanity. Certain countries, industries, and companies would lose out tremendously if this technology got out. For example, we now have the technology to use nanotubes and thin layers of graphene to convert seawater into freshwater with no toxic byproducts. Think of what that would do to the arid countries of the world, especially the warring countries in the Middle East. If they had enough freshwater, they would spend less time fighting and more time producing food to feed the people of their countries. World peace might break out, and the bad guys who are creating contention for their own nefarious reasons would be out of power.

"That's why if you were to divulge this information, and they were to find out, you would not only jeopardize your own life, but the lives of everyone else here. I cannot allow that to happen." Nicholas looked at her sternly. "At the same time, we are still moving forward with this without fear. As the earth moves to a higher dimension, this technology must come forward to help facilitate the Earth's ascension process. This knowledge is already seeping into the mass consciousness. My companies are not the only ones working with this technology, so it's only a matter of time.

"My instructions for you are that you continue in your individual ascension process, which will add momentum to the changing mass consciousness of the world. Then wait patiently until it reaches critical mass. It's going to happen, sooner or later."

Nicholas paused, making eye contact with each of his students. When his eyes met Taylor's, she could sense in the magnitude of what he was saying in his eyes.

Nicholas then turned to Alchesay, who got up and went back to the table where he had gotten the pad of paper from. He picked up a small metal container about the size of a shoebox. It had a handle on the top and two locking clasps on the side. He brought it over and placed it in front of Nicholas.

Without a word, Nicholas placed his hand on the box. At his touch, the clasps released. Opening the box, he pulled out a thin layer of what looked like bookmarks.

Taking the top one, he held it up.

"These wristbands may be your new friends for the next little while. They are on loan to some of you. The key word is *loan*. That means you will give it back to us when you're done. Is that clear?" He paused watching all of them nod in the affirmative.

Handing one to Alchesay, he held another up for all to see. It appeared to be a rigid piece of silver paper, about an inch wide and about eight inches long. Holding the end of it, with his fingers of his left hand, he tapped the middle of it on the back of his right wrist.

Instantly, it went from being straight and rigid to wrapping itself around Nicholas's wrist. He held up his hand, his palm forward for everyone to see. The wristband had wrapped completely around his wrist with no seam evident. Putting his finger underneath, he pulled it and the band went rigid and straight again.

Everyone watched in awe.

"These graphene bands are more advanced and have more computing power than any single computer in the world at this time. They use an interdimensional nano processor and are powered by the Earth's energy fields.

They work underground and underwater. They also work off of the sun's electromagnetic energy, even though they are not solar powered. Our sun is actually a massive electromagnetic plasma generator. These bands will remain charged anywhere in our solar system.

"Now if you go outside our solar system and are not near a rotating planet with an electromagnetic field, the bands will eventually discharge in about eight to ten months, depending on how much you use it." He smiled, "but if that's an issue you're dealing with, you probably have bigger concerns on your mind, than your wristband running out of power."

Some of the students laughed cautiously, but Austin got the impression that Nicholas wasn't completely kidding.

The lights in the room faded somewhat, as Nicholas snapped the band back on his right wrist. Turning his palm up, he tapped the back of the band with the fingers of his left hand.

Instantly an image formed about six inches above his hand. A three-dimensional picture of the wristband was floating in the air. As Nicholas moved so did the image.

"The band works as a communicator and an information device. It's better than any smart phone you will ever own. It is not connected to any Internet, but allows you access to a vast amount of knowledge. You can ask it questions and use it like a cell phone to call people.

"Unlike a cell phone, it does not transmit and receive using a microwave signal. Microwaves are actually harmful for people. You would never stick your head in a microwave oven when it's going. Long-term exposure to microwaves can actually damage the body. These bands do not transmit and receive using microwaves. The signals they use travel on neutron particles, not electrons. Because of the interdimensional processors within them, they transmit and receive, faster than the speed of light. Even if you are under the ocean on earth, you could talk to somebody under the surface of Mars, almost instantaneously. That is, assuming that the person on Mars had a band as well. Now the bands do have some help. One of the companies I own has several high Earth orbiting satellites to help facilitate better connections, especially when you're trying to contact somebody that doesn't have one of these bands.

"But don't be calling all your friends in India with this, Nathan," said Nicholas jokingly.

Nathan smiled sheepishly.

Nicholas tapped the band and the three-dimensional image disappeared, and the lights returned to normal.

"Alchesay will give you further instructions on how these things work. Some of you are going to be using them on this upcoming mission. Use them wisely. These prototypes are very durable, but treat them with respect. With great power comes great responsibility."

"Two more things about these bands," said Nicholas. As he cupped his left hand over the band on his right wrist, the band appeared to dissolve. He held up his hand. The band was gone. Cupping his hand over it again, it reappeared. "Don't bring any undue attention to the bands. They will still function in cloaked mode, so if you're out in public, keep them hidden. I am hoping to have enough bands ready for everyone before you leave, but as of now only the two team leaders will have them.

"One more thing: in manual mode it will function like a touch screen, either on the band itself or the three-dimensional image that it creates. It also has a voice mode. When you're on this upcoming mission, it will only work for you. If anyone else tries to use them, they won't work. And don't lose them, either. These cost a pretty penny to make."

Wow, that would be so cool to have. I hope I get one, Austin thought.

Chapter 54 – Grace and Demetri

The air mattress bobbed as it moved. Austin held Taylor's hand and pulled her along as they floated across the pool. Demetri, Grace and a few others were scattered around the pool or relaxing in the hot tub. A rare treat after the last few days. Nicholas sat a few feet away at a small table sheltered from the heat of the sun by the trees and shrubs that adorned the patio, a book in hand. Austin noticed Grace hesitantly walk to where Nicholas sat.

"Thank you for taking me off the ground team yesterday. I didn't have a chance to explain why. May I have a few minutes now?" she asked.

"Of course. Have a seat," Nicholas said, closing his book.

Austin floated closer, curious as to why Grace wanted a change of assignment. He heard something about issues with Talia and her concern about the Ark being in a different place than what her religious upbringing had taught. She was worried that Demetri was correct in his beliefs and that she was wrong.

"I don't want to lose my faith over this, and I am afraid I might."

Those are some serious concerns, thought Austin.

"Austin. Do you mind if we get out for a while?" Taylor's voice interrupted his thoughts.

They rolled off their mattresses, swam to the side of the pool and pulled themselves out. Austin handed one of the towels from the nearby patio chair to Taylor and used the other one. He watched Taylor spread her towel on the other lounge chair and lay down while he vigorously dried his chest and arms. Lying back on the towel, Austin closed his eyes and enjoyed the heat of the sun as it dried the rest of his body.

He was in the place of not quite asleep when he heard Demetri speaking with Nicholas.

"I mean no disrespect, sir," said Demetri. "But, I don't believe it's there."

"Why do you believe that?" asked Nicholas.

"Because in my father's faith, it's in a different location."

He's concerned about the mission, as well, thought Austin.

"You may be correct, and if so, this whole mission is for naught. But if it is where we think it is, we still want to do this mission. Why didn't you bring this up with me when I asked you to be a team leader?" asked Nicholas.

"Honestly, I didn't want to disappoint you," he said.

Austin cracked his eyes open and saw Demetri staring at the ground.

"Do you feel you can still perform your responsibilities as team leader, even though you don't believe it's actually there?"

Demetri paused for a moment.

"Whether it's there or not, I need you to do this. You are one of the most capable people here. You have great leadership skills. I need you to lead your team. Regardless of your concerns, can you do this?" asked Nicholas.

Demetri nodded.

Austin rolled over onto his stomach, closed his eyes and heard Nicholas ask again.

"Will you do this?"

"Yes, I will, whatever we find, and I will make sure everyone on my team makes it back."

"Thank you," Nicholas said as Austin drifted off to sleep.

"You're going to turn into a lobster if you don't get out of the sun," he heard Taylor say to him.

Austin slowly sat up. "Thanks, I think I fell asleep."

"Geri sent up some lunch, I'm going to get some. Do you want to come?"

"Sure," he said.

Taylor took his hand, and the two walked over to the food that was set up in the shade. Then found a table on the other side of the pool under a gazebo. They ate and chatted about their own reservations of the upcoming mission. When they were finished, Austin walked with Taylor towards the gate and set their dishes in a nearby container.

"Austin, could you join us for a moment please?" called Nicholas.

"I'll meet you later," said Taylor as she excused herself to go shower and get dressed.

Austin hadn't noticed Joseph's arrival until that moment. He was sitting with Nicholas when Austin walked up. The men sat relaxed on two of the three benches located in the grass not far from the patio. The warm summer air drifted shadows of leaves from the trees above, across them.

"Are you sure Austin needs to be here?" Joseph asked when Austin took a seat. "It's kind of personal."

"I think he does," said Nicholas.

Austin felt very curious now about the upcoming conversation.

"I found out some information that I think you should know about," said Joseph.

"What is it?" asked Nicholas.

Joseph eyed Austin warily. "Honestly, sir, I'd rather not say in front of Austin."

"Does it have to do with me?" Austin asked.

"Not really. Well, maybe, indirectly."

Nicholas looked up, not saying anything for a long moment. "I get a very strong impression that he does need to be here for this."

"My concern is not so much for him, but that he may speak of this information to another person," said Joseph.

Austin immediately thought of Taylor. *He knows something about her that I don't.*

"Austin, if we decide that what Joseph says should not be shared with anyone else outside of the three of us, would you be willing to keep it confidential?" asked Nicholas.

"It depends on what it is and who it's about," said Austin.

"That's the problem," said Joseph. "I don't think she should know."

It is Taylor. Austin began to feel frustrated that Joseph wouldn't come out and say it, whatever it was.

"It's okay," Nicholas finally said. "He needs to know about this."

"I still don't feel I can divulge this information with him here," said Joseph.

Austin was getting pretty tired of Joseph's attitude. *Just say it*, he thought.

"How about if I find out what it is first and then decide if Austin should know or not?" Nicholas asked.

"That's fine," Joseph said.

"Do you want me to leave and come back when he's told you or just plug my ears?" asked Austin.

"No, that won't be necessary," said Nicholas turning to Joseph. "We can do it an easier way."

"Hold the thought in your mind, Joseph. I'll do the rest," said Nicholas.

Joseph looked at Nicholas confidently and peacefully. Joseph acted like he was aware of what was happening and had done this before.

Nicholas stared, unblinking into Joseph's eyes. *Almost like he's searching his soul, searching his mind,* thought Austin.

After more than a full minute, a strange expression crossed Nicholas's countenance. He leaned back, his head resting against the tall back of the wooden bench. His gazed traversed the afternoon sky. "Well, that's interesting," he said.

"What?" said Austin, not doing well at holding back his curiosity.

"Do you see why I didn't want to tell him?" asked Joseph.

"I understand why, but I disagree," said Nicholas. "Not only do I think he can be aware of it, but that he should be aware of it."

"But what if he tells her?" asked Joseph. By this time Austin was dying from curiosity.

"Oh, he won't tell her," said Nicholas.

"Sure he will," said Joseph. "How can he not?"

"He's not going to tell her because you're going to tell her first."

Joseph cringed. "I can't tell her. She'll hate me. Or at least not trust me."

"All the more reason why you are going to tell her. For your own personal integrity, you have to tell her."

"Tell her what?" The need to know outweighed Austin's self-control.

"Do you want me to tell Austin, or would you like to?" asked Nicholas.

"If I have to tell Taylor, would you tell him?" asked Joseph.

"Yeah, I'm good with that," said Nicholas.

Austin saw the tension around Joseph's mouth relax.

"So," said Austin, "has Joseph talked to you about whatever this is before?"

"No," said Nicholas. "This is the first I've heard of it as well."

"Then if he hasn't told you before, then how do you know about it now?" asked Austin.

"Because I saw it in his mind," said Nicholas.

Austin remembered back to the experience when Nicholas had guessed what he had written on the paper in his underground office.

Nicholas turned to Joseph, "Correct me if I'm wrong on any of this, but it seems very possible that Taylor has multiple siblings."

Joseph sighed and sank back against the bench, nodding.

Austin, puzzled by Nicholas's statement, "Of course she does." The big revelation hadn't been all that revealing. "She has a brother named Connor. I've met him and she for sure knows about him."

"But it's more than that," said Nicholas. "Joseph, how did you find out about the other two?"

Other two! Taylor never said anything about any other siblings besides Connor.

"I helped her do a family history search as part of one of the classes I was teaching. We found some of her father's ancestors and she seemed really excited about that. But when it came to her mother, she became apprehensive."

"That's understandable," said Austin. "Her mother's a....she left Taylor and Connor years ago." Austin's annoyance could be heard in his tone.

"Taylor gave me her basic information, but then our time for the class ran out," said Joseph. "I thought I was doing her a favor, so I dug a little deeper and found out more information about her mother."

"And that's how you *accidentally* found out she has two additional siblings?" asked Nicholas, one eyebrow rising.

"Well, not exactly," said Joseph. "I got some help and dug pretty deep."

"What else did you learn about them?" asked Austin.

Nicholas held up a finger. "Wait a minute. Mr. Lee, what do you mean, got help?"

Joseph fidgeted in his seat, but didn't respond.

Nicholas stared at him more deeply. "You got Ahki's help, didn't you?"

"I thought I was doing her a favor," said Joseph.

"You know he has high-level clearance to the encrypted database at the Institute don't you?"

"I didn't see any harm in it," said Joseph.

"That's another story," said Nicholas, "that we're going to have to talk about later. But for now, keep going with Taylor's mother."

"Well," said Joseph a little sheepishly. "We accessed her Social Security number and some other records including birth records. Apparently about a year and a half after Taylor was born, her mother had another child."

"A boy or girl?" asked Austin.

"I'm not sure," said Joseph. "The record just said 'live birth' and 'father unknown.'"

"I don't think Taylor knows and if she does," said Austin, "she hasn't said anything about it."

"She doesn't know," said Nicholas. "What about the other one?"

"That's even more interesting," said Joseph. "The second one, which would be Taylor's third sibling was born this year, a boy, born March fifteenth, father unknown."

"That was just a few months ago," said Austin. "How old is her mother?"

"I don't remember her birth date, but probably in her mid to late forties is my guess," said Joseph.

Nicholas sat quietly pondering. Both Austin and Joseph waited for him to say something. He finally turned to Austin. "Last year when you and Taylor first came to the Estate it was in May. Correct?"

"Yeah," said Austin, not sure where Nicholas was going with this.

"And then in June of last year Taylor went to take care of her grandparents. Her grandfather had fallen and broken his hip."

Austin nodded remembering the previous summer.

"Let's just say her mother carried the baby the full nine months. As I recall, you went back to pick up Taylor the night of June thirteenth."

The date sounded correct, but even doing the Genius Training, Austin's memory wasn't anywhere as good as Mr. Ryan's.

"I believe that's right," said Austin. "Taylor's mom had shown up earlier that day and was trying to waltz back into their lives, apparently to get the life insurance money that Taylor and Connor got when their father died about seven years ago. I remember that night. Taylor was really upset."

Nicholas nodded quietly. "She wasn't pregnant before that."

"How do you know?" asked Austin.

"It's just an impression," said Nicholas. Austin had a feeling there was a lot more Nicholas wasn't saying.

"So, she tried to come back into the lives of her children to get the money," said Joseph. "And when it didn't happen, she left and got pregnant."

"Yep," said Austin. "It sure seems that way. I know Taylor was furious for quite a while after. She had to do a lot of emotional clearing. I'm still not a hundred percent sure she's over it. Better, but it still bothers her."

They both looked at Nicholas, his eyes moved back and forth and then up through the trees. "Is that really true?" he said quietly. "Wow."

This was the very first time Austin had ever heard Nicholas use the word 'Wow'. It just wasn't in his normal vocabulary.

"There is more to that story than it appears." Nicholas turned back to Joseph. "And by the way, Mr. Lee, you brought this up at quite the time, especially since we leave for Turkey soon. You better tell her before we go."

Joseph nodded, his eyes glancing to the right.

Chapter 55 – Simple Genius Training

"Do you want to know a secret?" asked Nicholas.

The question caught Austin off guard. Joseph had left moments ago to talk to Taylor, Austin assumed. He wanted to be part of that conversation, but Nicholas had asked him to stay.

"Sure," said Austin.

"If you promise not to tell anyone, I'll tell you."

"Agreed."

"I do the Genius Training with a lot of people: some world leaders and very high-end executives, including my senior staff that manages my many companies. I even offer a less expensive version of the Genius Training program for only five hundred dollars."

"I didn't know that," said Austin.

"I don't personally work with the ones doing the less expensive program because of the limitations of time. I spend most of my time with the higher paying clients and you guys here at the Estate. The higher-end program runs between ten thousand and a million dollars."

"Wow," said Austin.

"Do you know what the difference is between the two programs?"

"No, what?"

"They are almost identical, except for one thing, **accountability**. In the cheaper program, the person has to be self-accountable and be able to motivate themselves.

The person doing the higher end program is accountable to another, a mentor or an accountability coach.

"It really helps to keep you motivated, to stay committed when you know you have to report to someone else about your progress. You're often more determined to do the program. That creates greater discipline, which is what improves performance.

"If a person is self-motivated and disciplined enough on their own, they can do the same program for much less and still gain great results."

"I'm not accountable to anyone here, but myself, and I think I've done an amazing job at the Genius Training program," said Austin.

"And you did all that on your own?" asked Nicholas, silent laughter crinkled the corner of his eyes.

"I don't report to anyone. I do it all by myself. I feel I'm pretty disciplined."

"You did that all yourself?" Nicholas scoffed.

Austin, unsure of how to answer.

"Let me tell you the simple version of the Genius Training program," said Nicholas. "But just because it's simple doesn't mean it's still not powerful. Anyone can become a 'Genius' if they follow these five basic steps. The key is that they actually have to do the steps. That's where discipline comes in. Good intentions and half-hearted efforts won't create results."

"So what are the **five basics steps**?" asked Austin, a bit skeptical.

Nicholas smiled, "I'm glad you asked. These are not in any particular order. Each principle can be independent, but they also work together, creating a synergy.

"Number one, **learn broadly and thoroughly**. Read a lot about a lot of things. Reading at least three books on a topic will make you smarter than 90% of the population. And pay attention to what you read. Either high-light significant points or, better yet, take written notes. So read a lot, preferably every day."

Austin recalled the multitude of books he'd read. The topics contained a great deal of variation.

"Number two," continued Nicholas. "**Share the information** you learn with others. Your brain processes the information when you read, but it also processes that same information in a different way when you teach or tell others. You will understand more and your ability to recall will increase."

"Like when I learned to speak Spanish. Mia and I would have conversations," Austin said. "That was so much better than just trying to repeat the words from a recording."

"Exactly," said Nicholas. "It made your brain learn to process the information on a deeper level, at least three dimensionally, and it improved your recall. The memorization classes helped with that as well."

"Speaking of the memorization classes," said Austin. "Is that how you got such a great memory?"

"That's part of it," said Nicholas. "There are additional tools and techniques that help."

Austin nodded.

"The third principle to becoming a Genius is **reducing certain social media**. Especially the mind-numbing, endorphin-releasing habit of searching the internet for nothing in particular. It's like channel surfing."

"That's one thing I am doing really well at. I don't have time to surf. I only use my phone for communication and research," said Austin.

"That's one of the perks for being so busy here," Nicholas said. "The Fourth principle to becoming a genius is to **meditate at least five minutes a day** or more, with the focus on your breathing."

"I kept falling asleep when I first tried to meditate, but now I can do it a lot longer," Austin said.

"The length of time and the benefits will continue to increase with additional practice," said Nicholas.

"Fifth, **take care of body and brain**. Have you ever wondered why we eat the way we do here? And why we are so adamant about clearing out the negative thoughts and emotions? Keeping our bodies free of toxins of any kind is paramount to becoming a genius."

Austin relaxed against the bench and thought of how he ate and what his life had been like when he was back in college, before he met Mr. Ryan. The evaluation of his overall health made him cringe a little inside. He had treated his body and mind in a disrespectful and unhealthy way. Even last year at school his routines had slipped and he didn't feel as well as he did here at the Estate.

"Thank you again for allowing me to be here. I realize now that I couldn't do this on my own,"

The two men sat in companionable silence, Austin's mind wandered to how far he had come since being here at the Estate. He had made some significant life changes in the short time he'd been here. He looked over at Nicholas, feeling that there was more to be said.

"Let's walk," Nicholas said.

The direction they headed took them through the vast gardens and into the wooded acres beyond.

"Last year when I first met you, Austin, I thought you were such an arrogant soul."

Austin wasn't sure if that was an insult or a compliment.

"When we first met at that conference, and when you raced Joseph, then me, I thought you were so unaware, clueless and self-centered." Nicholas turned to him. "And I was right: you were. You were just like I was at your age and just like the rest of the *sheeple* in the world."

Austin wanted to speak, to defend himself, but chose not to.

"Then I watched you grow through last summer and this year as well, even when you hit my horse.

"You know, 95% of the population of the world is either unaware or not determined enough to do what it takes to become a genius. More than 4% that know about and want to be a genius may begin the process, but either get distracted, which is common, or don't stay committed because of the effort required. They're not determined or persistent enough to see it to fruition."

"What about the 1%?" asked Austin.

"The less than 1%, are the ones that are aware. They begin to acquire the knowledge and stay committed. They are determined enough to make it happen. They get excited about it. They gain more knowledge. They are self-motivated. These are the ones that get results, results in proportion to their efforts."

Austin had to think about that. "In all honesty if I wasn't here, doing these training programs with you, I don't think I would be part of the 1%."

"I know you wouldn't do it," said Nicholas. "Even after becoming aware of it, you would still be part of the 95%."

Now Austin was insulted. "How do you know that? I could do it on my own. I don't have to be here to still be a genius. I raised my grades and I kept the scholarship you gave me..."

Nicholas interrupted, "Sure, you *could* do it on your own. Most everyone has the potential to do it. That's the 90%, but that's my point. Without help, most never do it. When it was you alone, your grades were pathetic. You were failing. Then Taylor started to tutor you. You trained here last summer. You received a scholarship. My point is, you had to have help."

"But you did it without help," said Austin. "How are you the less than 1%?"

"I wasn't," said Nicholas. "I'm still not. I had help, and still do."

Austin looked at him questioningly.

"I have Rex and Dakota and others who assisted me to turn my life around. I got mentors and specialists in their respective fields. They help me stay motivated. I was accountable to someone outside of myself. And interacting with like-minded people helped me stay committed. It creates momentum."

Nicholas paused. "And then there's Vivian."

Austin wanted to say something, but decided it best not to.

"Having a partner that has similar goals and intention makes a significant difference, especially one who will stay with you during the hard times. Even when you're acting like an ass. Or so sick you can't get out of bed in the morning to go to work." Nicholas paused again as if searching inside his own heart and mind. He took in a deep breath. "I once asked her why she stayed with me through fourteen years of hell."

Austin had never seen Nicholas like this, so personal, so vulnerable. He stayed quiet, curious to hear more about the life experience of his teacher, his mentor. The man he had come to love and respect more than anyone else in his life, including his own father.

"Do you know what she said?"

The shake of his head answered Nicholas's question.

"She said before we were married, she had a dream or vision of sorts, where she saw me in the future, what I would become." Nicholas stopped speaking, still contemplative, a tear in his eye. "Yes, she saw the wealth and success, the things that I would do, but that wasn't what got her through the years of cleaning convenience store bathrooms. It was who I am. Who I Be."

They walked in silence for a long moment as Austin digested his mentor's words. He was filled with a sense of gratitude and closeness to this powerful man. *Wow,* he thought. *I've never before imagined anything like this in my life. It's almost like...*

Austin stopped, concern growing within him. Almost like this was the conclusion. The end of this amazing experience he had been having. *Is Nicholas going away? Am I?* He thought of the upcoming mission. *Is Nicholas or am I going to die tomorrow?*

"Austin," Nicholas's firm, but comforting voice drew him back to the world outside his head. "This is not the end. At least, I don't think it is."

Austin was somewhat relieved, but still felt a foreboding feeling that concerned him, like some significant experience was about to happen. So altering, that his life would never be the same.

"What are you saying?" asked Austin.

"Go back in our conversation," said Nicholas. "I'm saying that certain things in life are more important, even than life itself."

Austin was taken back, trying to shift gears in his mind to what Nicholas was intimating.

"Time and money, it's just energy, its fluid, constantly changing. The real essence of life, the real purpose to existence, is people. It's our relationships that matter the most. That is what goes with us beyond our mortal experience. It becomes us and we become it. It's part of our Being, because we are not separate from it." Nicholas paused. "I would never be where I am now if wasn't for Vivian. She didn't heal my wound. That was through my higher power. But after, I became whole and complete with her, and her with me."

Austin continued to search through his mentor's words, still not fully comprehending.

"Austin."

He felt the strength in the hand that came to rest on his shoulder, the power that seemed to permeate through him.

"For you, it's Taylor."

Chapter 56 – Time to Go

Austin took Taylor's hand as they made their way through the maze of hallways to the front door. The two ground teams were meeting by the SUV's that waited on the drive. Taylor could see Vivian close to Nicholas, his arm held her snuggly to his side. She would be staying behind while Nicholas escorted the two groups to the airfield and the hangers that contained the AW109 helicopters that would be taking them to their training.

Two helicopters waited by a large hangar. The double-doors were closed, but a small door off to one side stood open as if awaiting their arrival. Nicholas led them to the door where his pilot, Stephen, stood waiting.

"Everything is ready like you asked," Stephen said when Nicholas entered the building. Austin gasped when he stepped in next, Taylor by his side.

Inside the hangar was an oval-shaped craft, almost like an elongated egg. Austin could see Taylor's smile reflected in the silvery exterior. The eight blades that would give the craft its lift were connected at the outer edges with a circular band. In the tail section sat a smaller version of the blades.

Once everyone had entered, they gathered close while Nicholas explained what they were looking at.

"This is one of several prototypes created by my companies. It's called a Bumblebee. It uses Graphene technology and can fly very fast, especially for a helicopter. When the doors are shut, it's almost undetectable to most radar systems."

Nicholas asked Stephen to open the two doors nearest the group. Austin could see two seats up front for the pilot and copilot. The main doors behind were slightly wider and showed a passenger compartment. There was room for six passengers, four on the back seat, if they sat close, and two on the smaller seats that sat directly behind the pilot and copilot.

"The landing gear," Nicholas continued. "Is completely retractable; this also helps it avoid detection. In full stealth mode, it's almost completely invisible during the day. At night, it is completely invisible, visually. It gives off no heat signature because it does not use a combustion engine. It is completely electric and never needs to be refueled because it's powered by the Earth's magnetic field in a similar way that the wristbands are. It can fly indefinitely. It's also very stable due to the spherical design.

"Pajori and Logan have spent many hours with Stephen here learning how to fly these amazing craft. But for today's exercise you will be flying in the ones outside."

Austin suppressed his disappointment and followed the group out to the tarmac to the waiting helicopters.

Both teams spent the next few hours rappelling from the helicopters in the mountains west of the Institute. It was good practice for both them and the pilots.

The next day they flew to Torreys Peak and spent a good portion of the day in training exercises there, as well. They had the gear needed to spend the night and continue their training the next day, but Nicholas had sent word that they should return early.

It was a hum of activity when they arrived back late that night. Vivian was waiting for them in the entryway upon their return.

"Geri has a late dinner for you as soon as you get cleaned up. Your day is going to begin pretty early tomorrow. Mr. Ryan will meet you all in the dining hall in one hour, and I suggest you get right to bed after that."

The dining room was pretty crowded when Austin and Taylor entered. More than just the teams doing the training were there. Austin offered to get their dinner, and Taylor went to find some empty chairs. Uncertainty and curiosity worked its way into the conversations that occupied the room. They were finishing up their dinner when Nicholas walked in followed by Rex and Dakota. The three stood together next to the table where Austin and Taylor sat.

"It's time," Nicholas said, offering no introduction. "With the way the weather is right now in Eastern Turkey, we believe we will have a few days of good weather around our intended destination. We don't have much time to get there, so I need you all to be packed and ready to leave at first light."

Taylor and Austin got up with the rest of the teams and headed to their rooms.

"I'm glad I'm already partially packed," said Taylor. "It won't take me long to finish, and then I can get to bed."

"You could always come help me," Austin said with a tired smile.

Taylor leaned up, kissed his cheek, and went into her room.

It didn't take Austin long to pack. Soon he was in bed, thinking about what he'd be doing the next few days. Uncertainty filled his mind as he drifted off to sleep.

The line to load the trucks meandered down the drive, curved near the grass, and returned back to the main door. Austin found Taylor somewhere in the middle. It was unusually noisy for that early in the morning, but not chaotic given how many people were waiting.

"What are we standing in line for?"

"Mr. Ryan is having Alchesay check everyone's pack and equipment. He said he didn't want to have any surprises," Taylor said. "Mrs. Ryan is labeling all the non-essential items so they can be returned to our rooms once we've left. Can you believe people are bringing makeup and gaming devices? It's not like we're going on vacation."

The line crept slowly forward. Only two more bags, and then it would be their turn.

"I feel I should be able to take it," Will said.

"I don't know how you were even able to get it from the gun lockers, let alone think you could take it with you," said Alchesay, as he removed the 1911 45 ACP pistol and handed it to Vivian. She checked the safety and skillfully removed the clip. She turned from the group and made sure there wasn't a bullet in the chamber.

"I still think we should have at least one gun with us. We may need it," replied Will.

Alchesay and Will walked over to where Nicholas stood with Pajori. After a few moments of discussion, Austin saw Will nod and return for his pack.

"Talia and Demetri, would you join us?" Nicholas asked.

Austin couldn't hear their conversation, but got the idea that it was about the gun. Pajori and Talia got in the side-by-side and roared off in the direction of the gun range.

Once their packs were okayed, Austin and Taylor loaded them on one of the trucks and went to get some breakfast off the table Marti and Geri had set up on one side of the driveway. The temperature remained comfortable all night, so it wasn't chilly even in the early morning. The rising sun had swept the dew, leaving a cool, but dry spot to eat their breakfast.

Talia and Pajori returned, and the last of the packs were loaded. It wouldn't be long now before they would be on their way. Austin paid close attention to Nicholas as he talked to the group one last time before departure. He thanked them again for what they were about to do.

"Remember what you've learned," he said, before getting into one of the two SUV's that Pajori and the support groups were in.

When quiet settled over the group once more, Dakota asked if anyone had any questions before they left. Thirty-five minutes later they left for the Institute airfield. Two mid-size corporate jets sat ready at the end of the runway near the hangers.

With the equipment loaded, Austin and Taylor followed the others into the waiting aircraft. Everyone fit comfortably in the high-end jet. Its splendor didn't surprise Austin as he looked around the cabin. He could picture Nicholas relaxed in one of the many seats that filled the passenger section.

"I didn't see Nicholas on board," he said.

"I asked Alchesay where he was, and he said Mr. Ryan and the support teams went on ahead. There were things they needed to do before we arrived," said Taylor as she settled back into the comfortable leather seat. Seatbelts clicked as the craft made ready for takeoff.

Austin and Taylor spent the first leg of the flight in quiet conversation. It had been weeks since they were able to sit and talk without other distractions. They were asked to stay on board when they landed in North Carolina to refuel. It didn't take long. Soon they were on their way to Spain. This was the first trip to Europe for both of them.

Austin simply sat and watched Taylor for a while. She had fallen asleep after lunch. He gently moved a strand of hair that had slipped down over her face. It slid across her nose and cheek. His hand quickly pulled back when her fingers brushed the tickle away. He kissed her softly and smiled when she sighed and relaxed deeper into sleep.

He took the headphones out of the compartment beside him and scrolled through the meditations on his phone. He knew he wouldn't have the phone on the actual mission, but he was glad he had it now. He slipped his fingers around Taylor's, shut his eyes, and began to relax.

Waves rolled onto the white sand. Off to one side, rock piled on top of rock in an exquisite display of color and texture. The island was covered in lush green vegetation disturbed only by the small landing field where the two planes sat alongside waiting UH-1/T700 Ultra Huey helicopters.

Everyone willingly pitched in to get the gear and equipment transferred to the four waiting helicopters.

"Wow, look at that," said Will, forty minutes later.

Austin leaned close to Taylor to see what Will was pointing at outside the chopper window. There, floating on the shimmering blue-green water of the Aegean Sea, sat a magnificent mega-yacht. It was long, sleek, and black, and shimmered in the sunlight. They got a closer look as their helicopter circled the yacht a few times waiting for their turn to land on one of the two landing pads.

Nicholas met them as they exited the helicopters and said they had the evening to relax. Austin and Taylor dropped off their gear in their rooms and decided to explore the yacht. After a visit to the galley, they walked the carpeted corridor to the stairway to the next level. They moved through the French doors onto the patio. The blue water contrasted with a beautiful mosaic tile that surrounded the pool and hot tub.

"Let's get our suits on. I want to get in that hot tub," said Austin.

A warm breeze blew as the large boat moved swiftly through the water. The sun had almost set, leaving the sky behind them aglow with shades of pink and orange.

The jets of warm water softly pounded Austin's lower back, sending bubbles between and around them. Taylor sat close with her head on his shoulder.

"Can you believe we're here?" asked Austin.

"I know. So much has changed, especially the past few months," Taylor said. "We've been surrounded by some pretty amazing people: Nicholas and Vivian, Rex and Angelica Houston, Dakota and Kelly Kavanaugh."

Their conversation moved to the experiences that the next day might hold. Austin tried to quell Taylor's concerns and uncertainties and sensed his own, as well. As they sat relaxing to the sway of the boat, neither one realized the significance of what they were about to do.

"This is the control room where your support teams will be," said Nicholas the next afternoon.

The room in the middle of the yacht felt bright and airy even with the lack of windows. High-end computer terminals lined the tables that sat against the two walls. Large monitors hung mounted above and showed a satellite image of a long rectangular object covered in ice. It seemed like it was made of wood and hung out over a deep gorge.

"What's on that other screen?" Austin asked.

"Some of the satellites have sensors that can penetrate and detect objects below the ice further in the gorge." Nicholas said, pointing out three smaller objects on the second monitor. They were shorter than the first image, but almost as wide. You could make out the wood even through the deep ice that covered them.

"Hopefully what we need is not in one of those three lower sections. If it is, I don't think there's any way we'll get into them," said Aki.

"I agree," said Nicholas. "It seems like that section on top is more than half of the object. Can you get me a closer view?"

The upper section extended out over the gorge. Uneven ice cliffs sat above it. Austin was amazed at the detail. He stood off to one side with Taylor and had a good view of the monitors that hung on the wall.

"There appears to be three possible openings in the ice that may get us inside," said Shen, pointing to them on the screen.

Nicholas turned to Talia and Demetri. "What do you think?"

They stepped closer to the screens. The depth indicator showed what was hidden beneath the twenty five feet of ice at the farthest point, and the twenty feet of ice in the middle. The last indicator read zero feet.

"What's that?" asked Demetri. "Zero feet?"

"That means the wood surface is totally exposed. There is no ice on it," said Shen.

"How about that one, then" said Demetri.

The three took a closer look at the area on the monitor.

"Could you zoom in on that, Shen?" Talia asked, pointing to a spot on the screen.

"What do you think?" she then asked Nicholas.

Austin was impressed at how clear the image was. He could actually see wood planks connected tightly together. He could almost see the grain of the wood. "Are these images from your satellites?" he asked.

Nicholas nodded, his eyes fixed on the image in front of him.

"I don't think it's going to work," said Talia.

"Why not?" said Demetri. "We can get to it right from there."

"Pan back," she said. Shen made the adjustments. "Look behind it."

The wood of the object was more than forty feet wide. Only about three feet of the wood was actually exposed.

"That's a big drop," said Will, nervously.

"I agree," said Nicholas. "That's the Ahora Gorge. It's over a thousand feet deep at that point. What about the other two openings?"

"It's hard to tell," said Shen. "It's not a direct shot. It's around twenty to thirty feet to the object below the ice."

"And when we get there," interjected Demetri, "we won't know if there is an opening to get inside."

"Yeah," said Will. "And how do we get down there in the first place."

Nicholas turned back to the two groups. "All of these images will be downloaded to the graphene wristbands. The surface information will be in 3-D. But below about eight feet, were not exactly sure what to expect.

"I wish I had one of these for all of you," he said motioning to his wrist. "But right now all we have is the two prototypes. Each team leader will have one. The rest of you, make sure you take your headsets for your radios. They transmit and receive through your watch phones. Your watch phones won't be able to communicate directly with us here at Base One, because obviously there is no direct service, where you're going. But we can track your whereabouts even under the ice. The radios will, however, work for some communications, especially over short distances and in direct line of sight. Also, the wristbands will be able to receive audio signals from your watch phones, assuming they have enough power. Unfortunately, your watch phones won't be able to receive signals from the wristbands. And remember, make sure your radios and watch phones are fully charged tonight.

"The bumblebees will drop you off some three hundred yards above and to the west of those two openings. I've gone over the terrain with the Stephen, Pajori, Alchesay, and Logan. They will be flying you in." Nicholas pointed to another screen. "With the expected winds early tomorrow morning, we feel this is the safest place to drop you guys off.

"A-team will go in first," he said, looking at Demetri. "B-team will follow about ninety seconds later. It will still be dark at that time, so make sure your night vision goggles are all working properly.

"Once you're all safely on the ground and the bumblebees are away, check on each other, then on your gear. A-team will then proceed to opening number one," he said, pointing to the wide opening in the ice, on the screen. B-team will proceed to the second. Stay in contact with us at Base One at all times. We'll give you instructions as you go."

"I don't foresee any problems," said Demetri. "But what if we do happen to lose contact with Base One?"

"It's what we haven't foreseen that concerns me," said Nicholas. "If the team leaders lose contact with Base One or any member of your group, do what you have to to get back to the surface. The goal is to get in there, find the object or objects that we are searching for, and get out. But remember, the most critical thing is that all of you are safe."

Austin raised his hand. "Remind me again, what it is we're trying to find?"

"It's called an Ophanim. An artifact of significance," said Nicholas. "I'm not exactly sure what form it will take, but I believe you will know it when you see it."

"How will we know?" asked Taylor.

Nicholas touched a keypad and the images on one of the screens changed. "These are images taken from other expeditions." Pictures of long narrow passageways filled with walls of ice and wood planking appeared on the screen.

"This is the baseline," said Nicholas. "For the most part, this is what you are going to see while you're in there." The images continued to change, but appeared roughly the same, ice walls and wooden passageways.

"This is the norm," he said. "What you're searching for will seem very out of place."

"What do we do if...I mean, when we find it?" asked Joseph.

"It depends on what form it takes," said Nicholas. "If it is small enough to be retrieved, we will possibly go with that route. If it's something larger, then use the Graphene bands to analyze and record it. It mainly depends on what it is. But I believe you'll know it when you see it."

"Haven't other people been in there before us?" Mia asked.

"Yes," said Nicholas. "Over the past few thousand years there have been many who have been near or inside this vessel."

"Then how do we know that the Ophanim hasn't already been taken?"

"We don't," said Nicholas. "We do, however, have records of more than fifty encounters with this vessel over the past hundred years, and many more before that. In some cases, the insides were explored quite extensively. They probably would have removed any artifacts they would come across, if they found any."

"So what makes you think we are going to find something?"

"This is where multidimensional thinking comes in, along with logic and deductive reasoning. The tablet that some of you found with Rex and Dakota last summer gave us several clues. One of the main clues we learned from that tablet was that ancient recordings in some form made it through a planetary deluge on a large wooden vessel. I believe the records were intended to survive some major flood. From that, we are assuming the ancient tablets are correct and the knowledge of before that flood was recorded and brought with them on this vessel. If that logic is sound, then the records were there, at least anciently. Is it still on there today? Logically, I would say no. Either it was taken off sometime over the past few thousand years, or it could have been in the sections that broke off and is buried deep in the ice below. If that's true, then obviously we'll never find it."

"Then logically this whole mission is pointless" said Demetri. "This may not even be Noah's Ark."

"I don't care who built it," said Nicholas. "But I do believe, because of my experience with Austin and Master Kavanaugh that the information that this vessel once held is incredibly important and may still be there today. It needs to be revealed. We need to at least try."

"I still think we're taking a big risk for something that probably isn't even there."

Nicholas's eyes narrowed at Demetri. Sensing his displeasure, Demetri continued. "But on the other hand, as long as we're here, we might as well check it out."

"Double check your gear and get something to eat," said Nicholas. "You may also want to get some sleep. You'll be taking off right after sunset. The trip to Eastern Turkey will put you there right before sunrise."

Austin was a little puzzled. "Why don't we just do this during the daytime? It would be easier with the light."

"That is true," said Nicholas. "The problem with that is we don't want any undue attention. Ararat is near Russia and Iran in Eastern Turkey. The surrounding countries are not very keen on non-government sightseers."

"Are you saying," started Talia, "That we don't have permission to be there?"

"That's precisely what I'm saying."

"What if we're found out?" said Will.

"I'm not asking you to lie," said Nicholas. "If something happens and you get captured, tell the truth and cooperate completely."

"Captured!" said Will, looking at Talia.

"I didn't say this was going to be easy," said Nicholas. "If any of you want to bow out, now is the time."

Austin looked around the room at his friends and fellow students. The nervous faces he noticed moved sporadically, not lingering on any one person for too long. The silence remained.

After walking Taylor to her cabin Austin tried to get some rest. The time change was throwing him off. Even with the room darkened by heavy blinds, he struggled to shut down. This could end up being more dangerous than anyone thought. *We could get captured or even die.*

About forty five minutes before sunset, both teams were assembled on the aft deck. Their gear lay at their feet. All were dressed in the white clothing and the boots they were given before the high altitude training in the Colorado Mountains. Talia had reassured them at the time that even though they were lightweight, this was the best gear in the world.

Taylor tried to hide her yawn while she waited her turn for Talia to go over her gear and equipment with her. She had asked the members of her team to meet early to go over some last minute checks.

"You okay?" Talia asked her.

"Yes, but I am a little nervous. I've never done anything like this."

"I think there's more to you than you realize. Just remember your training and stay in communication. You'll be fine."

Taylor relaxed a little. She could see why Mr. Ryan chose Talia to be their team leader.

The sun sank further behind the horizon. Dark shadows moved across the water. All the lights on the yacht went dark except a single spotlight that shone on the edge of the landing pad. She could see her companions on the deck and wasn't surprised when Austin walked up and took her hand.

"Are you ready for this?" he asked.

"I'm not sure, but Talia thinks I am."

"Will was acting pretty nervous. I hope he'll be okay."

"I think once we get there and know what we are dealing with, it will be better. The unknown can be a bit nerve-wracking," Taylor said.

Ten minutes later, they heard a high-pitched sound. It appeared to be coming from the water off the west side of the darkened yacht.

Seemingly out of nowhere, a fuzzy image began to appear, rising above the aft section of the yacht. The team members saw the arrival of the first bumblebee. It gracefully lifted from just above the water to then touch down on the forward section of the aft landing pad. Everyone was so busy watching the first one land that they hadn't heard or noticed the second one come in right behind it.

"Cool," said Mia. "It really is like a bumblebee."

"This is going to be such a trip," said Mani. Reaching over he grabbed his pack and headed towards the first craft. The blades of both helicopters were still spinning as the team member's loaded into both craft along with their gear.

In the dim light of the aircraft, Austin noticed that Demetri and Talia were carrying a sidearm as they joined Nicholas. The rest of the teams continued loading onto the Bumblebees. After a moment, the pilots, Alchesay, and Stephen came over.

Austin moved closer into the shadow to listen to their conversation. Nicholas had a graphene wristband on each wrist. He removed them and handed them to Demetri and Talia.

"Use these, but don't depend on them too much. Follow your intuition first and foremost. You can do this," he said. "And remember the most important thing is that everyone is safe. Everyone makes it back. Everyone! Understood?"

They both nodded.

Taylor set her gear in the helicopter and walked to where Austin stood.

"Are you coming?" she asked.

"Yeah, just one minute."

She stood quietly next to Austin and saw Nicholas pull Alchesay and Stephen aside. She sensed a strong history in Stephen and wondered how he came to know Mr. Ryan.

"Stephen, are you up for this?" asked Nicholas, seriously.

"Yes sir. Absolutely."

"Thank you for doing this," said Nicholas. He turned his attention to Alchesay. "Whatever happens, bring all these kids back."

"Have I ever failed you?"

"No," smiled Nicholas. "Not once."

"Well, I'm not about to start now," he said with a smile. He confidently turned and walked to his awaiting craft.

Taylor and Austin moved to the craft. As the door began to close, Taylor saw Nicholas standing there, watching their departure. A powerful feeling came over her. She felt he desperately wanted to go with them. She even thought she saw a tear in his eye as the door shut and they lifted off the deck.

Nicholas watched as the two craft quietly melted into the darkness of the cloudless sky. "Please be right," he said, turning to head back to the control room.

Chapter 57 – Getting to Ararat

Austin felt like he was in some action or adventure movie as they moved swiftly in the darkness toward their destination. He, Taylor, Will, and Mia sat tightly pressed against each other on the narrow seat. Joseph and Talia sat across from them on their own small seats. Their gear was secured underneath them. The only light in the almost total darkness emanated from the console, at the front of the craft. It took only the slightest movement from Logan or Alchesay for it to become distorted with silent shadows that floated around the cabin.

"This is both terrifying and exciting at the same time," said Mia.

"Beta Bird. This is Base One. Systems check." Shen's voice came clearly through the radio. Austin listened as Logan and Alchesay talked with their support group back on the yacht. All the technical aspects didn't make much sense to Austin. *I'm glad they know what they're doing*, he thought.

"Approaching Antakya. I can see the lights of the city now." Logan's voice broke the silence.

"Al. Keep the cloak hot." The response was immediate. It was Nicholas. "We're detecting a lot of radar signals in your area. Stay on course."

"Roger that," replied Alchesay.

Austin could make out Taylor's profile in the darkness, he found her hand and gently squeezed. The radio became silent. Austin closed his eyes and intended to rest for a while.

Taylor heard the communication from Base One. She knew that the city of Antakya was in the middle southern part of Turkey, near its coastal border with Syria. She swallowed. She hadn't listened to the news of current international events recently but knew this part of the world wasn't the safest of places to be, especially flying in by helicopter on a covert operation.

Between Logan and Alchesay, Taylor could see a screen of some kind that presented a magnified, three-dimensional image of what lay ahead and below their aircraft. Directions and numbers were located on the 'head-up' display.

This really was an amazing machine, she thought. *I hope it can get us in and out safely.*

With her radio on silent, Taylor laid her head on Austin's shoulder and fell asleep.

Sometime later she felt Austin shift and squeeze her hand. Sitting upright she tapped her radio on.

"We just passed north of Van Golu," said Austin. "Talia said we'll be there soon."

The cabin lit up when Talia activated her graphene band. A three-dimensional picture of the terrain below appeared. As she moved her arm the picture changed. The side of a large mountain came into view.

"That's where we're going?" Mia asked.

"Yes," said Talia.

"ETA in fourteen minutes," said Logan.

"You guys ready back there?" asked Alchesay.

"We will be," said Talia.

A small red light went on in the back of the cabin. Talia did a quick but thorough check of the radios again and then had everyone retrieve their gear.

"Alpha Hawk is four minutes ahead of you," said Shen over the radio. "They're beginning their approach now."

"Get ready, you guys," said Talia. "It's going to get really cold and windy, fast."

Taylor checked her boots while Austin zipped up his coat. The cabin had been warm for their trip over, but the temperature had dropped in the last few minutes.

Austin's ears popped with the change in altitude. From the gauge in front of Logan, he could see they were cruising at a little below 15,000 feet and were beginning to descend.

"Hey Skipper," said Will, tapping Talia's foot with his. "Are we going to rappel down or land?"

"We're going to land first," said Talia,

They all could see the digital image of the first helicopter, from Talia's wristband, touchdown on the slope of the mountain. The doors on both sides flew open and Alpha Team scrambled out.

Austin saw two of the team biff it in the snow.

"Joseph," said Talia. "You're going first. We're going to keep the port side door closed. And be careful. As you can see, it's icy out there."

"Good call, Talia," said Logan. "Alpha Hawk is bouncing all over down there. The winds are worse than we thought."

"Can you get us down there?" asked Mia.

"Oh, I can get you down there,' said Logan. "It's just picking you back up, twenty four hours from now, that will be a bit tricky." That didn't make Austin feel any better.

"Everyone ready?" asked Alchesay.

"Will. Get your goggles on," said Talia.

"We've got to get you down now," Alchesay said. "The winds are starting to pick up."

"We're about ready," said Talia.

Austin and Taylor swiftly and efficiently helped each other secure their packs, ready to evacuate the hastily descending Bumblebee. The team held on to the seats as the chopper began to move down through the turbulent winds. All light vanished except for the faint glow from pilot's console and a red flashing light above the starboard door.

"When that light goes green, the door will open," said Talia. "Austin, you'll follow Joseph. Taylor, you're next, then Will, and Mia. I'll be the last one out. Get clear of the Bumblebee. Then wait for everybody else."

A few moments later the light flashed green. The door opened and they were greeted with a blast of frigid air.

Exhilarated by the cold and the jump, Austin leapt

out, giving Joseph mere seconds to get out of the way. He hit the ice and snow and rolled to a standing position. The maneuver ended up being more challenging with the night vision goggles on. He looked up to catch Taylor, but saw only Will barreling towards him.

The ground beneath his feet slid away with the impact. He rolled and slipped down the icy terrain. Chunks of frozen snow and rocks bruised his back as he quickly lost any handhold.

"Austin!"

He heard Taylor's frantic voice though his radio. His hands flailed. He grasped onto a small outcropping of jagged rocks, the only hold he could find.

"Dammit, Will," he said.

Each gasp of air echoed through his radio.

Joseph made his way to where Austin lay and helped him to the top of the ridge.

"Thanks, man," Austin said.

"Sorry, I didn't see you there," said Will. "You okay?"

Austin just nodded.

Mia gracefully flew out of the chopper and moved easily to where the others waited.

"Will!" Talia's voice carried through the cold air as well as the radios.

They all watched as she threw his pack to the ground and jumped out as the bumblebee began to pull away.

"Oh, hey, sorry about that," he said, and ran to

retrieve his pack.

"You're welcome," said Talia as she walked past him, annoyance blatant in her voice.

"Quit screwing around, Will," said Joseph. "This is serious."

Morning light began to spread, working its way through the clouds that dotted the sky. They could make out the cliffs where large rocks protruded out of the ice. The other team was high above them on the ridge.

"This is wild!" said Will.

Taylor wrapped her arm around Austin's waist, her goggles hanging around her neck.

"I'm glad you're okay," she said, comforted by his strong arm around her shoulders. He'd removed his goggles, so she could see the emotions written in his eyes. They didn't speak. They just stood there in awe at the majestic scene and amazed at where life had brought them.

Behind them Talia reported in. "Base One. This is Beta Team leader. All are safely on the ground and accounted for."

"Beta Team," came Nicholas's voice over the radio. "Everyone hook up. The wind and terrain up there is worse than it appears. Talia, do an equipment check and make sure all team members are connected. Then proceed to waypoint one."

"Roger that, Base One," said Talia. She went over to Will, took a rope out of his pack, and attached it to a carabiner on her belt. Joseph connected next and motioned to Taylor. Austin moved to fasten his carabiner when he heard Talia.

"Austin, I need you at the end."

Taylor smiled and shrugged when he stepped back and Mia took his place, leaving Will next to him.

They hiked along the icy ridgeline listening to the communications between Talia, Demetri and Base One.

It wasn't a long distance, but the icy steepness took them longer than they thought. The low amount of oxygen at that altitude made it hard to breathe. It was the hardest on Will because of his muscular build. He wanted to keep stopping, much to the annoyance of Mia and Austin.

"You're almost there, about another twenty yards to your left," Shen directed from the yacht.

The rope stretched and pulled as the group slowly made their way across the icy terrain. Taylor slipped to her knees when the line tightened painfully. Behind her, she saw Will and Austin pull Mia further away from the crevasse she'd unexpectedly found.

"Our sensors show that you're right on top of it," said Shen.

"Yeah, I think we found it," said Talia.

"Alpha Team has found their entrance and is proceeding in."

"Beta Team Leader. What do you think?" came Nicholas's voice on the radio.

"Standby, Base One," came Talia's voice.

Taylor was comforted by Nicholas's voice on the

radio and Talia's confidence as their team leader. *I'm glad she was in the military*, she thought.

She removed her night vision goggles, the advanced technology that created green, artificial vision, to truly see the sunlight breaking above the horizon as if for the first time. It slowly raced down the ridge before her. She inhaled the invigoratingly cold, aroma-less air as sight and smell became one. It seemed almost incomprehensible to her, but she allowed the majesty to form itself into one of those precious moments that she would remember beyond this lifetime.

Their larger packs were deposited on the snow a short distance away. The night vision goggles were put away and they were all soon securely strapped into their climbing harnesses.

It's quite windy at this altitude, but what an amazing view, Taylor thought. She watched Austin drive a long stake, looped on top, deep into the ice about ten feet from the opening. Joseph attached a long section of rope to it and handed Austin another stake. It sunk into the ice about five feet from the first. With the rope tightly fastened to the second stake, Talia secured it to her climbing harness.

Taylor made her way to where Austin stood and peered at the large crack. It was about ten feet long and no more than a few feet wide. The snow and ice sloped down to a dark hole just large enough for a person to slide through.

"Austin, you and Joseph hang on. Don't let me

fall," Talia said, half joking.

Taylor watched Talia's cautious approach to the edge. The crampons gripped the ice, keeping her feet from sliding. Austin and Joseph easily held her weight, even on the downward slope.

"Base One. I can see down about fifteen feet, but not much past that."

"Is it safe to go in?" asked Shen.

"Yeah, I think so," said Talia as she rejoined her team. "Who's going in first?"

"I'll go," volunteered Joseph.

After securing the rope Joseph descended into the hole in the ice. The light from his headlamp disappeared, and the only evidence of his movement was the rope that slowly moved at the entrance.

"I found some wooden planking and possibly an entrance." Joseph voice came clearly through the radio.

"Is this the real Noah's Ark?" asked Mia.

No one responded to her question as Talia reported back to Base One.

"Proceed," said Shen.

Taylor listened to the conversation on her radio as she tried to internalize Mia's question. *This really could be it.*

More stakes were placed in the ice and ropes attached.

"We're going to split into two teams," said Talia, "Joseph, connect to Austin and Taylor when they get in. Mia and Will, you're with me.

"You sure those little stakes will hold us?" asked Will.

"We'll go one at a time," said Talia.

As Taylor neared the entrance she slid her small pack off, lowered it to Joseph and then made her way down into the ice. The space she entered could hardly be called a room. It was more like an ice tunnel. She made her way through the uneven snow and maneuvered around the menacing ice sickles that tried to block her path. She could hear the rest of the team coming down behind her.

"The opening I found is this way," Joseph said.

Beams hung precariously from the wall, held in place by their frozen surroundings. Austin shined his flashlight around and off to one side a small opening became visible. Joseph attempted to slide down, but couldn't get past his shoulders.

"The opening is so small, maybe one of you girls could fit in," Joseph said. "I don't mean to be biased, but I think us guys are too big."

"We're going to have to do it head first," said Talia.

Taylor caught her gaze.

"I'll go first," she said.

The weight on her back lifted as Austin took her pack and set it aside. He held the rope that connected them.

"You ready?"

Taylor nodded and he lowered her into the small, icy hole. She got hung up on her hips, but with a little wiggling she made it through. She reached for the rope, flipped right side up and signaled Austin to let down more slack. The floor creaked when she landed. That was the only wood exposed in the snow covered space. The area she stood in was only about two to three feet wide and ten feet tall.

"It looks almost like a hallway or something," she called back to the others.

Upon the addition of another light, Taylor walked back to the opening just as Mia swung down.

"We're going to try to chip some of this ice away," Talia said.

Through the light of her headlamp Taylor watched the shower of ice fall to the floor. Packs, coats and even the guy's shirts came down next.

Austin grinned at Taylor when his boots contacted the floor.

"Figured we could slip in a little easier without the shirts."

Sweat glistened on Will's chest and arms when he dropped through. He stood in the narrow space, breathing heavily.

"Are you okay, man?" Austin asked.

"Yeah, it's just the altitude. I've got to breathe better."

The narrow space was filled when Talia and Joseph worked their way down.

Chapter 58 – In the Ark

Narrow corridors and uneven terrain made progress difficult. Their exploration was slowed even more by Talia, who was communicating with Base One and creating a Three-D map of the ship with her Graphene-band.

With Talia's approval, Austin, Taylor, and Joseph moved ahead down the snowy incline. The floor leveled out somewhat and continued into the darkness beyond the beam of his flashlight. Small compartments branched off on each side, evidenced by the fallen timbers that hung over the hallway, partially buried in the snow. Austin saw what may have once been a door frame. On closer inspection he saw precisely cut beams attached with wooden dowels. *If this is as ancient as Nicholas believes, they must have had some amazing tools,* he thought.

"Austin, look at this," Taylor said.

Her headlamp illuminated large cracks in the ice, revealing a compartment below. The light also showed a partial floor of wood. Snow and ice made up one side creating a way down.

"Talia wants us to continue our search on this level. We are to check in every hour. Even if we can't hear her, she'll be able to hear us on her wristband. She, Will, and Mia will try to find a way to the lower level. We're to contact her if we connect up with Alpha Team," Joseph said when he joined them. "By the way, here's a few energy bars in case you're hungry."

Taylor pointed out the entrance to the lower level while Joseph passed the information on to Talia.

The three continued deeper into the vessel as the space between the walls began to narrow near the top. There appeared an opening in the wall of ice and snow in front of them. They maneuvered their way through the maze of ice sickles and tangled beams.

The passage at the other side darkened with the light of only the three headlamps. Stagnant air reminded Austin of his grandparent's dirt root cellar in the early spring. He could see the outline of the gun that hung from Joseph's belt in the dim light. *I hope we don't have to use that,* he thought.

Austin reached out to steady Taylor as they made their way across the thick ice that hid the wooden planks beneath. A slimy dampness clung to his gloved hand as it moved along the icy wall. *Drip, drip, drip.* The high pitched sound echoed through the eerie darkness only to be interrupted by a low intense growl. Timbers creaked and the ice cracked and popped around them, sending down a shower of dirt and broken ice.

"What was that?" Taylor asked.

The sound began from deep in the vessel, rising in volume the closer it came. It sounded as if part of the ship was falling down around them. Austin found himself up against the cold, wet wall, Taylor pressed close to his side. His arm wrapped around and held her until the noise and shaking stopped.

"Do you think it is safe to move?" she asked.

"I think it's safe, but we don't have anywhere to move," said Joseph. "We're trapped."

Their lights took in the pile of debris that filled the space in front of them. Austin looked back the way they had come and saw a space on the far side large enough for them to get through.

"I think we should see if we can clear away the pile in front of us and keep going," said Austin. "There's an opening we can get through in case we need to turn back."

Sweat moistened Austin's back. Their small packs sat out of the way as they took time to clear some of the debris. The faint light that shone through became brighter when they made it to the other side. The source of light came from a large opening at the end of the vessel. The jagged timbers of the floor joined the frigid air and sunshine on a giant, mangled puzzle. A snow-capped ridgeline made up the other half of the vast gorge. Massive rock formations jutted out, dark against the white brilliance.

Austin and Taylor followed Joseph closer to the edge. The ominous crack was their only warning. The boards broke loose and Joseph started to fall. Austin lunged forward and seized his friends arm before it disappeared.

"Whoa! Don't let go of me!" yelled Joseph.

"I gotcha." Austin held tightly, unsure how he had gotten there in time. Inch by inch, he and Taylor pulled him up. As Joseph lay panting next to them, Austin could see the fear in his eyes slowly dissipate.

"Thanks, man," he said breathlessly.

"What do you say we go back the other way?" Taylor said.

When Joseph calmed down they retreated to where they last had radio contact with Talia. She and her group were working their way to the middle deck and directed them to find a way to the upper level. They lost radio contact when they found a space and squirreled their way up.

"It's a good thing I'm not claustrophobic," said Taylor.

"Yeah, me, too," said Austin, "but a place like this could really make a person that way."

"Will is claustrophobic." Joseph said a moment later.

"Now that you say that," said Taylor "he might be. I thought it was just the altitude, but he seemed really fidgety, more so than usual in this type of space."

Commotion from the level below got their attention. Joseph radioed Talia. No response.

"That's weird," said Taylor. "There are enough cracks in these boards that we should have easy communication with them."

The sound continued: methodical thuds and low growls. Austin felt a heavy weight slam against the floor beneath his feet.

"Let's get going," Austin said.

Beams crossed the ceiling and connected to walls, made of long, straight, horizontal boards. The corridor opened up exposing more and more of the timbers.

From below, they heard a chilling moan.

"That's got to be Will," said Taylor.

They tried to raise Talia again, but got nothing.

"Stop fooling around down there, this is serious," said Joseph into the radio.

"Guys, I don't think that was Will."

"Sure it was," said Austin. "What else could it be?"

"Whatever hit the floor beneath us, hit it hard. The ceiling of that compartment is over ten feet high. And that sound didn't sound human...." Taylor said.

The hair on Austin's neck stood up. "Are you saying that our two teams are not alone in here?"

"I think we need to get back to the others," said Joseph, still working with his radio.

"We haven't finished searching the top level yet," said Austin. "But if we're not alone in here, this would be a nightmare worse than any horror movie."

"Agreed," said Taylor. "Stay on your radio and get us in touch with Talia."

The trek back felt more difficult. Nothing seemed familiar the further they went. They'd heard nothing from Talia. They crossed to a second passage and continued searching for a way back down. Around the next barrier, they emerged to find themselves overlooking the gorge.

"Maybe we should wait here and see if the others find us," said Taylor. "We may have better communications out here in the open."

Austin and Joseph looked at each other. "Okay."

Taylor found a seat against one wall. She shut her radio off and set it beside her. Austin sat on the other side and shut his radio off as well.

"Might as well conserve the battery," he said.

Taylor pulled three power bars out of her coat pocket and handed one to Austin and Joseph.

"I'm going to look around some more," Taylor said. They had been sitting for quite some time, and she was getting antsy waiting.

"I'll go with you," said Austin.

"No, that's okay, I'll turn my radio on and not go far."

"All right."

Taylor left down the dark passageway. Austin kept an eye on her light as long as he could.

"Austin, can I talk to you about something?" said Joseph when she was out of earshot.

"Yeah, what's up?" asked Austin as he turned around.

"I need you to tell Taylor about her half-siblings."

"You didn't tell her?"

"No," said Joseph looking down. "And if anything happens to me, she needs to know. She trusts you, and it will be easier on her if it comes from you."

"Whoa, what makes you think anything is going to happen to you?" asked Austin.

"Just a feeling," said Joseph.

That's as far as their conversation went before

Taylor returned.

"Did you see anything important?" asked Joseph.

"No," said Taylor. "But I'm pretty sure that it wasn't Will or any members of our teams that made that sound."

"How do you know that?" asked Austin.

"I don't know, just a feeling, a very intense one."

"I think it's Will screwing around again," said Austin.

"Hopefully so," said Taylor. "But now I think we need to get back with the others. Let's see if we can find another way back down to the second level."

"Let me try the radio once more," said Joseph. He pulled his radio out of his pocket.

"Only five percent," he said to himself.

"How's the power on your radios?" he asked.

Austin and Taylor checked and found theirs were both slightly below fifty percent.

"Austin, leave your radio on for now, but on low power. Taylor, turn yours off," said Joseph. "We don't know how long we may need them."

They got ready to go back down the passageway when they heard a distant boom.

"What was that?" asked Austin.

"A gunshot?" said Taylor.

"No, that didn't sound like a gun, and it didn't sound like it came from inside the ship." Joseph tried to see out the opening towards the far side of the gorge.

Austin's radio crackled. He turned it up to full

power.

"Alpha Te..." The radio cut out again. The sound of another explosion came again from behind them. They glanced back, but couldn't see anything unusual except the wind had picked up a little bit through the canyon.

"That was Talia," said Taylor.

"Let's get going," said Joseph. "Something's up."

"No. Wait," said Taylor turning on her own radio. She walked closer to the opening. "I'm getting something," she said. She turned up the speaker on her radio.

"Taylor!" said the radio. It was Talia's voice. It sounded like she was running. Joseph and Austin came closer.

"Talia," said Joseph. "What's happening?"

"Alpha Team's in trouble." The radio crackled. "Base One has ordered a full abort. We are all to get to the surface for immediate extraction." The radio cut out.

Joseph tried to regain contact, but nothing. Austin and Taylor turned to him.

"A..." said Joseph.

Austin glanced at Taylor, who looked back confidently. They turned and surveyed the vast opening.

"Well, it's obvious we can't get out that way. Let's see if we can make it back and find the opening to the second level," Austin said, taking Taylor's hand. They turned and headed back down the narrow corridor, Joseph close behind.

There was a loud explosion above them. The floor

and walls began to tremble and quake.

"Watch out," yelled Joseph as snow and ice broke loose from the ceiling.

The force of the snow from behind made Austin lose his grip on Taylor's hand and propelled him forward to his knees. It only lasted a few seconds, but the rumbling had been deafening. Almost as loud as the silence that now hung over the snow laden space.

What light had come through the rift behind them was now extinguished. Austin tugged his arms free of the snowy mess and turned on his flashlight.

"Taylor?"

"I'm over here."

Clambering out of the debris, he crawled across the ice and snow to where she lay partially buried in the cold rubble. It took only moments to dig her out of the loose snow.

"Are you okay?"

"Yeah. I think so," she said.

"Where's Joseph?"

"I don't know, he was behind me when everything started shaking."

"Joseph," Austin yelled.

"I'm over here." They could barely hear his muffled reply.

Austin and Taylor climbed the pile of large chunks of ice and wood that had fallen behind them. It had created a barrier between them and Joseph. They tried fruitlessly to dig their way to him.

"Are you okay?" called Austin.

"I'm a little bruised, but I think I'm okay," said Joseph faintly. "Bigger problem is my radio is out of power."

"Joseph," Taylor said. "Try to get back to the opening. It may take us some time to either find a way back to the surface or down to the next level. We'll contact Talia and come back for you."

The quake had shifted the ice, blocking some areas, but opening others. They struggled to squeeze their way through the new openings and move deeper into the vessel. After a while, Taylor turned her radio back up and described their approximate location to anyone that might be listening.

"Are you guys all okay?" Talia's voice came through loud and clear.

"Yeah, we're okay," said Taylor, "but we got separated from Joseph."

"Where is he?" asked Talia. "I can't track his radio."

"I think his radio was out of power. He's on the top level heading towards the farthest section that's open over the gorge," said Taylor. "I'm not exactly sure where we are, but we're somewhere on the highest level."

"Standby," said Talia.

After a moment she replied. "Base One said that Joseph is moving towards the opening at the front of the vessel. You two are approximately 250 feet from the stern.

We are on the bottom level almost directly below you."

"Talia, what's happening out there?" asked Austin. "Was that an earthquake?"

"No," said Talia. "We got some unexpected company. Fighter jets were circling around above us, not sure where they're from. They fired higher on the mountain. I think they were hoping to cause an avalanche."

"Is that what that was?" asked Austin. "We were practically buried in it."

"No, the avalanche didn't happen until later. I guess Beta Bird tried to distract the fighters away from the mountain while Alpha Hawk extracted Alpha Team."

"Did they all get away?" asked Austin.

The radio was quiet for a moment. "Well, a... yes, they all got off the mountain," said Talia soberly. "But I think Alpha Hawk got hit taking off. Base One won't say."

"They won't say! What do you mean? What happened to them?"

"Shen doesn't know. He said there was some form of engagement over the north east side of the mountain and that Alpha Hawk was going down."

Austin and Taylor's eyes met.

"I guess Mr. Ryan left Base One immediately after that. His orders were to get all of us together and be ready for extraction as soon as possible."

"Where's Beta Bird?" said Austin.

"I'm not sure," said Talia. "The last I heard, it was trying to help Alpha Hawk. There was a large explosion on the ridge above us and I haven't heard from them since. I think the explosion caused an avalanche."

"Was the explosion Beta Bird?" asked Taylor.

"No, I don't think so. It seemed more like a missile explosion, but the fact that I haven't heard from Beta Bird since concerns me."

"What should we do now?" asked Taylor.

"We need to get to the surface so they can pick us up," said Talia. "The problem is we're having a hard time even getting to the second level. The way we got in collapsed in the avalanche."

"We have the same problem," said Austin.

"Talia," Taylor said, "with that avalanche above us, there's no way we're going to get out the way we came in."

The radio was quiet. After a moment, Talia came back on. Austin and Taylor could hear the sound of Mia crying in the background.

"I agree," said Talia. "I seriously doubt that's an option."

"What other choice do we have?" came Will's voice.

"I think our only option," said Taylor, "is the side that's open to the gorge."

Austin agreed. He just didn't know how they would get there.

"Seriously!" said Will.

"Agreed," said Talia. "You get to the forward most part of the ship. We'll meet you there. You will probably lose radio contact with us, but check in every ten minutes.

We should hear you. Base One is still tracking your location."

"Will do," said Austin.

"Oh, one more thing," said Talia. "If you come across Joseph, stay together."

"You got it," said Austin.

The radio went quiet.

"Let's see if we missed something." Austin and Taylor headed back to the cave-in. It was impossible to move enough of the ice timbers to get through.

"Well, I think we can rule out that option," said Austin.

"Yeah," said Taylor. "The only other way is to go back and see if we can find another way down to the second level."

They worked their way to the other side of the ship.

"Do you regret doing this?" asked Taylor.

"Now is not a good time to ask," said Austin trying to force a smile.

"Do you think Alpha Team is okay?" she asked.

"I don't know, but I hope so," he said.

They tried to keep their bearing as they moved through the labyrinth of corridors and compartments. Taylor was grateful for Austin's help over boards that had broken free and ice that had come loose.

"One thing I do know for sure," said Austin after climbing over a precarious pile of ice and wood. "Is that we will make it out, for sure."

"How do you know that?" said Taylor.

"With all the training that we've done with the Ryans at the Institute, I don't believe for one minute that things are going to end this way. It's an impression, but a very strong one. I don't know how things will turn out, but we'll make it," Austin said, taking Taylor's hands and helping her over a large ice chunk.

Taylor thought about when she first met Austin, how he was back then and how he was in that moment. "You've really grown a lot since I first met you," she said.

"Thanks," said Austin. "I've had to come a long way to get where I am now. I know I still have a long way to go, but now I actually have a purpose to my existence. All the things I've learned in the past fifteen months, I realized how much I don't really know. And actually, I'm okay with that, because I believe I will be so much more."

They continued on in silence for some time. The eerie stillness of the place was palpable.

"I need to tell you something," said Austin.

Taylor waited expectantly, having no idea what he would say.

"I spoke with Joseph earlier, and he told me I needed to tell you something. I was going to wait and make him tell you, but I think you need to know now."

Taylor sensed the soberness in his voice and knew this was serious. She stopped and turned to him.

"What's going on, Austin? You're starting to scare me. I think you better just come out and say whatever it is."

"After you left the family history class you had with Joseph, he found some more information about your mom. She has two more children in addition to you and Connor."

Taylor felt like someone had punched her in the stomach. She gasped, struggling for air. Austin pulled her close and she forced herself to breath.

"I'm so sorry. I know this is probably the worst place I could have chosen to tell you."

Taylor didn't respond. She tried to wrap her mind around what Austin had said. *Two siblings?*

"Is this really true?"

"I'm pretty sure. Joseph said he saw copies of the two birth certificates."

"Who is the father?"

"According to Joseph, the birth certificates both said 'father unknown.'"

Taylor felt comforted in Austin's embrace as she tried to process all the thoughts that ricocheted in her head. She took a deep breath and pulled herself from Austin's arms.

"I will need to think about this when we get back. We should keep moving."

Not far ahead, they found some broken floor boards. Together, they shifted them to create a space big enough for them to lower themselves through. Taylor could see that the compartment was taller than most of the others. The light in the room began to dim.

"Austin, I think my headlamp is almost out of power. We'll just have to use your flashlight."

A bright beam of light shone from Austin's flashlight as she removed her headlamp and switched it off.

Taylor checked in with Talia, but didn't hear a response, so she and Austin headed towards the forward section of the ship.

Ten minutes later, she tried again, this time making contact.

"Where are we now?" she asked.

"About fifty feet from the opening," said Talia.

"We can't be," said Austin. "We don't see any light." He shut off his flashlight. A faint shaft of light shone down the long corridor.

"The sun set about forty-five minutes ago," said Talia. "It's getting dark outside."

A cold wind blew stronger the closer they came to the opening. They huddled close along one wall and Austin yelled up to Joseph.

"You okay up there?"

"Yeah, I'm fine," said Joseph, "just sitting here by my lonesome, watching it get dark. I was wondering if you were going to come back for me."

"We thought about just leaving you," joked Austin. "But we were afraid the bogeyman would get you."

They could hear Joseph laugh. "My headlamp has finally died. I don't suppose you have a spare do you?"

"We do," yelled a voice from below them.

Taylor turned her radio back on. Talia, Mia, and Will were right below them.

"It's about time you showed up," said Austin into the radio.

"Is everybody all right down there?" Taylor asked.

"We're good, for the most part," said Talia. "Do any of you guys up there still have a rope?"

"Why?" said Joseph from above. "Are you looking to hang someone?" he asked, trying to lighten the mood.

"No. Not yet, at least," said Talia over the radio. "But we have two extra flashlights you can use if you want them. We just need a way of getting them up to you."

"Does anyone have a spare radio they could send up as well? The battery on mine is almost dead," Joseph said.

"You can have mine," said Mia. "We've got Talia's super wristband to keep us in touch."

"We still need to figure out another way to move these supplies if no one has a rope," Talia said.

"Does anyone have any food?" asked Will.

"I've eaten all mine," said Austin.

"I have two left," said Taylor.

Joseph didn't respond.

A mental list was created for all the supplies they had. There was still no way to move anything from one level to the other.

"Austin and I can go back and see if we can find my pack. It may have some things we could use," said Taylor.

They reappeared a while later, Austin with a small

pack on his back. It was Taylor's. Inside was a short rope that they used to rig a way to swing supplies to and from the bottom level. They were unable to get anything up to Joseph because of the overhang of top level.

"I just heard from Shen."

Taylor picked up her radio from where it sat next to her, when she heard Talia's voice. She and Austin had found a place out of the wind and were quietly talking when she heard the message.

"Mr. Ryan is working on a way to get us out of here in the morning. I suggest you all find a spot out of the wind and try to sleep."

"Any word about Alpha Team?" asked Taylor.

"I asked Shen, and if he knows something, he's not saying."

The radio went silent. Taylor turned hers off and moved back into the ship with Austin. She snuggled close to him and tried to find a comfortable position. A chuckle escaped her.

"What's so funny?" asked Austin.

"When I think of us sleeping together for the first time, this is not what I imagined."

There was quiet laughter, and then silence.

Chapter 59 – Next Morning

Austin awakened with a start. He swore he heard the cry of a mountain lion. Part of a dream or reality, he was unsure. He listened for it again. The wind continued to blow through the gorge, and he could feel Taylor breathing deeply beside him. Austin took a few moments and began to process through the thoughts and emotions he was experiencing. He kept getting distracted by the sounds of movement coming from deep within the vessel.

The uncomfortable wooden planks as well as the chilly night air made it hard to relax. He huddled close to Taylor and started to fall into a restless sleep. An image appeared in his mind. A large, beautiful, black cat and a brown puma seemed to stand guard around him, Taylor and their friends, as if protecting them from some great unseen monster. Even with the troubling images, Austin felt safe and fell into a deep sleep.

"Austin," came a voice in his mind. He tried to wake himself. He knew he was sleeping, and yet someone was talking to him.

"Get the other pack," said the voice in his mind. *What pack?*

"Near where you found Taylor's," said the voice again.

Austin recognized the voice. It was Nicholas. *Are you inside my head?*

"Yes," came the voice firmly.

Austin tried to focus, forming the words in his mind. *What should we do?*

"Get the other pack. I'm coming for you."

Bang! Bang! Bang!

The conversation vanished as Austin bolted upright, knocking Taylor in the process. His heart raced as the gunshots continued.

"What the..." said Austin leaping to his feet. He pulled a now wide awake Taylor with him.

The darkness slowly dissipated as the morning sun began its journey up the cold, dark gorge and the mountain beyond.

"Come on," said Austin.

He turned on his flashlight and went back into the ship to where they had found Taylor's pack. His light shone bright in the dark space.

"Look at that," said Taylor pointing to the large chunks of ice they had seen when they had found her pack.

"It looks like someone dug it out for us," she said.

"Yeah, someone or something," said Austin.

The light from the flashlight slowly crisscrossed the floor. Small spots of black were randomly splattered in the ice that had somehow melted to a gray slush.

"It looks like there was a struggle here," said Taylor.

A layer of fine ice particles had settled on one area of the floor after the avalanche. Taylor gestured to it. The paw prints of a very large cat were clearly imprinted on the floor. Austin crouched and touched the frozen wood. His hand was dwarfed by its immense size. The other print was smaller, but not by much.

"I think these were made by what we heard earlier."

Austin gulped as he looked at Taylor. "Let's get back to the others," they said in unison.

It was much brighter when they returned. Austin set the pack on the floor and opened it. The bulk of the space was taken up by an unassembled crossbow, three arrows and a long rope. It also held a spool of fishing line, a flashlight, some water bottles, but, unfortunately, no food.

"I've found your pack, Joseph. Where's the food?" yelled Austin.

"I've got a few more energy bars up here with me," replied Joseph.

"Well, let's see if we can rig this rope that was in your pack and pass supplies between us."

Taylor helped Austin tie one end of the rope to the harness he wore. She tied the other end to herself and handed the slack back. Standing back from the edge, she found a broken beam and looped the rope around it. Austin's careful steps took him closer to the edge. He had tied Joseph's pack with two water bottles inside to part of the line. Austin threw the pack. The boards above him began to crack under Joseph's weight. It took a moment for Joseph to find a safer plank. Austin could see his fingers and threw the pack once more. Success. The rope quickly moved up. There ended up being enough leftover rope to allow Austin to do the same thing for the group below. After tying the rope to itself, creating a loop, he took the end from Taylor and tied it to the other end he held in his hands.

"We need some food down here. Will is having a blood sugar fall off," Talia said.

It took a bit of work to figure out how to move the rope, but soon the food was down to Will.

"I just received word from Shen," Talia said. "Mr. Ryan is on his way."

"Wow, that was fast," said Taylor when the sound of a helicopter could be heard.

"That's not Mr. Ryan," Talia said. "It's a Turkish military chopper! Everyone, get out of sight."

They obediently complied, quickly backing away from the opening. Taylor realized she was holding her breath as she watched the helicopter make several slow passes before straying off.

"How are we going to get out of here?" asked Joseph once the sound faded.

"I don't know," said Talia. "But I'm sure Mr. Ryan will have found a solution. We just need to be ready when he gets here."

Austin and Taylor overheard Talia talking to Shen over the radio. "What's Mr. Ryan's plan?" she asked.

"I'm not positive. He's somewhere in Russia right

now and out of radio contact," Shen replied before signing off.

"So, how are we going to do this you guys?" asked Talia.

"Let's go back and see if we can find another way out through the third level, so we can get picked up on the surface," said Will.

"Is that an option, Joseph?" asked Talia.

"Not for me," he said. "The passageway is blocked on my level about a hundred feet back."

"What about you guys, Taylor and Austin?" asked Talia.

Austin looked over at Taylor who shook her head, an unsure expression on her face.

"I'm pretty sure the entrance we came through yesterday is blocked," said Austin.

"We can get back to the third level from here, though. Maybe a way opened up from there," responded Taylor.

"Check it out," said Talia. "We'll see if we can find a way to get to you."

"And I'll just sit up here and watch the sunrise," said Joseph.

Austin and Taylor hurried back to where they had found Joseph's pack. Sure enough, they couldn't go any further because of the snow and ice in their way. After climbing back, they checked the ceiling for openings. Some six feet above was wood planking fitted tightly together.

"Whoever built this thing really knew what they were doing," said Austin.

"There," said Taylor, pointing past the edge of the light. "That's how we got through."

Sheer ice covered one side and the wood on the other contained no handholds.

"Too bad we don't have a rope," said Austin.

"How would we get up there if we did?" asked Taylor.

Austin moved closer, shining his light around the opening.

"How about this?" said Taylor. "I climb onto your shoulders and lift myself through."

"Yeah, that will work, but then how will I get up there?"

"One thing at a time," she said.

Austin put his hands on the wall to steady himself. Taylor's grip tightened on his shoulders as she began to pull herself up. *She's not very heavy*, he thought. *I guess all the working out I've done is really making a difference.*

Balancing on Austin shoulders, Taylor pulled the flashlight from Joseph's pack out of her coat pocket and peered up through the opening. Sticking her arms through, she lifted herself up off Austin and into the empty space.

Austin watched her disappear. "What do you see?" he asked.

"Well, I don't see a rope," she said. "Give me a minute."

"Be careful up there Tay," he said.

Chapter 60 – Beta Bird Arrives

"Joseph, are you okay?" asked Talia from the bottom level. She and the others had heard a thud from above.

"Yeah. I'm right above you. I found something to pry up one of the loose floor boards and I'm on the second level, but Taylor and Austin aren't back yet."

"Sit tight. Beta Bird is almost…" Talia paused.

"What is it?" asked Joseph.

"Beta Bird is circling above us, but it's just Logan flying it."

"Where's Al?" said Joseph, the concern obvious in his voice.

"I guess he ordered Logan to drop him off on the far side of the mountain."

"Why did he do that?" asked Will

"There must have been a reason," said Talia.

"If we can't get to the surface, how are we going to get to the helicopter?" asked Mia.

The three stared at each other, unsure what to do. It was a voice from above that finally broke their silence.

"If we can't get to the helicopter," said Joseph. "He will have to come to us."

"What are you thinking, Joseph?" asked Talia.

"Give me a minute, I have an idea."

Joseph quickly assembled his crossbow. After, he unwound more than fifty feet of fishing line from the spool in his backpack. He then attached one end of the fishing line to one of the three arrows he had and connected the other end to the rope. Sharing his plan with Talia he looped part of the rope and sent it down to her. He then tied the free end of the rope to a solid beam.

"Joseph, you go over first," Talia said.

"I think you should. If Logan is flying alone, he may need some help, and with all your military training, I think you'll have a better chance."

She reluctantly agreed as she put on her climbing harness. Attaching the carabiner to the rope, Talia radioed Logan to move the Bumblebee as close as possible, explaining their plan.

Winds from the canyon blew the helicopter haphazardly when the doors slid open. With skill, he brought the powerful machine under control and flew closer to the open side of the Ark where the team awaited.

Joseph aimed the arrow just below the choppers blades and slightly above the door. The downdraft from the blades pushed the arrow down more than Joseph expected. It skimmed just above the floor and out the far side of the Bumblebee.

"Nice shot," said Will from below.

Joseph watched Logan struggle to keep the craft under control. Unbeknownst to them, the autopilot wasn't designed to be engaged with both doors open. Logan was still able to grab the fishing line before jumping back into the pilot's seat. He worked frantically, pulling the fishing line and rope as the chopper began to sway closer to the ark. After regaining control he activated the auto-pilot once more before securing the rope to the rappelling clasps that hung from the ceiling. Back in his seat he gently eased the craft over pulling the rope taut.

Time seemed to slow and they watched with raw nerves as Talia made her way over. Each slide of the carabiner took her closer and closer to the helicopter. If Logan took the Bumblebee too high, Talia couldn't pull herself up. If it was too low, the spinning blades could hit the rope or Talia.

Joseph didn't realize he was holding his breath until he saw Talia safely inside the chopper.

"You've got to get Austin and Taylor now," she said over the radio.

With a deep breath, Joseph hurried to find them.

Taylor searched the walls and ceiling meticulously. She covered only about ten yards of the narrow passage before turning back.

"You still there?" she asked down to Austin.

"Yeah. Anything?" he asked.

"Not yet. I'm going to try the other direction," she said moving down the corridor.

"What do you see up there?"

Taylor heard Austin's muffled question, but chose to investigate the generous opening she found in the floor instead. She knelt down and peered into the cavern below. The floor, free of ice and snow appeared to be about ten feet below her. Broken boards covered in snow and ice created a make-shift ladder which she used to climb into the room below.

Tightly connecting beams comprised the far wall. On closer inspection Taylor saw symbols and drawings that covered it.

This is it! She quickly scaled the beams and snow and made her way back to Austin.

"What did you find?" he asked.

"I think it's what we're searching for. I climbed down through an opening to the second level. There appears to be a huge map imprinted on the wall."

"How big?" he asked.

"It's about ten feet tall by twelve feet wide. I think it's on the other side of the ice blockage we found on the middle level."

"Did you see any way out?" asked Austin.

"Not yet. I'll look some more."

Back in the map room, Taylor stared at the image on the wall, trying to memorize what she saw. She only observed one side when the ground began to shake. She grabbed onto a narrow shelf that stuck out from the wall beside her when the trembling increased. Her glove knocked something from the ledge as she pulled her hand away. Without thinking, she picked up the object and stuffed it into her coat pocket.

"Taylor!"

Upon hearing Austin's frantic call, she struggled to scale the now shifting pile of debris up towards the opening. It seemed to be moving further away from her outstretched arms. *How am I going to get out of here?*

Strong hands gripped her arms and easily pulled her up past the now collapsing pile.

Austin kept one hand tightly around Taylor's while they hurried back through the passageway.

"How did you get up here?"

"I had some help," he said as they reached the place that led back down to the second level. "You go first," he said. She jumped down into the hole and into Joseph's waiting arms. He pulled her away as Austin hit the floor, rolling back to his feet. The three of them ran through the passageway back to the opening, dodging the ice and snow falling around them.

Austin saw the horror on Joseph's face.

"Where's the rope...the helicopter?" blurted Joseph.

"I don't know," said Austin. He gripped Joseph by the shoulders and looked into his fear-filled eyes. "We'll be okay, but we need to get Mia and Will." Austin let go when he saw Joseph begin to calm down.

The hum of the helicopter became louder as the Bumblebee rose into view.

"Joseph, do you read me?" came Talia's voice over the radio.

"Talia!" said Joseph. "We lost the rope."

"We've got it over here," she responded. "Shoot another line over and we'll get it back to you."

Austin helped Joseph as they attached another length of fishing line to an arrow. "Will this really work?"

asked Austin.

"I did it before. I can do it again," said Joseph as he carefully notched the arrow into the crossbow. "Tell Talia we're ready."

The doors opened as Logan maneuvered the Bumblebee broadside towards them.

Joseph took aim. The arrow flew straight and true, but a sudden gust forced the blades down into the arrow's path, destroying it.

"No!" cried Taylor.

The severed fishing line floated down. Joseph and Austin watched in disbelief.

Taylor dropped to her knees and pulled what was left of the line back.

"Do you have any more arrows?" she asked.

"Just one," replied Joseph as he reached into his pack. Drawing out the last of the fishing line, he secured one end to the arrow and the other to the line Taylor held.

"Talia, we're ready here," said Taylor into the radio. "Have Logan get as close as he can."

Another burst of wind forced the helicopter dangerously close. They saw Talia move out of the doorway in preparation for the next arrow.

Austin heard Joseph's loud whisper, "Help me make this shot."

He took aim again, and the three watched the arrow fly decisively through the waiting doors.

It took only moments for Talia to tie the fishing line to the rope. Austin smiled confidently at Taylor as they pulled it back. "We're getting out of here," he said.

"How are we getting across?" They heard Mia ask over the radio.

Austin looked at Joseph. "Can we do it the same way Talia did?"

"I don't think so," said Joseph. "At least not all of us."

"Hurry up, you guys," yelled Mia. "Shen says we've got company."

"We've got to try," said Taylor. "We're running out of time."

"Okay," said Joseph resolutely. "Everyone get your climbing harnesses on. We'll slide across."

Joseph looped the end of the rope around a large beam beside them, then swung it down to Will and Mia. "Hook your harnesses to this and we'll pull you up," he yelled.

The rope went tight, but there was no response from below.

After a long moment, Will's voice came over the radio. "Hey guys, we got a problem down here."

"What?" asked Joseph.

"My harness is broken," said Mia. "I got hung up, and Talia had to cut it to get me down."

"She's not strong enough to make it across without a harness," said Taylor.

"She can use mine," said Will.

"No," said Joseph. "You'll need yours to get up here."

"She can use mine" said Austin. "I'm strong enough to make it across without."

"I know you are, but she's going to use mine," Joseph said, disconnecting his harness.

Austin wanted to protest, but felt it was the right thing to do.

Joseph attached the harness to the rope by a carabiner and slid it down to Mia's waiting arms.

The Bumblebee continued to bounce less than fifty feet from the group. "You guys almost ready over there?" said Logan over the radio. "I can't keep this up forever."

As Austin looked out over the grand expanse, he realized what they were about to do. *This is not going to work*, he thought. *At least not for all of us.*

"Send Joseph over first," came a voice in his mind.

Austin put his hand on Joseph's shoulder. "If you're going to do this without a harness, then you need to go over first."

"No. I'm not going until everyone else..." Joseph stopped. As if searching inside himself, he began to nod. "Okay," he said. "Okay."

Stepping back, Austin yelled down. "Will! Is the rope tied tight?"

"Tight as I can get it. It won't come loose."

"Alright," Austin said to Joseph. "Take your time, but hurry it up."

Joseph smiled. "You're in charge over here now. Get everyone across." Adjusting his gloves, he took in a deep breath. The rope tightened as Logan gently pulled the aircraft sideways. Grabbing the rope, Joseph swung his legs around it and began his perilous feat.

Standing beside him, Taylor took Austin's hand as they watched their friend inch precariously forward. The scene moved into slow motion, like it was taking Joseph forever to cross the chasm before them. Then, time stopped completely, frozen as if it were solid. There are certain experiences in a person's life that change them. Pivotal points, that afterwards, your life is never the same. Defining moments of one's existence. Austin and Taylor both felt it there in that time and space, as if the universe had reached some great zero-point. It only took a microsecond, but lasted for an eternity.

Chapter 61 – Escape

Joseph's exhaustive ordeal came to an end when Talia grabbed his arm and swung him in.

Taylor let go of Austin's hand with a sigh of relief and picked up the radio.

"There's another chopper coming in fast, and I don't think it's a friendly," said Logan. "You can't do this one at a time."

Taylor looked at Austin questioningly.

"I don't know how else to do it," he said.

"Can we pull the others up here?"

"Yeah," said Austin. "Will. Untie the rope and we'll pull you up."

"It's too tight. I can't get it loose," said Mia.

Austin saw fear creep into Taylor's eyes. *I can't do this alone,* he thought. *What do we do?*

"Cut the line," came a voice in his mind.

"What?" he said out loud.

"Cut the line and re-tie it on the other side of the beam." It was Nicholas's voice speaking to him.

With a short glance at the beam, Austin knew what to do. He loosened his harness and got a knife out of his pocket. "Tell Logan to give me some slack."

Not understanding, Taylor just held the radio.

"I mean in the rope," said Austin as he unfolded the blade. He grabbed hold of the rope as it relaxed. "Hook your harness to it. We're all going over at once." He took a deep breath and sliced through the static chord. Dropping his knife, he grabbed the now loose end. *Glad I did that knot tying class back at the Estate*, he thought as he connected the two lines together with a double fisherman's knot.

Taylor clipped her harness below the knot as Austin tightened his. Before they realized it, the Bumblebee began pulling back.

"Austin!" she yelled, her arms reaching towards him. The chord was tightening, pulling her over the edge. He reached to clip his carabiner on, but it was too late. The rope was yanked from his fingers. He had no choice. He took a flying leap and grabbed a hold of Taylor as she began to descend. They dropped momentarily until the line tightened and they slid to the lower level. Mia pulled them in as Austin tried to catch his breath. He looked at Taylor, not sure what had just happened.

"Wow!" said Mia. "You two are amazing."

They both laughed nervously. "Let's *not* do that again," said Austin.

"Oookay," nodded Taylor.

"What's your plan to get us out of here?" asked Will from back in the shadows.

Austin tried to shake the shock from his mind. "We're all going over together."

"How?" said Mia.

Austin looked at Taylor.

"We can do this," she said, unclipping from the rope.

"Get the harness on Mia. Will..." said Austin peering into the darkness, he could see him sitting against the wall.

"He's not doing so hot," said Mia.

Austin knelt down next to him. "Will? We gotta go."

"I can't do this," he said, his arms wrapped around his knees.

"You don't have a choice," said Austin, pulling him to his feet. "Get your harness on!"

Smiling, Taylor watched Austin in amazement.

"Mia," said Austin commandingly. "Tell Logan to get as close as he dares and wait for our signal. Taylor, pull in some slack and tie a loop knot in the line. Then hook up to it."

Austin turned back to Will who was slowly putting his harness on.

"He's afraid of heights," said Mia.

"I'm not afraid," said Will emphatically. "I just don't like..."

Crack!

They were interrupted by a large fracture above them. The ceiling began to splinter about twenty feet down the corridor.

"Oh, shit! This thing is coming apart."

The floor began to shudder beneath Austin's feet, propelling him towards the opening. He lunged at the wall, trying to regain his balance. Seconds later, the trembling ceased leaving the section leaning precariously into the gorge.

Still holding onto the walls, they heard Talia on the radio. "Austin. It's collapsing above you. You've got to come over now!"

"Taylor," Austin ordered. "Hook up, then get Mia connected."

Taylor grabbed Mia and clipped her harness to the loop she had just tied. Then she tied a second loop knot, not far from the first. The click of her carabiner was silent beneath the wind and hum of the Bumblebee as she hesitantly connected her harness to the second loop.

"Come on," said Austin, pulling Will towards the opening at the same instant Mia's feet left the floor. Taylor tried to hold tight to the ten feet of slack in front of her as her feet slipped backward. Seeing what Taylor had done, Austin flipped two more loops in the chord and clipped onto the first, then he turned to help Will. He heard the click as the rope went tight and they all four lifted off the deck. The Bumblebee tugged frantically as Logan tried to pull away.

Hanging in the open space, Austin could see the upper level beginning to collapse. "Cut the line, Will! Cut the line," yelled Austin.

"I can't do this."

"Yes, you can," said Austin. "You have to or we'll all die."

Will pulled a fixed blade knife from his boot. Austin watched in disbelief as Will started to cut the line between himself and Austin.

Without thinking, Austin seized the blade with his left hand and smacked Will with his right forearm. They both spun around the rope. As Austin regained control, he flipped himself upside down. The razor sharp blade sliced the rope, freeing them from the collapsing Ark. They could feel the massive section pass them as they swung free.

Taylor's stomach plummeted right out the soles of her boots, her hands glued to the rope. She couldn't believe her eyes as she watched helplessly from above while Austin dangled about eight feet below her.

Even with the buzzing sound of the blades, Taylor could still hear Logan yelling to Joseph, "Get 'em up! Get 'em up!"

"They're too heavy," he yelled back.

Talia jumped from the copilot's seat to help.

Mia's gasps above her, made Taylor aware she was holding her breath. Closing her eyes, she focused her attention on her lungs. The frigid air made breathing painful, but helped calm her down. At least, until she saw the other helicopter.

It passed dangerously close below them. She didn't recognize the markings, but knew it was a military craft because of the twin machine guns mounted beneath.

Unable to pull them up, Logan moved the Bumblebee to the ridge. He found a relatively clear spot and the sloping ground rose up to meet them. Extending the landing gear, Logan laid the dangling rope and its occupants on the ice.

Will landed in a pile on the ground, unmoving. Austin landed on his feet, still holding tight to the rope with his right hand. Taylor and Mia briefly touched down as Joseph and Talia quickly pulled them up. Logan tried to hold the helicopter level while still keeping the blades from hitting the snow on the uphill side.

Joseph pulled the rope as Taylor saw Talia hoist Mia in. Talia then jumped back into the copilot seat. Joseph reached out and grasped Taylor's outstretched hand and pulled her in just as the ice behind her exploded. She held tight to Joseph when the Bumblebee rose unexpectedly. He had locked his leg through a cargo strap and was holding onto the rope to keep Taylor from being pulled out.

Taylor heard Austin yelling at Will until the other helicopter passed beside them. The thumping of its blades became deafening.

The tension in the rope relaxed when Logan touched down again. Taylor could see Austin struggling up the icy incline, the unconscious Will on his shoulder. Mia joined her and Joseph as they pulled the rope in.

"You've got to get them in!" yelled Talia.

The almost dead weight of Will's unconscious body caused Taylor to slide. She braced her foot against the door frame and pulled the rope with all she had. Joseph dragged Will inside when Austin heaved him up from below.

"Where are you going?" Taylor yelled to Logan as he moved the helicopter away from the hillside. "Austin's still down there."

The other chopper opened fire again. Bullets splashed around Austin's feet. Taylor's hand brushed Austin's, but slipped away when the craft lifted further into the air. She watched in horror as he flew around like an out of control kite, connected only by the two ropes she and Joseph held.

As Logan guided the craft away from the mountain, the Turkish chopper circled back around towards them.

Taylor and Joseph worked desperately to pull Austin up. He momentarily grabbed the landing gear, but lost his grip on its slippery surface.

The rope burned into Taylor's hands as she strained to bring Austin closer.

"Engage the cloak," yelled Joseph.

"I can't until the door's shut," said Logan.

"Get him in. Now!" Talia yelled over the chaos.

"Hope they don't have armor piercing bullets," said Logan. "Hang on!" he yelled as the other helicopter opened fire. He swung the Bumblebee broadside. Bullets sprayed the side along the closed door.

"Joseph, we've got to get him up," Taylor cried.

She didn't know where that last burst of strength came from, but with one final surge she and Joseph hauled him in. Austin lay gasping for breath on the floor beside her.

"He's in! Activate the cloak." The door slid shut as the Bumblebee picked up speed, accelerating away from the attacking helicopter.

Taylor, Joseph, and Mia worked quickly to untangle everyone from the ropes.

"Good to see you back," Joseph said when Will opened his eyes and shifted around. Mia reached over and helped him up onto the bench.

Austin remained on the floor, his breathing labored.

"Taylor. Are you shot?" asked Joseph.

Taylor gasped at the sight of blood.

"Who's been hit?"

"Not me," said Mia.

"I don't think I am," said Joseph checking himself.

"I don't know," said Will, eyeing the blood on his own coat.

Taylor unzipped Will's coat. "I think you're okay," she said when she didn't see any blood.

"There's a first aid kit under the seat behind me," said Talia.

Taylor immediately turned to Austin. Her eyes flew over him, searching for any evidence of injury. The sole of his boot was missing, but on closer scrutiny there was only a scratch across his foot. His left hand was covered in blood. She pressed the gauze pad Mia handed her onto the deep cut.

"Are you hit anywhere?" asked Taylor, struggling to hold back the tears that threatened to fall.

Austin reached up and wiped away the small stream that had broken loose and then moved to hold the back of her head. He brought her close and kissed her quivering lips softly. His head dropped back and his hand fell to the floor.

"My leg," he said, breathing heavily.

Taylor saw the blood stain surrounding a hole on his pants. After carefully exposing his calf, she saw where the bullet struck.

"He's been hit!" she cried.

Joseph tore open a sterile compress from the kit and pressed it against Austin's leg. "We need to lay him down. He may be going into shock."

After some shifting around, they got Austin stretched out on the floor. A jacket rolled up under his head and his feet propped up. Taylor spread the blanket Mia gave her over him. Then set about bandaging his hand and leg. Meanwhile, Joseph retrieved the oxygen mask and placed it over Austin's mouth.

"Base One, we have wounded on board, but have to go back and get Al. He ordered me to leave him on the mountain so he could divert the other helicopters," said Logan urgently.

"Negative. Return to Base One immediately," came the unwanted reply.

"Yes sir," he growled, then turned the Bumblebee and headed back to the yacht at full speed.

Taylor didn't say much once Austin was bandaged. She sat with her back propped against the door, her hand slowly stroking Austin's forehead. The oxygen mask had been removed and the color was returning to his face.

"I love you," she mouthed when she caught him watching her.

Chapter 62 – Return

The tension that filled the chopper dissipated the closer they flew to the safety of the yacht. The air pressure in the cabin slowly rose, and Taylor finally started to relax. Austin's hand felt warm in hers. She'd left it there when he'd fallen asleep. The adrenaline that fueled her system for most of the morning was soothed by his quiet breathing. She rested her back against the door and closed her eyes, relishing in the calm of the moment.

"We're five minutes out from Base One." Logan informed them.

Taylor opened her eyes and gently woke Austin. "We're almost there."

"Hold on to Austin, Taylor. We're going to be slowing down fast," said Talia.

Her stomach dropped as they did. The Bumblebee pulled up and slowed quickly as it turned and landed gently on the upper platform of the yacht. As the door slid open, they were greeted by a burst of moist Mediterranean air.

Taylor could see Dr. Mac and Kara coming towards them. After helping Austin onto the waiting gurney, Taylor followed them across the deck to where Sheena stood.

"Good to have you back," she said as they passed on their way to the infirmary.

Taylor stayed with Austin while Dr. Mac cleaned

and stitched him up. Miraculously, a bullet had only grazed the skin on his leg enough to draw blood, but it still required three stitches. Kara spent the next thirty minutes using Reiki on his left hand and right calf. He seemed to be doing much better after that.

Later, Taylor walked down the corridor slowly next to a limping Austin. Her arm rested lightly along his back.

"You lay down and I'll go find us something to eat," she said when they reached the door to his room. She turned and headed back down the hall after Austin went in. Ten minutes later, she returned with a tray holding two covered plates and two tall glasses of ice water.

The warm food was delicious. Austin had found his phone and turned on his favorite playlist. The relaxing sound drifted quietly in the background while they ate.

"I wonder where Mr. Ryan is?" said Taylor.

"I don't know. Joseph stopped by before you came back and said Sheena told him he would be back soon. Back from where though, no one will say."

Austin walked with Taylor to return their dishes and then strolled out onto the deck, basking in the warmth of the sun, his energy rapidly returning.

The pounding sound of a helicopter propelled them to the upper deck. The rest of their team was watching as a very impressive Russian helicopter flew in and landed abruptly. Austin swallowed nervously as two heavily armed-Russian soldiers jumped out with automatic rifle-grenade launchers hung over their shoulders. He couldn't make out their faces beneath the visors. His right calf muscle started to ache, but he forgot his pain when he saw them open the side door to reveal a joyful A-team. He and Taylor hurried over with the others to welcome their friends back as they piled out.

Two additional fearsome looking soldiers exited the chopper behind them. As they moved aside, a smiling Nicholas stepped out between them. They stood not far from the helicopter as the first two soldiers climbed back in and the chopper took off. Nicholas gave a salute as the accelerating helicopter circled the yacht and proceeded away.

Nicholas, an armed soldier on each side of him, walked up to Taylor, Austin, Talia, and Joseph.

The two soldiers simultaneously took off their helmets to reveal Pajori and Demetri. Without a word, they smiled as they sauntered past.

"We're so sorry. We failed you," Joseph said.

"Failed me?" Nicholas said.

"Yes. We didn't accomplish what you sent us out to do, what we had trained all this time for," said Joseph, looking down.

"You didn't fail me or let me down in any way. You did your best, everything you possibly could. That's all I asked. And you grew in very real ways that you cannot now understand."

Nicholas placed a comforting hand on Joseph's shoulder, the other on Austin's.

"It's all about your relationship with yourself and

others. You worked together as a team and learned about yourselves in a way that you couldn't otherwise."

Austin glanced over at Taylor. A smile lit up her face. She was proud of him. He knew it and he felt pleased with himself for what he had done.

"More than anything else, you all made it back. Everyone comes back. Everyone," said Nicholas."

"Well, not everyone," said Talia. "We heard what happened to Al, what he did for us. Running block so we could get away."

Nicholas didn't respond. He turned towards the landing pad and the open sea beyond.

Austin followed his gaze, searching the sky. The helicopter seemed to come out of nowhere. It decelerated as it circled the yacht once, preparing to land. It had Nicholas's company logo blazoned on the side. It landed on the pad in front of them.

Even before the passenger's feet touched the deck, Nicholas was there to greet him. Austin watched him help the limping, bandaged Al across the deck. He paused as he passed Austin.

"Everyone comes back. Everyone."

The End

Epilogue

Taylor and Austin wandered hand in hand along the trail, high on the mountainside overlooking the Estate. They'd been back only a few days. The trees and foliage of the hillside encased them. The call of a hawk floated on the current where it soared. Taylor plucked another wildflower and added it to the growing bouquet she held. It felt good to be back at the Estate, safe and warm. She turned her face towards the sun, soaking it all in.

"I spoke with Joseph earlier," Taylor said as they continued their walk. "He showed me the birth certificates. I guess I have a half-brother or sister, but a new baby brother, too? That took me by surprise. It's all so wild."

"Now that you know, what are you going to do?" Austin asked.

"I don't know. Nothing for now, I guess."

A log had fallen near the path, so it was a good place to stop and take a break. Off the hill below, the construction site was a hive of activity. Soil had been backfilled around a large square concrete foundation. Inside sat a white cement bowl like structure. It seemed to be about five hundred feet in diameter and probably two hundred and fifty feet deep in the center. They watched the activity below as they continued their conversation.

"Why did Nicholas want to see you this morning?" asked Taylor.

"He asked me about my goals and intentions here at the Estate."

"What did you tell him?"

"With everything that's happened to me, I think my goals are changing direction. Before, making money and having a high profile career was what I wanted. But now they don't feel as important as becoming a better person and creating lasting relationships."

What Taylor saw in his eyes amplified the words that she heard. She smiled at him and felt a faint blush paint her cheeks. Shyly, she looked away.

"I feel there's something much larger going on here than we realize, Austin," said Taylor, changing the subject.

"Are you saying you want to leave here?" he asked.

"No. Not at all," said Taylor. "But I wonder how *we* fit into all of this."

"I wonder if it has something to do with going to Ararat?"

"That ended up being more intense than we expected. I just wish we could have accomplished what Nicholas wanted," Taylor said.

"I kind of feel like we failed him," said Austin.

"Me to," said Taylor. "I know he's okay with everything because we all returned safely, but I still wish we could do more for him. He has done so much for us. If only I could remember more of what I saw in that map room. At least that would be something."

"You can't beat yourself up over it."

Austin's strong arm wrapped around her. Peace emanated from him and surrounded her as he pulled her closer. His fingers brushed up her neck and nudged her chin. His kissed her gently at first, but their kiss deepened as she entwined her arms around his neck. Time slowed as Taylor sank into the rapture of his kiss.

She felt slightly dazed when, with reluctance, Austin pulled back. Her hand slid from around his neck and settled over his chest. Neither one spoke, enjoying the moment together. The breeze picked up a strand of hair and blew it across her face. She tucked it behind her ear and then remembered the gift.

"I have something for you," she said as she moved slightly away.

"I found this in the map room and I wanted to give it to you before you left for school tomorrow," Taylor handed Austin the green stone she'd found in her coat pocket after their return to the Estate. "I know it's just a rock, but maybe something to remind you of our crazy adventure."

"Thank you for the gift." Austin paused, considering it. His eyes widened. "I've seen this before, Tay. The night I went camping with Nicholas and Dakota. I saw this."

Taylor stared at him in amazement.

"This isn't just a rock. I think it's what we were searching for."

She felt his bandaged hand caress her cheek when he gently cupped her face.

"I so love you," he said.

His lips moved softly over hers in the briefest of kisses.

Taylor rested her forehead against his and heard him whisper.

"We've got to get this to Nicholas."

References

References and materials included in Taylor and Austin's suggested Reading List.

Awaken the Genius (1993), Patrick K. Porter, Ph.D., Positive Changes Hypnosis, Virginia

Bringing Out the Best in People (1985), Alan Loy McGinnis, Augsburg Publishing House, USA

The Code of the Extraordinary Mind (2016), Vishen Lakhiani, Rodale Inc., New York

Executive Thinking (2011), Morris A. Graham, PHD and Kevin Baize, OD, iUniverse, Bloomington, IN., USA

Fat for Fuel (2017), Dr. Joseph Mercola, Hay House, Inc. USA

Get Out of Your Own Way (1996), Mark Goulston, M.D., and Philip Goldberg, Penguin Group (USA) Inc.

Golden Sapphire (Coming Soon), Rex Rian

How to Think like Leonardo da Vinci (1998), Michael J. Gelb, Bantam Dell, Random House

How to Win Friends and Influence People (1936), Dale Carnegie, Simon and Schuster, New York

Incognito (2011), David Eagleman, Vintage Books, Random House, Inc.

Knowing You (2019), Camile R. Rigby and Rex Rian

The Mind & The Brain (2002), Jeffrey M. Schwartz, M.D., and Sharon Begley, HarperCollins

Moonwalking with Einstein (2011), Joshua Foer, Penguin Group, USA

Power vs. Force (1995), David Hawkins, M.D., Ph.D., Veritas Publishing, Sedona, AZ, USA

Rezzimax, LLC.

The Talent Code (2009), Daniel Coyle, Bantam Books, Random House, New York, USA

Tapping the Healer Within (2001), Roger J. Callahan, PH.D., McGraw-Hill, New York

Wild at Heart (2001), John Eldredge, Thomas Nelson, Inc., Nashville, Tennessee

You are Not Your Brain (2011), Jeffrey M. Schwartz, M.D. and Rebecca Gladding, M.D., Penguin Group, New York

Golden Sapphire

Southern Cache Valley, Utah Territory, USA, July 1856

They stood 5,000 feet above the ancient bed of a great inland sea surveying the vast, landscape that lay before them. Far to the north they could barely make out what the French Explorers called the "Three Breasts," or the Tetons. To the west they looked out over a broad desert that surrounded an exquisite, sparkling blue, salt sea. As the Ancient One, my great-grandfather, gazed on its beauty, he remembered standing on this same mountain when water filled this huge basin, farther than the eye could see, even from this great height.

In my mind's eye I watched him admire, longingly, the beauty of this place. He knew his time here was quickly coming to a close, completing his mortal stewardship.

"They're coming," said Nantan.

I looked at my half-brother. He and what remained of our small tribe were frantically, but meticulously empting the archive.

"Are the wagons loaded?" I asked.

"Yes."

"Excellent. Get them moving, but quietly."

He smiled at me then turned and ran silently back down the hill. Ten full wagons waited for him. The horses seemed to fidget in anticipation of the long trek that awaited us. My people had acquired the wagons from the white men that had come from the east some nine years earlier.

The wind whipped at the wagons, pushing aside a cover to reveal our sacred cache: tablets of engraved stone, plates of metal, and stacks of animal hides. Some of the last remnants of the records of our people. The covers were quickly tied down as the wagons began to roll.

Nantan had mounted his horse, a beautiful bay mare that he adored. As he looked back at me, I felt his sorrow. Even at his youthful age of twenty-five years, the son of my mother had stayed close to my side as we assisted our great-grandfather.

As a young child, our great-grandfather watched 294 years ago as the demon wolves with round metal hats from beyond the great sea to the east came and destroyed our history. Vast halls of records were crushed or burned and melted down to send back to their queen. He had told us the story many times. I can still see the painful images in his mind.

"Keep these records safe at all cost" were his final words to us. And what a cost it has been. I am the last of my family. The light-skinned ones of our tribe. My darker-skinned sisters had all been killed or silenced into the white man's culture. My brothers, including Nantan, would soon suffer their same fate. But not before we completed our final task: hide these sacred works until the time comes that this knowledge should come forth. When Mother Earth is on the edge of death because of the darkness of her children, these records would bring light and life again to this dying planet, Life Eternal for all who would receive it.

With a wave, Nantan turned to follow quickly after the wagons. I was so grateful for him. He had been so loyal, so faithful. I would not see him again in this life, I knew it. But hopefully in another.

Grandfather had promised me that we would play a part in bringing this knowledge forth in a future time. I didn't know what that meant, but he did say others would help. He would even send Ashira, who would not taste of death until this work is done.

I watched the great white-headed eagle approach from the north. It was Grandfather's totem and guide. It swooped low above my head, then climbed steeply to the south. As I followed it to the mountain peak that the white men called Pisgah, I could see the dust beginning to rise. The settlers from the south were coming to inhabit the willow valley to the north. They were driving their cattle through the narrow canyon. They had sent scouts there before, but had left it. This time I knew, when they got there, they would never leave.

Even from this great distance, I saw the first of them, a lone rider going before the rest. He was no ordinary settler. He seemed aware of me; though I knew he couldn't see me.

I could sense his emotions: uncertainty, caution. His attention turned to the small hill almost totally surrounded by the dry lake. The same hill that once held our precious treasure. Confusion entered his mind. He saw the opening in the hill and the entrance to the caves. From there his eyes followed the tracks the wagons had made in the tall grass. At that same moment the last of our wagons disappeared behind the side of the mountain to the east.

Did he see them? I wondered. *No matter. I would be dead soon, but events had now been put into motion that no mortal could stop. In a little more than 160 years, I will finish this!*

About the Authors

Rex Rian is a Success Mentor, Life Coach, philosopher, and motivational speaker. As the CEO of 3 Peaks Institute of Energy and Wellness, he assists individuals and groups in their process of ascension. He finds great joy in helping others be their highest self. He lives with his wife and children in the Rocky Mountains of northern Utah.

Camile R. Rigby has found a love of writing that rivals her love of reading. She is a Foot Zone Therapist as well as a Reiki Master. She lives in northern Utah with her husband and family.

You're welcome to contact them at www.3peaksinstitute.com or following Rex on Instagram at mygoldencopper.

Made in the USA
San Bernardino, CA
28 January 2020